THE HUMMINGBIRD DAGGER

by Cindy Anstey

THE
HUMMINGBIRD
DAGGER

CINDY ANSTEY

Swoon READS

Swoon Reads | New York

A Swoon Reads Book

An imprint of Feiwel and Friends and Macmillan Publishing Group, LLC

175 Fifth Avenue, New York, NY 10010

The Hummingbird Dagger. Copyright © 2019 by Cynthia Ann Anstey. All rights reserved.
Printed in the United States of America.

Our books may be purchased in bulk for promotional, educational, or business use. Please
contact your local bookseller or the Macmillan Corporate and Premium Sales Department at
(800) 221-7945 ext. 5442 or by email at MacmillanSpecialMarkets@macmillan.com.

Library of Congress Cataloging-in-Publication Data is available.

ISBN 978-1-250-17489-5 (hardcover) / ISBN 978-1-250-17488-8 (ebook)

First edition, 2019

10 9 8 7 6 5 4 3 2 1

swoonreads.com

FOR MIKE, CHRISTINE, DEB, AND DAN,
ALWAYS STANDING BY MY SIDE.

Before

The dark, narrow room was rife with the fetid odors of mold and decaying fish. The only light came from a slit high above her head. Beyond its insipid glow were shadows, some deep and inert, others blurred and in motion.

In this cell of unknowns, only the dagger stood out. It swung from hand to hand, side to side. Words accompanied each movement, but the roar of panic obscured them.

All but the dagger ceased to exist.

Her eyes locked on its menacing beauty. The artistry was both simple and inspired, its form a study of opposites. The dark wood hilt gently curved into the shape of a hummingbird. The long bill that nature had fashioned to sip, man had fashioned to drink—to drink the nectar of life. And it was a thirsty bird.

Evidence of its last feed still dripped from the pointed steel beak. Dripped until it formed a red oozing puddle, small at first but growing steadily.

Blood. Her blood.

CHAPTER ONE

Disastrous Encounter

WELFORD MILLS, 1833

Guiding his horse to the top of a grassy knoll, young Lord James Ellerby toured Hardwick Manor and its grounds. The baron hadn't gone far when he heard the scraping of wheels against stone, and he jerked around to witness a curricle emerge from the stable yard in a rush.

Walter, James' younger brother, stood on the flimsy bouncing floorboard of a carriage, urging his horses from a trot to a run as he dashed pell-mell toward the manor's gate. Walter wasn't thinking of his safety or oncoming traffic. His friend Henry Thompson clung to the side rail, looking anything but confident.

"Walter, stop!" James yelled, though he was certain the noise of the racing curricle prevented his words from carrying to the fourteen-year-old boys. James' heart pounded as he watched, fearing dire consequences. Had Walter learned nothing from their father's accident and death a year ago?

Then James heard the jiggling equipage and thundering hooves of an approaching coach coming down the London road. He turned to stare down the hill at the large vehicle as it sped toward the Torrin Bridge—and Walter's emerging lightweight carriage.

James shouted again, but to no avail. He was too far away.

As Walter's carriage and the lumbering coach disappeared behind the trees, a great cacophony of crashes and screams rent the air. Heeling Tetley to a gallop, James' heart pounded in double time. Within moments, he jerked to a stop in front of the bridge.

The road was empty, though the wind was filled with the high-pitched terror of the horses. Snippets of foul memories flashed through James' mind. He saw the ruined body of his father in the wreckage of a different accident, his neck bent at an impossible angle.

In near panic, James called again. "Walter! Henry?" Guiding Tetley to the edge of the road, he looked down into the gully.

Walter's curricle sat to the left of the bridge at an awkward angle, but still on its wheels. The boys were wide-eyed and motionless on the bench, but otherwise appeared unharmed. The horses stood at the edge of the river. The shrill sounds of their distress abated as Henry crooned soothing words of comfort from his seat.

Walter looked up, meeting James' gaze. The color slowly drained from his brother's face and he swallowed convulsively. "I . . . umm . . . I . . ."

James exhaled a tortured breath and then huffed in relief. He wanted to shout at, pummel, and hug his brother all at the same time. Instead, he turned Tetley to the opposite, considerably steeper, bank of the Torrin.

The momentum of the near collision had propelled the larger carriage down the slope on an angle. It had almost overturned and now hung precariously. Mire covered the doors. The coach's horses were knee-deep in water, but other than being spooked, looked fine.

And then, James saw a figure on the ground—a very still figure. His stomach clenched and he jumped from Tetley, scrambling and slipping down the muddy slope in his haste.

A young woman lay on her back in the shallows of the river. Her face was pale, and long strands of brown hair floated beside her. James' view was partially obstructed by two squatting men at her side. One was only visible from the back. His great coat dropped from his broad shoulders to blanket the mud. The other man had a smudge of blood smeared across his cheek; his face was unremarkable except for a scar on his chin.

As he stepped forward, James' path was suddenly blocked by the coachman. The man's pockmarked face was flushed with anger, and his black-and-gray peppered head jerked in agitation.

"Is she all right?" James asked, indicating the figure in the water.

The coachman stared past James to where Walter and Henry watched from the roadside. His eyes narrowed. "Not to worry, sir. Her'll be right as rain in a tick." His harsh tone contrasted sharply with the reassuring words; he didn't even look toward the unconscious young woman. It left James unconvinced. "I needs 'elp rightin' me coach," the man said. "The sooner we gets this here coach of mine up, the sooner I can gets her to a doctor."

Glancing at the figures by the water, James frowned and then nodded. "Time is of the essence." He turned back to his brother and his friend. "Get down here!" he shouted, trying to instill authority in his tone. He pointed to the far end of the coach deeply embedded in the mud. "When I say so, push. And push hard!"

It was no surprise that Henry was the first to move, rushing through the mire, though Walter joined him quickly enough.

"Hitch your horses to the back," James told the coachman. A

lord expected compliance, even if he was only twenty years old and newly endowed with authority. "And get her out of the water!" he shouted to the men by the river.

At first, the men showed no signs of hearing. Then, without rising, one leaned over and slowly pulled her closer to the shore, into the mud.

"Are you *sure* she is all right?" James asked again. The words almost stuck in his throat. Memories of his father's broken body churned his mind yet again.

"A' course, sir," one of the passengers said. His cheek was red and bruised.

"Who is she?"

"Don't know." The man stood. "She got on at the Ivy in Ellingham. Didn't exactly introduce herself." He turned to the coachman. "Hurry up, man."

The coachman bristled. He had already unhitched the horses and rigged a line to the back of the coach. "You could always get your arses up here an' 'elp!"

The bruised man looked at the coachman with something akin to disgust, though he did take a position opposite to James, behind the coach door. The other man stayed by the water, nominally watching over the injured young woman.

James anchored his hands and shoved his shoulder against the filthy coach. His face was so close to the wood that he could almost taste the paint. Sweat trickled down his nose. He took a deep breath as much from disquiet as to prepare for the weight of the large coach. He shouted and the four men pushed while the coachman bellowed and pulled at his horses.

The coach was old and top-heavy; bandboxes and trunks

clung to the back, adding to the burden. The horses, nervous and fatigued, were almost at their limit. Then James felt a budge, a slight movement upward. James strained further and yelled to the others to push harder until, at last, the coach defied gravity and came to a standstill on the crest of the road.

Leaning over, hands resting on his knees, James gulped at the air, trying to regulate his breathing. Suddenly, the road was a hive of activity as half a dozen field hands converged on them.

"You needs 'elp, Lord Ellerby?"

"Yes, Sam." James nodded as he straightened. "Could you get the team hitched? They need to get to a doctor."

The coachman frowned at the good Samaritans and yanked the reins from Sam's hands when the laborer picked up the leathers. Incensed, James was about to deliver a set down, when he was distracted by the sound of wheels on gravel. A grocer's cart appeared on the far side of the bridge.

"Lud, Mr. Haines, am I glad to see you," James said as the small wagon drew up beside him. He leaned over the edge, assessing. Not big, but big enough. "Might we ask your help?" At Mr. Haines' nod, James motioned to Sam and another hand, Ned. "Clear room in the cart."

The coachman tried to block their way. "No, sir. I be almost done."

James sidestepped, slid back down the riverbank, and elbowed the ineffectual men out of the way. With one arm behind the injured woman's knees and the other under her shoulders, James lifted slowly and gently. She was no weight at all. James noted the dark red stain growing in her hair and across her forehead. It flowed freely, dripping on his boots.

His belly clenched. This did not bode well.

The bruised passenger dogged James' heels. "We will take her now."

James ignored the man, brushing past him without a glance, and carried his burden up the bank. Lifting the young woman over the side rail of the grocer's cart, James gently laid her down among the carrots and cabbages. Shucking off his coat, he covered as much of her as he could. "Take her up to the manor, if you would, Mr. Haines. I will be right there."

He turned back to the boys. "Walter, ride over to Kirkstead-on-Hill. Get Dr. Brant."

Brant was the only person James would trust with this dire a situation, someone trained as a physician and a surgeon. It didn't matter that Brant had only been in practice for a year; he knew what he was about and he was a good friend.

Walter jumped onto the seat of his curricle. Henry, mud and all, leapt up beside him. Walter turned the grays and hurried down the London road.

"Drive sensibly!" James shouted after them, likely to no avail.

The coachman was livid. "Y've no right, sir! To take away me fare."

"Your fare could die before your next stop. She needs immediate medical attention." James tossed a sovereign at the callous man. "That should cover the remainder of her fees."

The coachman caught the coin easily enough, but looked far from pleased.

"Sam, you and Ned get her trunks off the coach," James instructed, "and bring them up to the manor."

James mounted his horse and galloped after the wagon. He

quickly caught up to the lumbering cart as Mr. Haines negotiated the drive with diligent care.

James pulled Tetley to a walk.

In the full sun, he could now see the woman more clearly—she was young, perhaps eighteen or nineteen. Her face was smudged with dirt and covered with cuts and bruises, so much so that it was hard to discern what she really looked like. Her dress was ripped and soiled beyond repair. Her bodice was soaked, adding the possibility of a chill to their worries.

James sighed with impatience and concern—a contrary combination. He reached over and tucked the corner of his coat under her side. She did not look well.

"I will ride ahead, Mr. Haines, and get the household ready for her." James nudged Tetley with his heels. He didn't need to get the household ready as much as he needed to solicit his sister's help.

———

AT THE MANOR James tossed his reins to the groom and headed into the main hall.

"Where might I find my sister, Robert?" he asked the footman as the door opened. Feeling besieged, James *almost* wished his mother were here to consult . . . *almost*. The Dowager Lady Ellerby had not yet regained her equilibrium, which was tenuous at the best of times, since his father's passing. Fortunately, she was in Bath visiting her sister and not due to return until the end of June.

"Miss Ellerby is in the garden, sir. I believe she took her colors out there," Robert replied.

James nodded and quickly walked to the back of the hall and

into the saloon. His wide gait sped him across the floor of the large room, and then through the French doors to the patio.

At eighteen, Caroline was two years his junior and was, unlike Walter or his lady mother, of a steady, if somewhat unconventional, character. James had always relied on Caroline's good sense, never more so than his first year as Lord Ellerby. Just out of mourning, in her yellow gown, Caroline was easy to spot through the misty green lace of the new foliage. She was at her easel, not far from the sheltered arch of the conservatory.

"There was an accident on the London road," James said bluntly when he finally reached her side.

Caroline put down her brush and turned toward him. If she was surprised to see him covered in mud and without a coat, she showed no signs of it. "Was anyone hurt?"

"Yes, a young woman riding the London coach. With," he added in a tight voice, "no one to see to her welfare." The soiled, sodden face came to mind once again, constricting his breathing.

Caroline frowned. "Badly? Was she hurt badly?"

"I do not know. Mr. Haines is bringing her in his cart and Walter is fetching Brant."

"Is Walter involved?" Caroline stood and started toward the manor.

James followed. "I am afraid so. But he is fine. Even his ridiculous curricle is undamaged."

"That is almost too bad."

James chewed at his lip and nodded as he stepped through the door directly behind his sister.

Mrs. Fogel and Daisy were in the main hall observing the mud tracked across the tiled floor when Caroline interrupted their conversation. "Mrs. Fogel, Mr. Haines will be arriving at any moment with a casualty—a passenger from the London mail coach. Could you prepare one of the maid's rooms? Perhaps, Daisy, you could move in with Betty for a few days. Yes, I'm sure that's what Mother would recommend . . . if she were here."

No sooner had Mrs. Fogel rushed away to carry out her instructions, when James heard the squeak and rattle of the cart as it pulled up to the kitchen door. Help ran from every direction. Caroline shooed all but Robert and Paul, the groom, back to work.

"Poor girl. She does not look good," Caroline said as the men carried the young woman up the back stairs and placed her carefully on the bed in Daisy's room.

Caroline sat on the edge of the bed and lifted a lock of hair that had fallen over the young woman's bruised and bloody face. "Do not worry, dear. We will have you to rights in no time. Dr. Brant is an excellent physician." She patted the motionless hand as if the young woman could hear her.

James watched silently from the doorway, praying his sister was right.

———◆———

By the time Caroline heard activity on the stairs, she had begun to clean the young woman's rough, bruised hands. She could only imagine the difficult life this girl had had to live. When Dr. Adam Brant entered the room, he hurried past James with a perfunctory nod, almost filling what little space remained. A tall young man, he bent over to accommodate the slant of the roof.

Caroline backed away from the bed to give him room. "Thank you for coming so quickly, Doctor."

"She does not appear to have broken anything," Dr. Brant said after performing his examination. He opened his mouth as if about to speak and then closed it, shaking his head at some internal thought. Finally, he spoke. "While this," he indicated a cut on the young woman's right jaw, "*looks* nasty, this," he pointed to the wound on the side of her head, "might be a greater concern."

Caroline swallowed against the sudden lump in her throat and turned to meet James' troubled gaze. She offered him a tepid smile of reassurance and then turned back to watch as the doctor dressed the patient's gashed jaw. From the corner of her eye, Caroline watched James slip from the room, his expression grim and determined.

"I don't believe she has a broken head," Dr. Brant told her, "but we will not know for certain for a few more hours. Her pupils seem to be reacting to light, though it is hard to tell in this bright room." He looked over at Caroline. "I can wait with you, if you wish."

Caroline left Daisy to tend the patient and led Dr. Brant downstairs to the front of the manor. As they neared the central hall, they could hear a loud voice issuing from the library. Although James' words were indiscernible, his tone was not. Walter was being taken to task in no uncertain terms.

Embarrassed by the emotional display, Caroline steered Dr. Brant toward the drawing room. "Perhaps we should wait in here." She turned to the footman. "Robert, let Lord Ellerby know where we are, please. When he is free." She quickly closed the doors. The heavy oak did its job; the echoes of anger were now muffled and almost inaudible.

"James will be here in a moment," Caroline said needlessly. She led the physician to the settee and perched on the seat of an adjacent chair, pretending to be oblivious to the tension emanating from the library.

She sighed, feeling sorry for her brother . . . her *older* brother.

Being the disciplinarian was a new role for James—one in which he took no delight. But Walter had to be reined in, held accountable for his actions. For too long, he had run amok, coddled by their mother.

Caroline was certain that James would not lose the argument this time when their mother returned. Come September, Walter would be returning to Eton.

———•———

"WHAT WERE YOU *THINKING?*" James demanded. His words and tone might have been a tad loud as the question echoed around the room. Doing his best to temper his anger, James took a deep breath. While relaxing his stance, he tried to emulate his father's most severe expression. "There was no sensibility in the way you were driving, no propriety or modest behavior. All of which you promised!"

"Give over, James. It wasn't my fault . . . not really. The road is seldom traveled. How was I to know that the London coach was there?"

"Right," James said with more than a hint of sarcasm. "It's only lumbered down the road at the same time every day since before your birth . . . But how could you have guessed that today, of all days, it would do so again."

"I couldn't!" Walter glared at his brother for some minutes.

James stared back, giving no quarter. If he were not stern and unyielding, Walter would take advantage, pushing the limits, denying James' authority again.

Finally, Walter lowered his gaze to the floor. "I should have been more cautious."

James waited, hoping for an apology or a promise to never

again race down a road without checking first. But there was neither. Instead, when Walter lifted his eyes, his expression was of derision, his mouth partially open, a scathing comment undoubtedly at the ready.

James could see the strain on his brother's face as he fought the urge to argue, to shout that James couldn't tell him what to do. It had been Walter's contention since their father's demise. Hardly the truth, but the truth hardly mattered.

The standoff continued far beyond what was necessary, but eventually, James considered his point made. He crossed the hall to the drawing room, Walter shuffling in behind him with his shoulders bowed and his eyes glued to the floor. His younger brother crossed the room and sat down—well away from James.

"Sam and Ned left a trunk in the hall, Caroline," James said. "Where should it go?"

Caroline frowned. "Trunk?"

"The young woman's—from the coach."

"Oh, of course." She turned to the footman who stood by the door waiting for instructions. "Take it to the storeroom for now, Robert. Keep it to the front, though. I am sure she will want her things as soon as she awakens."

There was a brief silence after the door latch clicked.

"So, what have you been up to lately, Brant?" James asked, hoping to lighten the atmosphere. He knew he could count on his friend for florid and diverting anecdotes, something to keep Caroline distracted.

He, on the other hand, was restless and took a post at the window. There was nothing to see, nothing to watch except a large coach that lumbered down the road in the twilight hours. If James hadn't known better, he would have thought it to be the London stagecoach. But that was impossible. The mail coach from London only came through Welford Mills once a day and it had skated down the bank of the Torrin River, leaving behind a sorely injured young woman now resting in their attic.

CHAPTER TWO

The Enigma Awakens

Shadowed faces, in a twisted blur of colors and sound, lurked and menaced before her eyes. Echoes ricocheted through the chambers of her dreams. One moment was calm, the next brought fear. Struggling to break free, she reached out and up, her lungs giving vent to an unidentified terror.

When her eyes focused, she was sitting up in the bed of a sunlit chamber with whitewashed walls. The bed was hard, the linens rough, and her nightdress plain, but all were clean and smelled fresh. And the room was occupied not by shadows but by two women with very wide eyes.

The older of the two stood on the threshold. Her gray hair was tucked neatly beneath her starched muslin cap. Her face was firm but not unfriendly, despite the sharp nose. A black linen dress covered her ample form and her stance was that of authority.

The other woman, who had been leaning over the bed, was considerably younger. A full apron covered her flower print dress. A wet cloth, clutched tightly to her bosom, soaked into the upper bib.

"Gawd! Didn't you half scare the life out of me." The young woman shook the dripping cloth at her, and then she smiled. "Here, you lay yourself back down. Did I hurt you? Is that why you sat up screaming like that?"

"No, oh no. It wasn't you," the patient said absentmindedly. She allowed the young woman to grasp her by the forearms and lower her to the bed, distracted by a strange tightness around her head. She gingerly lifted a hand and fingered the wound cloth that she found there. It ran over her forehead and circled to the back above her ears.

The older woman stepped into the room. "Dr. Brant will be so pleased to see that you're awake. You gave us quite a fright last night. Lying so still, and then your fever started ta go up." Taking a deep breath, the woman straightened. "I'm Mrs. Fogel, the housekeeper, and this here is Daisy."

Mrs. Fogel reached over, taking the wet cloth, and shooed Daisy to the door. "Let Dr. Brant know that she's awake." The housekeeper dabbed at the patient's mouth with the cloth. "You won't be able to smile for a while, dear. Never you mind. It's a small concern. Everything's going to be just fine. Miss Ellerby will see to that . . ."

Mrs. Fogel's reassuring words had a lulling quality to them. The shadows dissolved in the nurturing warmth of the housekeeper's voice. Her eyelids grew heavy. Slowly the room faded, sounds drifted away.

Thudding footsteps grew louder. Fear filled her mind and her heart raced. Her eyes flew open and she gasped when a figure appeared in the doorway, but the tall man was a stranger, and a grinning one, at that.

"Good morning," he said. "You look *much* better." He had a slightly protruding chin and a crooked nose. "I'm Dr. Brant."

Mrs. Fogel shifted, trading places with the doctor so that he could take a closer look. He checked under the bandage on her jaw first. "Excellent, healthy pink skin. Yes, indeed, most excellent." His eyes were wide and excited. "If I weren't trying to maintain some dignity, I'd whoop. Yes, indeed, whooping is called for."

He looked expectantly at his patient, but when she didn't comment, he continued in a calmer tone. "You have a strong constitution. An infection started but it didn't take hold. It seems to have abated already." He replaced the wrapping and picked up her hands.

After toe wiggling, finger spreading, and even nose touching, the doctor declared that not only would sitting up be permissible but so would the consumption of that most restorative of elixirs, tea.

The recommended broth sounded less appealing.

JAMES SMILED AS he entered the small attic room. The patient was sitting up in easy conversation with Brant. Her straight brown hair was now neatly pushed behind her shoulders and some of the swelling above her ear was gone. Her skin was no longer ashen; her cheeks no longer rosy with fever. And her eyes were open, clear, and full of questions.

"Good morning," James said, standing at the end of the bed. His presence in the woman's room was rather untoward, but he had needed to see their . . . guest. See that she had, indeed, survived the night and was feeling better. "I am James Ellerby . . . Lord Ellerby." He flushed, still uncomfortable with the title. "And

I imagine you have already been told that you are at Hardwick Manor, just outside Welford Mills."

"Thank you for taking me in, Lord Ellerby. It was generous of you."

"You are most welcome."

James was pleased to find the girl articulate. More than articulate; her enunciation was cultured and educated. It contrasted deeply with the ripped and ruined gown that she had arrived in, as well as her bruised hands and dirty, broken nails; it was a bit of a puzzle. "It was the least we could do considering Walter, my half-witted brother, caused your accident." The recollection brought anger to James' face. "But enough of that," he said, unclenching his jaw. "We must let your people know where you are. They are probably frantic or at the very least wondering why you have not arrived with the coach. Were you destined for Exeter?"

The young woman stared at James for what seemed like a long time; her thin brows slowly pulled ever tighter together, and her eyes became distant. "I am . . . not sure. I do not know."

The room was still and silent. The sounds from the yard that had been drifting in the window muted. The young woman in the bed seemed to shrink. Her breathing became quick and shallow. She clamped a hand over her mouth.

Brant grabbed the basin just in time. He held her hair out of the way and watched helplessly until the young woman was spent. "Too much excitement all at once," he said. He tried to ease the patient to the pillow, but the young woman flailed as if pushing against her own distress.

"I don't know. I don't know," she kept repeating. Her eyes were wild. She searched their faces from one to the other, and back again. Then, her posture stiffened, and her chin rose. "I do not know who I am," she said, staring across the room.

Silence echoed resoundingly.

Brant took a noisy breath. "Don't be concerned," he said in a voice slightly elevated from its usual bass pitch. "Memory loss is common with injuries such as yours. It is usually temporary."

James watched as the young woman met the doctor's eyes; almost imperceptibly the patient shook her head.

James frowned, searching for a distraction. "Temporary." Then he nodded a little too enthusiastically. "We don't need your actual name right now. Why not just pick something for the moment, until you remember it? Young-woman-thrown-from-coach is a little too long," he said with false humor.

The young woman attempted a smile. It was wistful and accentuated her vulnerability. "The only name that comes to mind is Beth."

James' heart ached for her. "Beth it is."

"But I do not think that is my name."

"Beth will do for now," James said as bile churned in his stomach. He would have to eventually ask what she did remember, but slowly, with no pressure and without causing anxiety. To do otherwise might cause more damage . . . or so he thought. He'd best check with Brant about that—when not standing in front of the patient.

A rustle from the door broke the spell; Daisy entered with a tray. The teacup rattled against the bowl as she set it on the bedside table.

James met Brant's gaze and then he followed the doctor to the door. They gestured for Daisy to do the same and spoke in whispers in the hall.

"Stay with her, Daisy. Keep her talking, but do not ask any questions," Brant told the maid. "Not as yet. Keep it light . . . Talk about the weather or the retriever's new pups or your last half day, but do not mention her name or her family."

Daisy bobbed a curtsy and turned back to the small room.

James glanced in. Beth had not moved; the young woman stared, sightless, at a spot beyond the end of the bed. She didn't seem to blink or even breathe, and were it not for the occasional shiver there would have been no movement at all.

At the bottom of the stairs, James felt they were far enough away from all and sundry to speak candidly. "Is she likely to remember anything, Brant? Ever?"

"Hard to say. Best not ask her too many questions for a day or two. Give her mind a chance to relax and heal. You could send one of your footmen to Ellingham. Leave word at the inn for anyone who inquires."

"Yes," James agreed, though he was distracted. His mind had returned to the small upper room and the forlorn girl who had lost her name and her family in an instant. Her future was now as murky and uncertain as her past.

———◆———

LOCATED IN THE center of the west wall, the fireplace in the library was opposite the entry from the main hall. The elaborate design and proportion of the parquetry desk in the corner lent James the prestige and large surface required to oversee the running of the estate—his father's estate. No, he had to stop thinking that he was temporarily filling his father's shoes. It was a permanent condition—one could not get more permanent than dead.

James shook his head. Morbid thoughts, but James missed his

father terribly. He had yet to find solace in the role of Lord of the Manor. It would come in time.

James had anticipated running the estate in conjunction with a qualified land agent, but Old Dickens was still entrenched and the Dowager Lady Ellerby seemed disinclined to pension the man off. No, that wasn't true. His mother was more disinterested than disinclined . . . but the outcome was the same; the weight of over-seeing the estate was on his very inexperienced shoulders.

James frowned at the letter before him, trying to force his mind back to the seed tally. He was aware that the door opened; the swish of a skirt registered and announced his sister's arrival. However, Caroline was not alone. James watched as she and Brant made themselves comfortable in the burgundy leather chairs by the fire.

Scribbling a reminder across a paper, he placed the letter in a growing pile and pushed away from the desk. He joined his sister and friend, flopping inelegantly into a chair.

Caroline huffed. "This is a fine how-do-you-do," she said. "The girl cannot remember who she is or where she was going."

"Yes, I know. I was there when she realized." James shifted his gaze to Brant, not surprised to see his friend's relaxed manner; he was not fazed easily. Not as adept at appearing calm, James shook his head, deeply troubled. There would be people fretting, anx-ious for the young woman's return. Every day not knowing what had happened to her would be interminable.

"Her people will inquire after her, James," Caroline said, as if reading his mind. "I think we will be surprised by her circum-stances. Her voice and manner seem educated. She might even be a gentleman's daughter."

No bonnet or gloves, a torn gown and filthy hands, traveling alone. This did not sound like any lady that James knew. Still, he did find her direct gaze intriguing; it was almost a challenge. Yes, there was something about her, something . . . interesting.

Without a knock or a by-your-leave, the library doors burst open. Walter entered with great energy; Henry followed in his wake. Paying no heed to the fact that he was interrupting, Walter launched into a dramatic declaration.

"Life is so wild and unexpected! Life holds such excitement, especially in the spring. Do you not find?" he asked no one in particular and continued without hesitation. "Here I was in a fit of blue devils, for I was cruelly deprived of my curricle, suffered unwarranted criticisms, and then duties were pressed unjustly upon me. Bored and bored again, only to find Henry this morning with great news." Walter's drama was affecting no one but himself. "They have a guest at Risely Hall, Henry's uncle recently of the West Indies. Full of stories and adventures. I am revived!" He turned to leave the room, as self-involved as when he entered it. "I am off."

"Walter." James did not raise his voice. "Where are you going?"

Walter's smile slowly disappeared. "Why, to Risely Hall, of course."

James crossed his arms and, without taking his eyes off Walter, addressed Henry. "Thank you for dropping by, Mr. Thompson. Walter will, unfortunately, be unable to join you at Risely today. Or tomorrow."

Walter snapped his jaw shut.

Henry bowed without a word and stepped into the hall. The footman quietly closed the door behind him. Stealthy footsteps faded away.

"Now see here, James. You cannot keep me here twiddling my thumbs in penance. I did not mean to force the stagecoach from the road." Walter turned his appeal to Caroline. "Do not let him bully me like this, sweet sister. I will be miserable."

James watched Caroline struggle to maintain her composure. Her mouth opened and closed silently until the heat in her face flushed to the roots of her hair.

"How dare you! How *dare* you think of your own selfish wants while that poor girl lies in bed half demented because of your carelessness!" She rose and stood in front of her younger brother. Somehow she managed to tower over the taller boy. "You had better make yourself useful, not only to James and me, but more important, to the young woman that you injured.

"Her family and friends will be sick with worry, sitting up night after night watching and waiting, praying for some word of her safety. And you, you are worried about being *bored*!" Caroline sat down, shaking with emotion.

The room was silent. No one mentioned that only one night had passed.

Walter had the good sense to look contrite and cowed. "I had not thought of it that way. Mrs. Fogel said she was doing fine. I thought . . . I thought—"

"That is the trouble, Walter; you were *not* thinking." James shook his head, swallowing the lump of anger in his throat.

Walter's shoulders dropped, and he found great fascination in the pattern of the carpet.

Caroline took a deep breath and rose to her feet. "James, could you introduce *your* brother to our guest? I am in need of some fresh air." She turned to Walter. "You will do whatever you can to make her comfortable. You will talk to her, you will make her laugh, and you will read to her. You will ease her troubled mind and distract her. You will fetch her tea if she wants it." She raised her hand to silence him before he spoke. "Daisy has other duties. Beth will be yours. There will be consequences if I find you dallying."

Tight-lipped, Caroline left the room. Her careful footsteps and the swish of her gown could be heard through the doorway.

———◆———

DAISY BABBLED, her mind on other things. She had covered the pups, the weather, the horses, the kitchen staff, and her cousin that had moved to Exeter. Through it all, Beth had only nodded or made vague sounds of acknowledgment. When Beth suddenly squeaked, Daisy almost dropped the tray she had been balancing on her knee. "What?" she gasped. "What is it?" She glanced over her shoulder, expecting something large and scary coming through the door.

Beth touched Daisy's arm to regain her attention. "Can we get it? Right away?"

Daisy blinked, surprised by the change in Beth's expression; she looked excited. She sat straight up in bed, wide-eyed, and her teacup teetered, dangerously close to toppling.

Daisy recalled her last comment. "Oh, the trunk—the one from the coach."

"Yes! My trunk! It will have papers and records, perhaps a book with my name in it or, better still, letters! Daisy, I have been so worried that I would never learn my name, or of my family, where I'm from . . . my entire past."

"Calm yourself down, Beth dear. We can get yer trunk out when yer feelin' better. After you've rested a spell."

"There is no need of rest." Beth sat up as if to prove the point. "I'm feeling much better. Entirely better." She slapped her hand on the bed to prevent spilling forward.

"Entirely?" Daisy snorted a laugh. "I think not. Look at ya. You can hardly sit straight, let alone stand. You're tiltin'." She reached over, grabbing Beth by the shoulders, and maneuvered her into a balanced position. "There. That's better. Now, don't ya think I am goin' to have your trunk hauled up here anytime soon. You're not ready. Perhaps in a day or two."

"No, no. A day or two is a day or two too long." Beth shook her head adamantly, almost knocking herself over again. "The trunk will give me back my life. My memories are inside. My family . . . There might even be pictures. Oh, Daisy, please, if you won't bring it to me . . . bring me to it."

Daisy looked askance. "Bring you to the storeroom? In your weak and confused state? Most certainly not. If Dr. Brant didna give me a good dressing-down, Miss Caroline or Lord Ellerby certainly would. There would be a brouhaha—a loud . . . terrible brouhaha." She looked at Beth and bobbed her head as she agreed with herself. "Indeed. A terrible ruckus. So, let's hear no more about it. I am *not* bringin' up your trunk and that is that."

"Please, Daisy. No one has to be disturbed. I'll just—"

Beth put her foot down on the cold hard floor. Taking several short breaths, she exhaled and then slid her other foot off the bed. But before it touched the floor, Daisy grabbed her leg and pushed it back under the covers.

"No, no, no. You're not ready. You're goin' to have to wait."

CHAPTER THREE

A Proclivity for Melodrama

Beth knew that Daisy was right but, even as her belly roiled and her head felt cleaved in half, she couldn't stop resisting. She needed her trunk, needed her identity. "Please, Daisy. Just imagine how you would feel in the same situation."

Daisy stared at Beth's anxious face. "True enough . . . ," she said slowly.

"Whatever is the matter?" a voice asked.

Daisy turned to the doorway, still holding Beth in place. "Thank the heavens you are here, Lord Ellerby. She wants 'er trunk, sir. The one in storage. Can hardly blame 'er. Shall I see to it?"

Discouraged, Beth watched James Ellerby frown. Then he lifted his eyes and met her gaze. As their eyes locked, he smiled. It was a calm sort of display, not grandiose or frivolous. Then he nodded, and Beth thought her battle won, but his words proved otherwise.

"I will speak to Dr. Brant and if he agrees, perhaps this afternoon we will bring it to you." Lord Ellerby shifted to allow another figure to enter the room. "Until then, I have brought you a visitor."

Beth looked at the young man standing in the doorway. Was she supposed to know him? He was highly overdressed for a sick room, perhaps even for a country manor. Tall and broad shouldered, he had green eyes and dark wavy hair much like James Ellerby.

It could be none other than *Walter* Ellerby. Here was the author of Beth's misfortunes.

Beth held her tongue as James ushered his brother into the room, passed him a tray, and then departed. Wordlessly and awkwardly, Walter handed her the bowl of broth and a spoon. He grabbed a book from the reed chair placed beside the bed and slumped into it. She ate her soup in silence; he began reading in a bored, hard done-by tone. Eventually, Walter emerged from his self-involvement long enough to realize that she was not pleased by his company.

"It was an accident," he said, as if *that* were an apology.

"And therefore . . ." Beth paused, giving him ample opportunity to express his regrets. The silence lengthened until Beth harrumphed in disgust and passed him her empty bowl.

Leaning against the stacked pillows at her back, Beth's thoughts returned to the trunk in the storeroom. She did not want to ask Walter, of all people, for a favor, but she needed that trunk. It represented her identity, her past.

"Do you think your brother mentioned my trunk to Dr. Brant?" Beth asked.

He snapped the book shut. "How would I know?" Walter asked and then chuntered when she continued to glare at him. "I will check." With shoulders bowed and an expression of being overly burdened, he quit the room.

Time passed slowly—or so it seemed. Finally Beth heard movement on the steps, and she sat up in eagerness. However, it was not Walter's somber face that peeked into the room but the physician's.

"Do you really think you are strong enough?" Dr. Brant asked.

"I am exhausted," she admitted. "My head aches abominably and my belly does not want to stay still. But I need to know who I am."

Dr. Brant's eyes trailed from her clenched fists to her stiff back and then up to her tight lips. "You do, indeed. Walter is bringing your trunk up."

Within moments, a thump and thud rolled down the narrow corridor and burst into the room. It was followed by a loud *bang*, a few choice words, a sharp reprimand, and lastly, a scraping sound. James preceded the trunk into the room. The trunk preceded Walter. Or at least it would have but the room was now full. Walter found himself in the undignified position of watching the drama unfold from the hallway.

Beth glanced at James, meeting his gaze and sharing a look . . . of what she knew not, but it offered reassurance. Then they turned to stare at the trunk. There were no initials or labels, and it had certainly seen better days. For several moments no one moved, and then there was a scurry of activity as they all did. Dr. Brant pulled the trunk closer to the bed, James struggled with the buckles as the trunk moved, and Walter squeezed into the room and tried to turn the trunk so that the opening was toward Beth.

When they were done, Beth found herself reluctant to touch the lid. She bit her bottom lip and took a quick glance at the faces around her. Dr. Brant and Walter stared at the trunk. James watched her.

Beth braced herself and slowly lifted the lid.

At first she couldn't determine what it was that she was seeing. The swath of brown cloth turned out to be a cloak. Beth placed it on the foot of the bed. Underneath she found a lilac waistcoat, several shirts with winged collars, soft leather boots, a walking cane, ankle length trousers and toiletries . . . a man's toiletries.

"This is not my trunk."

Beth lay back on the pillows and closed her eyes. She raised her arms slowly and wrapped them around her bandaged head, hiding her face. The sound of scraping told her that the offending object had been dragged from the room. Whispers filled the air, and then footsteps announced the departure of the doctor and Lord Ellerby.

Beth knew that Walter remained in the hall. His muttered words echoed into the small attic room. He complained heartily as he threw the articles of clothing back into the trunk's cavern. The lid snapped closed, and the buckle jingled.

Another scrape indicated the trunk's relocation to the wall.

"This makes a very uncomfortable sitting stool. But do not worry about me. You just let me know if there is anything that you might wish. Oh yes, I will be right here. Waiting for your beck and call. Think not at all about my comfort. Oh no, I shall wait right here, just as I was ordered."

An unintelligible sound ricocheted through the hall. It sounded like a groan of frustration. It was followed by a mantra. "Boring, boring, boring."

Beth had a mantra of her own. *Go away. Go away.* "Go away!"

But Walter was too involved with his own misery to hear her.

LATER THAT AFTERNOON, Sam retrieved the trunk. He had been instructed to leave it at the post inn in Exeter, and inquire about any unclaimed luggage that might have turned up—however unlikely the possibility. So Walter, now deprived of his seat, had no choice but to reenter the sick room and try to keep company with the poor, broken lump that hardly talked.

Cook, in her infinite wisdom, had sent up a meal worthy of a feast—certainly plenty for a cautiously nibbling young woman and a ravenous, growing fourteen-year-old boy. Walter found himself once again perched on the reed chair, trying to distract Beth from her worrisome thoughts while he patted his satiated belly.

"I know what it is like to suffer as a result of a carriage accident," Walter commiserated. "My father was killed in one a year ago."

Beth lay passive on her pillows, staring in the direction of the window.

He shrugged to no one in particular and returned to his memories. "Both Caroline and James simply carried on. Can you imagine? My whole life had been turned on its end and yet they still expected me to go back to Eton. Well, that was what James wanted . . . expected. I persuaded Mother to let me sit in on Henry's lessons. Mother took to visiting relatives, not wanting to be here. Caroline was Friday-faced for months. And James, well, he stopped riding and shooting. He used to be one for a great lark . . . but no more." He sighed deeply. "It was *very* hard on me."

Beth shook her head at Walter's self-involvement. Concerns about family and fathers surged through her mind but without form . . . leaving her with more questions.

She chewed at her lip, trying to focus on the wisps of memory. "I believe I have lost someone as well."

Walter started. "Really? Who? Can you remember anything? Anything at all?"

Beth sighed. "Just what has happened in this room."

"Not even your favorite color?"

"Blue," Beth answered quickly.

"Your favorite sweet?"

Beth smiled. "Plum pudding."

Walter quizzed Beth on everything from pets to poets, countries to composers. Whenever she hesitated, Walter simply volleyed another question at her until she had an answer. It became a race as much as a discovery, and led to great mirth and merriment. When Caroline came in to release him, Walter was somewhat reluctant to go—although not entirely.

———•———

As the days passed, Beth slowly regained her strength. Her bruises healed and her appetite improved. Eventually only the deep cut on her jaw remained as a testament to her ordeal. However, her memories continued to elude her, and not a single night passed without a gut-wrenching nightmare.

It was always the same. A room full of shadows, a flutter of movement just beyond her sight, and a crushing fear pressing into her soul until she could no longer endure it.

———•———

The force of the thrust almost threw her past the large box that she had been directed to sit on. The sharp wood corner pushed into her corset and took her breath away. Fighting for air, she heaved herself up, slivers from the rough wood embedding themselves into her soft palms. The door slammed before she could right herself, and she was plunged into darkness.

She sat in the dank silence. The room reeked of filth and decay. She felt the gentle touch of a feather across her cheek and the hum of rapid wings; bile rose in her throat.

Unaware that she had moved, she found herself on the floor jammed into the corner, hands flailing. But now there was no soft menacing touch, no hum—just her own ragged breath. She dropped her arms, lifeless, into the sawdust at her side and she prayed for oblivion.

But her prayers were not answered. Instead sensibility returned and her eyes adjusted. She became aware of a dull glow; it came from a small slit in the wall high above her head. Beyond the lifeless beam it cast, were shadows, boxes and barrels stacked high and precariously.

After a time there was a flash of blinding light as the door opened and then closed behind three silhouettes. Nothing was said, but their presence was ominous. Shapes in motion, blurred from constant change. She was pulled back to the box and forced to sit. Her gaze directed toward a shape just beyond the glow of the beam.

There were no sounds in this small room overcrowded with malevolence. It was eerily quiet, as if she were suddenly and inexplicably deaf. But she was not blind, and what little there was to see was terrifying. A hand reached forward, toward her. It brought forth a shiny and honed form—a hummingbird whose sharp beak dripped with blood. In this room full of dark, the hummingbird stood out. It had found the light.

———◆———

IT WAS OFTEN a long, wailing scream that dragged Beth out of the depths of horror—her own scream. She would find herself sitting up in bed, her heart pounding. She was breathless and shaking, fearful of closing her eyes and even more of seeing a hummingbird— the tiny, iridescent bird that instilled terror in her.

The first night, her screams brought Lord Ellerby bursting through the door. He glanced around the room as if he expected monsters to be hiding in the shadows. But there were no monsters, just dreams, terrifying dreams.

"Are you all right?" he asked, out of breath, looking frazzled. "I was just going to my room when I heard you . . . You were screaming. What's wrong?" Again he glanced around, but there were still no monsters.

Mortified, Beth sat in bed, covers pulled up to her chin, a deep flush coloring her cheeks. "It was a dream, nothing more."

Taking a deep breath, James lifted his lips in a halfhearted attempt at a smile. "That must have been quite the dream."

"It was not pleasant. The stuff of nightmares." She laughed, realizing what she had said, and then shook her head. "I—"

"Beth, Beth," Mrs. Fogel called from the doorway. She had her hand to her chest and gasped as she dragged in a ragged breath. Her dressing gown was askew and hair fell about her face. "I heard you— Oh, Lord Ellerby? What are you . . . ?"

"Is Beth all right?" another voice called from the hallway. It sounded like Daisy.

Mrs. Fogel shooed her back to bed and then turned to Lord Ellerby. "Perhaps it's best if I take care of Beth, m'lord."

James slipped out of the room without another word, though he did glance back. He watched as Beth stared with haunted eyes at the empty space above the foot of her bed. She seemed unaware of Mrs. Fogel's arrival or his departure.

By the third night of nightmares, only Daisy arrived to sleepily inquire after her, and by the fourth, no one came at all.

Sɪᴛᴛɪɴɢ ᴜᴘ ɪɴ ʙᴇᴅ, anxious to be out and about, Beth rubbed her forehead and huffed a sigh. No matter how much she concentrated, the facts of her previous life eluded her. It was all well and good to remember favorite foods or color, but what about family, friends, where she lived? Did she have any siblings? Was she married? How old was she?

Dr. Brant had told her, many times, that her memories would return when she least expected them, when she was thinking about something else. But it was hard *not* to think of the past . . . or at least wonder about the past, as it was still a blank. A pristine slate, Lord Ellerby had said. She could fill it as she wished.

Still, Beth was almost certain that her past was painful—the circumstances of her arrival shouted of danger, disaster, and ruin. Her nightmares reinforced that foreboding. Yes, something had happened. Were her injuries all a result of the carriage accident or something else?

Something. The word kept coming up. It was so undefined, so nebulous. It was not in the least helpful. Something. She had to find out what . . . And she had to figure out why.

Jᴀᴍᴇs sᴛʀᴏᴅᴇ ᴀᴄʀᴏss the tiled floor of the white main hall as Caroline and Brant descended. Stopping at the bottom of the staircase, James' eyes were glued to a letter in his hand.

"I'm going to be called into London for a vote this summer," he said, swallowing with discomfort. "The House wants to stop the licensing of privateers. The vote is going to be tight and Lord Hanton has withdrawn." James frowned and snapped his tongue, demonstrating his disapproval. It was all bluster, of course. He wanted to exude confidence despite his trepidation. He had hoped his duties in the House of Lords would wait, that he could secure the advice of others first and make his way into the fold slowly.

"Perhaps Mama can suggest someone," Caroline said. "Such as Lord Levry or Lord Wolcher. Someone who can lead you through the proceedings. I know you are uncomfortable taking Papa's place in Parliament this soon."

James shook his head, still staring at the paper in his hand—his sister knew him well. "Let's not concern Mama. I will write Lord Levry directly and see what comes of it." James made a great act of folding the letter into quarters. "So, how is our patient?"

"Much better," Caroline and Brant answered together as they made their way into the drawing room.

"Other than the occasional headache, I believe she has recovered complete health," Brant continued. "I wish I could say as much for her memories." He dropped clumsily onto a chair.

"It would seem that her memories are not going to come back without some sort of prod," James said with a deep sigh. "And since no one has arrived to identify her, *we* must find her people. *We* must find the prod. Until we do, Mrs. Fogel will have to secure a place for her in the manor."

"James, we should bring her into the family wing until we know her background. I am convinced that she is a gentleman's daughter." Caroline smiled in that irritating manner she adopted when she was trying to get her way. "Talk to her; you will see what I mean."

"I have talked to her. Many a time." James didn't want to admit that he knew exactly what his sister meant. Beth had the demeanor, language, and attitude of a well-educated young lady. It complicated the matter tremendously; she *had* been traveling alone in a public conveyance wearing a filthy and torn gown. It was all very mysterious and confusing.

"I will send Beth to you this afternoon," Caroline continued to press. "So that you can assess her yourself."

James nodded, turning his face toward the fireplace.

———•———

"Welcome. Come in." James stood and waved toward the armchair by his desk. He tried to exude nonchalance, but it was difficult under the circumstances. Chuckling to himself, he recognized Beth's gown. It was one of Caroline's, covered with paint splatters, though still stylish and flattering.

Beth gracefully glided across the room and bobbed her head before sitting.

At a temporary loss for words, James tried to remember the point of their meeting. "Ah yes, Beth. We must decide on our next steps." He paused for a moment, watching as Beth licked her lips. "We had expected your people to make an appearance by now," he continued. "Inquiries at the post inn would have sent them our way. However as no one has arrived, we must start our own search."

"Indeed. Thank you, Lord Ellerby, for taking me in under such unusual circumstances." The silence that ensued was slightly uncomfortable.

James shifted uneasily. "It was the least we could do," he said finally, excessively aware of her gaze. "Have you had any recollections?"

James held his breath, waiting for her to answer. Hoping that she could offer something—a new memory, a sense of the past, a place in her childhood.

Beth dropped her eyes and huffed a sigh. "No, I'm afraid not."

James shrugged halfheartedly. "Worry not," he said. "We will not throw you to the wolves, but we will move you into the family wing for now."

"I appreciate your offer, but I would rather stay in the servants' hall. I'm not comfortable with the idea of giving myself airs only to discover that I'm a dustman's daughter."

James barked a laugh until he realized that Beth was serious. He swallowed his mirth with an audible gulp. "That is highly unlikely, but I bow to your wishes. There is no need to move out of the servants' hall if you are not so inclined."

"Excellent. Mrs. Fogel will find me something to do. I shall not be idle," she said as if to assure James of her usefulness. "Thank you, Lord Ellerby." Beth lifted her head and surprised James once more.

Beth's expression was not embarrassed or troubled. Had he given it a name, James would have said *determined*. It was a remarkable response, in a brave and impressive sort of way.

"I think I will ride over to Ellingham," he said casually. "One of your fellow passengers said you got on at the Ivy. We may not know much, but we do know where your journey began."

The statement rang hollow, for in truth, they knew nothing.

CHAPTER FOUR

Puppies and Impatience

James Ellerby sat in the corner of the Ivy, sipping a pint. Despite appearances, he was not there to relax. He was tense and frustrated and he wanted answers.

James had arrived on time, but the coach was late. And so he waited.

Finally, the sounds of jangling reins, pounding horse hooves, and grating wheels turned heads toward the door. Travelers stood and began to collect themselves.

Abruptly, the silhouetted form of a man stood in the doorway. "Goin' ta Exeter, leavin' in ten!" he shouted. He then moved out of the way to allow his new passengers through while he accepted a pint. He downed it in a gulp and was reaching for another when the innkeeper pointed him to James.

The man was tall and angular with brown hair and deep side-whiskers. "Can I 'elp ya, sir?" His attempt at a smile displayed more space than teeth.

James slumped. This was not the right man. "Actually, I was

waiting to speak to the driver of the London–Exeter coach of a fort-night ago." He tried to keep the vexation out of his voice, with limited success.

"That be me."

"No, no. I spoke with him when he had an accident by the Torrin Bridge. I need to ask him about one of his passengers."

"Oh no, sir, I didna have no h'accident by the Torrin. I lost me wheel near Ellingham. It took close on four hours to get it fixed."

James' frown deepened. "What time did you go through Welford Mills?"

"Well, I don't rightly know, sir. But it were gettin' on the dusky side. It were full dark when I hit Exeter."

Scrubbing at his face, James huffed in frustration. "Do you know a driver with black-and-gray hair with pockmarks on his face? He has a stocky build."

"No, sir. I don't."

James muttered a barely intelligible *thank you* and marched to the door.

<hr />

JAMES CHUNTERED MOST of the journey back to Hardwick. Frustration ate at his thoughts. Certainties, in fact, were not certain at all. The driver of Beth's coach had lied. The coach was *not* the post from London; the trunk wasn't Beth's trunk. Even her name was . . . well, not her name.

James felt his gray stallion turn; they had reached the drive of Hardwick Manor. The arching bridge over the Torrin was just beyond. Guiding Tetley back to road, James drew nearer to the accident site. The rain had softened—almost obliterated—the sharp cuts from the carriage wheels.

Jumping from his saddle, James draped the reins over the parapet of the bridge. He slid on the soft earth to the bottom of the bank and squatted by the water's edge. He stared into the gently lapping water, looking for answers, knowing he would find none.

An object just below the surface caught his eye. He reached into the water, pulling up a shapeless mass.

A coiled dirty mess. Rope. Just rope, cut and now useless.

He dropped it back into the water but, as he did so, a glint caught his eye. Soaking his cuff in the effort, James pulled up a blackened silver button. It had likely been encased in the mud for eons, uncovered when they had churned up the bank. He slipped the tarnished object into his waistcoat pocket for a closer look some other time.

———————

As THE GROOM led Tetley into the Hardwick stables, James' curly-coated retriever, Jack, greeted him with great enthusiasm—jumping and wagging with fervor . . . a little too much fervor as James stumbled back into someone who had been kneeling by the last stall. They nearly landed in a heap.

"Lord Ellerby?" Beth braced herself on the open gate.

Embarrassed, James offered his arm to help her rise. "My apologies, Beth. I did not see you."

She dropped a cursory bob. "I have a tendency to be in the wrong place at the wrong time." Then she caught his eye and continued in a rush. "I heard that you were going to Ellingham today. Did you visit the Ivy?"

Beth's eager expression was painful. "No news I'm afraid, Beth." He preferred to discuss the ramifications of the wrong coachman with Caroline first.

A pucker briefly appeared between Beth's pretty hazel eyes and then she turned the corners of her mouth up in mechanical-like increments. James breathed heavily through his nose; it sounded dangerously close to a sigh.

Fortunately, the exuberance of six fat pups behind Beth could be used as a distraction. James smiled. "So this is what drew you here."

He reached down into the straw-covered stall and lifted one of the squirmy bodies to his chest. Jack hopped over the board that sequestered them from the myriad of hooves, and was welcomed in style by the curly pups and Amber, their mother.

"Indeed. They are little bundles of curiosity wanting to explore the world. Playing at full tilt one moment and fast asleep the next." She pointed to one pup, bulkier than the rest, dozing in the corner, completely oblivious to the tugging and pouncing of its brothers and sisters. Beth knelt again and placed a puppy on her lap. "This one is my favorite."

The pup was identical to the others. James laughed and squatted beside her. "How can you tell? They all look alike."

Beth grinned. "Well, it's actually easy to tell. She always greets me first. She is almost the tallest, and she is almost the skinniest."

James snickered. "In other words, you can't tell at all. You simply guessed."

"Of course I can tell." In a conspiratorial manner, she looked right and then left. She dropped her voice to a whisper and reiterated her conviction as if imparting a secret. "Of course I can tell."

She lifted up the right forepaw of the wiggling pup. One white claw stood out from all the rest.

James smiled. He met, and then unintentionally locked on to Beth's eyes. A few moments or seconds passed. It was only when the pup tried to lick Beth's chin that they came out of their reverie together. Surprised and uncomfortable, James realized that his behavior was not appropriate.

"I am glad you are enjoying the retrievers, Beth." He dropped his squirming bundle back into the straw, rose, and dusted off the paw prints. "Good day."

James called to Jack and left Beth still kneeling in the straw.

———•———

TWITCHING WITH IMPATIENCE, Caroline sat with the appearance of calm on the edge of an overstuffed chair, ready to pounce. She knew that James would wend his way to the quiet warmth of the library as soon as he had changed. And this was where she intended to confront him.

Caroline was resolved that neither was going to dine until James agreed that Beth should move into the family wing. Beth's manner, speech, talents, and countenance all indicated that she was misplaced in the servants' hall. And now, after this afternoon in the garden, there was no doubt. James had to listen.

So intent on formulating her arguments, Caroline missed the sound of the opening door.

"Relaxing with a good book, are you?" James eyed the closed novel on her lap. He reclined into the facing chair.

"Oh, James. I wish you wouldn't creep about so. You scared the life out of me."

"Did I? Next time I'll have Robert announce me."

"Very funny." Swallowing and then taking a bracing breath, Caroline delved straight into the cause of her disquiet. "James, I must speak to you about Beth."

"By all means, Caroline."

"This afternoon I was painting in the garden. The crocuses are up as well as the tulips, by the by. And as much as I adore florals—as well you know—today, I was inspired to do a landscape."

James blinked and then tilted his head, as if to see her better from a different angle. "Most excellent . . . And this regards Beth how?"

"Well, I felt like doing something different. I wanted to do a vista. It started out just fine . . ."

"Ah, we are still talking about painting." James raised his eyebrow questioningly, wordlessly reiterating his query about Beth's involvement.

"But I decided to put leaves on the trees," Caroline continued, ignoring his rejoinder. "I could not make it look right. Beth was at one of the upper windows and heard my frustrated mutterings." She shifted back in her chair and lifted her chin as if preparing for an onslaught. "She came down to help me. James, in less than a quarter of an hour she showed me three ways to render the impression of full trees without painting each leaf, which is what I had been trying to do. The first method was to take the fan brush and tip it in not one but three colors—"

"I am sure, Caroline, the point of your story is *not* to teach me how to paint leaves."

"No, indeed not, James. I simply wanted to assure you of my confidence . . ." She swallowed awkwardly, exuding anything but confidence. "I want to assure you that Beth is a gentleman's daughter. I am all but certain. That we do not know who this gentleman is should not prevent us from providing the proper shelter for her until such time as her relatives come looking for her. I would like to ask her to be my companion."

"She would be a welcome addition to our small clan."

Caroline laughed and relaxed into her chair. "You had already decided she belongs with the family, hadn't you?"

"Yes. Staying in the servants' wing was Beth's suggestion, not mine," James admitted. "But I could tell that you had gone to a lot of thought. Worked yourself up and all that. I wasn't about to steal your thunder."

"You brute." Caroline threw her book at him without much force.

He caught it handily and then dropped the abused novel on the table between them. He sighed—rather deeply, world weary-ish. "There is more to this accident than meets the eye, Caroline."

"What do you mean?"

"Beth was not on the London stagecoach."

Caroline sat forward again, listening to James describe his visit to Ellingham.

"There was no one waiting in Exeter," he said, "because that was not her destination."

"But where, then?"

"That is the trouble, Caroline. I have fewer answers now than before."

"But, James, you said one of the men at the accident mentioned the Ivy."

"Yes, one of the passengers on the coach. Now I know that he lied. If the carriage was not the post or stagecoach, it had to be a coach for hire. But I am beginning to think I should not assume anything. It is a baffling business, Caroline, make no mistake."

"Will we tell Beth?"

"Perhaps not. It is unsettling, to say the least."

"We could ask Dr. Brant what he thinks. I will send a note. Invite him to sup with us tomorrow." Caroline stood, nodded absentmindedly to James, and quick-stepped into the hall. She wanted to speak to Beth before dinner.

CHAPTER FIVE

Fellow Confederate

Caroline strode down the small hall and into the servants' wing with a skipping sort of gait. To be proper, she should have rung for one of the maids to find Beth, but Caroline was too excited to wait. Fortunately, Beth was descending just as Caroline approached the back stairs.

"Beth, might I have a word with you?" Caroline asked.

The girl stared wide-eyed, as if expecting bad news.

Silly widgeon.

Caroline swept her arm toward the front of the house and gestured for Beth to follow. Marching into the bright morning room, Caroline closed the door with more force than she intended, eager anticipation making her ham-fisted. She bounced over to the settee, dropped down on the cream brocade, and turned with a gleeful smile. Patting the seat beside her, she encouraged Beth to join her.

Wary and watchful, Beth sat stiffly, looking anything but comfortable.

Caroline leaned forward, grinning. "You do not belong in the servants' hall, Beth. Your manners, sensibility, and obvious education speak for themselves. If Mother had been here, I'm sure she would have insisted that you join the family." She said nothing about Beth's resolve to be placed with the servants and ignored Beth's frown and confused expression. "Since Mother left a month or so ago," Caroline said, steering their conversation to a safer topic, "Hardwick has had plenty of boyish pomposity . . . more than enough." She shook her head as she thought of Walter.

Her mother's flair for melodrama had been fully realized in her younger son. Losing the staid, steady guidance of Father had taken its toll, and her mama's extended visit with Aunt Beatrice had not helped anyone but Mama. Caroline frowned, pushing her thoughts back to the problem at hand. "Gentlewomen are few and far between in this household at present. It would be quite agreeable to talk of music and books, to paint, to laugh, and be engaged in easy conversation again. Well, what I am trying to say . . . Might I persuade you to become my companion?"

Beth opened her mouth but only produced an unintelligible squeak.

"I know the loss of your memory is a great trial to you. But when—and I say *when* because I fervently believe that the day will come—when your memories return, I will simply call you by another name. Still, I would like to think I will always call you my friend."

Beth swallowed visibly, her expression no longer wary but dejected. "I am very grateful, Miss Ellerby—"

"Call me Caroline."

"I'm very grateful, Miss Ellerby, but you do me too much

honor. There are many circumstances in which . . . I might have the appearance of being gently raised."

"Indeed."

"But that does not make it so. I might have thwarted my parents and run away . . . or I am a disgraced governess."

Caroline snorted in a most unladylike fashion. "Perhaps we won't enumerate all the possibilities of your situation—it would require more time. It shall have to suffice that I believe we would get along rather well no matter what your circumstances. So, what say you?"

Breathing deeply, in almost a sigh, Beth stared at Caroline.

"Does Lord Ellerby know of this change?"

"Yes, Beth. Not only does he know, but he supports it."

The clock on the mantel chimed loudly in the ensuing silence, and there was a soft knock on the door.

"One minute, please," Caroline called without taking her eyes off Beth. "What do you think?"

"I feel like a charlatan. Unworthy of your company." And then she smiled. "But you seem certain—"

"I am. And determined."

Beth chuckled. It was the first time that Caroline had heard her laugh. Caroline grinned. "Yes?"

"Yes. Thank you. I will accept your generous offer. I will be your companion."

Caroline jumped to her feet, pulling Beth up with her. "Wonderful. We are going to have such good times together." She gave her new companion a quick hug, ignoring the girl's stiffness. "Enter," she called to the door.

It was Mrs. Fogel. "Dinner is ready, Miss Ellerby. And Miss Beth's things have been removed to the green room."

Caroline glanced guiltily at Beth. "I was fairly certain that I could persuade you."

Beth laughed again. "Apparently."

Turning to Mrs. Fogel, Caroline ignored the housekeeper's lack of expression; there had been approval in her tone.

"Did Daisy help determine which were Beth's possessions?" Caroline asked.

"No, Miss Ellerby, the girl hasn't returned from her half day yet. But it was clear enough and little to pack." The housekeeper glanced in Beth's direction and smiled. "I'm sure Miss Beth will let us know if we mistook anything."

"Thank you, I'm sure she will." Caroline glanced again at the clock and sighed. "Oh dear, the boys will be ravenous. Mrs. Fogel, would you show Miss Beth to the green room and have a tray sent up?" She squeezed Beth's hand. "It will give you the opportunity to get used to your new circumstances. No need to rush; tomorrow will be soon enough to join the family." Caroline nodded enthusiastically and left the room.

———•———

BETH DROPPED BACK onto the settee, staring and blinking at the carpet for some minutes.

"Are you all right, my dear?'

Beth looked up and laughed. "Yes, actually, I am quite well. I'm just astonished. I could never have imagined this turn of events."

"Well then, dear, you are the only one. It was all too obvious that you belonged upstairs. Not that we can blame Miss Caroline or Lord Ellerby, but you can't make a sow's ear out of a silk purse."

With a grin and a shake of her head, Beth rose again. "I believe the expression is you can't make a silk purse from a sow's ear."

"Just trying to say you can't hide quality under a dirty dress. And speaking of which . . ." Mrs. Fogel turned Beth around, undoing the strings of her apron. It was dingy and limp with age—a spare found in the ragbag. "You won't be needing this anymore," she said. "Now, I believe I'll take you up the main staircase so that you'll be able to find your way back in the mornin'." Mrs. Fogel squared her shoulders and strode from the room.

After a few moments, a disembodied voice drifted through the doorway. "Miss Beth, would you care to join me?"

Beth came out of her reverie and stepped out the door. She met Mrs. Fogel in the elegant, white-tiled main hall. The sounds of muted voices and clicking cutlery drifted under the closed door of the dining room.

Tomorrow, Beth would join them.

How would Lord Ellerby feel looking up at breakfast to find the face of a stranger sitting across from him? Would he be uncomfortable and stilted? Worse still, would he think she had manipulated the situation—used Caroline to her own ends? Beth could protest her innocence but . . . the less said soonest mended.

Yes, she would simply be as unobtrusive as possible. Until she knew who she was and where she came from, it would be best not to step on anyone's toes—especially not on those of an accommodating young lord.

———•———

JAMES LOOKED UP when Caroline entered the dining room alone.

"Our guest shunning our company?"

"Hardly, James." Caroline looked across the linen-draped

rosewood table. The silver candelabra offered a generous amount of light, illuminating Walter's empty seat. "Speaking of shunning, where is Walter?"

As if on cue, Walter entered the room with an affected gait—implicit grandeur with a hint of military posturing.

"Are you all right, brother dear?" James asked. "You seem to be limping."

Lifting his chin in haughty distain, Walter missed the center of his chair and almost tumbled to the floor. With a casual swipe at his hip, Walter secured his seat and adopted an unconcerned expression. "Henry and his family have expressed their interest in my company tomorrow," Walter said. "They asked me to dine with them at Risely Hall. And I would like to go. No, I *need* to go. I have been at Beth's beck and call for a fortnight, a whole fortnight. I have paid my penance."

Caroline frowned into her soup, pursing her lips as if the broth had suddenly turned sour.

Walter continued to monopolize the conversation, switching to particulars about the West Indies, waxing on about the marvels of large spiders and coffee plantations. Stories no doubt gleaned from Henry about his uncle.

Eventually, Walter's blather wound down; it gave Caroline a chance to speak. She began with a huff. "Fine. You may go. But do *not* take the curricle."

Walter harrumphed in protest. However, when James shifted in his chair, Walter quickly accepted the limitation. "Thank you, Caroline. I had no intention of traveling the main roads. The freer paths for me." Having attained his goal, Walter rose and quit the room, leaving behind his affected gait as well as his surprised siblings, who were waiting on the next course.

UPSTAIRS, BETH PACED. The green room—though lovely—was overwhelming. It was large with a high ceiling, full of substantial furniture and swirling color. The walls were busily covered in ivy and mauve clematis paper. Two huge corner windows offered her prospects of the park and the gardens. Hardly threatening. Across from the deep green draperies of the windows was a four-poster bed with heavy matching linens and hangings. The effect was one of tradition and quiet elegance.

In the mahogany wardrobe hung Caroline's hand-me-down dress; it looked forlorn and out of place, just as Beth felt. She snapped the door shut, unable to bear its recriminations.

A fire had been lit earlier and the room was cozy and comfortable, but still Beth paced. She had only nibbled at the dinner brought to her by Mrs. Fogel. Her dinner tray sat, barely touched, awaiting its return to the kitchen.

At first blush, this social elevation had seemed a godsend. The expectation of spending her days in Caroline's company—talking, painting, helping with charitable works, and planning meals—was a pleasurable one. But the moment she was left alone, she felt inadequate, bewildered, and confused.

With deliberate will, Beth slowed her pacing and stopped before the windows. The sun had just set and the sky was painted a soft rose-pink. Staring out, she gasped in alarm. A flock of silhouetted birds dipped and reeled against the glowing backdrop. Not hummingbirds. No, not hummingbirds. Swallows, looking graceful and lithe.

There was nothing in their smooth flight to remind Beth of her nightmares and yet fear found her nonetheless. Her limbs started to shake and her breath quickened. In her mind she could hear the flap of beating wings—humming. She wanted to look away but was caught, spellbound.

It was fortunate that, at that moment, she heard a distracting knock on the door. She took a calming breath and bade, "Enter."

"A lovely view of the gardens, don't you think?" Caroline asked, joining Beth beside the window.

Beth nodded, continuing to watch the birds as they soared across the sky.

"We have something important to discuss," Caroline said after a moment. "I have detected a lack of style in your wardrobe." She bounced her eyebrows up and down.

Beth chuckled. "It is *your* dress."

"Indeed." Caroline nodded with a grin. "That is the problem. I have never been all-the-crack, as Walter would say. No, it will not do. We shall have to visit Millie Couture; she is a modiste in Welford Mills. Country fashion, I'm afraid," Caroline sighed. "But it will have to do for now."

Beth liked pretty dresses as much as any girl, but the expense was a little overwhelming. "I don't need anything new."

Caroline ignored her protest. "Cast downs will not be sufficient. You must have new gowns. Can't have you looking like a ragamuffin." Her smile denoted mischief, a hint of humor, and pleasure from the prospect. "Bonnets, gloves, stays, petticoats . . . Oh yes, this is going to be quite enjoyable."

Inwardly sighing, Beth wondered how she would ever pay back this generosity.

COWERING ON THE CRATE, oppressive silence besieged her. The room was dark and reeked of filth and decay. Something waited in that dark silence, waited for her, threatened her.

She felt the gentle touch of a feather across her cheek and the hum of rapid wings. Bile rose in her throat and she jerked away. Now on the floor jammed into a corner, her hands flailed. But the feather touch was gone, as was the hum; only her ragged breath disturbed the silence.

Time passed, a little . . . a lot, she hardly knew. She became aware of a dull glow, seeping from a small slit in the wall high above her head. Beyond its feeble beam were shadows, boxes and barrels stacked high and precariously.

Silhouettes approached. Shapes blurred from constant motion.

Hauled from the floor, she was dragged back to the box and forced to sit. Her head was held in place, forcing her gaze toward a shape illuminated by a slit of light.

There were no sounds in this room laden with malice. It was unbearably quiet, as if she were suddenly deaf. But she was not blind, and what little there was to see was terrifying. A hand reached forward, toward her. It held a dagger. Its dark wood hilt gently curved into the shape of a hummingbird. Its long bill was razor sharp. Evidence of its last feed dripped onto the floor. A puddle formed and grew. A puddle of blood.

Her blood.

Beth awoke, screaming.

———◆———

JAMES AWOKE WITH a start. He sat up, trying to clear his head. Had he heard a cry, a scream? The creaks and groans of the manor were familiar friends. Nothing felt amiss and yet his heart pounded in alarm.

Slipping out of bed, James found his robe and slippers. He lit a candle and opened his bedroom door in silence. In the corridor, all was as it should be. He glanced toward the main staircase, then turned in the opposite direction. As he neared Beth's room, James heard movement and a soft sound . . . a sob?

Gently tapping the door, James opened it a crack. "Beth, is all well?"

The reply was muffled and inarticulate.

Pushing the door farther, James could see that Beth was still abed; she had pulled a pillow over her face, held in place with her knees. Her shoulders shook with emotion.

James glanced down the corridor in both directions, thankful that the passage was empty. Beth's reputation would be ruined if he were seen standing by her door in the middle of the night. As he decided on his next course of action, Beth sobbed again, and James rushed through the door without thought. As he approached the bed, he slowed, not wanting to startle her. He gently lifted her hand from the counterpane and cupped it, crooning soothing nonsense.

Soon the only sounds in the room were the wind scratching at the window, the creak of the shifting floors, and the squeak of movement on the bed. James could feel Beth take a deep breath before she lifted her face from the pillow. "Thank you," she said in a hushed tone, almost a whisper. "I am sorry I disturbed you . . . again. It's rather embarrassing. Could we not pretend that nothing is amiss?"

James pulled an upholstered cream-colored Chippendale chair

closer to the edge of the bed. "Perhaps. But you were screaming rather loudly," he said. "Have your nightmares come back?"

Beth hiccupped a laugh—a giggle of sorts—that was more embarrassment than amusement. "They have never gone away." She shifted as if she were uncomfortable, either with her position or her words. "It's nothing," she said without conviction.

"Clearly it is something, and if you think that I am going to leave before I know what this is about, then you are sadly mistaken. Even if you could induce me to leave—which you cannot—I would not be able to sleep a wink. Do you want me heavy lidded in the morning? No beauty rest for these weary bones?"

Beth's smile was halfhearted, likely meant to reassure, but James' uneasiness continued to grow. "Please, tell me."

Beth swallowed. Her voice dropped to a whisper. "I dream that I am in a putrid, narrow room. It is filled with moving, changing shapes, but in the center of the room is a beam of light. I want to curl into a little ball. I want to disappear, and actually pray to do so." Beth stopped; she met James' gaze.

"You fear the light?"

"No, what the light shows. A dagger—in the shape of a hummingbird. It's dripping blood . . ." Beth lifted her eyes to stare at nothing on the far wall. "My blood." Tears slid unnoticed down her cheeks.

James was shattered, witnessing the depth of her fear and sorrow. He wanted to jump into the nightmare and rush at the bearer of this dagger and exact revenge. Instead, he leaned forward, offering her a handkerchief. "It is just a dream," he said, repeating her words. "A horrid one, but a dream nonetheless."

"It might be more." Her eyes filled with tears again.

James brushed Beth's hair back behind her shoulders in a wordless display of solidarity and caring. As he did, his gaze caught the scar just under Beth's chin. "You think it's a memory."

"It might be." Beth's tone was studiously unemotional.

James nodded, leaned back, and then stood. "I have invited Dr. Brant to dine with us tomorrow. Why don't we see if he has any ideas?"

Beth flushed. "I don't think it is important enough to mention."

"Fustian nonsense, he won't mind in the least. He is always looking for a way to impress us with his knowledge."

He left Beth staring with deep concentration at her counterpane. It was a pretty quilt with an intricate design but hardly worth an intense study. She was lost in thought, still caught up in her fears, her nightmares, and James could hardly fault her for that. If he knew the source of those horrid dreams, he could dispel her concern with logic, or at the very least call in Brant with some medical explanation. Something, anything, to erase the haunted melancholy in her eyes.

———◆———

"Beth!" Walter sauntered into the morning room, greeting the new companion with his usual lack of decorum. "Have you deigned to join our ranks?"

Beth held firmly to her cup and saucer as Walter danced around her. It was already late morning, and breakfast was well and truly over—the kippers cold, James' paper read, and Caroline's menu for the day not only planned but given to Cook. The congenial atmosphere of the room had caused the time to pass quickly, and they had lingered over their morning meal beyond their regular habit. Beth had only just risen to refresh her tea again from the sideboard.

Walter ignored his own lack of punctuality, piled his plate with what was left of the ham and biscuits, and accused others for his ignorance. "Why wasn't I told?" He glanced up at James with an attempted piercing stare. "I would have been down here directly this morning."

"No, you would not. You would still have been late." James folded the *Times* with care. The blazing headline House in Uproar became the bland news of House in. "Besides, last night you monopolized the conversation and left us without a by-your-leave. So when would we have mentioned Beth's transfer upstairs?"

Walter ignored his brother and fixed his eyes on the table.

"So, what do you think?" Caroline asked, returning to the subject at hand before Walter's grand entrance.

"I do not know if I can ride. What would be the point of ordering a riding costume if I cannot ride?" Beth replied.

"Easily solved, Beth: We will teach you."

Beth laughed. "Are you going to solve all my problems?"

"Absolutely." Caroline smiled and then continued, "So, as you can surmise, James, Beth and I will be out for a few hours after luncheon. Would you be so kind as to greet Dr. Brant should we be late? I did mention his note arrived this morning."

"Yes, you did." James pushed his chair out from under the table. "A few times. Walter will be joining me at the Havershams' this morning, but inspection of the new barn and fields should be completed well before midday. That is, as long as his nibs here tarries no longer and finishes his breakfast sometime before noon."

Walter looked up. "Oh, tare an' hounds. I forgot. I won't be here for you, Beth. I am to dine at Risely tonight. It will be top of the trees. You, however, will be entrenched in"—Walter's tone expressed his distaste—"*liberal conversation*. But worry not. I shall make it all come right. Tomorrow, I shall tell all. Every detail."

Beth saw Caroline cringe. She managed a nod and smile that was only a little off-kilter before she rose. Beth and James followed suit.

"Please excuse us, Walter," Caroline said. "We don't want the day to be carried off without us."

The three stepped into the hall together but diverged by the main staircase. The women were headed to the storage space in the attics while James would wait for Walter in the library.

Mr. Evans, the wizened house steward with bowed shoulders and a hesitant walk, stepped forward the moment the group appeared. He asked for a private moment with the master.

As Beth stepped onto the first tread of the staircase, she glanced over her shoulder to see the men enter the library. James' expression was somber but unconcerned. She turned back to meet Caroline's gaze, exchanged a shrug, and then they continued up to the attic.

CHAPTER SIX

Introducing Miss Dobbins

Although curious about the steward's twitchy behavior, Beth followed Caroline up the stairs. Upon reaching the second level, Caroline swept her arm toward the back stairs that preceded to the storage attics. Finally they stopped in a dusty, trunk-laden corner under the eaves.

"What do you think has happened?" Beth asked, her uneasiness getting the better of her.

Caroline wiped the cobwebs from the lid of a sizable trunk and shrugged. "Oh, don't worry, Beth. It's likely a small, meaningless incident . . . something having to do with the estate or one of the tenants. Had it involved the manor, Mr. Evans would have spoken to me."

Beth nodded, trying to hide her continuing disquiet. It was unlikely that Mr. Evans' request to speak with James had anything to do with her and yet . . . shaking the troublesome thoughts from her head, she exhaled noisily, helping lift the heavy trunk lid. Inside lay several carefully folded gowns.

"Miss Overton, my governess, was never extravagant—she couldn't afford to be—but I persuaded Mama to provide a bolt of cloth for a riding costume last year . . . just before she, Miss Overton, shuffled off her moral coil." Caroline touched the lace of the topmost dress. "She was well regarded by all of us; in fact, she was going to stay on at Hardwick. I sincerely wish she had not gone to Nottingham." Caroline pressed her lips together for a moment. "She caught the typhoid and I never saw her again."

Caroline looked across at Beth and smiled—albeit weakly. "I gave away all but her favorite gowns to the poor, but I couldn't part with these." In one motion, Caroline pulled a plum silk dress from deep in the chest and held it before Beth. She stretched the bodice across Beth's midriff and shoulders, and then glanced down at the hem. "As I thought. This will do quite nicely. I think Miss Overton would be pleased that it was passed on."

Beth touched the beautiful material reverently. "So, we won't be visiting the seamstress in Welford Mills after all?"

"Yes, we will." Caroline's voice was muffled, her nose half buried in the trunk once more. "You'll have a day dress and an evening gown from here, but only to use while waiting for the new ones."

Caroline continued to root around. "There it is!" she finally called out. She straightened and pulled a deep blue velvet riding habit from the trunk's depths. She held it high above her head, but still the skirts trailed to the floor. "However, this was the last costume she had made. I believe she only wore it a few times." Caroline stared sadly at the habit.

"It's difficult to lose someone," Beth said, squeezing Caroline's hand in empathy. "I understand. I lost my mother when I was quite young."

The words were out of Beth's mouth before she realized what

she had said. She stood motionless for what felt like an eon, then slowly turned to find Caroline staring at her.

Beth felt an urgent need for a chair. She sat with a thump on an adjacent trunk, oblivious to the dirt and grime.

"Beth! Do you remember something?"

Fisting her hand into her temple, Beth tapped at her brain as if to make it work. "Who—when?" She furrowed her forehead and squeezed her eyes shut in an effort to think. But to no avail; the passages of her mind were still clouded. "No," she said, groaning in disappointment.

Caroline pulled Beth from her seat. "It is a beginning, though, a breakthrough." She laid the habit across Beth's arms and put two other gowns on top of that. "They will come. Your memories, I mean. You'll be thinking of something else and *voilà*, there they will be. Best not belabor them until then. Anxiety will only make them hide."

Beth nodded and then smiled weakly. "Very likely." She gulped and wiped the emotion from her eyes. "Yes, very likely," she repeated.

Caroline squeezed her arm in commiseration. "I'm very sorry about your mother."

Beth nodded again, fighting tears and empty memories.

"A distraction is in order." Caroline reached out and closed the trunk lid with a clang. It echoed down the narrow hall as Beth followed Caroline to the stairs.

"A trip into town might be just what you need. I'll run and get my bonnet, and I'll grab one for you, too," Caroline called over her shoulder. "Daisy can air out Miss Overton's gowns while we are gone."

Beth smiled as Caroline quickened her pace, humming and all but racing down the stairs.

As it was nearing midday, Beth was not surprised to find the bedroom floor quiet. There was no sign of Daisy, and it took a few minutes to find one of the other maids.

"Don't know where she be, an' don't care—dawdling while the rest of us work," Harriet grumbled. And then, likely remembering that Beth was now a guest, Harriet abruptly stood straighter and swiped at the dirt on her apron. "'Ere, give them ta me. I'll make sure they gets an airin'." Harriet reached forward, relieving Beth of the gowns.

Rather than head directly back to the family rooms, Beth skipped up the back steps to the servants' quarters. She wanted to verify that nothing had been overlooked in the removal of her few possessions.

The room was as bright and cheerful as ever, but a tad stuffy. Beth opened the window to allow the breeze and sounds of the yard to penetrate the stale air. In a glance, she could see that nothing had been left behind.

Beth turned, catching sight of Daisy's apron still hanging from the bedpost. Behind the door, she found Daisy's work dress and a brown cloak. It seemed rather odd. Shouldn't Daisy be wearing her work clothes? She certainly wouldn't be wandering around naked.

With a snort, Beth shook her head. If she worried about every little exception, made mountains out of molehills, and jumped away from her own shadow, she would be of no use to anyone. Questioning everything was paranoia at its best.

She would talk to Daisy this evening. There would be a simple explanation. Then Beth forced a smile to her lips; Daisy had likely gotten a new dress and apron. New clothes were always agreeable.

With that cheery thought, Beth slipped downstairs and headed toward the front of the house. She didn't want to keep Caroline waiting.

STROLLING ARM-IN-ARM DOWN the quaint and less-than-bustling main street of Welford Mills, Caroline and Beth were enjoying their outing immensely. Beth's anxiety at meeting new people in unfamiliar surroundings had been overcome almost immediately with a welcome at her first encounter.

No sooner had they alit from the carriage than a tall, husky woman approached them, a genial expression on her generous face, and a plethora of indiscernible words on her lips. Mrs. Edith Cranley was all that a man of the cloth's devoted spouse should be. According to Caroline, she was friendly and charitable and knew when to chat, when to demur, and when not to ask questions.

Caroline, obviously familiar with the good woman's concoction of thick Yorkshire and hollow nasal resonance, greeted her enthusiastically. "It is good to see you, Mrs. Cranley. I must tell you, Reverend Cranley's sermon last Sunday was unparalleled."

This combination of good will and Caroline's unruffled responses gave Beth the uplift that she needed. It cleared away the butterflies running amuck in her belly.

"Elizabeth, I would like you to meet Mrs. Cranley. Mrs. Cranley, Elizabeth Dobbins."

Beth was startled to find that she had gained a last name, but only missed the flowery welcome by a few words. The ensuing conversation, while about Beth, required very little input on her part, allowing her the time to absorb her role as seen beyond the gates of Hardwick Manor.

It was likely that the rumor mill of the village was already rippling with Beth's arrival at the manor. Few outside the household staff knew of her missing memories, but her unconventional trip in Mr. Haines' wagon would have been discussed six ways to Sunday. Caroline did her best to establish Beth as a friend of the family. If nothing else, it gave the populace of Welford a guideline to follow.

This approach proved worth the effort, for after their brief conversation with Mrs. Cranley in front of the apothecary, and short foray therein, Beth was not only greeted politely but by name in each subsequent shop.

At the dressmaker's, Millie Couture was overjoyed at the honor the ladies had bestowed upon her. Her great enthusiasm carried them all through the taking of measurements, deciding styles, and choosing materials. No comment or observation was made pertaining to the ordering of everything from dresses to gloves to smallclothes. They left Millie with assurances that all would be finished within the week and a sense of a job well done.

Smiling contentedly, the two nodded their way down to the milliner's to make their final purchases. As they stood before the large window admiring the vast array of bonnets, Beth finally had enough privacy to ask, "Why Dobbins?"

Caroline shrugged. "It was the first name that came to me when I realized that introductions would be necessary." Her smile reflected in the glass. "Isobel Dobbins is a school chum of mine. It will be assumed that you are her sister." Quite satisfied with her reasoning, Caroline entered the shop.

Beth remained outside, staring at her reflection, trying on the name Dobbins. It didn't trip lightly across her mind, but stumbled and limped. She stared deeply into the eyes of her mirrored self, and then noticed that hers were not the only eyes in the glass.

Another pair, eerily disembodied, stared with unmasked hostility from over her shoulder.

Beth met those eyes in the reflection and then whirled around to meet them in truth.

No one stared back.

The street was awash with ambling couples and dirty-faced urchins. There was no unsolicited scrutiny, no expression of disapproval. Beth looked back at the glass. She blinked and tried to imagine what it was that had misled her. She could find no staring eyes a second time.

Inside the shop, the atmosphere was congenial. Caroline purchased a lovely high-crowned bonnet, after obtaining Beth's good opinion, and they returned to the street.

The carriage ride home was quiet. By keeping her own counsel, Beth felt that she was protecting Caroline from her overactive imagination.

It was ludicrous, ridiculous, pure melodrama. No one was watching her. Why would they?

Beth almost laughed at her wayward thoughts, but glanced at Caroline and contained the urge. It would have been tainted by a touch of hysteria.

THE WIDE CARPETED staircase of the main hall made the perfect backdrop for a grand entrance. Caroline had dressed in a soft shade of green that contrasted faultlessly with her white skin and dark hair. The embroidered pattern of her skirts was echoed on her headband that wound throughout her unruly curls.

Beth's plum evening gown, having been hung out and ironed, was as rich in color as Caroline's was not. Her hair was dressed with loops, and her shoulders unadorned. She looked both simple and elegant at the same time.

Caroline was pleased with the effect. Her protégée looked wonderful, despite the cast-down clothes. She couldn't wait to see James' reaction.

Unfortunately, their grand entrance went unobserved. James and Dr. Brant were waiting in the drawing room, absorbed in their conversation. Taking it in stride, Caroline sashayed with Beth to the chairs beside the fireplace. They gracefully lowered themselves and settled their skirts, awaiting comment or compliments. None were forthcoming. The young gentlemen were far more interested in their discussion.

"What burglary, James?" she asked, having finally become aware of the subject.

"Break-in, Caroline, as I was just explaining."

"I was not privy to that conversation, James. We have only just arrived."

Somewhat belatedly, the gentlemen awoke to their presence. The sudden recognition of their want of proper manners was almost comical in their attempt to recover the girls' good opinion. They both bowed hastily and began to speak at the same time. James' enthusiastic delivery overshadowed the diminutive attempts of the physician. What remained unexplained, however, was the meaning behind James' sudden heightened color or his inability to stand still. He was not prone to blushes, nor was he usually twitchy.

The polite niceties having been served, they could now return to the problems at hand.

"What burglary?" Caroline asked again.

James shifted his weight from one leg to the other. "The boot boy was awakened last night," he said finally, "by the sound of breaking glass in the back hall. He rushed to Evans' quarters. However, by the time the old man had been alerted, so had the thief. Robert gave chase, but the intruder had the edge, not having been just roused from sleep."

Despite the light timbre of his voice, Caroline knew her brother was troubled. "Why would a thief break a window in the servants' quarters? The silver is kept locked up in the dining room. Why—"

"Caroline," James interrupted. "This is Beth's first evening in our company. Perhaps this discussion could wait?"

Beth shook her head and laughed. "Unlike your window, I am not made of glass. I will not break. I have lost my memory, but it does not follow that I have also lost my reason or my ability to think." She looked to Dr. Brant for agreement.

"Beth does not show signs of a weak mind, James."

Frowning, James nodded as if reluctant to do so. It was a moot point, as dinner was called, and all theorizing had to wait until they retired from the table.

———◆———

The ambience of the drawing room was so congenial that James was reluctant to resume the pre-dinner conversation, but the servants were busy cleaning up after the meal, and their privacy was once again assured. Beth, almost immediately, returned to the subject that had been left hanging two hours earlier.

"Has the manor ever experienced a burglary before?"

Slight, almost invisible, changes indicated that the occupants of the room were no longer relaxed. Shoulders straightened, eyes no longer drooped, and fingers stopped their idle tapping. The atmosphere had become alert.

"Well, yes actually, it has." Caroline turned to James, who was about to deny any other theft. "I believe you to have been in Oxford at the time. Stop huffing and puffing, James, I know it's irrelevant, I was merely answering Beth's question."

"True, but I believe Beth was really asking if there was another break-in that could be tied in with this one. What treasure do we possess that lures men to the darker side of their nature, and all that." He turned to Beth. "Right?"

She laughed. "Yes, but without the melodrama."

James relaxed against the back of his chair. "Nothing that I know of beckons thieves here more than any other manor. Evans thought he recognized one of the men, though he was half hidden in the shadows: Hugh Derrydale. Walter and I went round to the Derrydale cottage this morning, but Hugh is no longer in Welford. He has been in London since the fall, working at the docks. Mrs. Derrydale suggested looking, instead, to Jeff Tate, who has the same height and hair."

For a time the room was quiet, only filled with the movements required to sip from crystal and stretch toes toward the fire.

"So, James, what is your theory on the errant coach?" Brant asked. Whether he felt the subject of the burglary spent or that they needed another distraction, his leap of thought brought a start from Beth.

"My coach?" Beth asked.

Staring at the flames, James shifted uncomfortably. He had hoped to delay this conversation. "Yes. I'm afraid your coach was not, as we assumed, the regular London stagecoach. I cannot trace it, or your coachman, or your luggage. At the accident, one of your fellow passengers said that you got on at the Ivy, and yet it appears that he was . . . wrong."

"Or he lied." Beth frowned, her eyes troubled. "Why was I was traveling alone?"

"Perhaps one of the gentlemen, who was more intent on continuing his journey than your well-being, was your escort." James allowed his tone to show his disgust.

"Oh, James, how can you say so?" Caroline protested. "Who would desert a young woman in such circumstances?"

"There was a slight unsavory air about them, sister dear. It was only in hindsight that I picked it up."

"Or imagined it," Caroline argued.

"That still leaves the ragged aspect of my clothing unaccounted for." Beth absentmindedly sipped at her ratafia.

"Your gown was of a quality material," Caroline said. "It had just seen hard times."

Brant nodded in Beth's direction. "Trying to fit you into a mold of anything that we consider normal is not going to work. We have to concede that you come to us from a less than ideal background." Brant sighed as if reluctant to form the words. "You could have been escaping an abusive situation. You could have been fleeing a father, uncle, brother, or employer. The list is—"

"Or husband," James added quietly.

"Too young for that, surely. But you see what I mean. Her outfit might have been a disguise. There was no one to meet her, as she was not expected. No one to follow, as they know not where she had gone. Beth's memory loss could be the combination of distress at having to make her way alone in the world, as well as the accident. Enough to do anyone in."

The occupants of the room sighed in unison. James was reluctant to agree, but he found this the most plausible theory yet.

Finally, Caroline spoke up. "Something in that order might explain the nightmares, Beth."

Beth flushed and stared at the fire. "Yes, I suppose so. That might explain the fear, but . . . What about the dagger?" She spoke softly, almost a whisper. "What does it mean?"

"Mean?" Brant frowned. "Oh, you speak of the dream itself. There is no meaning in dreams, Beth, just in having them."

Caroline lifted her eyebrows and tilted her head. She opened her mouth as if to speak but then closed it.

"We need to break the cycle. Perhaps a drop of laudanum before bed." Brant chewed at the corner of his lip as he watched Beth shake her head. "Speaking of sleep, I must away. Don't want to outstay my welcome."

Caroline accompanied him to the door.

The echo of their voices slowly diminished as they passed out of the little hall and left Beth and James deep in thought by the fire. It was a comfortable silence at first, but as it grew, so did their inability to break it. What was perhaps only a few moments dragged into an eon before Caroline returned. She had only just settled back on her chair when the drawing room door burst open.

Walter entered with no decorum, and surprisingly, no affectation. He was an unpretentious mixture of breathlessness, excitement, and horror.

"They found a body in the bay," he announced.

CHAPTER SEVEN

Conspicuously Absent

"I was coming back along the shore road," Walter said in a rush. "I was about to turn off at Shepherd Lane when I saw Mr. Hodges up ahead. He and young Foster were staring over the cliff and pointing. I couldn't make out what they were shouting at first—the breakers were thundering—so I took a closer look."

James heard Caroline's sharp intake of breath.

"Oh, Walter, you didn't see—"

"No, indeed, I couldn't make out a thing—a white smudge. The moon is only a quarter and their lantern didn't reach the base of the cliff. Hodges said it was a body. Only they couldn't get at it until the water settled. They'll be waiting all night."

James sat back in his chair with relief. "I think you are not the only one around here with an overactive imagination. Mr. Hodges is likely awaiting a pile of laundry."

Walter's face fell momentarily and then brightened again. "Do you think it's a French spy?"

"Really, Walter." Caroline shook her head. "Where do you get these ideas? James is right; this is a great deal of fuss for something that will turn out to be rubbish. Spies simply do not wash into Torrin Harbor. They have better things to do." She tried to stifle a yawn.

"A wrecker or a convict who jumped ship. Yes, that's it, he was being transported to Australia," Walter continued.

Caroline rolled her eyes. "The best way to end this unsavory speculation is to deprive you of an audience. As it has been a long day and I am entirely wilted, I shall turn in." She rose and wished everyone a good night.

Although not as eager to bring the evening to a close, James rose as well, followed by Beth. In silence they paraded through the hall and up the stairs.

Just as they were about to separate, James turned to Beth. He wanted to say something of comfort, something to ease her mind. Walter's wild speculation would likely add to Beth's troubled nightmares. But somehow the look in her eyes blocked the connection between his mouth and his brain. He couldn't think of anything useful to say. Instead, he gently took her hand and kissed her fingers. He bowed to Caroline and continued to his room.

———◆———

BETH STARED AT her hand for a few moments, enjoying the residual warmth and tingle of Lord Ellerby's touch. Reluctantly she dropped it to her side. When she looked up again, she met Caroline's puzzled eyes.

Lord Ellerby's action begged to be explained, but what was Beth to say? As much as she appreciated the gesture, she did not understand it; certainly, not any more than his sister, who had known him for all her eighteen years. Wordlessly she smiled and disappeared around the corner to her room.

For the first night since awakening in Hardwick Manor, Beth did not dream. No shadows or fears came to her in the night. Perhaps it was the congenial evening and two glasses of ratafia. Or, could it have been the distracting heat that she felt as James bent and placed his lips tenderly on her hand?

"HE HAS BEEN to the colonies as well as all the islands in the West Indies, a regular out-an'-outer."

Walter had surprised one and all when he had arrived to breakfast with the rest of the family. Seated next to Beth, leaning in toward her, he was waxing on—as promised—of his evening at Risely.

Mrs. Thompson's brother had captured most of his attention, and therefore all his conversation. "He owns one of the largest sugar plantations in Jamaica, has a letter of marque, and three large privateer ships. He took a liking to me, and asked me to visit. With Henry, of course."

James tensed and frowned above his paper at Caroline, who, like him, bristled with indignation.

"Privateers are pirates, Walter," Caroline said. "To talk of them with such careless admiration is unworthy of you. They steal, plunder, and kill under state license. The letter of marque is nothing more than villainy. It needs to be stopped." She sat straight and ridged, her eyes spitting fire. "Your brother will be joining the parliamentary debate against this practice. The only acceptable dialogue of piracy under this roof is that of its vile nature and how to rid the world of its scourge." Turning away from Walter as if she could not bear to look at him, Caroline locked her eyes on a spot halfway up the wall.

Looking confused and then contrite, Walter stared at his plate for a moment. "Sorry, Caroline. You are right. I . . . I forgot myself."

"You certainly did," she snapped, still staring at the wall.

Having all but finished the *Times*, James took a glance at the social page. He blinked and drew a quick breath, rereading a remark partway down the page.

> *It should be noted that Pamela Barlow, youngest daughter of Sir Desmond Barlow, has been conspicuously absent these past weeks. She neither appeared at Lady Dalruin's ball in her honor, nor the Lydenne Assembly three days prior. Is Miss Barlow already tiring of the social set, having only just entered it?*

"Caroline," James called down the table in a tone that was not meant to alarm. It did not distract, either. "Caroline," he said a little firmer. Still there was no reaction.

With measured impatience, he folded the paper, the article still visible. He rose with his cup and dropped the newspaper beside Caroline's empty plate as he made his way to the sideboard. He poured his tea, motioned to Robert to clear, and returned to his seat. Caroline was staring at him by the time he had placed his serviette back on his lap.

James nodded his head when Caroline surreptitiously motioned to Beth, but shook it in negation when she indicated Walter. They would wait for Walter's departure before speaking of the matter.

However, Walter still had to finish his account and his breakfast. When it looked as if his brother was going to retell all his stories again, James interrupted. "Walter, I have a job for you." The argument in the boy's eyes forced James to alter the request, giving the task a twist. One that James knew would draw Walter out. "To help Beth."

Beth blinked at him in puzzlement.

"We were discussing Beth's arrival yesterday and I realized that while there were no clues of *her* identity in the trunk that we returned to Exeter, there might be of her fellow passenger. That *gentleman,*" James said the word awkwardly, "might know more. We need to take another look at his trunk. Perhaps in finding him, we will learn more of Beth. The bag will still be unclaimed in Exeter."

Walter's face brightened. "I'll fetch it without delay." He straightened his back and pushed his chair away from the table. "Well, perhaps a slight delay. Thought I'd drop in on Mr. Hodges to ask after the *laundry* in the bay."

Walter glanced at Beth, misinterpreting her frown. "Do not be concerned, I'll have the trunk back by tea." Squaring his shoulders, Walter lifted his chin and marched from the room, giving all the impression that he would don a shining suit of armor and leap atop a white stallion to complete his noble quest—had they been available.

"Was it necessary to send Walter off on a goose chase?" Beth asked as soon as Walter had quitted the room.

"Not really a goose chase, Beth. There *may* be clues in that trunk." Caroline passed the folded paper to Beth and pointed to the small paragraph. "But this is what we wished to discuss."

Beth read it quickly, glanced at her companions, then back to the paper and read it again. "Is that me?" she finally asked. "The name is not familiar."

"I do not know the Barlows." Caroline switched to Walter's seat. "It might have nothing to do with you or—"

"Everything," James completed the sentence for her.

"But I am left with more questions." Beth's voice rose slightly in timbre. "Why would the daughter of Sir Barlow be traveling alone in a soiled dress in a hired coach? If, as we speculated, I was taking flight from an uncomfortable situation, from whom was I running? Sir Barlow?" She rose and walked to the window, then back to where Caroline and James still sat. "And if I was trying to flee, do I want to dance up to the front door and ask after myself? I could be returning to the very plight from which I escaped." Beth plunked back into her seat. "What am I to do?"

"We, my friend, we." Caroline patted Beth's hand. "We need not rush into anything. We will start with a few tactful inquiries. Our best avenue would be to find a friend of the family or even an acquaintance, someone who would be able to describe the girl." Caroline took Beth by the shoulders and firmly but gently turned her so that they were looking eye-to-eye. "Beth, don't worry. No matter what we discover, whatever it is, you do not have to leave us unless you want to. I will only lose you to a happier situation. Nothing less will do. Do you understand? Nothing less."

Beth nodded without conviction.

James rose and after giving Beth a baffling smile—lifted lips with a puckered brow—he patted the still-seated Caroline on the shoulder. "I'm afraid that those inquiries will have to be yours, Caroline. If I were to ask about the Barlows' daughter, it would cause a great commotion. Speculation and rumor would be rife." He bowed deeply and left the young ladies to their discussion.

Caroline wrung the bell and sent Meighan, her lady's maid,

up to her apartment for writing implements. She pulled a straight-backed chair from the corner and placed it in front of the delicate desk that sat before the low windows. The view was that of the lush greenness in the conservatory.

In no time at all, Meighan returned and Caroline busily scratched out her letter. "I think just one or two inquiries would be best," she said as she wrote. "Although it will seem an eternity for the response. We simply have to be patient."

Beth took up some needlework while Caroline pondered her wording; a gentle tap on the door interrupted them both.

"Yes, Robert."

"Mrs. Thompson wants to know if you're home to callers, Miss Ellerby."

Caroline blinked in surprise. The early hour of the call presumed a nonexistent familiarity. Still, one had to make allowances for one's neighbors' peculiarities. "Of course we are. Please, show Mrs. Thompson in."

As the footman turned to deliver his message, Caroline motioned to Beth and whispered, "I was afraid that our trip to town might promote a visit. I do apologize for Mrs. Thompson, but there is no harm in her."

With those words, the door opened again to admit said person. The lady had dressed elaborately for the occasion. Her gown was flounced in three tiers and was largely puffed at the wrists. The feather in her enormous hat almost folded against the door-jamb as it tried valiantly to enter with its wearer. Gray hair with the occasional shock of black spilled out in all directions.

As Robert closed the door another figure, hidden previously, was forced to step out from the shadow of their corpulent neighbor.

Caroline rose and dipped a polite curtsy to each of the ladies. "Sophia. So nice to see you, as well."

Sophia Thompson was as diminutive as her mother was large. Only a glance was needed to discern that the two visitors were opposites. There was intelligence in Sophia's eyes, character on her face, and she wore a gown much more suited to a morning call.

After introductions, the four ladies perched firmly on the edges of their chairs and began an important discourse on the weather. This discussion lasted a good five minutes and threatened to continue for at least that again.

Caroline interrupted—the less-than-fascinating monologue comparing the weather of each passing year—by expressing her thanks to Mrs. Thompson for her hospitality to Walter the previous night.

"Oh my, Miss Ellerby, it was nothing indeed. My brother is quite taken with him—such an entertaining young man," she added confidentially. "But, oh my, he does have a tendency to wild ways. Not to worry, though, my Henry keeps him in line."

Caroline bit her tongue and pursed her lips to prevent any wayward comment about *Henry's* wild ways.

"We would so like to have you dine with us, too," Mrs. Thompson continued, unaware of her rudeness. "You must meet him—my brother, that is—before he returns to the West Indies."

"Is that likely to be soon?" Caroline tried to sidestep the invitation, but Mrs. Thompson was not easily distracted.

"I would so like you to see the new ruins. It has just been completed, and Gilbert—Gilbert Renfrew, that's my brother—says he has seen none better. Oh my, but doesn't your park remind me of our own before the improvements. You must come to Risely and see what can be done."

Caroline pinched her lips tighter and glanced at the clock.

Sophia's entry into the conversation startled them all. "Have you heard that a body was pulled from the channel?"

"Sophia!" Her mother sharply called her daughter to order. "What can you be thinking? That is no subject for a young lady to discuss." Thus having noted its impropriety, she proceeded to do just that. "Oh my, it was just this morning that I learned. Poor soul. Battered up against the rocks, or so I'm told. So sad. The high sea brought it right into the bay, skirts floating all over the place, or so I'm told. Can you imagine—?"

"I am trying not to, Mrs. Thompson." Caroline cut the discussion off before the description became detailed. "It, as you say, is not a subject for gentle conversation." She glanced toward Beth. "Most unseemly." It was more of a rebuke than was her norm, but Caroline was disturbed by Beth's color . . . rather, lack of color. She had gone quite pale.

"Yes, quite." Mrs. Thompson sniffed, doing her best to impart the notion that a woman of breeding should not interrupt her elders. "Tell me, Miss Dobbins, are you one of the Brightly Dobbinses or one of the Midhurst Dobbinses?" Mrs. Thompson turned to Caroline. "I have such a large social circle. I am sure that I am acquainted with at least one member of Miss Dobbins' family."

Caroline watched her neighbor's eyes focus on the newspaper sitting on her desk. A sly expression on Mrs. Thompson's face replaced the one of feigned interest.

"A large circle can be a burden at times. For only just this morning I received news, poor Charlotte," Mrs. Thompson said, lowering her head as if in deference to the absent woman. "Lady Charlotte Dalruin, of course. She went to such extraordinary lengths to accommodate Miss Barlow . . . from what I understand. Such lengths. Can you imagine the shock she must have endured when Miss Barlow did not appear at her *own* ball?

"I have not actually met the Barlows, but my maiden aunt, Miss Penelope Morris, has spoken of the Barlow family in such glowing terms that I feel as if I know them. Whatever can have occurred to deliver such an undeserved slight to poor Charlotte?"

Fortunately for both Beth and Caroline, the requisite quarter hour drew to a close, without further discourse of either the Dobbinses or a reiteration of the dinner invitation to Risely. Neither Beth nor Caroline was sorry to see the door close on the yards of flounced silk.

"I should, of course, return the call by week's end. Mrs. Thompson will consider it a slight otherwise." Caroline sighed with resignation. "Perhaps we will encounter the worldly Mr. Renfrew and thereby negate the need of an introductory meal."

"*Was* a body pulled from the bay?" Beth asked.

Caroline blinked in surprise at the non sequitur. "I haven't heard any such thing, as yet. Though the possibility is fairly high. Rumors often have some truth to them."

"I am very sorry, Caroline. You are likely to know who—"

"Yes," Caroline interrupted before the discussion became overly sentimental; it would do neither of them any good to speculate on the identity of the body. "I'll ask James to look into it," she said, staring at the door.

Beth nodded, picking up her needle and canvas when Caroline returned to her desk.

Caroline touched her quill as if she were going to draw it from the well. She looked down at the neat, incomplete letter on which she had been working before the interruption. She picked it up and rent it in half, then quarters.

The frown and questioning look on Beth's face prompted Caroline to explain. "Mrs. Thompson's visit was not as worthless as it seemed, Beth. I am well enough acquainted with Penelope Morris that a note from me would not be out of turn. As she *is* on friendly terms with the Barlows, we can begin our inquiries without appearing to do so."

Beth's nod of understanding was somewhat lackluster, but Caroline felt her companion would react somewhat differently when the reply came in. Caroline pulled out a fresh piece of paper and began her missive anew.

BETH SETTLED HER skirts across the back of the spirited roan, Bodicia, and reveled in the natural feel of the saddle. She had swung her leg over the sidesaddle horn with the ease of practice—she *could* ride, skillfully and comfortably. There was no other explanation for the feeling of excitement and anticipation as she had placed her foot in the stirrup. The afternoon could be enjoyed in the fields and forests; lessons were not required.

Caroline had come to the stable with Beth and James to see them off. Ned would accompany them for propriety's sake, though at a discreet distance.

Bodicia danced and skittered across the cobbles, until Beth had the mare under control and Caroline nodded with satisfaction to see Beth's skill. James was pleased as well, and claimed not to be surprised. Beth thought she detected a hint of admiration in his eyes.

Following James out of the yard, Beth smiled as Jack preceded them, barking and chasing squirrels through the thickets and hedges. The path was worn, and well able to handle a dog and two riders abreast.

Beth urged Bodicia forward as James had done with Tetley. They rode in silence, breathing in the fresh spring air. The smell of newly turned earth mixed with a tinge of salt air was familiar, but not distinct enough to be a memory.

Beth laughed, watching Jack bound deep into the grass and then bob back up to check on them, to make sure they were following.

And still no word or comment passed between the riders.

Beth shifted in the saddle. She was slightly uncomfortable and it had nothing to do with the horse. She tried not to look at James; when she did her heart beat faster and her face flushed of its own accord.

Instead, she started running conversations through her head, looking for a witty but comfortable topic. Something that would impress.

"Lovely weather we are having." Well, perhaps impressive was overrated.

"A bit blustery, and a tad on the cool side. But yes, overall, a perfectly reasonable day." He snapped his mouth shut, likely realizing how awkward they both sounded.

Beth stole a glance at the handsome young gentleman who sat so straight and tall in the saddle. He stared back at her. Intelligence reflected in his eyes, and his smile was warm and gentle. Beth felt another uncontrollable flush begin at her toes and make its way up her body. She tried to look away before it reached her face, but his eyes wouldn't let her go.

And then Jack barked, with great insistence.

Beth smiled and they both looked toward the dog. He was chastising them for falling behind.

———◆———

JAMES HAD AN unexpected desire to be witty, to make Beth laugh and watch her eyes sparkle. He wanted to tell her about his plans for the future of Hardwick. Why did he want to be frivolous in her presence? Romping with Jack in the grass suddenly held great appeal.

James swallowed and pulled his thoughts back to firmer ground. "I'm learning the rotation method of farming, but there have been new developments in germination . . ." He focused his mind on the fields and well away from any visions of frolicking.

———◆———

BETH FELT RATHER windswept when she and James ambled back through the fields and park. The vista from the southernmost tip of the estate had been breathtaking but rather breezy. Still, the view from the cliffs had provided Beth with a better understanding of the locale.

The manor had been difficult to see over the treetops. They had had to alight and stand in close proximity for a better view through the trees. Beth tried not to be aware of that closeness. However, it had taken some time for the rooftop to be discernable; she was rather distracted.

James seemed to be having a hard time concentrating as well, and stammered out a suggestion that they return to the manor to keep Caroline company.

As they entered the stable yard, Beth noticed an open carriage approaching from the drive. Caroline must have seen it as well, for she joined them from the manor.

In silence the group watched the curricle's progress. Two figures were visible.

Caroline squinted. "Who is that?"

"Walter, of course."

"But then, who is with him?"

"I asked Sam to accompany him," James explained. "Didn't want Walter getting into any more hot water." He looked across to Beth. "At least, not until this fiasco is cleared up." He looked away quickly when she frowned.

Caroline shook her head. "I'm not altogether sure that the man accompanying Walter is Sam Biddlesport." She squinted again, and then straightened. "It is not," she whispered under her breath as the curricle pulled around the final curve. "It is Mr. Hodges, the shoemaker."

Caroline glanced toward Beth. "Mr. Hodges assists the justice on parish matters," she explained. Her grimace was replaced with an uplifted mouth and a show of teeth, but it was not a smile. "Good afternoon, Mr. Hodges. How nice to see you," Caroline said when they came into hailing distance.

"Good afternoon, Miss Ellerby," Mr. Hodges said as the horses pulled to a stop and he stepped down to the ground. "I was hoping to speak privately to Lord Ellerby." Mr. Hodges was a quiet-spoken, somewhat gaunt man.

"Where is the trunk?" James frowned at Walter.

"James," Caroline tried to interrupt politely.

"You did go to Exeter didn't you? And why—"

"James, Mr. Hodges would like to speak to you," Caroline pressed.

"I beg your pardon, Mr. Hodges. If you would await me in the library, I will be but a moment. I am sure Robert will be able to direct you."

Mr. Hodges bowed in acquiescence.

James returned his attention to Walter while Caroline led the old man into the house. Beth clutched Bodicia's reins, thankful for the excuse to remain.

"The trunk wasn't there," Walter finally answered.

"What do you mean not there?"

"Gone, missing, taken. Not there." Walter paused dramatically. "Apparently our pockmarked friend came looking for it two days ago. He simply claimed it and left. All with barely a word spoken, civil or otherwise. I spent the better part of two hours asking after the man but to no avail."

"What does Mr. Hodges want?"

"How should I know?" Walter huffed. "I dropped Sam off by the north field and picked Mr. Hodges up by the front gate. Said he had to talk to you 'in the capacity of parish constable.' Sounds ominous."

James pursed his lips and then frowned. He passed his reins to Paul, pivoted, and walked into the manor.

Walter didn't seem perturbed. He merely lifted his shoulders in a slow shrug. Beth, on the other hand, felt a sense of disquiet. With the recollection that Mr. Hodges had barely glanced in her direction, she cast aside the rising fear that the man's visit was related to her situation.

Still, all was not as it should be.

CHAPTER EIGHT

Warning Signs

Called to the library half an hour later, Beth found Caroline distraught, James stoic but visibly upset, and Mr. Hodges conspicuously absent.

"Caroline, are you ill?" Beth rarely saw Caroline lose her composure; it was unsettling. James hovered beside his sister, holding and patting her hand.

"Oh, Beth, please excuse my display. Mr. Hodges has brought the most horrid news." Caroline held a tightly clutched handkerchief to her red-rimmed eyes.

Beth swallowed slowly and pressed her palms into her skirts. "Is there anything I can do to help you?" she asked, standing stiffly, preparing for the worst—though she didn't know what the worst could be.

Caroline motioned to the chair beside her. "No, Beth, I am sorry, for this is going to affect you as well." She waited until Beth was seated before saying any more. "They have identified the body that was pulled from the bay."

Puzzled, Beth's brow folded briefly. Why would Caroline believe that she would be upset? Saddened by any loss of life, yes, but her circle of friends was so small that had Walter and Dr. Brant been in the library with them, it would have been complete. Not quite—because, of course, there was Daisy.

At that moment, Beth realized just how much Mr. Hodges' news *was* going to affect her. She swallowed hard and looked up, not at Caroline but at James. "Daisy?" Though she'd spoken barely above a whisper, he heard and nodded.

Beth lowered her head to hide her flood of emotion. Visions of Daisy sprang to mind: Daisy sitting on the bed laughing with Beth about the antics of the footmen; Daisy's face when Cook suggested making jellied eel; and Daisy's dreamy expression when she spoke of Jeff Tate.

James touched Beth's shoulder gently and then quietly slipped from the room, leaving the girls some privacy.

"Mr. Hodges believes that she slipped going over the Torrin River," Caroline explained as she passed Beth a handkerchief, using her own to mop up around her eyes. "Daisy was last seen on her way to Risely, anxious to spend some time with Jeff Tate, who is . . . *was* her young man. Probably tried to step across the Torrin instead of using the bridge. But it is spring runoff and what with the rain and all . . . Mr. Hodges supposes that the stream took her down to the basin and then out into the channel. High tide must have brought her back in."

"I see," Beth said, seeing all too well an image of Daisy's body caught in the ebb and flow of the waves, banging against the cliff. Despite trying to swallow her grief, Beth soaked the handkerchief with tears.

IT WAS UNFAIR that the day of Daisy's funeral and subsequent burial should burst forth so bright and sunny. Nature felt askew. As they gathered by the lowering coffin, the birds had begun to sing. It felt rude and highly unnecessary.

Upon returning to the manor, Beth knew she was not yet ready to sequester herself indoors. The walls felt insufferably close; the air was heavy with memories. She told Caroline that she needed to go for a walk.

"Would you like company?" James offered.

But as much as Beth found great comfort in his presence, she needed some time alone. "I will not go far," she promised.

"You'll stay in the park and not approach the Torrin?"

"Yes." Beth almost smiled at his protective attitude. "I'll stay far from the river."

"James, leave the poor girl alone." Caroline motioned for Robert to open the door.

Beth nodded and started down the stairs.

"Solace is derived from different sources, brother dear. And while your concern is admirable, it is also excessive," Caroline chastised James as the door closed.

Beth walked through the gardens and along the path to the shore cliffs. As she broke from the shelter of the trees, the wind became bitter and damp, but Beth ignored it, found a resting place, and indulged herself in a flood of tears. Now she sat, emotionally drained. The salt wind played and pulled at the pins in her hair. Her borrowed bonnet hung by its ribbons in her hand. Beth stared at the thick black felt hat and its veil; her hand involuntarily brushed across the front of the unadorned black crepe dress.

A heavy fog that had been hovering a few miles off the coast crept ever closer. It pushed a steady and strong wind that nibbled at the bright sunshine still clinging to the shore. The wind was clammy, and the mossy stone hard and cold. Its chill permeated through Beth's many layers of skirts and petticoats, and yet she didn't move. The inner chill that Beth felt far outweighed the mere coolness of her mortal core. She was heartsick and troubled.

Deep thought and concentration muffled the sounds around her, even the wind whistling by her ears. It was some time before Beth recognized the sound of someone or something approaching. At once, the skin on the back of her neck began to tingle. The sounds emanated from just beyond the trees, to the right of her makeshift chair.

"Hello?" she called out.

There was no answer, but the crackle in the underbrush halted.

"Hello?" she called out again.

No reply, only the sounds of the wind.

Beth rose from the boulder, placing her back to the water. She felt her pulse begin to quicken. "Is anyone there?" She could hear the fear in her voice. She tried to see into the dark shadows of the trees. "Is anyone there?" she asked again.

"Yes, indeed!" The words came from up the hill.

Beth turned to watch James approach, leading Tetley and Bodicia down the path. "How did you know I was here?" he asked.

Beth looked back into the underbrush where she had thought the sounds had originated. Still nothing moved. She must have been mistaken.

"That is not the question, Lord Ellerby." She gathered her skirts and met him at the crest of the path. "The question should be: Why are you here?" She placed her arm through his and glanced back into the shrubbery. No waving branches, no snap of twigs. "I hope you are returning to the house," she said, lengthening her stride, forcing James to keep pace. "For that is where I am bound."

Once inside the protected shelter of the trees, the wind was rendered impotent and Beth's hearing was immediately more acute. There was nothing untoward in the rustling of the leaves and *certainly* not in the lark's song. She slowed her pace, and as a consequence, James did as well.

"Actually, I thought a ride might be a distraction," he said, swallowing as if he were uncomfortable. "You enjoyed your ride so much the other day . . . And being a natural on horseback . . . I thought it might . . . help," he said lamely. "But I could be wrong."

Beth lifted her mouth in a poor imitation of a smile. "That was very kind of you. A ride might be just what I need. A distraction . . . giving me the opportunity to think of happier times. Yes, thank you." She crooned as she took Bodicia's reins and ran her palm down the horse's soft cheek. "Shall we go for a ride, my sweet?" Then she noticed that Tetley was saddled and stomping, eager to move, too. "Would you like to join me?" The invitation to James was not really necessary as it was highly unlikely he would let her go off on her own, but it did seem politic.

James nodded readily. "I thought you might want some company." He guided the horses to a collection of rocks that Beth used to step up into her saddle and then he slipped his leg over Tetley's back.

They rode in silence for some moments, as James guided them farther away from the cliffs. "You will always miss her, but in time the pain will lessen," he said.

Beth sighed from the depth of her soul. "My mind is full of 'what ifs' and 'if onlys.'" She stared at the path ahead. "Life is so fragile. But you are right, each passing day will bring me closer to acceptance and I shall leave behind these shadowed thoughts." She fashioned her mouth into a smile and watched his frown disappear.

———◆———

"JEFF TATE KILLED HER!" Mrs. Bartley was not only feeling the loss of her daughter but also the weight of the neighborhood gossip.

"Please calm yourself, Mrs. Bartley." Caroline led the widow to the carved rocking chair sitting by the cottage stove. "Daisy wasn't murdered. It was an accident." It was Caroline's third visit in as many days, and the accusation had yet to change. "Here. We've brought you a shoulder of pork and some vegetables. Cook also sent along a pot of soup, so you can feed the little ones with hardly a fuss. Now, just sit there for a moment and gather your thoughts while Beth and I lay these out for you."

Caroline and Beth worked silently around the neat but small cottage that housed Mrs. Bartley and her three younger children. The woman had two others out working, and despite being without her good man—he having passed four years ago—she was far from a charity case. Caroline would soon have to leave off her visits or run the risk of humiliating Mrs. Bartley with her kindness.

"Our Daisy was a good girl." Mrs. Bartley rocked with such force that the chair threatened to tip her out. "If she hadna taken up with that Tate boy, she'd still be here today. He threw her in the channel. I feels it in me bones."

Caroline ushered the children out of doors and turned to the distraught woman.

"Mrs. Bartley," she said gently. "You've lived here long enough to know that rumors can start from nothing."

"It were that Tate boy, I tell ya. Never was any good. Always up ta mischief, him and that Derrydale boy."

Beth passed Mrs. Bartley a strong cup of tea from the pot perpetually brewing on the back of the stove. The strong blend had a revitalizing effect; she had regained her color and was no longer muttering by the time they left.

They had only just mounted their horses when Nora, one of Daisy's younger sisters, approached. "Excuse me, miss." The sweet-faced girl with a smudge of grime on her chin held in her arms a brown bundle. "This here cloak, it weren't Daisy's, miss." She passed it up to Beth. "They brought it from the manor with the rest of her stuff, but it weren't hers." She glanced back toward the cottage door. "Ma woulda given it back to ya, but she's not thinking clear these days."

"There's soup on the stove and some foodstuff on the table," Beth said, tucking the cloak into her empty basket.

The girl nodded and thanked them prettily. She was still standing by the door of the cottage when Beth and Caroline rounded the bend, screening her from view. With the turning of the next bend, the mill would be in sight, along with the river that rushed by its great wheel.

Deep in thought, having given their horses their head, neither paid attention to the warning signs of trouble. Beth heard but discounted the crashes in the underbrush, the chatter of annoyance from disturbed squirrels, and the protests of encroachment from the jays.

Then, out from the thicket, two rough men leapt onto the road and lunged for their bridles. The man attacking Bodicia missed and grabbed Beth instead. Nearly torn from the saddle, Beth screamed as the thug clutched and pulled at her skirts. She held on and kicked out. The man ignored his bloodied nose, sneering at her with a toothless maw.

On the other side of the road, Caroline swung Cotton around, dragging the man that had caught her reins. She urged her horse backward, giving the villain no chance to regain his footing. "Let go!" she screamed at him.

Bodicia quivered in terror, lurching as Beth held on to the saddle. The toothless man reached forward without freeing her skirts and grabbed again for the bridle. This time, Beth pulled back on both reins, encouraging Bodicia to rear. Beth kept her seat easily, leaning forward. Bodicia's hooves slashed at the air inches from the villain's face but the man was not rattled in the least.

"Come 'ere, love." His gravelly voice was eerily calm. He reached up to loosen her grip on the reins, then hesitated. Something, some movement or noise, on the road ahead had caught his attention.

Beth turned to follow his stare.

Hatless, a rider raced pell-mell toward them, hooves pounding the dirt. "Unhand those ladies!" Walter shouted. The words echoed across the narrow road and filled the air with his command. Arm raised, Walter brandished his crop.

Walter flew past Caroline and struck his whip across the head of the monster clutching at Beth's skirts. "How dare you!" he shouted and struck again.

The man dropped Bodicia's bridle and dove for the underbrush in a sprawling escape.

"If you ever try that again, you'll get more than a whipping!" Walter screamed after the fleeing figure. Yanking his horse around to help his sister, Walter found Caroline staring into the brush on the other side of the road. It had been a double retreat.

Quickly pulling together, the three riders formed a defendable group with Beth in the middle. They twisted this way and that, watching, waiting, and listening.

Nothing seemed out of place. It was almost as if the attack had never happened.

Walter lowered his crop to his side and finally took a breath. "What was that all about?"

Caroline shook her head and urged her horse forward. "Let's put some distance between us and them before we discuss it." She clicked her tongue and Cotton broke into a gallop. Beth and Walter did the same.

Around the bend, the miller was repairing his sluice, his wife hanging up laundry as their children chased one another across the field. It was all so normal.

The Ellerbys raised their hands to reciprocate the miller's wave, but continued apace until they came to the junction of the London road. There, they slowed the horses but did not stop.

Walter leaned back across the croup of his horse. "Lud, I thought we were in the suds." He let go of his reins and flung his arms out.

With the reins still tightly clasped across her palms, Beth leaned forward to stroke Bodicia.

Caroline barely moved. Her posture was rigid and unyielding as she stared straight ahead. "I assume it was a purse they were after," she finally said.

Both Beth and Walter straightened and stared at Caroline, not for the words that she had uttered but for her manner of speaking them. Her voice was unnaturally high and raspy, as if her throat were constricted.

Walter was the first to express concern. "Caroline, are you well?"

She blinked as if trying to understand what Walter thought an uncomplicated question. "Yes. Yes, of course. But I do feel a pressing need to sit down."

"You are sitting down, Caroline," Beth pointed out.

Caroline frowned and glanced down at her saddle. She giggled in a very un-Caroline-like manner. "Oh. So I am."

"I think we should make haste, Walter," Beth said, leaning down to grab Cotton's reins. That Caroline did not protest was worrisome. "Might you go ahead and prepare everyone for our arrival?"

Slowly but emphatically, Walter shook his head. "It is you who must go ahead. I will not leave two ladies, who were just attacked, meandering home. Even if I could find it in my heart to do so, I know that James would wash his hands of me."

Breathing deeply—and rather noisily—through her nose, Beth nodded as she passed Cotton's reins to Walter. "You are right, of course."

Walter watched Beth heel her horse into a run, admiring her grace and fortitude, then turned toward his sister. Her color was quite high.

"Come, Caroline," he said, encouraging the horses forward. Her continued silence was rather alarming.

CHAPTER NINE

Flights of Fancy

James would normally appreciate the sunny warmth of Caroline's small boudoir, but it was a tad overcrowded. Caroline reclined on the settee surrounded by pillows, sipping a cup of tea. With less color in her cheeks and a calm manner, she did not in the least resemble the red-faced young woman who had walked into the manor with a wobble in her knees. Beth sat at her side, while Brant was perched on a chair at the far end.

Between sips, Caroline discussed the day's happenings in a rambling sort of manner. "Why were we attacked? Perhaps they sought a heavy purse—well-dressed ladies could be carrying valuables. But we were on our way back from charity; our pockets and baskets were empty." Caroline frowned, sipped, and began again. "Awaiting us just beyond the Bartleys' could only mean that they were aware of our situation. No, their intent was more personal. Their purpose was to injure. I saw it in the eyes of the man clutching my reins. There was more than greed in his eyes; he didn't look away. There was hunger and enjoyment of my terror. They were the eyes of a killer."

"*Eyes of a killer*? Isn't that doing it a little brown?" James leaned into the wall, staring out the window. His casual posture belied the fact that he, too, thought the circumstances of their attack unfathomable. "I agree that they were bold, but if they meant to rob, they were imbeciles as well."

Caroline sighed and looked at Brant over her cup.

"Can it not be labeled an unfortunate happenstance and be put behind us?" Brant asked.

"Perhaps we could if it were not for . . ."

Beth straightened. "Not for what, Caroline?"

Caroline glanced around the room and laughed. It had a hollow sound. "I think we are being watched. I felt someone staring in Welford when we were shopping and then again at Daisy's funeral. You know, that uncomfortable prickly sensation on the back of your neck?"

Beth nodded. "Yes, I do know. At the milliner's I caught a staring reflection in a store window but when I turned around . . . nothing. No one was paying the least bit of attention to me." She straightened as if bracing her back. "I told myself that I had an overactive imagination. That I was being melodramatic."

James couldn't imagine a less accurate description.

"And then, yesterday when I was sitting by the water," she continued, "I heard something rustling in the bushes—something large, and close by—and yet nothing was visible. I had an uncomfortable sense of a presence. Someone was there, but when I called out, they did not say anything."

Caroline scowled at her friend. "Why did you not mention it earlier?"

"For the very same reason that you were reluctant to say anything just now. Nothing happened. It seemed like a flight of fancy."

Silence echoed.

James gritted his teeth and fought the urge to kick something . . . anything. He wanted to tear these monsters apart. How dare they imperil his family! "This puts a very different complexion on today's events," James said, doing his best to sound calm, in control. "What *are* they after?"

Beth huffed a sigh. "Me."

"Rubbish," James said, regretting it immediately. It wasn't that he didn't believe these men, these monsters, were after Beth . . . it was just that he did not want it to be true.

With a bewildered expression, Beth tipped her head to the side, as if trying to see James from a different perspective. "And yet these incidents revolve around me, and did not start until my arrival. It seems a natural conclusion."

"I—" he started to say, searching for words of apology. "That's not what I meant."

Beth frowned and, with a shake of her head, stood. She turned toward Caroline. "I really must change for dinner, or Cook will never forgive my tardiness. Mrs. Fogel is having a tray prepared for you. I'll come to visit after dinner." She left the room without glancing in James' direction.

Caroline glared at him. "Well done, brother dear."

"But, Caroline, it does not make sense."

"Nothing has made sense since Walter forced Beth's coach into the river."

"True enough." James frowned at his reflection in the window. "Have you received any replies to your inquiries?"

"Not as yet. And there has been no further mention of Pamela Barlow in the *Times*."

"Yes, I know." James had checked every day, too, since discovering the article. "Has Beth had *nothing* of her memories return?"

Caroline looked at him with incredulity. "Well actually, yes, James. Yesterday, she recalled that she was princess of the Nile on her way to join the circus. I just forgot to mention it."

James did not appreciate Caroline's levity or Brant's barked laugh that followed.

"Is Beth still having nightmares?" Brant asked, an expert at deflection.

Caroline's expression softened. "Yes, I am afraid so."

"A colleague of mine from Edinburgh is making a study of injuries of this nature. I will write to him for recommendations."

"Thank you, Brant." James nodded. "I think the sooner we know who Beth is, the sooner she, and those around her, will be safe."

———◆———

BETH SAT BY her bedroom window, lost in thought, steeped in humiliation. One of her new dinner gowns had been laid out on the bed and she had only to ring for Harriet to begin her preparations. But Beth had plenty of time to change before dinner; claiming the need to rush had only been a pretext.

What had possessed her to blurt out like that? Of course it sounded incredible. How could a mundane person such as herself be at the center of this tumult? Why would anyone want to follow or hurt her? Beth looked down at her unadorned hands.

She had nothing.

And yet there was no doubt in her mind that she had been the target—of the watchful eyes *and* of the roadside villains. And it was to those horrid men that her mind kept returning. Might they know who she was, her name? Might they know why she was traveling alone, and to where? The attack didn't feel random, there was a purpose to their actions—or so it seemed.

Yes, those leering, lawless men had to be caught—caught and made to tell all. And what better way to catch them, than to offer that which they had been ready to steal? Beth could draw them out again. Indeed, she could make it easy . . . lure them, taunt them. She could use herself as bait.

———————

BETH LAY TUCKED deeply beneath the counterpane. Her thoughts were foggy from sleep and her eyes half shut. The overcast sky did nothing to encourage her from bed.

"Good mornin'," a pert voice greeted her.

Beth sat straight up, half expecting Daisy to appear before her, but it was Harriet who carried the warm pitcher and bowl to the side table. It was Harriet kneeling by the fire . . . not Daisy.

"Good morning, Harriet. How are you today?"

"Fine, miss." She didn't look around but remained where she was, trying to draw life from the coals. "An' you'll be happy ta know that Miss Ellerby is right as rain, too."

"Excellent." Beth roused herself enough to swing her feet to the floor. The room had a slight nip to it, but with each lengthening day the chill abated.

"An' Mrs. F. were wonderin' what to do with the cloak, Miss."

"What cloak?"

"Mrs. F. says Paul brought it inta the manor. It was with your baskets."

"Oh yes, that cloak. It was mistakenly included with Daisy's belongings and should go to the rightful owner."

"I'll tell 'er, miss." Harriet crossed the room and opened the doors to the newly stocked wardrobe. Beth used the water in the pitcher while it was still warm and then hurriedly dressed.

Caroline emerged from her chamber just as Beth rounded the corner.

"Oh, most excellent, you do look better," Beth said, linking their arms.

"And ravenous," Caroline laughed as they descended the stairs together.

The bright yellow of the morning room shook the dullness from the day and instilled it with cheer. The smells emanating from the sideboard increased Beth's appetite. Taking her filled plate to the table, Beth noticed it was set for three.

One of the gentlemen had already been and gone.

Caroline raised her eyebrows. "Robert, has Lord Ellerby already breakfasted?"

"Yes, miss. He ate earlier and then set off fer Welford Mills. Said something about Mr. Hodges, I believe."

"Yes, of course," Caroline replied just as Walter sauntered through the door.

"Good morning! Your hero has arrived." He wore a traditional white shirt with a winged collar, a pale blue waistcoat, beige trousers, and brown jacket.

"Walter?" Caroline questioned. "I didn't know you owned a plain waistcoat. Where did it come from?" She looked her brother up and down as if he were an unearthly specimen. He was dressed with decorum and sporting almost no affectation.

"Is that any way to greet the gentleman who saved your life?"

"You look very distinguished, Walter," Beth remarked.

Preening, Walter tossed Beth a grin over his shoulder. "The very essence that I wanted to portray. How very astute."

Caroline glanced at Beth with her eyebrows raised.

Walter filled his plate to overflowing, pulled his chair closer to Beth's end of the table, and began his morning meal with relish. "And how are we this morning?" he asked between bites. "Did you sleep well, my dears?" His tone was condescending. It was likely meant to be sophisticated or, at the least, elegant. It wasn't.

Caroline ignored her brother's pomposity. "I thought we might return Mrs. Thompson's call this morning, Beth. It will be considered a slight if we leave it much longer."

"Will she not understand our delay?"

"It will be her impatience to discuss Daisy's demise that will increase her pique."

"You will, of course, wait for James' return," Walter stated . . . as if he had the right.

Caroline nodded, staring out the window in the general direction of Welford Mills.

They didn't have long to wait, as James sauntered into the morning room a little less than an hour later. The table had been cleared of breakfast by then and returned to its position by the wall. Caroline sat at her mother's desk, again staring out the window.

Beth had taken up her post on the settee with her stitching in hand, and Walter sat next to her, reading snippets aloud from a novel. The scene was domestic and had the aspect of a congenial and relaxed gathering, but the undercurrent was guarded.

"Good morning." James took a chair by the door. He threw a

quick glance Walter's way, blinked at his outfit, and then shrugged. After fluffing the cushion behind him, James settled himself comfortably. "I am returned," he finally said, stating the obvious. "And, of course, I have returned with more questions than when I left."

"Have you *any* answers?" Walter pressed.

"I'm getting there. Have patience." James bowed his head in Beth's direction. "First, I apologize. There is little doubt that you are the focus of this unsavory attention, for whatever reason that may be."

Beth bowed her acceptance and then grinned when he winked.

"Now, as to Mr. Hodges. Setting the law on the tracks of the thugs was prevented by Mr. Hodges' refusal to believe that an attack had taken place."

"What!" Walter bristled.

James raised his hand, palm toward Walter. "His standing was—take note of the word *was*—that in the sleepy parish of Welford Mills there had been both a burglary and a death. That was enough for any community."

"So you said 'Sorry to disturb' and went on your way." Caroline's tone was blasé.

"Exactly. My way involved a visit to Justice Walker, and I politely recommended that he either remove Mr. Hodges or appoint a deputy."

"Mr. Hodges is a cousin of the justice, you recall," Caroline said.

James nodded slowly. "Yes, I do."

"So the parish of Welford Mills has a new deputy."

"How astute of you, Caroline. Yes, Derrick Strickland is now a deputy, and as such, he will be joining me later this morning."

"Did you suggest Mr. Strickland?" Caroline asked before turning to Beth. "Mr. Strickland is the apothecary," she explained, "and a good choice for deputy. He seems to be a fair man with some intelligence."

"I will admit that I helped Justice Walker with his decision. Mr. Strickland is an efficient man. We will review the break-in of the manor, I will put him on the scent of the villains who attacked you, and I will even ask him to make inquiries about Daisy."

Caroline frowned. "Daisy? Whatever for, James?"

"To ease Mrs. Bartley's troubled mind and settle Tate's innocence. Beth mentioned the vicious gossip last night at dinner. I think Tate has suffered enough without having the town treating him like a leper."

"What additional questions?" Walter asked. "You said that you had returned with more questions."

"Yes, a most curious incident." James paused, looked pensive for moment, and then continued. "Mrs. Cranley accosted me just as I was leaving town. She was almost beside herself with excitement. Apparently an elderly gentleman was asking after a young lady yesterday throughout Welford. He described a person such as you, Beth. When she told him that the only new arrival in the area was an Elizabeth Dobbins staying at Hardwick Manor, he abruptly ended the conversation and rode off."

Caroline frowned. "Are we to be excited, apprehensive, or disinterested?"

"I have no idea. I mean to mention it to Mr. Strickland."

"Before you go, James, I thought you would want to know that Beth and I will be driving over to Risely Hall this morning. We have to return Mrs. Thompson's call."

James flicked a piece of lint from his trousers in an overly casual manner before speaking. "Please take the closed carriage." He stood and pulled down his waistcoat. "Enjoy," he added with a hint of sympathy.

⸻

BETH STARED OUT the carriage window. The tranquil scenery did nothing to alleviate her apprehension. James' news of a stranger making inquiries coupled with the assault confirmed her fears. A proper lady was not hounded; a sensible woman did not travel alone. She might regain her memories and wish to God that she hadn't. The longer she had no name, the longer she endangered the family.

"They are quite pretty."

Startled, Beth blinked and allowed her eyes to refocus on the view. The carriage had passed through Welford Mills and was making its way up the slope to Risely. The hall before them was smaller and newer in comparison to Hardwick Manor. The portico was grand, although a trifle overlarge for the hall's size, but the trained ivy softened the edges. It was a plain but noble Palladian-style manor.

Beth turned from the Thompson residence and cast her eye in the direction of Caroline's comment. A small distance from the main road, a path guided the viewer toward a ruin. It was meant to mimic an ancient stronghold with all but one wall tumbling into dust. The distance disguised the newly cut stone, and in a few years, the shrubs and bracken would have filled in enough to give it an air of antiquity.

"I am surprised. It is well done. I had not expected it of Mrs. Thompson." Caroline nodded in approval.

Beth smiled and offered her friend a one-shoulder shrug as

their carriage pulled under the portico. "If you want a *new* ruin," she said.

Caroline sent Robert in with her card. She expressed a quiet hope to Beth that she had picked the right time to call. Unfortunately, she hadn't. Mrs. Thompson was, indeed, available for visitors.

A footman led them into a small, overstuffed drawing room. Pastels had been used with abandon and a multitude of pillows covered the settee and chairs. The room was stiflingly hot due to an overstoked fire blazing on a warm spring day.

Sophia bounded to her feet upon their entry with such energy that Beth felt the younger girl's desperate need for distraction. The interest and shine in Sophia's eyes after completing the customary curtsy gave Beth some regret that their visit would not be long.

Then Mrs. Thompson spoke. "Oh my, I had thought the worst. It's been nigh a week since last we chatted. I had begun to think you had done yourselves an injury."

Caroline stiffly addressed her neighbor. "I regret the delay, Mrs. Thompson." She perched on a free corner of the settee. "We have been dealing with a difficult situation at Hardwick."

"Oh my, yes, Daisy Bartley," Mrs. Thompson said bluntly. "Such a shame."

Beth pushed an ornate paisley cushion aside and dropped down onto the settee beside Caroline. She glanced around the room in a bid to hide her surge of anger brought on by Mrs. Thompson's callous comment.

"We feel her loss still, Mrs. Thompson, and would prefer not to discuss it as yet," Caroline said firmly.

Mrs. Thompson frowned and closed her mouth with a snap. Sophia took up the conversation with comments about the weather, but her mother quickly recovered from the set-down. "Oh my, it is a shame that you delayed your call. My brother is not here today. He is out visiting friends, as we are to London within a fortnight. We shall have to forgo the pleasure of your company for a month or two. But fear not, we shall have a grand affair when we return."

"We are to begin arrangements for my coming out." Sophia's eyes sparkled.

"Yes, indeed. My brother, Mr. Renfrew, petitioned Mr. Thompson on Sophia's behalf. I myself have mentioned it to Mr. Thompson well over two dozen times."

"Perhaps you'll be seeing the Barlows in town," Caroline added casually, ignoring the snip at Mr. Thompson. "The girls must be of an age."

"Oh no." Mrs. Thompson barely disguised her horror. "The Barlow girl is older, nigh on twenty. Such a shame about her looks. Rather insipid from what I hear, though I have never met her. Hair so pale it is almost white." She looked across at Sophia's dark curls. "It would be unfair to outshine the girl."

Caroline glanced at Beth and then at her brown hair. Beth shook her head pointedly while they endured an uncomfortable lull in the conversation.

"Did you see the new ruins?" Mrs. Thompson asked eventually, waving toward the window. "Are they not the very thing? I am sure such a building would vastly improve your grounds. I could set you on the heels of our builder. Although, I am told he is very busy. It was, in fact, my brother who undertook the project, when it threatened to fall through."

"It even has a dungeon," Sophia added.

"Dungeon?" Caroline looked amused.

"Yes, indeed. A folly has to be authentic."

Beth almost lost her composure. An authentic fake! She stared at the fire for a moment, trying to get her amusement under control. She dared not look at Caroline. Glancing instead at the ornate clock sitting on the mantel, she observed that it been a quarter hour since their arrival; duty had been done, penance served.

———◆———

THE CARRIAGE HAD only just started down the Risely drive when Beth turned to Caroline. "I am not Pamela Barlow." Beth pulled at a small tuft of hair that had escaped from the bottom of her bonnet.

"It would seem not, but Mrs. Thompson might not be our best source of information. Let us wait upon Miss Morris' reply before deciding."

Beth glanced at Caroline, hesitant to speak but feeling compelled to do so. "I have been wondering if perhaps I was not a good person."

"Whatever makes you say that?"

"Why would this man, asking after me in town, not march up to the front door and demand to see me? It seems rather furtive. And who were the men on the road? Who has been following me?"

"It could be that we were reading more into the attack than was meant. That would be my fault. My imaginings and weakness might have enlarged a trifle event. The men looked desperate enough that they may simply have wanted our horses." Caroline patted Beth's restless hand and then relaxed against the seat back, allowing the motion of the carriage to rock her.

Beth turned back to her window, ignoring the curious glances of the townsfolk as they crossed through Welford again. She was lost in thought—planning and, yes, scheming—without her friend's knowledge. Caroline would not approve a plot to ensnare those that, even now, she could feel watching and waiting—like a vulture waiting for its carrion.

CHAPTER TEN

The Post

Inside Hardwick's library, James and Mr. Strickland sat in contemplative silence. Mr. Strickland—a quiet-spoken man in his mid-fifties with a broad face—sported pure white hair and a matching mustachio of grand proportions. The spectacles that he wore pushed tightly to his face magnified the crow's feet at the corners of his eyes. His clothes were well made, but older in fashion, and gave off the slight aroma of camphor.

James had spoken of the burglary, assault, and Beth's mysterious origins, as well as Mrs. Bartley's accusations. Lastly he had brought out the silver button, which Mr. Strickland was still considering.

"In the water, you say?"

"Yes, just at its edge."

"Well, it weren't there long, no weathering to it at all. Could be a remnant of the accident. This here etching looks to be quite detailed. If I may, I'll take it with me. Try to identify it."

"By all means."

Mr. Strickland dropped the button into his waistcoat pocket. "Would it be all right with you, Lord Ellerby, if I spoke to the ladies about the assault, or would it cause a difficulty?"

James smiled when he thought of how resilient Beth and his sister were. "Not at all, they are quite recovered and, in fact, paying Mrs. Thompson a call this morning." With only a few strides, he crossed the room. "I will see if they have returned."

James opened the door slightly and was about to call for Robert when he saw Beth and Caroline descending the stairs. They were chatting easily, and it disheartened him to think that his request was likely to introduce a touch of disquiet. Caroline caught his movement and gesture. Within moments they were both greeting Mr. Strickland with the formality that was dictated on such occasions.

"I apologize for the interruption, Miss Ellerby, but if I'm to investigate and—God willing—catch these here villains that waylaid you, I best get some details."

"I'm afraid there is not much to tell, as the man that hung on to my horse was so very ordinary," Caroline said. "He had brown eyes, was covered in dirt, and in need of a shave. He wore workman's clothing, was of medium height and build. His jacket was brown and mended. No scars, rings, not anything of value . . . It happened very quickly; that is all I recall."

Caroline's voice had taken on a strained note. It drew Mr. Strickland's attention. "Not to worry, Miss Ellerby, we'll get these blackguards. Strangers are not hard to find in a town such as Welford Mills."

Caroline smiled. "I think you are in your element, Mr. Strickland."

The mustachio curled upward. "I didn't know it until this

morn, miss, but I believe I have always wanted to be a parish deputy." The fleeting expression of pleasure was again replaced with a serious demeanor. He turned to Beth. "Could you describe the man who attacked you, Miss Dobb . . . ?" He hesitated, suddenly uncomfortable. "Your name isn't Dobbins."

James watched the mild expression on Beth's face dissolve and a flush creep across her cheeks.

"My sister has a friend by that last name," James answered for her. "She thought it would elicit fewer questions if Beth had a name that might be recognized."

"And the name 'Beth'?" Mr. Strickland asked.

"It was the first name that came into my head."

"Dear, dear." He turned to James. "Was a man not seeking the location of a young woman matching Miss—Be—her description?"

"Yes."

"He might have been put off by the name. He has no reason to know that the young lady is without her memories."

Caroline bit her lip and frowned. "In trying to protect you, I have unwittingly prevented your return to your family," she said with a shake of her head.

Beth reached over for Caroline's hand and squeezed. "Do not distress yourself, Caroline. The circumstances of my journey were cagey at best. Anonymity *is* my protection."

"Perhaps." Caroline glanced to James for reassurance while Beth began her description.

"The man that tried to seize me was substantial but not corpulent. His hair had been cut in a ragged fringe. Filthy, dressed in rough work clothes. And toothless . . . yes, toothless." She shuddered.

"Yes, indeed. This is most interesting." Mr. Strickland looked over at James, who had taken up a position near Beth's chair. "I will cast about town for strangers, both the ruffians and the elderly gent what came by, and I'll speak to Mrs. Bartley. Think that will make a beginning, and then I'll take it where it leads."

James walked the new parish deputy to the main door. He surprised Robert by waving him away and opening the door himself. He continued to the drive with Mr. Strickland and waited with him until his pony-chaise was brought around.

———•———

BETH WATCHED THE men quit the room and rose with Caroline to make her way to the back of the manor. As they rounded the corner and entered the little hall, they found Mrs. Fogel awaiting them in front of the morning room door. Dressed primly, as always, she had a brown cloak slung over her arm and the post in her hand.

Caroline acknowledged the housekeeper. "Yes, Mrs. Fogel?"

Passing Caroline the post, which required no explanation, Mrs. Fogel held up the cloak, which did. "The cloak, Miss Ellerby, appears to belong to no one."

"I beg your pardon?"

"I have asked all around." She looked at Beth, indicating that she had followed Beth's request. "But no one claimed it."

"How peculiar. Where did it come from?"

"We thought it was Daisy's, Miss Ellerby. It had fallen beside her bed. Harriet hung it behind the door."

In an instant, Beth remembered the brown cloak. She reached out, relieving Mrs. Fogel of the heavy garment. "Thank you for your trouble, Mrs. Fogel. I have *just* recalled where it came from."

Mrs. Fogel nodded, turning back to the servants' hall.

Head down, Caroline flipped through the post as she walked into the morning room. Following her, Beth sat down on the settee and began searching the pockets of the cloak.

"Here at last." Caroline sounded triumphant. She cast aside the other letters and quickly broke the seal of one. Unfolding the page, Caroline squinted at it. "Oh dear, Miss Morris doesn't have the best of penmanship." She huffed a sigh and began to read.

While she did so, Beth searched. She had yet to find more than a square of white cloth within the folds of the great cloak. However, she knew there to be another pocket, as she could feel the crispness of paper beneath her probing fingers. She just had to find the right fold among the many.

"Aha," Caroline crowed. "*In answer to your question in regard to Pamela Barlow. It is unlikely that the young woman you met last year is my Miss Barlow, as Pamela's complexion is not dark but very fair. Her hair is a soft blond, her eyes bright blue. She has indeed disappeared, but the mystery of that disappearance is but a ruse. The sweet child has ruined herself and eloped with a penniless charlatan.*" Caroline stopped reading. "That is a wonder."

Beth was unsure of Caroline's meaning. "What is?"

Caroline looked up with a broad smile. "A wonder that Mrs. Thompson was right."

Beth chuckled. "Yes, a wonder indeed." She continued kneading the cloak.

"What are you doing, Beth?"

"I believe this cloak came from the trunk—the one that wasn't mine. It must have slipped behind the bed unnoticed."

"What a happy accident." Caroline dropped the letter on her desk and crossed the room to Beth. "Have you found anything?"

"Not so far, but I know there to be another pocket somewhere, as I can hear the rustle of paper. See—" Beth ran her hands along the brown material and produced a faint but distinct crinkle.

"Let us spread the material out." Caroline took one corner while Beth took the other and spread the cloak out like a sail between them.

Just then James entered the room. "Have you seen the post, Caro— What on earth are you doing?"

"Sleuthing."

"I beg your pardon?"

Caroline laughed. "This cloak was in Beth's mysterious trunk. We are checking the pockets." She explained how it had come into their possession.

James shrugged, clearly intent on other matters. "Have you seen the post?"

"There," Beth exclaimed. She lifted a slip of paper into the air as if it were a grand prize.

She dropped the cloak, and it fell into a puddle at their feet. Caroline, with more haste than grace, sat beside Beth.

James found the letters and began opening them and then tossing them aside. "Anything?" he asked, looking up from the mail.

Beth stared at the scrap of paper and sighed deeply. "It is just a calendar of appointments. It looks to have been torn from a log or ledger." She dropped her corner, allowing Caroline sole possession. Picking the cloak up from the floor, she slung it across the top of a chair.

Caroline sighed, too. "Perhaps the only mysterious aspect of this list is that it is a woman's list in a man's pocket."

"How do you know that?" James' voice was distant and distracted.

Caroline leaned closer to Beth as if it were she who had asked

the question. "This is a milliner, this a glove shop. In fact, James"—
she stood to show her brother—"all these shops are in London. I
know of a few, and have even frequented Fitzroy's."

James glanced over from the letter that had taken most of his
attention. "Does it have a date on it?"

"This might be a reference." Caroline pointed to the *A15*
scrawled at the bottom of the paper. "But it doesn't give a month."
She passed it to her brother for a closer look.

However, James didn't give it another glance, but folded it with
the letter in his hand. "I will see if any of these shops retain records of their clients' appointments. Perhaps we will be able to
return the cloak to its rightful owner after all." He smiled at Beth's
puzzled look. "He might find himself appreciative enough to
answer a few questions about the coach and its occupants."

"Are you to London?" Caroline asked.

James lifted the letter in his hand. "Indeed. I must talk with
Lord Levry and Lord Wolcher about repealing the letters of
marque. I believe I mentioned it earlier. Worry not, we will have
heard from Mr. Strickland before I have to go."

Beth's stomach flip-flopped and her heart raced uncomfortably. It was the loss of James' clear thinking and helpful involvement that sent her spirits plummeting. She knew it *couldn't* be the
thought of his absence that filled her with despair.

———◆———

"My, how you've grown."

Beth giggled as the pup she had come to adore climbed all over
her, licking and squirming. Looking around the stable yard, Beth
tried to determine the best place to release the wiggling creature,
but found the decision moot when the puppy squeezed out from

under her arm and dropped, first to her quickly bent knee, and then to the ground. The little retriever raced around the corner in the blink of an eye, trailing the rope meant to keep her under control.

"No!" Beth yelled futilely, giving chase. She nearly collided with a tall young man on the other side of the yard. He was holding the puppy's lead.

"Would this be yours?" Walter asked with mock disinterest.

Panting in a most undignified manner, Beth nodded. "Tem . . . porarily."

"Does she have a name?"

"No. Indeed. Not." She took a deep and calming breath. "That would be most presumptuous. She is not mine." Beth knelt down and patted the dog, who greeted her as if she had not just run away.

"I don't know why you say so; the dog clearly thinks you are hers."

"She is but three months old and has a lot to learn."

Beth turned, and with a slight tug on the rope, directed the pup to follow. Walter fell in beside her and the three strolled into the gardens. "You have only to ask. I'm confident James would give her to you."

"He might, but asking would be unconscionably rude."

"I will speak for you."

"No, Walter," she laughed. "Thank you, though, for the offer."

They wandered through the newly planted beds in silence. The tulips, mostly spent, were drying, and soon the gardeners would begin their overplanting.

"I wish we could take a walk by the water. It would be more private." Walter sounded wistful.

"You know your brother has forbidden it. Unless, of course, I take seven grooms, five footmen, ten field hands, and a partridge in a pear tree."

Walter grinned.

"However, it's of no consequence," she continued. "The garden is lovely and I am sure our culprits will be caught soon." Now was the time to lead in to her request, but she was not sure how to do so. Fortunately, Walter gave her the opening that she needed.

"I wish there was something I could do."

"Yes, I feel the same way." She looked across at him as he swung his arms loosely. "I have thought of something that we—you and I—might try."

Walter's arms stopped moving and slowly came to rest at his sides. "Yes?" His eyes sparkled with interest.

"I had thought that, if Mr. Strickland had no luck . . . that is, if the ruffians were not found . . . I might . . . entice them. Provide an opportunity for them to reach me again." But even as Beth spoke the words, self-doubt intruded. It left her wondering if it was wise, or safe, to involve Walter.

"Bait! You want to use yourself as bait!" Walter stared at her, mouth gaping. His expression was of dismay, not eagerness, and then his lips lifted in a slow, lazy smile. "It is a foolish, idiotic, and asinine idea. Indeed." Then he grinned. "Something *I* might suggest." He laughed heartily. "You almost had me. I thought you were serious for a moment. But no, you would not be so impetuous. James would have our guts for garters if we tried any such thing."

Beth nodded, realizing that Walter was right, and she was right. It would not be prudent to include Walter in this confrontation. "Well done, Walter. You caught me." She chuckled. It sounded hollow and forced, but Walter seemed not to notice. Quickly turning to another subject, Beth unwittingly increased his good opinion by asking about his curricle, Henry, and then, best of all, his wardrobe.

———————

JAMES FROWNED OVER the ledgers. The walls of the library pressed in against him, shutting him away from the other members of the household. He had no desire to sequester himself there; he preferred company today, especially the company of a young lady with straight brown hair and an intoxicating laugh. But the accounts were not being cooperative. Knowing that he would get through the wretched sums faster if he were undisturbed, he informed Robert that he was not to be interrupted.

Therefore, he was greatly surprised, and annoyed, when Robert did not comply.

"M'lord, there is a gentleman here who would like to speak with you. He says it concerns his sister."

"Has he the right direction, Robert?"

"I believe so, m'lord. He asked to speak to you directly."

"Very well. Show him in." James tried to complete the sum he was working on before the man entered, but didn't quite make it. The man waited by the door.

James closed the book and set it aside. He pointed to one of the chairs before his desk.

The gentleman bowed slightly and took the offered seat. There was an unsavory air about him, although James could not divine its source. He was dressed well enough, in apparel of a reasonable quality, although his boots were muddied. The hat that he held to his lap was new with a narrow rim. His hair, straight and dark, was brushed forward on the sides. His face was unremarkable and common, except for the goatee sported below a clean-shaven lip.

James waited for the man to state his business.

"Martin Paterson, m'lord. I have come in search of my sister, Diana."

James frowned. There had been a slight hesitation to the man's words. "And why would that bring you to my door?"

"I believe she is housed within."

James started. The superiority of the man's attitude felt contrived, but his reference had been clear enough. Could this man, just barely passing for a gentleman, be related to Beth?

"Can you describe your sister?" he asked.

Paterson smiled as if it were a joke. "Of course. Straight hair, hazel eyes, considered pretty by some, and a scar under her jaw."

James stood, doing his best to exude a calm, casual manner despite his racing heart. He straightened his waistcoat. "Please excuse me." He bowed slightly, very slightly, to the man seated before him, and left the room. He closed the door with more force than he had intended.

"Robert, could you find Miss Ellerby and direct her to the library right away. Not Miss Beth, *just* Miss Ellerby." He then reentered the room with his thoughts in turmoil. He sat back at his desk and leaned forward, hoping to intimidate.

"First I must say, Mr. Paterson, that we have a person such as you have described under our roof, but she is not known to us by that name."

"Little minx, I'll give her credit. Changed it, has she?"

Just then, Caroline opened the door and stepped in. James introduced the two and waited until Caroline was seated before he explained why she was summoned.

James watched Caroline swallow a few times before she spoke. Her voice was devoid of emotion. "How is it that you lost your sister, Mr. Paterson?"

"She has been missing nigh on three months. We had quite given up hope." Mr. Paterson shifted in his chair. "Perhaps I should start at the beginning."

"That would be helpful." Caroline sat back incrementally from her perched, straight-back position.

"Diana's a good girl an' all. But she's slightly touched."

"Nonsense," Caroline interrupted. "We cannot be talking about the same woman."

"She has nightmares. Night after night."

James could hardly hear over the noisy pounding of his heart. Thoughts flooded his mind, questions screamed.

"Diana lives with us," the man continued. "She helps my wife around the house in small ways. Our mother used to keep her but—God rest her soul—my poor mother passed away last year."

James recalled Beth's assertion of her mother's demise and felt his stomach sink. Beth had suspected her mother's passing was a childhood event, but her memories were far from reliable.

Beth couldn't possibly be this man's sister! James didn't want it to be true.

Mr. Paterson held his hat to his chest for a moment, as if in supplication. "Our Diana has a hard time dealing with change. She didn't settle in with us as quickly as we would have liked. One day, she just vanished. We heard from the vicar that he saw her catch a ride in a wagon. Thought that she might have tried to return to Pencombe, where she lived with our mother. We have had agents looking for months. Yesterday, we got word that she had been found." Mr. Paterson's eyes flashed. "Can I see her?"

CAROLINE LIFTED HER hand and thought for a few moments before speaking. She looked over at James, but received no message from his furrowed brows and pensive expression. "Perhaps it would be best to explain that the young woman who may or may not be your sister is suffering from loss of memory."

"Matters not." Paterson shrugged. "I'll know her to see her."

Caroline frowned and met James' eye. "We don't want to startle her. Perhaps we should contact Dr. Brant."

"Not to worry, Miss Ellerby, I always knows what's best for our Diana. Two peas in a pod, our ma used to say."

"I am not so sure. Did you know that she was in a carriage accident? She received quite a knock to her brain."

"But well enough to go to town. That was how my agent found her. And if she's well enough to shop, she's well enough to greet her nearest and dearest." Mr. Paterson showed his teeth.

"And yet, she has no memories from before the accident."

Finally the man seemed to comprehend. "None . . . none at all?"

"That's what we have been saying," James snapped.

Mr. Paterson glanced from one to the other. "Diana is all right, isn't she?" He gathered the great coat that he had lain across his lap, and replaced his hat. It was a little overlarge. "I demand to see her."

Caroline rose and opened the door to the hall. The footman was there immediately. "Robert, could you inquire as to Beth's whereabouts but do not disturb her?" she said. "I only want to know where I might find her."

"She is in the garden, Miss Ellerby. I saw her out there not twenty minutes ago," the footman assured her.

"Excellent." Caroline waved her arm toward the door, gesturing for Mr. Paterson to follow. She led Mr. Paterson through the main hall into the saloon. At the far end of the grand room, there were three sets of large French doors. They looked out on a patio and the gardens beyond that.

Caroline held aside the draperies and they gazed out at the shrubbery. A charming picture met their scrutiny. Walter and Beth were alternately laughing and conversing as they strolled casually along the paths. Beth's pup pulled this way and that, promoting more merriment.

"Diana!" Mr. Paterson shouted as he reached for the door handle. He was outside before either James or Caroline could stop him.

"No!" Caroline called after him, but the man did not listen. In fact, he scurried—in a most undignified manner—over the patio and straight through the flower beds.

"Diana! Diana!" he shouted. His arms spread into a welcoming posture.

James grabbed Mr. Paterson's shoulder from behind. "No farther, Mr. Paterson." His tone brooked no argument.

But the damage was done. Beth and Walter were very aware of their presence.

"But it is she," Mr. Paterson declared. "Our Diana."

"Mr. Paterson, as my sister quite clearly explained, Beth will not remember you. You will frighten her. I am sure a brother of such devotion as yourself would not want to cause her distress."

Paterson straightened. "Lord Ellerby, I want my sister returned to me. I will not lollygag around here waiting until you feel she is fit to venture an introduction. She is my sister, and I know what is in her best interest. The sooner she is surrounded by all that is familiar, the sooner her memory can return. I intend to quit this house immediately with Diana at my side. My pony-chaise is waiting."

CHAPTER ELEVEN

The Familiar Stranger

A hush fell over the garden. Walter ceased talking and Beth stood motionless, her heart rhythm accelerating. Even the active puppy sensed the disquiet at the other end of the lead and plopped down onto a burgeoning plantain lily.

Not far from where they stood, an animated conversation was taking place. Nothing could be heard of that discussion, but the gestures and postures did not appear friendly. A stranger kept waving in her direction. The scene was peculiar, and Beth was greatly disturbed by the visitor. There was something uncomfortably familiar in his bearing. Beth swallowed, her mouth suddenly dry. The man frightened her, though she didn't know why.

After what felt like an eternity, Caroline came toward them. James led the man back through the French doors and into the manor.

"What a glorious day." Caroline's words were stilted, her smile forced. She bent down to pat the pup that leapt and circled around her ankles. "Could we have a moment, Beth?"

Beth felt the blood drain from her face and her knees threatened to drop her to the ground.

"Walter, might you return this adorable bundle to the stable?" Caroline asked before Beth could respond.

"I should have known!" Walter scooped the puppy up in a firm but gentle hand. "Once more, I am to know nothing! You don't trust me!" He glared at Caroline.

Caroline snorted and shook her head. "Really, Walter. That's not my purpose, not at all. I will explain shortly, but at this time I feel Beth needs a private conversation."

Walter straightened his shoulders, wiggling them as he did so. Then, bowing with infinite grace and dignity, he set off to do just as he was told.

Caroline led Beth through the doors of the conservatory to the white wicker chairs grouped under two large palms. The fresh smell of earth and flowers, the lush greenery, and the twittering of caged birds created a calm facade.

Caroline faced Beth, but sat for some moments with her brow creased and her mouth partially open, as if she was having trouble forming her words.

"Perhaps, it would be best just to come out with it, Caroline," Beth said. "Can your news be that disturbing?"

Caroline snapped her mouth shut, sighed, and then shrugged. "No indeed, if it is true, it is happy news."

Beth noted the qualifier. "*If* it is true?"

"Yes. The gentleman that you observed, just moments ago, has arrived to claim his sister. He has it in his mind that you are she. His name is Martin Paterson; his sister is called Diana. He claims she disappeared three months ago and he has been looking for her ever since."

Beth was taken aback. His sister? There was nothing similar in their stature or appearance. It couldn't be true, could it?

"I am not comfortable with his explanation." Caroline looked toward the door. "However, his description of Diana was very much like you, and he mentioned . . . nightmares."

Beth started. "His sister suffers them as well?"

"He said so." She paused for a moment before continuing. "He says she ran away."

Her mind awash with a torrent of questions, Beth sat silent and overwhelmed. When she finally spoke, her voice was barely audible. "What was she running from?"

Caroline tried to laugh. "He claims Miss Paterson to be touched."

"Touched?" Beth didn't feel unbalanced. Her brain seemed to work perfectly fine, if she overlooked that small problem of memory loss. No, she was not touched. "That is too convenient."

"I thought so as well."

"By claiming her to be touched, Mr. Paterson has control of her—or rather me—if he is to be believed. Any claims I might have, or denials, can easily be discounted."

"Yes, those were my thoughts exactly."

"How did he find me?" Beth had felt no comfort when looking at the man. If he were her protective brother, would she not feel something? Something other than horror?

"Apparently, it was his agent asking questions in town the other day."

Beth slowly shook her head. "Caroline, when I saw him in the garden just now—"

"Yes?"

"I felt a spark of recognition and . . . fright. If he is my brother, we are not on good terms. I do not want to go with him. It doesn't feel safe."

"I quite agree. I have a plan." Caroline patted Beth's tightly laced fingers. "I am going to have another conversation with Mr. Paterson. You are going to develop a sick headache—"

"That is true enough."

"Might I then suggest the quiet of your room for the time being?"

Beth nodded and rose with Caroline, straightening her skirts. Caroline led the way through the narrow opening in the corner of the conservatory to the manor's back hall. The servants' stairs were just beyond the entrance. They allowed Beth to reach the floor above without entering the main hall, where Mr. Paterson might observe her. She was not going to take the chance of encountering the man who claimed a right over her.

———•———

IN THE LIBRARY, an uncomfortable silence permeated the room. James sat at his desk with the appearance of calm, reading his correspondence, while Paterson impatiently squirmed and shifted in the large wingback chair. He cast James a furtive look, and then glanced to the doors and the windows.

"It shan't be long now, Mr. Paterson. Miss Ellerby was going to speak with Beth directly. Perhaps you need something to do in the interim." He gestured around the room. "You are in a library. There must be something here that would interest you."

Paterson glanced from side to side at the tall cases of thick tomes. He turned back to James with a look that could easily be attributed to abject indifference. Without comment, the man returned to squirming and shifting.

James frowned. Strange that Beth's "brother" would find the written word of so little interest when she treated books with fascinated reverence. James lifted the letter before him, trying to understand the incongruities of the man.

By the time Caroline returned to the library, Mr. Paterson was stomping across the room, pacing. It irritated James excessively.

While the expression on Paterson's face held suppressed anger, he greeted Caroline with a tone that masked his rancor. "Now that Diana is acquainted with my arrival, I assume she is packing, and my pony will not have to wait much longer."

"Would that it were so easy, Mr. Paterson."

The man's complexion began to redden.

"Beth is not well and has gone to lie down," Caroline explained. "She has a sick headache."

"Nonsense!" Paterson shouted. "Diana is just avoiding me."

James watched Caroline raise her eyebrow and fix a silent questioning stare at the visitor.

"Our last words to each other were, perhaps, not as affable as usual, but she need not avoid me." Paterson looked back and forth between the Ellerby siblings, apparently unsure who would respond best.

"Nonsense!" Caroline echoed Paterson's words. "Beth is not avoiding you, nor does she remember those caustic words. Beth has *lost her memory*." Caroline stepped closer to James and then took a deep breath. "Beth will not be going anywhere today, Mr. Paterson," she said firmly.

Paterson's reaction was less explosive than James expected. The man's heightened complexion dissipated and his posture relaxed. If anything, Paterson was quieter and calmer than James had seen thus far.

"Why would that be, Miss Ellerby?" His voice was akin to ice.

"As I mentioned earlier, Beth was in a carriage accident, and I do not believe she should be doing any lengthy traveling without seeing her physician first. I will request his attendance, but the afternoon is already half gone. It will not be until tomorrow that he will be able to examine her." Caroline glanced over at James.

He nodded his approval. Caroline returned her gaze to Paterson with her chin slightly elevated. A cagey expression formed on the man's face. "On the morrow then."

"We cannot possibly be ready in so short a time, Mr. Paterson."

"We?"

"Yes, we. I promised Beth long before *your* arrival that I would not let her go to any situation in which she was unhappy," Caroline said coolly. "I cannot keep that promise unless I accompany her and see for myself."

"Are you suggesting that I would not do well by my sister?" Paterson's volume began to increase once more. "That is insulting."

"It has nothing to do with you, Mr. Paterson."

"Do you expect me to twiddle my thumbs while the two of you pack at leisure?"

James had had enough. "Sit down, Mr. Paterson," he barked. "It would appear to me that you have four choices, and none of them involve taking Beth away anytime soon. You could return home, content to have found your sister in safe hands. Then you could either return for her at a later date, or give us your direction and I would accompany Miss Ellerby and her companion to your home. Your third choice is obvious. She could stay here."

Paterson opened his mouth as if to speak, but James raised his hand to indicate that he was not finished speaking. "You may also accept our hospitality and stay with us for a few days while the proper preparations are made. Hardwick is not known to be a difficult place in which to while away time."

Paterson fixed James with a glare. It was likely meant to be intimidating, but it merely increased James' resolve.

Paterson took a couple of sharp breaths. "I am expected home," he muttered after swallowing several times in succession.

"Really, Mr. Paterson, have you no imagination?" Caroline smiled without warmth. "A letter will arrive just as quickly as you would have done."

"Perhaps." Paterson twitched and then swallowed again. "I believe I will accept your kind invitation and thank you for the care and attention you have shown Diana." His smile was mocking.

James was not impressed, not intimidated, and not convinced.

Caroline quietly slipped away as James began to organize the visit. James would rather have traded places with Caroline and gone to Beth. He wanted to reassure her, comfort her, and tell her how much he . . . the family . . . cared. He could and would be her protector. There was no need for her to worry—he would do it for her.

———•———

CAROLINE SLUMPED DOWN onto the settee in her boudoir. She curled her feet up and leaned her head against the ornate carved edging. The deep grooves and swirls were uncomfortable but allowed her to remain in repose without enticing sleep. A book of verse lay open on the table at her elbow. It would serve as a distraction until James arrived, if James arrived.

She was almost certain that James' elaborate "good night" had been fashioned to persuade Mr. Paterson that the evening was concluded. If the man was not a total boor, he should now know to keep to his chamber.

Mr. Paterson had been placed in one of the state apartments that faced the drive. It was a well-appointed room with a huge four-poster bed and its own sitting room. It was more than Mr. Paterson's rank dictated, but it was the room farthest from Beth. Ned was assigned to keep watch from a small alcove in the hall.

Caroline had only read the first line of a Byron poem when a light scratch on the door of her bedroom parlor caught her attention. James did not wait for a reply. He entered, crossed the room to the chair opposite Caroline and dropped into it. He mirrored Caroline's relaxed pose by lifting his heels to the corner of the settee. They sat wordless for some moments, staring into the abyss of their own minds.

James was the first to articulate his turmoil. "Well, this is a bloody mess!"

The vulgarity of his words in her company surprised Caroline and offered her a clear picture of James' frame of mind. His thin-lipped scowl completed the picture.

"We are in the suds!" he continued in distracted tones.

"Not really, James. I think our contrived delay has put Mr. Paterson into a lather. Despite his languid posturing, there was a sense of desperation to his dinner conversation. Did he not claim that his wife is in her confinement, and Beth—or Diana, as he insists—is needed to help immediately? Then he recalled his pony-chaise was hired and had been promised to be returned on the morrow." She smiled at her brother with the recollection. "So clever of you to suggest he do just that. Though I am not sure he liked it overly. It was not surprising when he declined."

James shook his head as he stared at the floor. "He even utilized

Walter's polite inquiries to further his point." He brought his eyes up to Caroline's. "If one were to believe Mr. Paterson, catastrophe is about to befall his entire clan, and only Diana can remedy it. I do not give credence to that."

"James, I do not believe Beth is Diana any more than you do. In fact, I doubt there is a Diana Paterson. But in all fairness we have to entertain the idea that there might be a sliver of truth in what he says."

"Why do you think so?"

"He described Beth without seeing her—"

"Beth has been to town. Any number of observers could have given him her description."

"He knows of her nightmares—"

"Are you not the one who is always complaining about gossip?"

"Beth recognized him."

James sat up abruptly. "She *recognized* him?"

"Calm yourself, James." Caroline waved him back to his slouch. "Not as her brother, just as someone she finds familiar. But his presence caused her great discomfort."

"So you believe there to be something factual in what Paterson says?"

"A fraction, perhaps."

"I am hard-pressed to believe any of it." James replaced his feet on the settee. "But his explanations answer a fair number of our questions. His depiction of what transpired—an argument that led to her sudden departure—would explain how she came to be in the coach in soiled clothing with no escort, funds, or baggage. Was it a public conveyance or had she been *assisted* by strangers giving her a lift to the next town? Their purpose might not have been honorable—hence the lies and evasive behavior of the men in the accident. And then, Paterson's search extending around the area of her youth is logical. It is likely that a frightened young woman would seek asylum with a family friend or retainer. But Beth is not touched!" He stared blankly at his feet. "Quite the opposite, I would say. Besides, her diction does not match that of Paterson—Beth's elocution is far superior. She is an intelligent young woman with a lively and enthusiastic character. Her inability to adjust to a new home does not hold true as the reason for their disagreement and her sudden departure."

Caroline nodded and sighed. "And if the Patersons make their home in Cheltenham—as he told Walter at dinner—a distance that must encompass a journey of at least three days' hard ride, then how did he get to Welford Mills within a day of his agent's discovery?"

"You are right. There is a connection of some sort, but what it might be has me baffled."

"We can delay."

"Yes, but not forever. I must go to London, do not forget. Besides, delay without action is pointless. We must have a plan."

Caroline uncurled her legs from beneath her and placed her feet firmly on the floor. Likewise, James' boots were placed with conviction under him.

"Send a note to Brant as we said we would do," James began, "but include an explanation as to why we are seeking his advice. Request that he inquires after the Paterson family in Pencombe before he arrives."

"Yes, and I might include in the request that he not step into Welford until he knows something. We need no other excuse to delay than waiting for Beth's physician to arrive. However, if

Dr. Brant finds nothing, we must have another excuse on the ready."

"You could pack but become indecisive."

Caroline smiled. "Yes, I might even see the need to add to our wardrobes."

"Excellent thought." James nodded enthusiastically. "I will go into Welford Mills to ask Mr. Strickland about his progress and get his opinion on Mr. Paterson."

"I shall keep Beth sequestered and continue to ask that man a barrage of questions. It is not likely he will let down his guard for us to see his true relationship to Beth, but I can try."

"Yes." James rose and made his way to the door. "It gives me great pleasure to envision your innocent questioning and the irritation it will cause."

Caroline feigned shock. "James, I am surprised. I believe Mr. Paterson to have found no favor with you. And he a man of such varying . . . temperaments."

James snorted and silently stepped into the hall.

———◆———

An unremarkable and common face darted in and out of the shadows. Hands clawed at her. Beth tried to protect herself but her limbs would not move; they stayed lifeless at her side. Even as she watched the dust dance from one side of a light shaft to the other, she became aware of the hum. It grew in volume until it eclipsed all else.

Then suddenly the creature was in front of her. The wings fluttered too quickly for Beth to see them in anything more than a blur, but its brilliant body shone in shades of green and blue. It stared at Beth with knowledge and understanding, and even as Beth watched, it began to cry. At first the watery tears dripped slowly onto her lap, but as she watched the puddle spread and flow down her legs, it began to take on a rosy hue and then the tint deepened to bloodred. Soon she was drenched in its oozing stickiness.

Off in the distance she could hear a strident, continuous sound, like a siren, or the wail of a babe.

———————

BETH GASPED FOR AIR, jerking straight up in bed. The echo of her scream crashed against the walls and then faded into the inky darkness.

The night was deep and the manor silent.

Beth shuddered and gulped for some moments as she tried to control the tremors that shook her body. Perspiration dripped down the back of her nightdress. She pulled the counterpane up to her chin and listened to her own ragged but easing breath. After a time, Beth forced herself to inhale deeply and then slowly exhaled. She was about to do so again when she heard a noise.

A creak.

Beth froze and listened. She strained against the silence and waited. She closed her eyes to concentrate. She prayed that the noise was natural and her fear was just a product of all her wild imagination.

Another creak . . . and then another.

There was a furtive rhythm to the creaks, a hesitance. The only consistency was their approach—an oncoming herald played out in the groaning of the wooden floor.

Beth leapt from the bed, raced across the floor and slammed into the door, pawing for the handle. The instant her fingers touched the cold metal she turned the key. Even as she heard the lock click home, she felt the handle turn. And then it squeaked.

The handle stilled as if the noise had alerted the intruder. But it didn't return to its normal position. Beth waited—a mere three inches of oak protecting her. With her ear and shoulder to the door, Beth stood for what seemed like hours.

Then the handle squeaked again and continued to turn. There was a soft thump on the other side, as if the door was being pushed. A louder thump followed, and then, almost instantly, another. This one was accompanied by a crack, as if the jamb was about to give way.

Terror shot through her veins. Beth grabbed the desk by her elbow and dragged it nosily across the floor. She braced it against the wood, kicking the spilled papers and books out of the way as she did. Quickly, she turned and sped over to the heavy armchair by the corner windows. She tugged it over the carpet, creating so many hampering folds that she had to heave the chair over them. The chair screeched its protest as she towed it across the bare wood and slammed it against the desk. Finally, she dragged a small table from beside the bed and wedged it against the chair.

Beth would have continued rearranging the furniture but for the fact that silence had returned. The door no longer groaned and the handle no longer squeaked.

Beth backed into the wall opposite the door and stared. Her haphazard renovations looked like glorious sentinels, guards, and protectors. She allowed her legs to give way, dropping to the floor, and clasped her knees to her chest. Her eyes never strayed from the door.

The stranger was on the other side; Beth was certain. He must have slipped past Ned. No one else would have tried to invade her room in the dead of night. The man would be forced to answer for his actions in the morning. James would see to it the moment he heard about this intrusion.

The misplaced furniture before her began to blur and Beth felt the warmth of pent-up tears trickle down her cheeks. The combination of exhaustion and terror proved too much for her. She cried long and hard, and saw the sun rise above the trees long before she crawled back under her covers. Drained by fears and emotions, Beth finally found the sweet oblivion of sleep.

CHAPTER TWELVE

Leave Taking

Caroline was not in the least troubled by the absence of their uninvited guest at breakfast the next morning. Beth was not expected, either, as they had agreed that she would avoid Mr. Paterson for as long as possible. Consequently, the Ellerby trio enjoyed a relatively relaxed meal, until Harriet's light knock and inquiry.

"Mrs. Fogel asked for a moment, miss." Harriet looked at Caroline's empty plate. "Whenever you're done."

Caroline peered into the hall. "Come in, come in, Mrs. Fogel. Since when do we stand on ceremony in this household?" She smiled her welcome as the stout woman replaced Harriet and crossed the room with some rapidity. Caroline's smile faded with recognition of the serious look on Mrs. Fogel's face. She belatedly realized that the housekeeper had been looking for a private interview. She pushed her seat back, planning to quit the room.

James glanced up from his newspaper. "Is all well, Mrs. Fogel?"

Mrs. Fogel shifted her weight. "Well, m'lord, Harriet informs me that Mr. Paterson was not in his room when she went to see to his fire. I thought him an early riser, perhaps, seeking a breath of the morning dew. But Paul informs me his pony-chaise is gone as well. He seems to have slipped past Ned early—very early—this morning." She looked back to Caroline with raised brows. "I had been under the impression that he would be staying some days."

James frowned and swallowed visibly. "We were under the same impression, Mrs. Fogel. Whatever could have caused his early departure? Is anything missing?"

"Not that I am aware of, m'lord."

Caroline turned to stare at the door as if doing so would help her see into the hall and up the stairs. "Is all well with Beth?" she asked.

"Harriet weren't able to stoke her fire, either, Miss Ellerby."

James jumped to his feet with such force that his chair fell to the floor behind him. "What . . . what?" he sputtered. "What do you mean?"

"It seems Miss Beth locked her door last night. And there's a great crack running down the door what weren't there yesterday. *And . . .*" Mrs. Fogel hesitated, squeezing her hands together tightly. "There seems to be something blocking the door. I couldn't get it open."

———

WALTER WAS THE first to arrive at Beth's door. He pounded the oak, rattled the handle, and called to Beth so loudly that James had to quiet him to listen for a reply.

There was a collective sigh of relief when they were answered from within. However, the scraping and moving of furniture renewed Caroline's anxiety. It seemed forever before they heard the lock groan. When the door opened, Caroline saw dark circles under Beth's eyes and fear contouring her face.

"What has happened?" James asked as he stepped ahead of Caroline, leading Beth to the chair by the window. He watched as her shaking subsided and she no longer gulped at the air. Lifting her hand, she placed it on his arm, giving it a quick squeeze. And then Beth tightened her dressing gown belt, smiled weakly, and described her harrowing night.

"This does, in some way, explain the disappearance of Mr. Paterson," Caroline said when Beth finished.

"He is gone?"

Caroline dropped onto Beth's bed, swinging her legs back and forth in a relaxed manner. "Yes, he cannot be located within our walls and his pony-chaise is missing. Good riddance!"

"But we have lost a valuable source of information." Beth sighed. "Who knows what we could have wrung from him after last night's intrusion?"

"True, true. But it is moot now." James waved his hand in the general direction of the door and misplaced furniture. "Do not worry about the mess. I will have the furniture put to rights while you eat breakfast. All is well." His reassurance sounded more theatrical than realistic, but it seemed to calm Beth.

———•———

EVEN WITHOUT HELP, Beth was ready in a twinkling. Mr. Paterson's departure was a godsend, and her relief so acute that her fingers had wings. Still, her excitement to rush downstairs had as much to do with James as Mr. Paterson. James was her refuge and her security. Which was redundant but she didn't care; he offered the sense of safety that she so desperately needed.

Beth had only just stepped into the main hallway when she encountered the handsome young gentleman of her thoughts. Skittering to a halt, Beth tried to appear unruffled by his presence. It likely didn't deceive Lord James Ellerby.

"Are you well? Truly?" James leaned across the banister, straightening as he spoke. "I feel as if one of the family should be with you at all times from now on . . . for protection." He met her gaze and held it for a moment or two. His expression was enigmatic.

Catching her breath—for somehow her lungs were empty—Beth nodded. "Thank you for your concern, Lord Ellerby. It was a harrowing night, but it is over now. Normality might once again enter these hallowed halls." Beth swept her arms in an arc with the flourish of melodrama that Walter often adopted.

"If he had hurt you—"

"I am fine," Beth interrupted, "and we are all the wiser for it." She hated seeing the hesitation and anxiety behind his eyes.

James stared over her head for a moment. "How can we be wiser when the man spoke not a word of truth? And how did that wretched worm even know where your chamber was? It was not mentioned at dinner, and none of the servants would have divulged your location."

Beth shrugged with feigned nonchalance and hooked her arm through his. They slowly traversed the hallway to the stairs. "It is my own fault, I believe."

James stopped short. He looked at her, glanced toward the wall for a moment and then back. "How can you say that? I will *not* have you . . . criticizing yourself." He cleared his throat as if uncomfortable with his outburst.

Beth snorted and tugged him forward. "Not intentional, of

course. He knew of my nightmares and my screaming led him to me."

"Well, yes, that is possible. I heard you from my room and the scoundrel was just opposite." They continued down the stairs in silence for a moment. "The hummingbird again?"

Beth laughed without humor. "Yes, the bird that becomes a dagger." She swallowed and looked away. She no longer saw the elegant marble stairs but the bird that terrorized her dreams.

"I know it to be a hummingbird, for I have heard them described and seen a picture or two." Her voice was hollow, lifeless. "Though I doubt they drink blood." She shuddered and then continued. "It frightens me. Can you imagine this beautiful little bird—for it is quite small—frightens me? The eyes glaze over, the wings fuse, and blood dribbles from its beak. Suddenly, it is no longer a beak but a dagger." Beth looked up at James. "I try to block the fear but it consumes me."

When they reached the bottom step, Beth shook herself as if to erase her tormented thoughts. She glanced at James, once again placing a cheerful expression over her bleak one. "I usually start screaming when I realize I am about to die."

She released his arm and smiled as if she had just been discussing the weather.

"You are safe, Beth," James said, ignoring her feigned nonchalance. "It is possible these dreams are caused by a sense of insecurity. But you know, or at least you should know, that the family is here for you, in whatever capacity is needed to keep you safe and sound. We are your friends and your protectors." He took a deep, ragged breath. "I'm here for you." His last words were spoken in a hushed tone—almost reverent.

Beth blinked, dumbfounded by his fervor, and shifted her gaze to the floor. She was lost in the memory of their shared looks, the joy she felt in his presence and the bliss of his laughter. While her affections were most ardently given to the entire Ellerby family, Beth realized that her feelings for James Ellerby were stronger than affection—much stronger.

It was going to be difficult when he left for London.

AFTER BREAKFAST HAD been cleared away, Beth took up what had become her usual position on the settee, embroidery in hand. Walter perched on the settee's arm beside her, trying to be helpful. He made thread color suggestions and exclaimed great distress over nonexistent stitching errors. Caroline sat at her desk composing a letter to Dr. Brant.

Settling back on the settee, Beth sat with her shoulder turned slightly so that she might be attentive to the door without appearing to be doing so. She noticed that Walter glanced constantly in the direction of the windows.

It was no wonder, for the day was a delight. The morning dew and heavy skies had broken into a heated spring day. The air was fresh with the smell of new blossoms. Beth was not surprised that Walter found it hard to concentrate on anything but his desire to be outside.

"Beth, how about a drive through town?" he finally asked. "We could take the curricle, chat up a few of the locals. See if anyone has encountered Mr. Pat—"

"Perhaps now is not the best time," James said, entering the morning room.

Beth felt a rush of pleasure at his sudden appearance. Her heart beat faster, and she had to remember to breathe. She drank in the sight of his profile but dropped her eyes when his head turned toward her. His sigh elicited a brief glance, but when Beth saw that James was still looking her way, she quickly returned her eyes to her stitching.

James cleared his throat. "I have been giving it some thought and . . . well, I believe we should head to London."

Caroline scratched out another line on her note and then signed with a flourish. "Yes, James," she answered absentmindedly. "It is *when* you are going that is in question."

"I said we, Caroline." He glanced at Beth. "I'm certain I said we?"

She nodded just as Walter jumped to his feet. "All of us?" the younger gentleman exclaimed. "To London? We are to make a holiday of it?"

"Yes, indeed. I thought a change of scenery might do us all some good."

"This is capital! Capital indeed!" Walter bounced around the room.

James smiled at Walter. "Within a fortnight or so."

"Wait till Henry hears this! He'll be wild with jealousy! Mrs. Thompson and Mr. Renfrew are taking Sophia into the city without him and now," Walter added with great glee, "he'll be beside himself."

Walter was halfway through the door when he called back over his shoulder, "I'm off to Risely."

Caroline dropped onto the settee beside Beth, forcing James onto the ornate and undersized parlor chair across from them. He dusted a nonexistent piece of lint from his trousers.

"Why?" Caroline asked without preamble.

James hedged. He regaled them with the splendors of the city such as the opera, balls, and assemblies. He spoke of the need to purchase goods at some finer shops, and the chance to meet friends.

None of it rang true.

Beth, like Caroline, remained silent—hands neatly folded on her lap. Her face, again like Caroline's, was devoid of emotion. Finally, their passive nonacceptance bore fruit.

"Paul found a note in the stall that contained Mr. Paterson's pony." James pursed his lips and handed Beth the piece of paper. "It was not addressed to anyone, but the words make it plain that the note is meant for the family, and you in particular, Beth."

Beth opened the folded paper. The message was hastily written but succinct.

You will pay dearly for this charade.

Caroline squeezed Beth's hand. "I think London an excellent plan, James."

"We are just prolonging the agony." Beth stood and began to pace the room. "Paterson could easily follow us to London, if he has a mind to."

But while James and Caroline agreed in principle, they argued that it was unlikely. And so Beth marched from one end of the morning room to the other, and then back again, thinking. While she was aware that James and Caroline were arranging the journey to London, Beth took no part in the discussion. She had devised an alternate plan.

CAROLINE PLUNKED HALFHEARTEDLY at Beethoven's Piano Concerto no. 5 in E-flat Major. Her mind was not on the music but on the list of preparations for what James thought might encompass as much as a two-month stay in Town. Had the journey been for other reasons, the prospect of spending the last of the Season with the Ton would have been exciting. However, July in the heat and stench of London was another matter.

Caroline thought that a simple change of residence would not be enough to deter those pursuing her companion. She had suggested to James that she take Beth to their mother in Bath instead. James and Walter could take up residence as expected in Berkeley Square, hopefully confounding their adversaries. James had been against the idea. Caroline did not assume it was *her* company that he could not do without.

Should Dr. Brant come to dinner, Caroline hoped that he would be able to make James see reason. With that thought, a light knock alerted Caroline to a visitor.

"I had not expected you so soon," Caroline said, leaving her position at the piano and greeting Dr. Brant with affection.

"Your missive arrived just after luncheon, and as I already had it in mind to pay a call, I felt no need to delay."

Caroline tried not to look disappointed. "Oh dear, I had so hoped for news about the Patersons in Pencombe."

"Well, that is the beauty of it. I did not need to pay the town a call to learn of them. Our cook was born and bred in Pencombe and was a veritable fountain of information."

Caroline brightened. "Is there such a creature as Diana Paterson of Pencombe?"

"There are no Patersons in Pencombe. Cook went so far as to say, nary a one in the whole parish." Dr. Brant laughed. "I now know that Matilda Prattle lives in the town proper, and her two sons Douglas and Stephen are out to sea. Molly and Dillan Patney are beyond—"

"So," Caroline interrupted. She was both relieved and disturbed by Dr. Brant's answer. She led him out of the music room toward the drawing room. "Everything, every word that spilled from his lips was nothing but a lie."

"No surprise to any of you."

Caroline nodded. "True enough."

Dr. Brant looked around the drawing room as they crossed the threshold. "Should we speak to Ellerby? Let him know?"

"Yes, indeed. But, unfortunately, Mr. Strickland sent James a note. He left a quarter hour ago, looking quite grim." Caroline sighed heavily.

Dr. Brant looked grave. "You have had darker days and survived," he said, alluding to the tragedy of her father's death and her mother's . . . well, desertion. "You can only take each day as it comes."

Caroline nodded with little vigor. "There is one more piece of news I haven't related to you as yet."

"And that is . . . ?"

"We are to London."

"This is marvelous! I am as well. Dr. Poole has agreed to come out of retirement while I'm gone. We shall make a party of it."

"Really? Why are you to London? Are your parents well?" Caroline knew Dr. Brant to have a distaste of city life.

"Yes indeed, quite well. Although, my mother *is* suffering from acute boredom. Every year she must attend part of the Season. See and be seen, as she puts it, only to find the tedium of gossip and the marriage market overwhelming. No, it is not for their sake that I am bound to make the journey, but for Beth."

"Beth?" Caroline frowned slightly. "How so?"

"While I was waiting for an answer from Edinburgh, I received word of Dr. Stewart Fotherby in London. His specialty is the study of injuries to the head. I thought I might present Beth's case to him and ask his advice. With Beth in London, she could see him in person."

"That is splendid." She smiled and then turned toward the doorway as footsteps quickly approached.

Walter burst in on them. His new staid manner of dress was slightly offset by the return of a wild waistcoat. This particular one was a patchwork of bright colors, but he was not there to discuss fashion, for a change.

"Dr. Brant." Walter nodded a greeting and then turned to his sister. "Where might I find Beth?"

"I believe she mentioned the conservatory, something about an orchid in bloom." Caroline winked at Dr. Brant, knowing Beth to be ensconced in the gallery.

"I've looked. There, and the morning room and the gallery and the music room." He raised his eyebrows. "Any other suggestions?"

Caroline was surprised to learn that Beth was not in the gallery. "Just the obvious. I am surprised that you have not checked the stables."

Walter's face brightened. "Of course. The puppies." He turned without a by-your-leave and left.

"The stables?" Dr. Brant's question drifted over Caroline's shoulder as she stared after her brother.

"I hope so, because I don't know where else she might be." Caroline tried to ignore the catch of fear in her throat.

CHAPTER THIRTEEN

Fluff and Feathers

Without guidance, Tetley cantered through the front gates of Hardwick Manor and turned toward Welford Mills. James was deep in thought, mulling over Mr. Strickland's short note requesting his presence. It was most disturbing and had far-reaching implications.

> Lord Ellerby,
>
> I found the questioning of Daisy Bartley's death to be worthwhile. If it is your convenience, I would meet you at the foot of Old Risely Road.
>
> Derrick Strickland, Parish Deputy

Just after the Torrin Bridge, the east-west London road veered south, toward Welford Mills and the coast. The byway to Risely had been abandoned decades ago to a newer, finer drive past

Welford Mills. Consequently, grass had grown to some length between the old wagon ruts, and the forest bracken had encroached on the road. As it continued up the hill, the road became no more than a widened horse path, Old Risely Road.

Spotting Mr. Strickland's pony tied nearby, James dismounted, called Jack back from where he was exploring the bracken, and tethered Tetley.

Instantly, Jack leapt to James' side and around his master's legs. "What are you doing, you foolish dog?" He patted the enthusiastic creature and calmed him with a command.

James looked around the small clearing. The sun was making its descent in the sky, and thus its rays entered the forest on a sharp angle, casting deep shadows. An outcrop and large boulder pushed the trail into an arc, narrowing the rough road further. Surrounded by an unnatural hush, James stood in the silence for some minutes, trying to catch a glimpse or sound of the deputy. Nothing was evident.

James patted Tetley's flank, called Jack to heel, and started up the hill.

"Aha!" a voice rang out, cutting through the quiet. "Just as I thought."

After a moment—needed to settle his startled heart—James continued to climb the hill. His smile was forced. "What are you doing, Mr. Strickland? Playing a game of hide-and-go-seek?"

Mr. Strickland met James on the path. "Not at all, Lord Ellerby. I was testing a theory." Pulling at his mustachio, he pointed toward the path just past the narrowing. "This is the site of an ambush." He paused, shook his head as if to clear it, and pulled a wad of paper from his breast pocket. "Thought I'd deal with young Daisy Bartley's death first."

James slipped his top hat off with one hand and raked the other through his hair. He stood silent for some moments in preparation. "What have you learned, Mr. Strickland?"

"First off, Daisy Bartley drowned. Doc Triden says her lungs be full a *salt*water." Mr. Strickland pointed to his paper. "As you know, the Torrin is fresh, so she didn't drown in the river or a well or even a bathing tub. So we can *conclude*"—he nodded at the word—"that Daisy Bartley drowned in the channel."

Strickland walked to the edge of the boulder and peered around it before looking back at Ellerby. "The poor girl was right some mess when they finally got hold of her. She had been crashing against those rocks for hours afore they could bring her in. And who knows how long she had been hitting the shore afore she were noticed."

James shuddered and swallowed against the lump in his throat.

"She had bruises all over her body. You don't bruise up when you be dead. She coulda fallen down the cliff and tried to get back up. Yet, some a those bruises didn't make sense—especially round her neck. Doc Triden thought someone strangled the poor thing." He glanced up at James.

James swallowed again. He wanted to yell *stop*, but fought to keep his face passive; he nodded for the man to continue.

The mustachio twitched as Mr. Strickland's head bowed once more over the paper wad. "Just afore Daisy left her ma's, her sister, Nora, gives her a parcel. A pillow she'd stitched herself. Wrapped it up with red wool." Mr. Strickland snapped his tongue. "Last they saw a her, she be heading into Welford Mills past the mill." Mr. Strickland patted the retriever sniffing at his leg.

"Daisy were supposed to meet Jeff at the bottom of this here road." Mr. Strickland waved his arm about but didn't look up.

"And a Sparks boy saw her doing just that. She were waiting, humming, an' hugging that there parcel."

A frown clouded the deputy's face. "Jeff didna meet her, as one of the Thompson horses had the colic. He figured Daisy'd come looking for him, and when she didn't arrive, he figured she were mad."

James recalled Jeff Tate at the funeral, standing before Daisy's newly dug grave, distraught and alone—locked in grief.

"So, when she tired of waiting, she either continued on to Welford Mills, or she headed up this path to Risely." James tried to sound calm, not impatient.

"Or she could have returned to Hardwick, but you had men working in the fields and they didna see her. I asked round town and no one seen her there, neither. If she'd come through, people would have been a whispering for some reason or another. Nobody can sneeze in this here town without someone figuring it's their business."

James nodded.

"So as I see it," Mr. Strickland continued, "she decided to head up to Risely. But . . ." The deputy hesitated and looked farther up the path. "Here, I'll show ya." He motioned for James to follow.

James stepped around the boulder and found that the path widened just beyond. He called several times to Jack, who was engrossed in the multitude of scents in the bushes, and proceeded. It was a relatively steep climb but not long, and within a few minutes the two men were standing at its peak.

The vista was expansive. The sheltered woods behind them gave way to the clearing of fields and gardens; beyond, Risely Hall stood out boldly against the horizon. This was the manor's service face, the kitchens and stable yards clearly visible.

"It be an active house with the hands in the fields, gardeners tending flower beds, and laundry maids in and out of the wash-house," Mr. Strickland said. "So . . . I can't figure on how she got into the bay. Past all them servants."

James stared at the large manor, searching for a theory but coming up short. He veered away from his empty thoughts. "What of the ambush you mentioned?"

"Oh yes, come see." The deputy headed back into the woods and down the path. They stopped just before the sharp bend. Mr. Strickland hunkered down beside the large rock and pointed to a large patch of flattened grass. "Someone sat here waitin', an' I found more trampled grass opposite. There be two a them."

James shook his head. "But why? Why would someone wait for Daisy?"

"Heaven bless us, Lord Ellerby, so many reasons: an old beau, someone she owes money, or now that she's known to be walking out with the Tate boy, it might have had something to do with him. A foe from his wilder days? Almost anything. Almost anything."

"But none of those are reason to . . ." James had a hard time saying the words. "Strangle her."

"True, I haven't quite got me head around that one yet. But that's not the biggest problem. If someone did grab Daisy here, how did she end up in the bay?"

James cast his eyes slowly through the woods on all sides of him. The underbrush was thick and shadowed. Why would the killer not simply dump her body in the brambles? Why take her out to the water? Bewildered, James shook his head. "Nothing makes sense."

"Not yet, but it will. I'll keep investigating, Lord Ellerby. Just thought you should know the direction I'll be heading."

"I appreciate that." James half turned. "Have you had a chance to look into the assault on Mill Road? That *was* an ambush."

Mr. Strickland looked up quickly, brows again drawn together. "On my list a things to do."

He again reached into his pocket. "And I'll ask 'round town if there be strangers dillydallying about." As he patted the folds of his coat, he came up with the silver button that James had pressed upon him at their last meeting. "This here button." He held it out. "I see no clue in it."

James nodded and dropped the useless trinket into the pocket of his waistcoat. He whistled again for Jack. "Where has that mutt gone?"

Just then the curly-coated retriever burst out from the bracken sporting a limp piece of rag proudly between his jaws. As he approached his master, Jack whipped the object back and forth with relish, bits of red fluff and feathers floating in a trail behind him.

"Leave," James commanded, and the dog spit the bits and pieces onto the dirt. Despite the dog's reluctance, he called Jack to heel and was about to depart when he saw the deputy squat down by the soggy mess.

There were remnants of material and paper mangled together. Betwixt the tatters, wool and feathers stuck out at odd angles. Mr. Strickland turned it over; a childish hand had stitched what remained of an embroidered prayer.

"Think I'll be talkin' ta Mrs. Bartley again. This might be the pillow Nora were talking about." The deputy looked up significantly. "The one Daisy were carrying when she were last seen." He gingerly mashed the pieces into a lump and placed it in his greatcoat pocket.

They both stood and stared at the shrubbery where Jack had emerged. It was overgrown with bushes and ferns, but Jack's form had parted the branches enough to make a small but discernable trail. It didn't take long to find the site of Jack's treasure. The ground was covered with feathers and paper. What time and rains had started to ruin, Jack had finished. The largest portion remaining was the one lumped inside Mr. Strickland's pocket.

As James studied the ground around the ravaged pillow, it became apparent that the trail continued. He followed Mr. Strickland in tandem through the broken branches and across the trampled ground. Almost before they realized it, they were out of the woods.

There the trail ended and a surprising vista presented itself. The view was that of the park and the hilly grounds before Risely, intersected by the circuitous drive. But whereas the fields, garden, and house dominated the landscape above, they were only suggestions here, hidden behind hedges and ivy-covered rock walls. Between them and the drive, the ruins of the new keep looked contrived and ill-advised. But what mesmerized James was the sight beyond the drive and the grounds on the far side.

A lightly clouded horizon met a deep gray-blue span of water. The sun reflected across the crests, which occasionally glittered white in bright contrast. Thunderous but muffled crashes reassured James that what he was seeing was, indeed, the English Channel.

James squinted. "I had no idea the land turned in so much at this point."

"Me, neither, m'lord. It almost meets itself coming."

They stood there for some time, breathing the salt air, watching the drive, the channel, the keep, and the park. The rhythmic swelling of the waves and the steady wind from offshore provided the only movement in the scene before them. Of human life, none was evident.

"I see now how Daisy could have gotten to the water without being noticed," James said quietly, almost a whisper.

He continued to stare as if spellbound by the tranquility and beauty of the view, while a tumult of thoughts raced through his mind. Then he turned and followed Mr. Strickland back to the trail. Jack bounded ahead, a small feather embedded in the fur behind his ear.

———— ·•· ————

ONCE AGAIN ASTRIDE, oblivious to his surroundings, James' thoughts and emotional turmoil eclipsed the quiet beauty of the countryside. Before leaving Mr. Strickland, James had informed the deputy that a man claiming to be Beth's brother had appeared . . . and then disappeared in quick order. The older man had taken notes, but remained silent through the tale with the exception of agreeing with James' decision to get Beth away.

While London had its unsavory boroughs, Mayfair was not one. Protected by abutting neighbors, far fewer windows, and a walled garden, the Ellerby residence in Mayfair could provide a safe haven. James would speak to the staff—warn them to be wary of strangers, to be vigilant. He could safeguard Beth in London; he could not if Caroline had her way—running off to Bath. Really! Caroline knew their mother and aunt would be socializing constantly, people in and out, the house full of strangers. Ridiculous suggestion!

Beth needed him nearby. None would stand vigil as he would.

Well, perhaps that was an overstatement. Walter had certainly grown fond of Beth. Caroline, too, had formed a tight bond with their mysterious young lady, but . . . well . . . that was irrelevant.

James snorted. *Mysterious.* A more erroneous descriptor could not be found. Beth was sunshine and laughter. She was strong, independent, traditional yet outrageous, and confused yet clear-headed. Fascinating, not mysterious.

Tetley, restless from his long wait, broke into a canter. As they crossed the Torrin Bridge, the clatter and rhythm of hooves echoed under the bridge, amplifying the sound and distracting James from his musing.

On the other side, James pulled Tetley to a standstill. He stared down the bank at the tranquil setting—idyllic. A soft breeze hovered on the air, replete with birdcalls and the gentle lap of the water.

Jack barked at him impatiently.

James urged Tetley forward but, as he did so, he recalled his first sight of Beth lying in the muddied edge of the river. He remembered the man with his back turned making a swiping motion. Taking a sharp breath, James nodded to himself. Yes, that made more sense. The bundle of rope he had found earlier, the man had cut it . . . and then there was Beth's chafed wrists and bruised body. No one had been injured in the accident save Beth. She had suffered the worst. She had not been able to brace herself as the coach careened off the road, for Beth had been tied. She had been a prisoner on that coach, not a passenger.

James dug his heels into Tetley's sides with unaccustomed force. His only thought was of Beth; for now, more than ever, he feared for her safety.

———◆———

WITH AS MUCH decorum as one can accomplish while trying to keep apace a running sibling, Caroline queried Walter again. "Why do you believe Beth to be in danger?"

Caroline followed Walter through the manor, completely disregarding the startled glances of the staff. The fastest route from the drawing room to the stables was through the kitchens and that, apparently, was Walter's target.

By the time they had stepped out of doors, Caroline was quite breathless.

"Walter, stop and explain yourself!" Dr. Brant demanded. He had been following close on their heels.

Walter did stop, but with visible difficulty; he twitched with pent-up energy. "Not in the manor or gardens. Not in the stables. Bodicia's gone, too."

Caroline grabbed his sleeve to prevent him from running off again. "Walter, she has just gone for a ride. I am sure she will stay close."

"She knows someone is after her."

"I am sure she has taken Ned with her."

Walter shook his head. "Other than Tetley and Bodicia, the stable is full."

"Paul had to have saddled Bodicia for her. He would not let her go off alone."

"I cannot find him to ask." Walter peeled Caroline's fingers from his sleeve and once again ran toward the stables. He skirted the grocer's cart that had pulled into the yard.

"She would not leave." Caroline turned to Dr. Brant. "Would she? Where would she go?"

"Fear can make people do strange things," Dr. Brant replied.

They rushed into the stables to find Walter saddling his horse and cursing the absent groom. In frustration, he shouted for Sam and Ned.

Caroline was almost overwhelmed by the thought of Beth alone and unprotected. She couldn't just stand there. "You head east on the London road. I'll head into Welford Mills." She reached for a blanket and entered Cotton's stall.

"You will not!"

Caroline looked up in surprise. Dr. Brant stood at the foot of the stall as if to bar her way.

"It was not just Beth who was attacked the other day, if you remember correctly," he said.

"Walter can't be everywhere at once," Caroline pointed out with annoyance. "He'll need help."

"Of course he will. Me." Dr. Brant started out of the stable toward the paddock and his grazing horse. "Where in God's name is the stable man? Paul!"

"Walter—" Caroline started, but the sound of approaching steps gave her pause.

Walter lifted his foot into his stirrup just as the lined face of Jim, the under-gardener, rounded the corner.

"So sorry. I didna hear ya callin' till just now." The man curled his lip in self-disgust. "An I says to Paul, I'd 'elp 'im fer certain." He reached toward Walter's cinch strap.

Walter batted the man's hands away and swung himself up. The horse danced momentarily but Walter reined him in. "Where is Paul and why would he ask you to help? Why not Ned or Sam?"

"Used to 'elp out now an again when I was a lad." The under-gardener smiled, quite oblivious to the tension around him. "He an' t'others went wiff da young lady to the Point."

"Miss Beth? Paul, Sam, and Ned all went to the Point?"

Caroline let out her breath and lay a steadying hand on Cotton. "There! See, tempest in a teapot." She patted the horse's flank and stepped out of the stall. "I knew Beth would not be so foolish as to try to make her way without someone with her." She returned the blanket to the rack.

Walter was strangely silent as Caroline went to the stable doors to call back Dr. Brant.

"Were they mounted?" Walter asked after a few moments.

Caroline turned. She knew the stalls were full.

"Oh no, sir. Theys went on foot. Said somethin' h'about catchin' somethin' at da cliffs."

Caroline looked up at Walter with a frown. "Whatever could that mean?"

"I believe she means to catch the villains who are after her . . . by using herself as bait."

Caroline felt her stomach turn over. "Walter, you can't be serious. What would give you that idea?"

Walter urged his horse forward. The clatter of the hooves on the cobblestone almost overwhelmed his answer. "Because she mentioned it to me before, but I thought she was teasing!"

Just as Walter burst out of the stables, Caroline saw James gallop up the drive. She watched helplessly as one brother quickly disappeared, while the other was still too far away to hear her shouts.

Caroline picked up her skirts and ran to intercept James.

━━━◆━━━

BETH WAS BORED, tired, and sore. Her lower body was numb from the immobility of the past hour. If she shifted her limbs in any direction, she would have knocked either Sam or Ned sitting at her feet.

Beth was perched atop a boulder overlooking the English Channel. It was where she had come to seek solace after Daisy's funeral. And it was here that Beth was sure that persons unknown had approached her. So, naturally, it was to this very place that she returned to capture said villains.

When Beth had spoken to the men of her plan, their willingness to help reassured Beth that she was doing the right thing. Getting away had not been a problem. Beth informed Caroline of her desire to sit in the gallery—a seldom-visited section of the house—then slipped through the French doors of the saloon. She had rounded the gardens and met the men in the stable yard.

James was out and Dr. Brant had just arrived to occupy Caroline. The under-gardener had offered to watch the stables while weeding the kitchen garden; all was ready.

Beth had sent Sam and Ned ahead. She described the rock's location and suggested that they hide behind it. She was not sure that both men could fit but, while practically sitting in each other's laps, they had done so.

Then Beth had mounted Bodicia, and with Paul walking beside her, slowly ambled, humming all the while, through the park and past the tree line to the open cliff top. She had kept apace with Paul on her left side since the earlier disturbance had been to the right. When she had reached the clearing, Beth tied Bodicia to a tree, and left Paul hiding among the bushes. He had a good view of both her and the woods behind her.

Seemingly without a care, Beth had sauntered over to her rock, spied Sam and Ned waiting behind it, and casually stepped between them. She sat down and spread her skirts to hide any telltale body part that her arrival might have exposed.

The stage was set, the minor characters were in place, and they awaited the stars. They waited and waited. Every rustle of the wind set her nerves on edge. Beth could almost feel the tension pulsing from the men at her feet. They were ready to pounce, to bring down these heinous criminals who cast fear into the hearts of the entire household.

But as the time passed, the villains did not appear, and no unexplained sound emanated from the forest. The peace and tranquility of the place calmed their heartbeats and replaced anxiety with boredom.

"It seemed such a good plan at the time," Beth finally whispered to the men below her.

They didn't answer or move. Beth wasn't sure if they had heard.

"I don't think we will capture anyone today," she sighed a little louder.

Sam shifted and looked up. "I thinks ya might be right." He started to rise.

Ned, too, stiffly got to his feet, offering Beth a hand.

"It was a good try." She smiled her thanks. In a louder voice, she released Paul from his sentry duty in the woods. The groom sauntered over to Bodicia and then brought the animal forward to help Beth mount.

Beth sighed as she watched the three men amble down the path to the manor. She patted Bodicia's neck when the horse snorted and then shook away a fly. Straightening, she frowned at the rock. She would have to come up with another, better plan.

Pulling Bodicia's rein, Beth wheeled around to face the water. Just as she did so, there was a sharp retort from the woods and a loud buzz. Bodicia reared and Beth grabbed for the horse's mane but missed. She tumbled off Bodicia's raised back, hitting the ground with a heavy thud as a red mist filled the air.

CHAPTER FOURTEEN

Walter's Lament

James raced Tetley down the cliff road, catching up to Walter's mount with ease. He glanced at his brother's grim expression and determined posture. It likely mirrored his own.

Turning the last bend before the clearing, they galloped past Paul, Ned, and Sam. The horses were almost free of the woods when they heard the sharp retort of a musket and its echoing reverberation.

Watching in horror, James was deaf to all but Beth's scream as Bodicia reared and flung her to the ground. His mind went numb, yet somehow he made it across the clearing. Somehow he was kneeling beside her prostrate form.

He lifted her gently, cradling her in his arms. Then, slowly, tenderly, he pushed the hair from her face. Her skin was frighteningly pale, her eyes closed and droplets of blood covered her neck and bodice; worse, there was a growing stain of red on her skirts.

Beth lay still. Very, very still.

Raising his eyes to the pandemonium around him, James

watched as Paul chased after Bodicia, who was spooked and beyond reason. Sam and Ned crashed through the underbrush as if in pursuit, and Walter knelt with James on the other side of Beth. His brother's mouth was moving, but if he was speaking, James could make no sense of the words.

Then a hand, a soft delicate hand, cupped his chin. James looked down into clear hazel eyes. They stared at each other, mesmerized.

Suddenly, the world was right again. James swallowed and stared and thanked God, over and over. He clasped Beth tighter in his arms and rocked back and forth. He kissed the top of her head and whispered her name.

FOR A MOMENT Walter was too shocked to move. When he did, it was to rise and stand over the entwined couple. He almost laughed, but knew it would sound hysterical.

Walter felt a shove as Dr. Brant pushed him away from Beth and into the role of bystander. Even when Caroline ran to the group, she all but ignored her younger brother and launched into a flood of questions directed at Dr. Brant and James.

In a daze, Walter forced his eyes around the clearing. Paul was returning with Bodicia, holding a blood-soaked cloth to the horse's shoulder, and Sam and Ned shuffled out of the brush empty-handed. Mr. Haines' grocery cart stood nearby where Caroline had abandoned it, the pony's reins flung heedlessly over a branch. Walter watched a bag of carrots slide off the back and onto the ground.

Of the mysterious assailant, there was no sign.

Walter knew the tightly knit group surrounding Beth hid all

evidence of her well-being. He was about to reassure the men when he stopped. He was acutely aware of eyes in the woods.

Sam and Ned might not have found their villain, but Walter was all but certain that the assassin was watching. He could distinguish nothing unusual but, as Beth and Caroline had described before, he knew the feeling of being watched.

What if the villain learned that Beth was not fatally injured? He would try again—Walter knew this with certainty. However, if Beth were . . . dead . . . the assassin would *not* return; there would be no need.

Walter looked back to the crowd around Beth and shifted his weight. He swallowed and stared, and then forced his eyes out to the channel.

Then he waited. It took forever!

At least a minute or two.

Eventually all three of the hands joined the group on the ground, although Paul refrained from getting too close with Bodicia. When the look of relief crossed their faces, Walter acted.

"Oh Lord!" he wailed loudly in his most plaintive voice. "She is dying."

All eyes turned on him, including Beth's.

"Cut down in the prime of life!" he wailed even louder. He then fell to his knees, threw his arms heavenward and broke into deep theatrical sobs.

———◆———

EVEN THOSE OF his family who were used to Walter's melodrama and twisted humor found this in bad taste. Caroline knew Walter had seen that Beth was conscious. She was about to scold the foolish boy soundly when James stilled her. It was a simple shake of his head, almost imperceptible, but Caroline understood the motion and immediately after, understood the reason. She had never been so proud of Walter, nor appreciated his quick intelligence so much, until that moment.

"Beth come back to us," Walter continued, his gaze still skyward.

Not wanting Walter to overdo it and thus ruin his good intentions, Caroline called him over.

James whispered to Beth to close her eyes and relax. Enlisting Walter's help, the brothers carried her to the cart. Dr. Brant held a cloth to her bodice that draped down to her leg, where he applied pressure to the real injury.

Caroline swept what remained of the jostled vegetables to the ground to make way for Beth and James. Bodicia and Tetley reached over to nibble a carrot as she tied their reins to the back of the cart. She would have to compensate poor Mr. Haines, who had not only lost his groceries but was undoubtedly mystified by the cart's disappearance. He had left it by the kitchen door and was likely unaware that Caroline had taken it in the interest of speed.

Dr. Brant climbed up onto the seat beside Caroline, facing away from the horses, as if watching over his patient. Caroline took control of the ambling pony.

The returning pace of the cart was in complete contrast to the one that had left the manor. James sent the men ahead in preparation, and had already lost sight of them before reentering the woods.

━━━◆━━━

BETH'S LIMP FORM was carried, bloodied and dirty, through the kitchen door of Hardwick Manor, much as she had been the day of her accident. However, on this occasion James carried Beth directly to her room in the family wing—without any help.

Mrs. Fogel clucked and fussed, and anxiously shooed everyone back to work before rushing into Beth's room.

Caroline closed the door behind the ashen-faced housekeeper. "I am sorry that we frightened you, Mrs. Fogel. Beth will be fine."

The housekeeper glanced at the bed. Beth grimaced as she shifted but then smiled, albeit weakly.

"We are just being careful. Trying to hide Beth's true condition." Caroline lightly touched Mrs. Fogel's hand. "A musket ball grazed her leg."

Mrs. Fogel blinked. "Not an accident?" Her voice squeaked.

"No, I'm afraid not. Attempted murder, Mrs. Fogel. The fewer persons who know she was not mortally wounded, the safer she will be. We shall simply say that Beth is very ill and leave it at that. You might have to be inventive, Mrs. Fogel."

"Fabricate? Lie?"

"I'm afraid so."

The housekeeper nodded, smoothed her apron and straightened her skirts. "That should not be a problem, Miss Caroline. Excuse me while I fetch some cloth and fresh water."

Caroline ordered her brothers to the far side of the room while Dr. Brant made Beth comfortable on the pillows. Together, they pulled up the counterpane. Caroline held it up to afford the patient some privacy as the physician uncovered her right thigh. Mrs. Fogel came and went with the required water and bandages, and Dr. Brant methodically set to work.

When he had removed the matted fibers and cleaned the wound, Caroline saw relief in his eyes.

"It is long but not deep," Dr. Brant announced.

Caroline smiled up at James and watched *some* of the tension drain from his face.

"That was quick thinking on your part, Walter." James slapped Walter on the back in that manly sign of approval. "Should keep the rats from our door for some days."

Caroline glanced at them from the bedside, nearly laughing at Walter's expression. He looked flabbergasted. "Are you well, Walter?" she asked, though she was fairly certain she knew the cause of his surprise. He was staring at James as if he were confused by his brother's compliment and undisguised pride.

Oblivious, James knocked Walter shoulder to shoulder. "Yes, indeed," he said. "Well done."

Walter stammered his thanks and then blinked, puffed up his chest, and grinned. "Of course."

The doctor's procedure complete, Caroline lowered the counterpane, allowing James to return to Beth's side.

———◆———

"What on earth were you doing? How could you possibly believe that using yourself as bait was a sensible thing to do?" James asked, trying very hard to keep his tone even—trying to hide his frustration and concern. "Foolishness beyond measure."

"Perhaps not a brilliant plan," Beth agreed. "But I thought my recapture was their intent . . . Apparently I was wrong."

"But they didn't want to recapture you. They wanted to kill you."

"Exactly."

The room was silent except for the swishing of water as Dr. Brant wrung his cloth out in the bowl. Beth was tired; her wound throbbed and all her muscles ached. But more than anything else she was disappointed—gravely, gravely disappointed. It had all been for nothing. She *still* did not know who she was or why someone was menacing her.

James tightened his grip on her hand and leaned closer. "If you had waited, I could have told you of their *deadly* intents."

Dr. Brant's hand stopped moving and Walter slowly turned to look at his brother.

"Why?" "What have you learned?" they both asked, one question on top of the other.

James straightened but he did not drop Beth's hand. "Daisy's death was not an accident."

Beth closed her eyes. *No. Oh no.* She swallowed against the ache in her throat; her eyes swam, awash in unshed tears.

"Nothing suggests Daisy's death is tied to Beth's villains, but . . ." James left the sentence hanging as if he did not want to complete the thought. "When I looked around just after Beth's accident, I found a small bundle of cut rope in the water where the carriage had been mired. I thought it insignificant," he said. "I didn't, at the time, understand the marks and bruises around Beth's wrists."

Dr. Brant studied the floor for a moment, and then nodded. "That would explain why she was the only person injured. She was tied up, and as a captive, Beth would not have been able to hold on to anything, or brace herself as the carriage went over the embankment."

Walter sat with a *thump* on the window ledge.

"But until today," Beth said, "there was no intent to murder. I would have been an easy target on Mill Road, but the villains tried to grab us, not kill us. And Mr. Paterson meant to run off with me. If they could murder Daisy, why then did they hesitate with me?"

"You must know something," Walter said. "And they must have suspected that you had shared confidences with Daisy as well as a room."

The raw ache continued to eat at Beth. The thought of causing Daisy's death was devastating. She took a deep breath to steady her emotions. "But I have no memories to share."

"Perhaps that's what changed," James said with a pensive nod. "Until Mr. Paterson's visit, the villains believed your new name was meant to be a deception."

"James, if that is true, then Beth is in greater danger now." Walter's voice began to rise. "My little game, our little game, only delays. They still know where she is."

Caroline nodded. "We have to get her away from here and the sooner the better."

"They are definitely wily, I must say." Brant shook his head as he, again, related his discovery about the decided lack of Patersons in Pencombe.

"They might not be watching tonight," James said. "They would not expect us to regroup so quickly, especially as Beth has been *mortally wounded*." He glanced at Walter and nodded.

"True," Caroline agreed. "They will think the job done. Even if the shooter didn't stay to see Beth placed in the cart, wagging tongues will spread the word of her injury."

James straightened, his figure rigid. "Tonight might be the best opportunity we have to get away cleanly." He squeezed Beth's hand but addressed his friend. "Can she travel?"

Dr. Brant hesitated. "It would be better if she didn't, but all things considered—if she was to keep her leg horizontal—"

"Good," James interrupted. "We'll head to London tonight."

"JAMES, how on earth can we possibly be ready in time?" Caroline stared at her brother with something akin to panic.

"Pack as much as you can." James strode toward the door. "I'll arrange the carriage with Paul. The household is expecting my departure and we will have Mrs. Fogel hide the family's as long as possible."

"I am not going," said a voice by the window.

James stopped and turned with the doorknob still in his hand.

"I have decided to stay here," Walter rephrased his rebellion.

James shook his head; he did not have time for this. "Why?"

"The carriage only seats four on a long journey, and, if Beth is to be accommodated properly, it seats three. More important, I can keep the pretext up longer." He glanced at Brant. "The doctor and I can discuss Beth's continuing battle with anyone willing to listen. I'll race through the lanes, as if all were routine, and Dr. Brant can visit daily. It will appear normal."

"But you cannot take the women to Berkeley Square," Brant added. "It is the first place they will look after they realize that Beth is gone. Then all this subterfuge will be for nothing."

James frowned at his friend. "Beth could simply remain indoors at Berkley Square. A hotel is as bad, if not worse."

"What about Aunt Ophelia?" Caroline asked, referring to their father's sister. "She would be pleased to have us."

"Yes, but her place is only a stone's throw away from the Ellerby townhouse."

"You could go to my place in London."

Caroline turned back to Brant with a smile. "I am sure your parents would be overjoyed at the arrival of their son's guests without their son. Thank you for the offer but no—"

"No, not the Brant residence, my own . . . on Harley Street."

"Your own? I did not know you had a London residence, Dr. Brant." Caroline's eyes widened.

"When my great uncle, Warren Newby, passed away last fall, his estate was divided in such a way as to provide me with a small London home and an allowance to keep it. My association is not well known and it is not on the usual beaten path. It, in fact, is in Marylebone, not Mayfair." Dr. Brant turned to face James. "It would be even more of a hideaway, if you were to reside as usual at Berkeley Square and avoid Harley Street."

"Really?" Beth sat up. "Would Lord Ellerby *need* to do that?"

Caroline pursed her lips and then nodded. "James must visit Lord Levry and Lord Wolcher while in London," she answered. "He would be recognized and followed, we would be found again."

Beth lay back against the pillows and huffed a sigh, a forlorn expression on her face.

"Secrecy *is* your best protection," James said quietly from the door.

———•———

THERE WAS LITTLE time and few hands, but somehow the work was completed before the hour of their secret departure. As the dust settled, James swore a few more persons to secrecy, but they were chosen with forethought.

Caroline, having decided that her lady's maid was to accompany them, enlisted Meighan to help pack the ladies' belongings as well as her own. Sam and Ned carried down the trunks and bandboxes with more stealth then they had hitherto shown. And Paul had the carriage quietly ready and waiting only a few hours into the new day.

All was in their favor, as the sky was deeply overcast. There were no shadows from the moon, no glimmer of a star, just pitch-black silence that the lightly treading feet barely disturbed.

James carried Beth, swathed in a black cloak, into the carriage before the others, and consequently, could place a gentle but quick kiss upon her brow unnoticed. He stepped back out to assist Caroline and Meighan up the step. They took their place across from Beth. Meighan reached across to settle Beth's skirts as James closed the door.

Tetley seemed unaware of the unusual hour and snorted in pent-up anticipation. James settled him with a pat and placed his feet in the stirrups. Ned climbed up beside Sam on the driver's box and the procession was underway.

———⋄———

BETH WOULD HAVE preferred James' company in the carriage, if for no other reason than she felt him vulnerable atop the large black horse. But as the wheels continued to roll and the distance between the gates of Hardwick Manor and its master lengthened without incident, her fears began to subside.

The rock and the rhythm of the carriage lulled Beth into a state of relaxation and reflection. It was hard to believe that a day could hold so many changes. A day that had dawned in fear and circled through relief, nervousness, boredom, pain, enlightenment, and then—unfortunately—returned to fear.

At times, life was too complex to fathom. But what remained

clearest in Beth's mind was the change in her relationship with James. While there had been no time to speak privately, there was almost no need. James had confirmed through his actions—sometimes a simple connection of their eyes—that his attachment to her had grown. Where they went from here, Beth was not sure. But the prospect was exhilarating.

CHAPTER FIFTEEN

Change of Scenery

Caroline lounged, with all appearances of calm, in the drawing room of No. 26 Harley Street, Cavendish Square in London. Leaning back against the arm of the settee, her mauve day dress gathered and tightened as she twisted herself into place.

From her position by the window, Caroline could see the bustling carriages and the busy street below. At this hour of the morning, traffic was at its peak. There were callers, tradesmen peddling their wares, and sauntering walkers out for a breath of air. Hidden behind the draperies, Caroline could watch three sides of the square, observing without being observed.

The square's park offered the only respite to the continuous activity and noise of the city dwellers. Its greenery and weaving paths served to remind the populace of the existence of life outside barriers of stone and glass. Partially obscured by sprawling euonymus and spiked barberries sat a bench facing Wigmore Street.

A toddler and woman in service occupied the seat, but as

Caroline watched, a young man dressed in the plain muted style of a laborer joined the pair. His movements were not furtive, but relaxed and unremarkable. Only his slightly turned position gave hint to any interest of the goings on at No. 26.

Caroline was grateful for his vigilance.

It was as if Ned felt personally responsible for letting Paterson slip by him and the fiasco on the cliff road, and he meant to restore the family's faith in his abilities. While James *had* asked him to guard the women, he had not specified how. Ned had taken it upon himself to monitor the residence from without.

In the past three days, Ned had watched and waited from many different positions on the street and in the park. He had gone wandering through the mews behind the large Georgian terraces, looking for any sign of something irregular. He had reported that nothing seemed out of place.

They had succeeded in fleeing Welford Mills undetected.

The first few hours after crossing through the gates of Hardwick had been harrowing. Poor brave Beth had been stoic. She had implied that compared to her fears and concerns, the jarring motion of the carriage was almost welcome. She had done her best to dismiss the throbbing of her leg but Caroline knew better.

Caroline's other worry had, of course, been her brother. James had placed himself off to the side of the road, studying the countryside and occasionally stopping to listen for any signs of pursuit. They had been gone three interminable hours before he had ridden forward to inform the women that all was quiet.

As a new day dawned, it became evident that—at least temporarily—their greatest foe was to be boredom. Stopping periodically for a quick meal, and then long enough at an inn to rest their stiff muscles and collect a few hours of sleep, they reached the outskirts of London just after the sun had gone down on the second day.

At Harley Street, Caroline and Beth had waited for James to acquaint the housekeeper with the situation. He carried the requisite note from Dr. Brant. Once accepted, James had briskly picked Beth up in his arms and whisked her up the stairs to the drawing room.

Caroline had entered the townhouse tired and travel weary. She plodded through the expansive main hall and climbed the elegant staircase, joining Beth in the drawing room. James made quick work directing the unloading of the coach, and as soon as a room was prepared, carried Beth to her chamber. Their good-byes were brief and Beth's dismay left Caroline certain that her friend had hoped James would linger.

But it was not to be. James had a purpose and resolve. Now that he had admitted the folly of remaining close, Caroline knew he would be steadfast to their decision. He and Sam were soon on their way to Berkeley Square.

———

FOR THE NEXT five days, the reclusive young ladies saw none but the Brant staff. At first Beth remained in bed, the wound greatly irritated by their journey to London. Caroline had feared the necessity of calling a surgeon, but Beth's strong constitution had pulled her through. She was, in fact, tucked comfortably on a twin settee across from Caroline, lost in the last pages of a novel.

"Excuse me, Miss Ellerby." Meighan stood just inside the door and bobbed her curtsy.

Caroline dragged her gaze away from the crowds outside and into the calm room behind her.

"I've made the list you requested." The maid crossed the floor, placing the paper in Caroline's waiting hand. "I believe it's complete now."

Caroline nodded her appreciation as the maid retreated. When she looked up from the list, Beth's interest had shifted to the paper in Caroline's hand.

"Our hurried packing has left us in want of a few items," Caroline explained.

Beth frowned. "You are not going out, are you?"

"Yes, actually," Caroline answered in an overly casual manner. "I think I need some air and a little exercise. Regent Street is only steps away. Don't shake your head, Beth. I'll take Meighan with me and go veiled." She swooped her arms around as if to encompass the neighborhood. "Better to go now, while it is crowded, than later when I might be observed."

"Can we not get by? Make do until we are certain that we were not followed, that we are safe?"

Caroline rose and placed a reassuring hand on Beth's shoulder. "We *are* safe."

"But—"

"I will keep an eye open for a bookstore or circulating library while I am out. I think you must have read and reread that book to monotony."

"I would rather you just got what you needed, and came right back."

"Very well, but if I happen upon—"

"Please," Beth sighed. "Just be as quick as you can."

Caroline tripped lightly up the stairs to change. She was being stubborn; not from anxiety or nerves but rather a pressing desire to do something. Regent Street housed many of the shops on the appointment list from the brown cloak. James had the list, but Caroline remembered that Fitzroy's had been mentioned. It stood but a block or two from Harley Street.

Caroline descended the main staircase to find Meighan leaning against the wall of the entrance, trying to stay out of the way of the workmen laying Italian marble. As best they could, the girls stepped gingerly to the door. Caroline pulled down her veil before stepping out into the busy world.

The crowd and noise were a little overwhelming. Born and raised in the country, with little time in the city, Caroline had no appreciation for the urban way of life. While the press of a ball or assembly was often close and confining, she found the rush of wagons and carriages just inches from where she walked more than a little unsettling. However, by the time she had crossed Chandos Street, she was beginning to feel the rhythm of the masses and her heart no longer raced. A cautious glance behind confirmed that Ned had followed them, furthering her comfort.

Once the two young women had gained Regent Street, Caroline dispatched Meighan with the list and a time of rendezvous. There was a slight protest on the maid's part, but Caroline quickly dissuaded Meighan of the idea that she was needed for protection. Meighan, being fine boned and rather timid, would have been no obstacle for anyone wanting to cause Caroline an injury.

———————

FITZROY'S, as Caroline remembered, was only two blocks south, near Oxford Street. The gentle tinkle of a bell announced her presence and drew a smiling merchant from his inner office. The shop was not full, but the other salesmen were busy showing customers the skill of their designs and quality of their leather.

"Can I help you?" asked the salesman. He had calculating eyes beneath his spectacles. He looked Caroline up and down—no doubt taking in her country styles. There was an arrogant air about him; he was likely the manager.

"Yes, indeed." Caroline had prepared a story. It was a stretch of the truth but not enough to be considered a lie. "I was hoping to help one of your customers."

No surprise or puzzlement interfered with the bland expression on the man's face. He remained motionless except for a barely perceptible lifting of his chin.

Caroline took a deep breath. "A package of some value was left upon my doorstep by mistake." She mentally apologized to Beth for calling her a package. "The only clue as to the gentleman to whom it might belong was a list of appointments that had accompanied the package. It was stamped with your address."

The manager tipped his head to the side with his eyebrows lifted. "Yes, of course, one of ours." He led Caroline to the back of the store, disappeared briefly and returned with an appointment book. "What day would that be, and what time?"

"Two o'clock on the fifteenth. April fifteenth." Although even as she said so, Caroline realized that A15 had a plethora of possibilities, none having to do with a date.

The manager leafed through his book and then ran his finger down the page at which he had stopped. "Oh dear," he sighed dramatically. "No name." He made as if to shut the book.

"No name at all?" Caroline craned her neck to see for herself.

"None." The manager turned the book to face Caroline. "As you can see, just the initials 'R. & E.H.'" The book closed with a snap.

"Who might R. & E.H. be?" Caroline tried to keep her voice level, while at the same time wanting to give the man a good shake.

"The hand is not mine but that of my wife."

"Could you ask your wife, then?"

"She is not here today."

Dejected, disappointed, and dissatisfied, Caroline huffed. "Perhaps—" she began, then felt a hesitant tap on her shoulder.

"Miss, Miss Ellerby? I can't find that lavender soap what Dr. Brant's housekeeper wanted," Meighan said, obviously forgetting the request not to use names while they were out and about. "I just wanted you to know that I'm going to try another shop. I'll just be a tick longer than expected."

Caroline felt a surge of alarm. "Yes, yes, by all means, do so." She motioned the maid back to the door before the girl mentioned Beth as well.

Caroline followed, thinking a general retreat was in order.

The manager raised a curious eyebrow as he walked with her to the door. "Miss Ellerby, are you certain it is a gentleman that you seek? My wife serves only our female customers."

Caroline swallowed, uncomfortable with the man's use of her name.

The departing tinkle of the store's bell did nothing to hide the anxiety in her voice. "No, not certain." She closed the door and stood on the step for some moments. She chastised herself for making assumptions and wasting an opportunity. A look through the window showed the manager scribbling on a piece of paper.

Oh dear, Caroline thought, *it could be worse than a waste of time.*

———

WALTER AND HENRY raced halfheartedly down the drive toward the Welford Mills Road. They felt disinclined to flaunt. Gone was

Walter's desire to create havoc; it had been replaced by a sense of authority. As the man of the house, decorum was more to his taste.

Walter reined in his grays and set them to a more comfortable pace. Careening just didn't have the same appeal as it used to. Besides, the task was to be seen; racing was unnecessary.

The manor was empty; no voice of disapproval awaited, but neither did the evenings of laughter and excitement. Mrs. Fogel, tasked with his care, was not a great conversationalist. Walter's desire to impress was rendered impotent by the lack of witnesses.

For the past seven days, Walter gauged the town's gossip, listening for hints of the Ellerby escape. He had been pleased to answer questions regarding Beth's health and Caroline's new reclusive tendency. Nothing to date had given him the idea that the irregularities within the manor had been noted.

"A word, Mr. Ellerby." Mr. Strickland stepped in front of the curricle. This would normally have been a dangerous endeavor, but as Walter had been paying more attention to his thoughts than his driving, the horses were barely moving.

Walter pulled up and allowed the deputy to cross over to his side.

"I must speak with you and Lord Ellerby." There wasn't even a hesitation. "Might I drop by later this afternoon?"

Walter knew that Mr. Strickland must have news to impart and was reluctant to wait. Still, without lifting his head, Walter was aware of the many eyes that were upon them. "Yes. Of course." He nodded and flicked the reins. "Carry on," he called to the horses.

The quick jaunt about town was quicker than usual and, if Henry saw anything amiss in it or the gossip they had gleaned, he said nothing. Henry was compliant when Walter recalled random duties that needed his immediate attention. He dropped Henry back at Risely and hastened to Hardwick. Once there, Walter retired to the library, James' desk, and his own thoughts.

Mr. Strickland did not appear for an hour or more, and Walter had plenty of time to convince himself that the jig was up. The plan had been to keep all in ignorance for as long as possible. Seven days was not long; a new plot was required.

Lost in thought, Walter was surprised when Robert opened the door to admit not one but two gentlemen. It was clear that Mr. Strickland and Dr. Brant had only just happened upon each other; their first words, as they crossed the threshold of the library, were in greeting. They made themselves comfortable across from Walter, and if they saw anything improper in his sitting in James' chair, they said nothing about it.

Dr. Brant was the first to speak. "Well, Walter, everyone knows James is gone, and there is a lot of speculation that the young ladies are gone, too. You can bet the races that those whom we were wishing to deceive have heard the rumors as well."

"So the jig is well and truly up."

"Afraid so. I heard the tale from three different patients. All very hush-hush, of course."

"Of course," Walter sighed and shook his head. He turned to Mr. Strickland. "Is that what you wished to discuss?"

"Well, Mr. Ellerby, only in part. Mostly, I wished to notify you, and Lord Ellerby, of a few . . . things. There be few strangers in town; most are gone. They was brought in to build that there keep up at Risely. What was wrong with our own tradesmen, I can't tell you. Two men in particular was hanging about for, as some put it, 'no bloody good reason.'" Mr. Strickland's upper lip twitched as he quoted. "They was close to Miss Ellerby's description of the blackguards who waylaid 'er and Miss Beth, but not exact-like. So

I still don't know if they were part and parcel of them troubles. They've been gone for two or three days now." He looked significantly at Walter. "Enough time to have been involved in the shooting."

"So we are no further ahead." Dr. Brant's chair squeaked as he leaned back into the leathered wings.

Walter lifted his chin, speaking with authority . . . Well, he tried to emulate authority. "Except, if the men only left a few days ago," he said, "they weren't following the carriage."

"True enough, true enough. Oh and that there pillow Lord Ellerby and me found on Old Risely Road . . . You knew about that, right?" He nodded, agreeing with himself and continued. "That there pillow were, indeed, Daisy Bartley's. Messy though it be, the little one recognized it." A cloud passed over the deputy's face and he pursed his lips for a moment.

Walter waited, twitching with impatience.

"And lastly—" Mr. Strickland took out his pad and flipped through it. "The man what come into Welford looking for a lady somewhat like Miss Beth . . ." He looked up.

"Yes, Mr. Paterson's agent," Dr. Brant encouraged.

"Well, now you've just hit the nail on the head. It seems he weren't working for Mr. Paterson. Mrs. Cranley says the man were hired by an uppity-up titled gentleman or so he said. Not only that, the butcher remembers him mentioning London; the feller didn't come from Cheltenham or Pencombe." Mr. Strickland reached into his greatcoat and, after some rooting around, produced a letter addressed to James. "I put it all down for his Lordship, but I didn't know if you were going to join him or . . ." His voice trailed off.

Walter didn't take the letter. He stared at it.

Dr. Brant took the note from the deputy and then leaned toward Walter, note extended again.

Walter continued to stare. "I do not think I am going into Town anytime soon." Joining the entourage in London would mean losing his freedom again, being ordered about by James. Walter quite enjoyed being his own man.

Dr. Brant lowered his arm and with it the proffered note. "Not to worry, I'll take it. I will be leaving for Town tomorrow." He dropped the paper into his waistcoat pocket. "Now that I am no longer needed as an alibi, I will see how the renovations are proceeding in my house." Dr. Brant raised his eyebrows. "I'm already packed; my practice is covered. I will leave in the morning."

Just blocks from St. Katherine's Dock, James fought the urge to open the carriage door and walk ahead. He knew Sam was doing his best to press on, but the traffic had reached a bottleneck.

Wagons, carts, and coaches provided a steady stream of movement both in and out of the narrowing gate under the warehouses. Once through, there would be ample room to move about, but until then, patience was his only choice.

James' arrival in London had coincided with a short recess of the House. After a long and contentious debate renouncing the letters of marque, all parties agreed to take a break. The delay suited Lord Levry's needs; they were inching toward James' twenty-first birthday, when he would be able to add his vote in the House of Lords to end the privateering.

A note from Caroline had reached James just as he had been departing for his gentlemen's club, Brooks's. Her request for assistance with a difficult supplier was hardly the inconvenience that she believed it to be. James was quite happy to take on the task of acquiring flawless marble; if nothing else, it kept his mind away from Beth. Was she safe? Why had someone tried to end her life? When would he see her again?

Yes, with Beth no longer on his mind, James could concentrate on Brant's floor—a floor that Beth walked upon daily, as she wandered about the townhouse . . . without him. James shook the images from his mind's eye and refocused on the marble. He was prepared to chide the troublesome merchant who was taking advantage of Brant by furnishing inferior tiles. He was pleased to note that his sister had not taken it upon herself to resolve this problem and remained in seclusion as they had agreed.

———————

AT LAST, the Ellerby carriage passed through the gates and made its way toward the warehouses. The large quays were busy with docked ships and barges of every size and description, but not nearly as varied as the humanity that surrounded them. Riverside laborers encompassed the majority of the bustle, including coopers, rope makers, carpenters, stevedores, and day workers. Cargo was raised out of the ships' holds and directly placed in the ground floor of the warehouses. Sugar was transferred from the measured hogsheads into barrels. And there was an overabundance of noise and indiscernible smells, some rich and others fetid.

James alit and cast about for the offices of Treviso and Ferrara Importers. With the direction of a customhouse officer, he found Mr. Ferrara on the third floor of a warehouse, sitting behind a desk that did nothing to hide his bulk. Their conversation was short but satisfying; Mr. Ferrara agreed to replace the defective marble tiles immediately.

James had only just stepped back into the bustling fray, when he saw a figure approach his carriage. It was a stocky man with a deeply tanned face. James recognized him and quickened his pace.

"Mr. Derrydale! Hugh, how are you?"

The Welford Mills native turned, somewhat startled by the greeting and the person from whom it emanated. "J-just fine, Lord Ellerby," he stammered.

James clapped Hugh on the back, surprising him even further. "Your parents mentioned that you were working on the docks. A cooper, they said. Well done."

Hugh's chest rose slightly. "I be a regular." He jerked his thumb toward the gathering of barrel-makers behind them. "Me cousin got me the job. Ma thought it best, considering . . ." Hugh had a reputation for mischief that would not soon fade.

James motioned for Sam to open the carriage door and smiled with a benevolent expression learned from his father. "Very wise of her. It will be some time yet before your *adventures* are forgotten . . . or forgiven. Every time there is something amiss, your name is *still* mentioned. People will eventually forget. Unless you can create mischief in two places at the same time."

"Some think that I can," the cooper added with bouncing eyebrows. "I'm oft mistaken for me cousin. He be older and had the pox, but he has the same Derrydale looks and he be a wild one. He's off drivin' a coach now for some hoity-toity nob—" He swallowed visibly. "Pardon, m'lord."

James frowned and stared over Hugh's head for a moment. Had he heard Hugh correctly? He and his cousin shared the Derrydale looks? "Is your cousin in London?"

"No, m'lord. Exeter. Gone since April."

The bustling hum of the dock faded into the background.

James was aware of Sam closing the carriage door and the vehicle's jerking start, but his mind was locked on the words of the cooper, and the description of his errant cousin and what it might mean.

"Stop. Stop, Sam!" James shouted and was halfway out of the carriage before Sam could pull up. He jumped to the ground and jogged back to where Hugh still stood, staring with mouth agape.

"Be there a problem, Lord Ellerby?"

James took a gulp of air to calm his racing heart and then straightened. "I think your cousin might be up to no good," he said. "He's been seen making mischief in Welford." Mischief indeed, if breaking into the manor could be called such.

"Not surprised in the least, sir. He be foolhardy at the best of times. But I'm thinking he landed on his feet a few months back. Least ways, it sounded like it. Greg got into a spot of trouble an' were let go here at the cooperage. He be livin' hand to mouth when he met one of the passengers coming off a merchant ship, looking for a driver."

James shook his head. "I can think of better places to hire a driver."

"Indeed, sir. Ya got that right. Greg bragged about pullin' the wool over this gent's eyes. The gent mentioned Welford an' Greg said his people, the Brills, were from Welford Mills." Hugh laughed with little amusement. "That be stretchin' it more than a bit. Greg Brill be London born and bred. He dinna know Welford at all but he dinna say so."

"Rather naive," James interjected, shaking his head at the gentleman's folly. "And where might I find Greg Brill, Hugh?"

"Not seen Greg, not hide nor hair, since he headed out in the coach, whippin' up the horses like he knew what he was about."

"Oh," James said with great eloquence and a huff of frustration. He was no further ahead at all. "Might you see what you can learn about this gentleman from the ship, Hugh?"

"Certainly, m'lord. I'll do what I can."

Nodding farewell, James returned to his carriage and signaled to Sam. They were soon rolling down the busy streets of central London with James lost in thought.

CHAPTER SIXTEEN

Magnetic Forces

*S*he sat in the dank silence. The room reeked of filth and decay. She felt the gentle touch of a feather across her cheek and the hum of rapid wings, and bile rose in her throat. A dull glow shone from a small slit in the wall high above her head. Beyond the lifeless beam it cast were shadows, boxes and barrels stacked high and precariously.

There were no sounds in this small room overcrowded with malevolence. It was eerily quiet. A hand reached for her. It carried a shiny and honed form—a dagger shaped like a hummingbird. It glistened in the light.

A whisper broke into the silence. "Beth," it called over and over. "Beth, dear." The voice grew louder until the roof floated away and the soft glow of a candle illuminated a friendly face.

———◆———

"Caroline?" Beth croaked.

The face smiled and then nodded. "Are you all right?"

Beth pushed the coverlet back and sat up, trying to focus. The room was dark except for the glow of Caroline's candle. "Is it morning?"

Caroline laughed quietly. "We retired only a few hours ago."

"Oh no. Was I screaming?"

Caroline placed her candle on the bedside table and straightened the covers. "No, merely restless. I had not yet fallen asleep when I heard you thrashing about." She motioned for Beth to lie back down and she tucked her in like a child. "Back to sleep now. And *pleasant* dreams."

Beth lay back briefly and then sat up again. "You could not sleep?"

"No," Caroline sighed. "I do not think I am active enough to get tired."

"I am wide awake now, as well." The thought of returning to that dark, dank room of her dreams was terrifying. Her small but comfortable bedroom was filled with the hushed and muffled sounds of a house at rest. Then a carriage rolled past the terrace windows, and with it the echo of a laughing couple.

Caroline glanced toward the window. When she looked back, her eyes were full of mischief. "We need not force ourselves to sleep." She disappeared through the door. "I will get some cards." Her disembodied voice drifted from down the hall and across the threshold.

By the time Caroline returned, Beth had lit all her candles and smoothed out the bed. She was curled up on it, and Caroline joined her there. They ignored the table and chairs primly waiting in the corner, too customary for a rebellion. They laughed, played cribbage, and read the occasional poem well into the wee hours. Beth felt roguish and more carefree than she had for some time.

JAMES SAT, comfortable and relaxed, with a book in hand. Occasionally he glanced up, drawn by the laughter or chatter of those around him. Greeted infrequently, and overlooked for the most part, James found the atmosphere of Brooks's lively and democratic, much to his taste this evening.

White's was undoubtedly the smartest and most exclusive of the St. James Clubs, but while it was the most aristocratic, Brooks's was the most interesting. It was known to be the breeding ground for Whig politicians, stomping grounds for advocates of reform. It had thick carpets, marble fireplaces, rich upholstery, beautiful looking glasses, and most important, comfortable wingback armchairs and enough pandemonium to distract James from his brooding.

A burst of chortling drew James' attention. Movement, just beyond the backs of cavorting young men, pulled his gaze even farther from his paper. He was both pleased and disturbed to see a familiar figure wending its way toward him. He stood and greeted Brant with enthusiasm.

"I did not expect to see you in Town so soon." The statement held many layers of questions.

"Only just arrived," Brant said casually, looking around to see that they were alone in their corner of the club.

"And how are they?" James asked, trying to keep the intensity out of his voice. Avoiding Harley Street was proving to be much more difficult than he expected.

Brant knew James' true concern. "She is much improved, James. Walking about, granted with a limp, but no longer in pain."

He lifted a shoulder and added. "If anything, our young ladies are bored."

"Bored? Bored is good," James said. "Better than frightened or hounded or . . . Yes. Bored is just fine. So, why are you here, in Town? Is anything amiss at Hardwick?"

"Nothing unexpected," Brant said, and then related his and Walter's conversation with Mr. Strickland.

James grumbled his disappointment upon learning that their ruse had been discovered. "I had hoped for a fortnight at least," he said.

Brant nodded thoughtfully and then reached into his waistcoat pocket. He handed James Mr. Strickland's note, but rendered it pointless by explaining all that it contained.

"So, if the men dawdling in Welford *were* our villains, they left Welford Mills before it was common knowledge that the family had disappeared," Brant concluded.

The two young gentlemen lapsed into a companionable silence, watching the spirited club patrons make great cakes out of themselves. It was all wild hilarity and high jinks.

"I happened to be at the St. Katherine Docks the other day," James said casually, avoiding the subject of flawed marble tiles. "And came upon Hugh Derrydale." He shrugged, again trying to maintain the appearance of nonchalance. "He has been working the docks for six months—nowhere near Welford Mills. Anyway, Hugh mentioned something that I found . . . most curious. His cousin, on occasion, is mistaken for Hugh—albeit an older and pockmarked version."

"And?"

"Well, several things struck me as odd in our discussion. Hugh told me his cousin, Greg Brill, was hired as a driver for a merchant ship passenger. Apparently, Greg embellished his abilities, but the man seemed more interested in the fact that Greg's family came from the southeast coast."

"And that means?"

"I am not sure really, but the boot boy thought he recognized Hugh when we had the break-in . . . Greg and Hugh look much alike. And it struck me that Greg Brill, who could also answer to the description of the numskull that abandoned Beth at the accident, was hired around the time that her coach came roaring through Welford Mills on route to Exeter."

"But Beth's coach was not Exeter bound. We know that."

"No, we only know that the coach was not the stagecoach. Who can say where it was headed? I asked Hugh to find out what he can about the man off the ship, but until he does, I have nothing to follow."

"You know, James, we might think about going to the peelers. They could be of some service. They have people that are used to dealing with this sort of thing, investigators, or detectives, or some such. Mr. Strickland is inexperienced, and we are in quite over our heads."

"I know. I have thought of it, several times, in fact. But our information is ambiguous and the peelers are likely to intimidate Beth, frighten her."

"I agree that she will find it unsettling, but not overly so. She is amazingly resilient, James."

Brant raised an eyebrow at James' knowing smile. "Still," he continued, "perhaps you are right. Better to be safe than sorry. I will visit Dr. Fotherby straightaway. See what he thinks about Beth's mental recovery. We can decide about the peelers after that."

James sat back, staring at the space above Brant's head. "Yes, after that," he repeated in an inattentive manner.

"Come dine with us tomorrow." Brant made it a statement rather than an invitation.

Acceptance on his tongue, James paused as he rethought the matter. He gulped and curled up the corner of his mouth. "I am not sure that is wise." He had not meant to sound so deflated.

"You would normally visit your good friend when he is in Town. It would be notable if you were not to do so. Only the staff know that our ladies have taken up residence as well."

"Yes, quite right. It would look odd indeed." James tried not to grin. "I *will* dine with you tomorrow, thank you."

JAMES' HEART POUNDED as he stepped across Brant's shiny new—flawless—marble floor, following the butler, Reeves. They paraded up the stairs and into the large saloon that served Brant's London residence as a drawing room. The walls were bright with a fresh layer of soft yellow paint. Not many pictures had yet found themselves a home on the refurbished walls, but of the few that had, there was a profusion of hunting and horses.

James was informed that Dr. Brant and his guests would be down directly, and then was shut in to wait. He did not perch on the settee but paced energetically around the room. He was both eager and uncertain.

The sound of running feet caught his attention and arrested his movement. His heart pounded with the immediate concern of danger, but then as the sound approached the door, the steps became regular. Beth entered at a calm pace, if somewhat breathless and flushed.

Her evening gown was a rich cream, with a gauze overskirt; beaded rosettes were embroidered across the low collar, matching those circling her hem. Her hair was swept up into a loose chignon and a matching cream band wove in and out of its thick brown tresses. She was beautiful.

"You look well," he finally said, coughing and blushing at his meaningless and bland words. He tried to start the conversation again. "Your wound no longer troubles you?"

Beth's smile broadened. "It is quite well, thank you. Dr. Brant can perform miracles. Even my limp is improving." She stepped closer, as if to demonstrate her ability . . . or to shorten the distance between them.

"That is wonderful." Again, banal. His heart spoke such a different language from his tongue. It was full of eloquence, devotion, and passion intertwined with excitement and dreams. His words were formal and staid and brainless.

A scuffling noise echoed in the hallway. It drifted through the still partially opened door, warning them of impending company. Beth jumped back, but not as far as James. By the time Caroline entered the drawing room on Brant's arm, James was standing at the window. He looked out to the street in a studied manner . . . and hoped that his flush had faded.

"Lovely evening," Caroline commented, her gaze volleying between her brother and her friend. She lifted one brow in an unvoiced question.

James ignored the query. "Yes, lovely," he said, being careful not to look in Beth's direction. Caroline knew him too well; she could easily guess his . . . affection by his expression. It was something he was not ready to share with anyone, least of all a teasing sister.

Dr. Brant led Caroline to the settee opposite and they sat, perched on the edge of their seat.

Finally, Dr. Brant broke the awkward silence. "Is all well?" He glanced around, fixing a lingering look on Beth.

She squirmed under his scrutiny, doing her best to hide her awkwardness. Now, if James were to stare at her for as long . . . well, that would be a different matter.

"All is well." Beth lifted her shoulders. "Did you have any success this afternoon with Dr. Fotherby? To secure an appointment?"

"Oh yes, indeed. Dr. Fotherby saw me quickly in between patients. He is quite excited about your case." Dr. Brant nodded. "He has never had one of full amnesia before, nor a patient who dreams of a menacing hummingbird."

"Do you trust him, Dr. Brant?" Beth felt a twinge of nervousness. "Do you have faith in his abilities?"

"Yes, Miss Beth, I do. But if you are uncomfortable with the idea of talking to him, we can look elsewhere to recover your memories."

Beth shook her head slightly. "No, Dr. Fotherby is fine."

"Excellent, yes indeed." Dr. Brant's enthusiasm echoed throughout the room. "You have an appointment tomorrow. It was a great kindness on his part; the good doctor was booked for the next fortnight. However, as soon as I explained, he felt treatment should be started sooner rather than later."

"Is that wise?" James asked. "Would it not be best to postpone the appointment until we are certain, beyond any doubt, that the thugs from Welford Mills have not followed us to Town? Perhaps Dr. Fotherby could come here?"

Caroline snapped her tongue. "It has been more than a week, James. Ned has seen nothing untoward. There have been no suspicious persons lurking about. We have had no break-ins, assaults, or mysterious relatives."

Dr. Brant came to the true crux of the matter. "Besides, Beth needs relief soon. She cannot live with these terrible uncertainties much longer. We must establish whether or not Dr. Fotherby can help, for if he cannot, we shall have to scout further."

Beth nodded, appreciating the doctor's understanding. "I will wear a veil and cloak. No one will be able to recognize me."

"I hope it is worth the risk, and the man can be of *some* assistance," James said with a sigh, a very deep sigh.

Dr. Stewart Fotherby's outer office was a tasteful room, if not overly large. The walls were mahogany and lined with bookcases. It had the aspect of a library as much as that of a doctor's office. Beth enjoyed books. That fact alone should have brought her comfort, but it didn't.

The last patient had just departed. Beth would soon have to face her fears, large and small: shadows that loomed, birds that hummed, tiny creatures with wings that beat so fast . . .

She pulled a fan from her reticule, snapped it open, and fanned herself at an accelerated rate.

"Are you unwell, Beth?" Caroline was perched on the seat opposite. "You are a vile shade of green." She looked over to Dr. Brant waiting by the window, but before she could speak further, a voice called across the room.

"Miss Elizabeth Dobbins?"

Beth stood, swallowed, and stepped forward, glad—exceedingly glad—that Caroline had agreed to accompany her. Dr. Fotherby followed them over the threshold and closed the door.

"Welcome, welcome. So glad you could come. I have been looking forward to seeing you ever since talking to Dr. Brant. Good man, good man." He motioned for the girls to sit.

Beth took a chair positioned in front of the desk. She drew a deep breath and lifted her veil.

Dr. Stewart Fotherby was a diminutive gentleman with white hair. He had rosy cheeks and wire-frame glasses perched on the tip of his nose. When his eyes met hers, she found them bright blue, twinkling, and kind.

"My dear, my dear." The doctor could hardly miss her shaking limbs and green-tinted complexion. "This is not an execution. I promise not to hurt you. You are safe. No need to fear."

Instead of taking the chair opposite, Dr. Fotherby dropped onto the chair beside her. He gestured for Caroline to take the one behind his desk. The unorthodox nature of their positions was enough to bring a smile to Caroline's lips, and Beth momentarily relaxed.

"I am not sure what you are expecting, my dear. Perhaps I should explain. Your magnetic forces are confused. Your memories, thoughts, and dreams are all jumbled together, mixed up from your accident. And I am going to lead you through the tangles.

"We are going to realign the magnetic forces of your body through trances. Simply put, we are going to talk, you are going to relax, and we will talk some more. You see? Nothing to fear."

Beth lifted the corner of her mouth in a halfhearted attempt to smile.

"Let us start at the beginning, shall we? First, am I to understand that you suffered a knock to your brain?"

Dr. Fotherby proceeded to lead Beth through the past—everything pertinent since she awoke without memories. With his many questions, the process took a fair amount of time. Time in which Beth could not—did not—relax.

"You are as jumpy as a cat." Dr. Fotherby patted her lower arm. "Always remember you are safe here. Look around the room; there is nothing for you to fear. No birds of any kind. Certainly not a hummingbird. Dr. Brant told me about your dreams."

Beth did as directed, looking from the paneled walls and bookcases to the full couch opposite. Warm gas lamps added to the soft glow from the partially shaded windows and lit the charming landscapes and seascapes that decorated every inch of the walls. There were no hidden corners, no other doors, and no hummingbirds.

"Now, we will relax." Dr. Fotherby lit a candle and asked her to stare at it until her eyelids felt heavy and they closed of their own volition.

In the lengthy silence that followed, Beth suspected that the doctor had gone to sleep, as she was near to doing. She jumped when he spoke, but his voice had a lulling quality and she quickly relaxed again.

"First, let us think of happy times. Breathe in and out slowly. You do not have to describe them to me, just think of something that would bring a smile to your face."

Beth thought of James.

"Now imagine a little girl; she is doing something fun. What is she doing?"

"Playing with her dolls by the fire."

"Excellent. Is anyone with her?"

"Yes, her mother is sitting in a chair reading."

"Excellent. Are there any other children there?"

"Yes."

And so it continued for some minutes as the doctor guided Beth through imaginations, not memories. They went from the dolls to pets, and a smiling father. Beth had reached her most relaxed state while still awake when the good doctor startled her with a simple question. "When you close your eyes at night, what is the first thing that fills your mind?"

Beth immediately saw the hummingbird with blood dripping from its beak.

She cried out, but the doctor had anticipated her reaction and patted her lower arm in a comforting manner. "You are safe, my dear, nothing in this room to fear. Remember that you are in my office, no matter what your mind presents to you. Close your eyes again. Yes, there you go. Do not look at the hummingbird, my dear, but what is around it. What do you see?"

"A dark room full of boxes. Everything is covered in filth, and the stench is bad enough to make me gag."

"Is there anyone around you?"

"Three men, but I can only see the man ahead of me, and him only partially."

Slowly, Beth directed her thoughts in and around the dream. She described herself, and where she was sitting, covered in filth, bruised and cut, dress ripped, and gloves lost. She described the shape of the man just beyond the candle glow.

Strange, she hadn't recalled that he was short with broad shoulders before, but she heard her voice tell the doctor just that. She had called a name, a name she didn't understand. It echoed through the small, dark room of her imagination. It felt as if it echoed across Dr. Fotherby's office.

Beth told him more about the dagger, her voice calm, until in her mind's eye blood started dripping onto her lap. She wiped at her skirts, pushing it away in jerky movements, her voice growing shrill.

"Oh dear," the doctor said, trying to pull her out of her memories. "Best end this now and we will continue next time."

But it was too late. The cycle had begun.

The dark wood hilt of the dagger curved into the shape of a hummingbird. Wings pounded the air; eyes of cool steel stared, devoid of feeling. Closer and closer the bird swept until at last she felt the pain, saw the spray, and watched life ebb into the sawdust.

Beth gasped. Her eyes flew open and she ran for the door before Caroline or Dr. Fotherby had a chance to react. She swept past Dr. Brant in the waiting room and left overturned chairs in her wake.

CAROLINE RUSHED AFTER BETH, leaving Dr. Brant to make their excuses. She found her friend outside, shaking, with her forehead leaning on the carriage. Whether this was for support or to hide her face Caroline was not sure, but it was attracting a number of glances. She quickly turned Beth around and drew down her veil.

Dr. Brant arrived breathless, stammering questions.

Caroline shook her head. Wordlessly, they entered the carriage. Beth hunkered into the corner, her troubled stare fixed above their heads. Caroline knew Beth needed some time to regain her composure. She raised a finger to her lips should Dr. Brant not realize her purpose. He nodded and turned his eyes to the window.

Not for the first time, Caroline wondered about the name Beth and why her friend had chosen that particular one. Was it her name or someone she knew . . . or was it simply a name in a book or an article she had read? More important, why had she called out *Beth* as she had run from the room?

———◆———

As THE CARRIAGE pulled away, those hovering nearby quickly lost interest. The strange antics of the veiled girl cloaked in black had been mildly entertaining but easily forgotten. For everyone, that is, except the slight young gentleman dressed in a dated coat. He had been in midstride when he had seen the girl's uncovered face.

He had stopped so abruptly that the woman walking behind had fallen into him. He had not offered a helping hand or an apology. Oblivious to all but the sight that had captured him, the gentleman stood with his mouth agape. His astonishment was so complete that he had to fight to act.

Raising his hand, he hailed a cabriolet. "Follow that carriage!" he yelled as he jumped inside. Now was not the time to worry about cost; this was an emergency.

CHAPTER SEVENTEEN

Announcements

May 1833

To the Right Honorable, Lord Ellerby,

Justice Walker feels I should let you know what is happening here in Welford Mills.

Another player to this here game arrived two days ago at the Horn and Thistle. He has been asking many a question about Miss Dobbins. The young man calls his self Joe Smythe. I dropped by to check him out and found him cagey like. He did not answer a single question straight up.

I need to know what you want me to do now. Do I put the screws to this here gent or just watch him?

Derrick Strickland, Parish Deputy

Walter, the only—and lonely—soul inhabiting Hardwick Manor, not counting the twenty or more staff serving his needs, carefully folded and resealed the letter addressed to his brother. When Mr. Strickland had dropped off the note for James to be posted, he had said nothing about it not being opened.

It had been fourteen days since the family's departure, and in that time Walter had made good use of the first seven. Since then he had been brooding, anxious, and bored. Why had he volunteered to stay behind? The exhilaration and freedom of having the manor to himself had faded. The daily monotony made the glorious spring days dull and lifeless.

Walter attributed Beth's lack of pursuers solely to his acting abilities, particularly on the cliffside—not to mention the first days of the family's departure. He was excessively proud of his contribution to her well-being, but piqued that it might be at an end and a boring end at that.

Instead of dropping the resealed note back onto the silver tray for the outgoing mail, Walter made his way to the library. He placed the dispatch on James' desk with the missives that were due to be posted at the end of the week.

If Walter were to be of any service, he would need time. The letter would require a slight delay, if he were to include an addition of his own news. He needed a few more days, that was all. Then he could announce the true purpose of this fellow called Joe Smythe. It would impress James. He would marvel that Walter had taken it upon himself to investigate and had done such a fine job.

Walter felt better than he had in some days. He sent for his curricle to be prepared, donned his tallest top hat, squared his shoulders, and set out on his next adventure alone. Although, he thought, he might pick Henry up on the way.

James rubbed at the creases between his eyes and then his throbbing temples. It was not often that he came down with a headache, but traipsing from shop to shop in a vague pursuit of the man in the brown cloak was proving entirely pointless.

Once again, he looked down at the list. There was nothing unusual in the lettering; the hand was competent and practiced, the characters well formed. The list itself was organized. It read like a map, up one side of Regent Street and down the other. The shops had been varied—everything from a confectionary to a linen and lace wholesaler—but they all had a decidedly female aspect.

James was no longer convinced that any clue could be wrested from this coded scrap. Still, he was not yet ready to toss it aside—especially since he had only just arrived on the doorstep of Fitzroy's. It was the only shop that had included a time.

Gingerly easing his top hat back on his head, James climbed the few steps to the merchant's door.

The gentle tinkle of the bell as he entered announced his presence, but drew no more than an inquiring eye from the busy salesmen. The shop was not large and was currently overcrowded with customers of every size and complexion. James had, clearly, not come at a good time. He would have to return later. It was not much of a hardship, as it would give his aching head a respite.

James put his hand on the doorknob. He did not, however, open the door, for he was immediately accosted by one of the busy salesmen—leather samples still dangling from his fingers. The man simpered and offered assistance, no doubt observing James' finely cut coat and high-quality boots.

"Yes, I have come about an appointment." James glanced down

at the paper in his hand to verify the time. Suddenly, without a by-your-leave, the list was jerked from his grasp. Incensed by the man's audacity, James loudly protested. The mousy man ignored him, threaded his way to the back of the shop and disappeared.

He returned moments later with a parcel under his arm.

"There you be, m'lord." He passed James the large package wrapped in brown paper. "Been ready for some time." The salesman's voice held a hint of disapproval. "We are known for efficiency." He tucked the list under the string of the parcel and scurried back to his impatient customer.

James looked down at the parcel and sighed. *Well, this is just grand.* Now he had someone else's package. He glanced around, hoping to catch the mousy man's attention, but James was studiously ignored. Clicking his tongue and huffing did little to alleviate the situation.

Feeling the parcel, James wondered about the contents. Boots, he guessed by the shape and size, but would there be a bill of lading, a receipt of some sort tucked into the toe? Did it have anything to do with Beth? Was it all a mistake? Or would he be throwing away a golden opportunity if he dropped the parcel by the door and walked away?

James looked around the room again. It was still overcrowded and busy. He could return the parcel at another time, when it wasn't so hectic. He would cite a mix-up.

"Excuse me, m'lord."

James turned, slowly and with great condescension, toward the man behind him. He was a severe-looking man with large nostrils . . . or so they seemed as his nose was lifted in the air. He introduced himself as the manager of Fitzroy's.

"Yes." James clutched the package tightly, not wanting to give it up now that he had decided to keep it—briefly.

"There was a young lady here a few days ago looking for information in regard to your parcel."

James was relieved to know that his subterfuge was not the cause of this interruption. "Information?"

"Well, m'lord, she said she was looking for a man associated with your appointment. Naturally, I gave her no intelligence. I did, however, overhear her name and direction." He passed James a folded scrap of paper.

Calmly, with exaggerated disinterest, James took the paper and slipped it into his pocket. He nodded ever so slightly to the man who was now holding the door ajar.

"Good afternoon."

James hid his excited anticipation, managing a normal walking pace down the street to his waiting carriage. Then he leapt onto the seat, slamming the door behind him, and reached into his pocket. He unfolded the slip of paper and read it.

Clamping his teeth to prevent a shout of outrage, James' anger threatened to boil over. He called up to Sam and, with a tight voice, directed him to Harley Street; he was about to ring a great peal over his sister.

EXCEPT FOR THE clatter of the horses' hooves on the stones, the jiggling of the harnesses, the squeaking of the leather-backed seats, and the shouting of the street vendors from without, the hired carriage was quiet.

When Beth finally turned a calm face to her companions, she

was met with Dr. Brant's concerned expression. "I am a ninny goose." She sighed, shaking her head in self-disgust. "I apologize for my unorthodox sprint to the door and give you permission to catch me next time."

"I am so glad to hear you say that, my dear. I thought you might not wish to see Dr. Fotherby again. You are a brave young lady."

Beth snorted at his praise. She felt anything but brave. "I wonder if Dr. Fotherby will even see me again. I could not have given him a good impression."

"Not to worry," Dr. Brant reassured her. "I secured an appointment for you before I left." He grinned sheepishly. "I was going to convince you of the need to continue. Dr. Fotherby has already set aside time the day after tomorrow."

"Why did you call out 'Beth'?" Caroline asked.

"I did? I didn't realize." She huffed a weary sigh. "I must know a Beth. After all, it was the first name that came to mind when I awoke."

Dr. Brant sat back and leaned his head against the leather wall. "Dr. Fotherby believes the mind makes up things to explain what it doesn't understand. Calling out 'Beth' and dreaming of a hummingbird must mean something."

Beth was amazed at how open Dr. Brant was to the idea that dreams and nightmares were not to be dismissed. Had he not, just a few weeks ago, assured her that the content of dreams were irrelevant?

Beth relaxed into her seat as well. "That is not at all hard to fathom, Dr. Brant. I know what the hummingbird represents—a dagger. A razor-sharp dagger, dripping blood," Beth said calmly. Her companions shared a quick glance.

"I see." The doctor cleared his throat. "And what does the dagger represent?"

"Just that: a dagger. A weapon. A killing tool."

Once again, Beth saw the puddle of death in her mind's eye, and shuddered.

THE CONGENIAL CONVERSATION, tinkling laughter, and unconcerned voices of his nearest and dearest almost checked James' determination to take Caroline to task. The party of three knew of his arrival; James had heard the echo of his name on the lips of Reeves, just as they entered the house.

It was not surprising that Beth entered the drawing room first, rushing up the stairs ahead of the others. But James barely had time to nod his greeting before the entrance of Caroline and Brant.

His sister was the first to speak. "How wonderful to see you, James. Have you come to see how we fared with the doctor?"

"Yes and no," he answered abruptly. Beth gave him a quizzical glance, which he deflected with a shake of his head.

The newly arrived sat. Caroline relaxed on the settee while Beth perched. She folded her hands on her lap and glanced his way. The plain wrapped parcel, resting on the side table, drew no interest.

James swallowed, grumbled under his breath, and began to pace.

"Whatever is the matter, James?" Caroline smoothed her skirts. "Have you made a discovery?"

James nodded, staring sightless at the far wall. "Yes, indeed. I have discovered dishonesty and subterfuge, right here in this very room." James heard the touch of melodrama in his pronouncement and wondered if he had more of his mother in him than he thought.

Shock straightened the backs of all those seated and brought furrowed brows together. But, James noted, no disclaimer or utterance of surprise.

James pulled a gold braided armchair from its position by the wall and placed it directly in front of Caroline. With exaggerated grace he reclined, eye-to-eye with his sister.

Caroline half smiled and looked uncomfortable. "Are you to explain this accusation or are we to guess?"

James drew a slip of paper from his pocket. "I was given this at Fitzroy's."

Caroline took it. There wasn't much to read. "All this melodrama, and this is what has put you in such a lather? Really, James, swallow your spleen. It is not like you to take on so." She swallowed several times and would not meet his eye.

James turned his head slightly in Beth's direction. "Did you know?"

"No she did not, James," Caroline snapped. "What is it you want? An admission? Fine, I should not have gone investigating on my own. It was a trifle impetuous . . . but just a trifle."

"You what!" Brant showed his lack of duplicity by being suitably outraged.

James motioned toward Brant. "You see? It is not as insignificant as you would have us believe."

"Most decidedly not." Brant continued to huff and puff.

"I will not sit around doing nothing." Caroline's tone was far from contrite. "Besides, I thought that I was incognito." Caroline lifted her eyebrow at her brother.

A discreet knock at the door distracted them all and James

leaned back in his seat while Reeves explained the interruption. Ned entered the bright room with cap in hand. He lowered his head to all present and then his eyes went straight to James. "Lord Ellerby, I's sorry to disturb you, but I saw something you might want to know about."

James bade him to continue.

"I were watching from the corner of the park, m'lord. Saw the carriage pull up an' everyone goes in. But then I saw this here other carriage stop two doors down." He lifted his shoulders, using his hands to express himself. "Only no one got out. It sat there for a few minutes then rushes off, quick like. Pell-mell."

James glanced over to Beth and was pleased to see that while keenly interested in Ned's account, her complexion was neither too pale nor too ruddy. She was not fearful or overwrought. "Thank you, Ned, I appreciate your good eye and vigilance. Take Sam—"

"And two or three of the house staff," Brant broke in, his voice firm and his eyes worried.

"And post them around the terrace, front, and back," James continued. "Try to be as inconspicuous as possible and report anything unusual."

Ned hurriedly quit the room.

"In all likelihood it means nothing," James said, realizing it was not just a platitude. "A late appointment, incorrect address, a forgotten item . . . The possibilities are endless."

"Packing, then, might be a little premature," Beth said with a shrug.

"Tell us what you have bought, James." Caroline indicated the parcel on the tablet.

"Lud, I almost forgot." James picked up the package with a suddenly guilty face. "I know I should not have taken it when it was offered. But I thought there might be a clue in it." He held it out to Caroline. "From Fitzroy's. This was what was to be picked up on April fifteenth at two o'clock."

She took it from him. "The appointment wasn't kept."

"Obviously not," he replied.

"Well done. Excellent job. And what is his name?" Brant sat forward on his chair expectantly.

"I am afraid I have come away with only the package, no name. I was hoping it would be included, but as you can see there are only the initials 'R. & E.H.' on the wrapper."

"Perhaps there is a receipt inside," Beth said, sliding to Caroline's side of the settee and helping her to carefully undo the brown paper. The men loomed over them, watching the proceedings with great interest.

However, when the parcel lay open, it revealed two elegant pairs of riding boots of different sizes. They were made of fine black leather with smooth fitted calves and wrinkled ankles, but there was no bill, receipt, calling card, or any other identifying marker.

Beth dug into the toe of each boot, and while she did find paper, wrinkled and torn, they were only old newspapers. She held the last boot aloft, still upended upon her arm. "These are not a man's style." She turned it about. "Nor a man's size."

"Bother!" James sat with much less ceremony than usual, almost a sprawl. He took the list from the table and crumpled it into a ball. He batted it to Brant, who returned the volley. "Two steps forward and three back," he said. "Why would the owner of the brown cloak have a list of a woman's appointments? Just as we think we are gaining, we find ourselves falling behind. Each clue leads to more questions."

The room was silent except for the occasional sigh and creaking of the chairs on which they were poised. Outside, the street noise was constant and familiar, a comfort for the time being.

———•———

As the evening progressed, the ease of those gathered in the townhouse increased. Dr. Brant had invited James to dine and enjoy the evening together. Their congenial banter had not been interrupted by any of the men lingering out of doors on their behalf. Relaxation became the order of the night.

When the party returned to the privacy of the drawing room, it was to continue the conviviality—perhaps Caroline might be persuaded to play for them on the piano. Yes, all in all a pleasant way to end a topsy-turvy day.

Beth sighed in contentment as James joined her on the settee, albeit at a respectable distance. Still, their shared glances brought a flush to Beth's cheeks and she found it difficult to stop her mouth from grinning—a silly, besotted grin.

"Excuse me, sir." The butler addressed Dr. Brant from the doorway. "I regret to inform you, sir, that there is a police person who wishes to speak with you. Calls himself Inspector Davis. I have shown him to the study."

Beth stiffened, eyes wide and distressed. Did this have anything to do with her?

"Really?" Dr. Brant frowned. "In the study? A peeler?"

"Yes, sir," Reeves said with great dignity.

"Well, there you go." Dr. Brant lifted one shoulder. "Wonder if R. and E.H. want their boots back."

The teasing fell flat. The room was solemn and quiet.

"Why would a policeman be at your door?" Caroline looked

to Dr. Brant and then at the mantel clock. It was a quarter of ten. "And at this hour?"

"Could it be another ruse?" Beth asked, tamping down her urge to flee.

Dr. Brant hovered by the door.

James rose, tugged at his waistcoat needlessly, and joined his friend. "There is no point in speculating," James said. "If it is another trick, we shall set the true peelers on him."

"Right!" Dr. Brant agreed as the young men exchanged glances.

"We will be back directly. Worry not." Though James' words were spoken in general, Beth had no doubt that the reassurance was meant for her.

The gentlemen left the room with carefully cultivated untroubled expressions.

Wordless, Beth and Caroline stared after them. They listened to the men's footsteps as they crossed the hall and heard the creaky study door open. Dr. Brant's greeting was delivered in a rather blunt manner before the mighty oak swung closed, preventing any tone, phrase, word, or even vowel from seeping through its cracks.

JAMES DID NOT know what to expect, as he had heard little of the newly formed London police force. Inspector Davis was a man of indiscernible age. His face was strong but had no dominant features other than a cleft chin, and his mode of dress was insignificant. He stood calmly watching them as they entered. He did not seem surprised that while he had asked after one gentleman, he had been delivered two.

Brant introduced himself and then James. Again, no surprise registered on the expressionless countenance of the man.

"I do hope, Inspector, that your business is of enough urgency to take me away from my drawing room. It is late."

"Yes, Doctor, it is." The man's voice was his only defining characteristic; it was deep and gravelly. He pulled a wad of paper from his pocket in such a manner that it reminded James of Mr. Strickland. "How many number in this household, sir?"

"Eight staff, two guests, and myself. What is the purpose of these questions, Inspector?"

"Could I have the names of all those within, please, sir?"

"No, you may not."

James was surprised at the effrontery of the man. His tone and manner were almost arrogant. He was still in a quandary over the inspector's claim of authority. Was he or was he not a true peeler? Did this arrogance add credence to his claim or proof of subterfuge?

"Perhaps you would be so kind as to answer some of our questions first?" James' tone was intentionally disdainful.

"M'lord?" The inspector didn't deign to look up.

"What district do you cover and who is your superior? What proof do you have of who you are and your position?"

The man calling himself Inspector Davis looked up slowly. He shook his head slightly, scratched at the stubble on his chin, and rubbed his eyes.

James was not sure if the inspector's gestures were to control his agitation or give the man time to think of a feasible answer. Either way, it was soon irrelevant as a heavy knock at the door interrupted the proceedings. The hammering was repeated before those within had time to react.

"Yes, Reeves, what is it?"

The door opened not on the expressionless countenance of the butler, but the worried, almost frantic face of Ned.

"We're surrounded, m'lord. They got Benny and Sam, and I has no idea if they got the two round back."

"Be sure that we have."

James and Brant whipped their heads toward the gravelly voice. "What is the meaning of this?" shouted James, trying to warn the women.

Just then, the door below slammed open and a stream of men rushed in, colliding with Reeves, sending him arse over teakettle. They were dressed in blue uniforms with brass buttons. Without hesitation, they started up the stairs.

All thoughts, questions, or even emotions were rendered impotent as James and Brant raced across the hall and burst into the drawing room. They almost collided with Beth and Caroline who were rushing toward the door. Their escape was blocked by the onslaught of blue uniforms, forcing them back into the bright, cheerful room.

Looking for a weapon, James grabbed up a brass vase from the mantel and tossed the fireplace poker to Brant. They held their arms outstretched in both a threatening and protective stance. But they were well outnumbered and retreat was their only option.

As the wave of uniforms surrounded them, Beth and Caroline pushed tables and chairs into the paths of those approaching but were forced continually backward. Ultimately, they were pressed into the corner by the windows. James grabbed the coat of the man closest and threw him to the ground, placing himself between the ladies and the attackers. Brant joined him, shoulder to shoulder, their chests heaving, weapons held high, ready for a fight.

Suddenly the room was still. The men no longer advanced.

The inspector parted the blue coats and came forward. "You

cannot escape, you know." He addressed first Brant and then James. "We have you."

"Who *are* you? What do you want?"

The inspector ignored the questions. He looked to Beth and Caroline, who were standing in the shadows behind James and Brant.

"Come, ladies." The man smiled and reached his arm out.

With a slash, James brought the vase down, narrowly missing the man as he jumped back.

The inspector faced James, his face now a ruddy glow, his mouth a firm line. "You will desist immediately! You are well and truly caught! There is nothing to do but submit and allow the ladies their freedom."

"Allow the ladies their freedom?" James repeated. "What in God's name are you talking about?"

Puzzlement flashed across the inspector's face. "We have it on good authority that these ladies are being held against their will."

Beth gasped in surprise.

Inspector Davis glanced in her direction and then called out. "Sergeant! Sergeant Waters, get Mr. Osborne."

James straightened and lowered the vase—marginally. "I believe there has been a mistake, Inspector."

"Perhaps."

A slight young man was led forward. His head was bowed at first as if intimidated by the proceedings. However, when he looked up there was determination in his eye.

"Mr. Osborne, are these they?" the man calling himself Inspector Davis asked.

James felt the movement of both Beth and Caroline. He knew

them to have stepped forward and peeked out beyond his and Brant's protective backs. Beth placed her hand on his arm as she did so.

Mr. Osborne looked at Caroline and frowned. Then he turned to Beth. His face lit up and his immediate step forward attested to his conviction.

"Becca! Oh, thank the Lord, it *is* you!" When Beth did not react, his smile faltered. He pointed to himself. "It's me . . . Jeremy Osborne . . . your cousin."

Just then a calamitous noise could be heard from the hall. It was the sound of scuffling and shoving and voices saying over and over, "No, m'lord, best stay here."

"Davis! Osborne!" a deep and raspy voice bellowed. "Where are they?" It was obvious that whoever the men below were trying to restrain was slowly advancing up the stairs, despite the obstacles.

Inspector Davis shook his head. "Leave him be," he ordered loudly, and the footsteps came on more quickly.

Like a parting of the Red Sea, the peelers stepped out of the path of the tall, broad-shouldered, gray-haired man. James was surprised to recognize him.

"Lord Hanton?"

"Do not talk to me, you filth." Lord Hanton's eyes blazed with fury. Without turning, he addressed the inspector. "Davis, where the devil are my daughters?"

CHAPTER EIGHTEEN

Renewed Hope

James relaxed his hold on the brass vase to the point that it dropped from his fingers with a clunk and rolled across the floor. Another clang indicated that Brant had dropped his poker as well. Grinning, James turned to his companions.

Laughter and bedlam broke out. There were half sentences, words on top of words, on top of claps. Caroline grabbed Beth and hugged her, kissing one cheek and then another. Beth smiled broadly and then gulped; she had a name, a cousin . . . and possibly a father.

"What is going on?" roared Lord Hanton.

"Sergeant Waters, clear the room!" Inspector Davis shouted above the pandemonium.

With a great deal of shuffling, but little time, the room emptied. Soon the only interlopers were Davis, his sergeant, and Lord Hanton; even Mr. Osborne had been ushered to the hall. Davis directed the doors to be closed and turned to face the four still holding fast to one another in the corner.

"There is an explanation here, Lord Hanton." James started to guide Beth forward but was distracted by her resistance. "Beth, whatever is the matter?"

"Beth? Whatever are you talking about, man?" Lord Hanton made as if to grab Beth and drag her from the protection of her circle, but she screamed.

The inspector and his sergeant grabbed Lord Hanton's arms, holding him back.

Davis struggled with the large man. "Please, m'lord. Are you certain it is she?"

Lord Hanton yanked his arms from his inferiors and pulled his waistcoat straight. He addressed Beth, who was still partially hidden behind James. "Come forward then. Let us have a look at you."

Beth clutched at James, then lifted her chin, and stepped out of the shadows. She was not prepared for the reaction.

The harsh, cold countenance of the broad-shouldered man instantly dissolved. A sequence of sentiments rushed across his face; it started with recognition and ran through relief, calm, and great felicity. Emotion rushed to his eyes. When the momentary storm had passed, his face held infinite joy.

Lord Hanton stepped forward, wrapped his arms around Beth and lifted her from the floor. Her hand was pulled from James' and the room began to spin. The man twirled her round and round.

"Please, sir," she tried to say. The fabric of his coat muffled her voice.

Lord Hanton loosened his grasp, allowing Beth to breathe.

"Please, *sir*?" His voice sounded puzzled. "*Sir*? What is this 'sir'? I am your dear papa."

He held her aloft as if to allow her a full view of him. "Becca, dear. Thank the Lord you are safe. But where is Elizabeth?"

"Are you certain, sir?" she asked.

"What do you mean?" Lord Hanton frowned. "What is this?" His jaw clenched and his face tightened, but his voice was still smooth. "Becca, you are most certainly my daughter. Do you not know me?"

Beth shook her head with downcast eyes. She pinched her lips tightly, trying to control her emotions. "No, sir. I know you not," she finally said in a quavering voice.

She pulled herself from Lord Hanton's grasp. She backed away slowly, retreating until she felt James' muscular, safe body against her. His presence gave her strength. Without taking her eyes from the viscount, Beth addressed the gentleman behind her. "Lord Ellerby? Are we certain of Lord Hanton?"

James ignored the surprise on Hanton's face and turned Beth so that they might fix their eyes on each other, and disregard all else. He was heartbroken to see the fear and uncertainty that covered every contour of her face.

His voice, just above a whisper, was meant for her alone, but the silence of the room was such that his words echoed. "Yes indeed, this is Lord Hanton. He is not such an unknown as was Mr. Paterson. If Lord Hanton says that you are his daughter, we need not fear a lie. There is no doubt that you are she."

For some moments Beth and James were locked in their own private world. James was rewarded when realization and acceptance relaxed the expression on her face, but with it came tears.

Beth closed her eyes for some moments and then reopened them to find James smiling gently with a touch of sadness. "You are the honorable Misses Hanton. Rebecca Hanton."

"But I know him not," she whispered, swallowing hard again, trying to fight the hysterics that were constricting her breath. "I had thought—" She brought her hands together in front of her mouth, clasped as if in prayer. "I had thought," she tried again, "that to know who I am, my name—to know that I am Rebecca Hanton—to meet my family . . . well, I thought that my memories would return." Again speech was momentarily impossible. "But . . ."

James had to strain to hear her.

"But I do not. I do not know him."

The familiarity between the two was more than Lord Hanton could stand. "You scoundrel!" he shouted, and once more pulled the two apart. He swung his arm wildly, and as he did so, was rewarded with a connection.

James fell hard to the floor, his nose bloodied, but there he stayed. No hint of retaliation glinted in his eye. Instead, vexation and anger emanated from another source.

"How dare you!" Rebecca shouted. She knelt beside James, took his arm, and helped him to his feet. She held her hand beneath his nose to catch the dripping blood, and then exchanged it for the handkerchief offered by Dr. Brant.

"You should be thanking God for this man. It was he who came to my rescue and with a lot less theatrics than this." She swept her arm toward the helter-skelter around the room, upended tables and couches, and broken ornaments.

Rebecca could feel the outrage building in her and she opened her mouth to give it full vent.

But Lord Hanton smiled at her. Smiled? What new trick was this?

"There is the Becca I know." His eyes sparkled and he smiled again. "That's my girl." He half turned toward the inspector, waving his arm in her direction. Then his eyes met James', and they hardened. "Where is Elizabeth?"

"*Who* is Elizabeth?" James asked, looking mystified. "If Beth is Rebecca, who is Elizabeth?"

"My other daughter, you fool!" Lord Hanton shouted. "I have two!"

James took a step back from the angry eyes, startled as much by Lord Hanton's words as by the suffused emotion in his shout. Rebecca gasped and reached out to him for support.

"My sister?" she asked in a whisper.

Glancing down at Rebecca, James placed his hand on hers and glared a reproach at the older gentleman.

"Please," Caroline entreated, looking at Rebecca, watching the color drain from her face. "We need to sit." She stepped forward, kicking bits of pottery from her path, and halfheartedly pulled at one of the settees, trying to right it. She sighed and looked around the room, shaking her head.

"There is much to discuss. Let us adjourn to the dining room," Dr. Brant said. "Where we will be able to talk in comfort; certainly, more comfort than this." He glared at the inspector.

Before anyone could respond, Dr. Brant held his arm out to Caroline and he led her to the door. It left the others with no choice but to follow. Lord Hanton offered Rebecca his arm, but she ignored it. In a blatant snub, Rebecca reached over to James and placed her arm lightly—with intentional ease—on his. James removed the cloth from his nose and saw that it was no longer bleeding. He crumpled the stained cloth into his pocket and led Rebecca forward.

Reeves waited in the outer hall with the inspector's men. Only his slightly askew tie attested to the evening's trauma.

"We will have tea and brandy in the dining room, Reeves," Dr. Brant addressed his butler.

Reeves bowed.

"Please," the doctor added, "have Mrs. Sagor put the drawing room to rights in the morning." He then led Caroline through the throng of uniforms without a backward glance.

Reeves scurried ahead of them to light the ornate silver candelabra waiting in the center of the large mahogany table. The light proved ample to dispel the shadows from the corners of the less-than-cavernous room.

No one spoke while the ladies were seated and Reeves scurried away. Rebecca made a ceremony out of placing her skirts just right, and resting her hands on her lap. James stood behind her and, likewise, Dr. Brant placed himself behind Caroline.

Rebecca appreciated the show of solidarity.

Lord Hanton pulled a chair away from the table and the small group. Sergeant Waters waited by the door and Inspector Davis paced before the sideboard.

"As Beth's—Misses Hanton's—physician," Dr. Brant began, "I feel that it should be noted that Misses Hanton is suffering from amnesia." He hesitated as if expecting a disagreement. "Well, that, I suppose, was patently obvious." He cleared his throat again. "She was in a coach accident that rendered her unconscious for a time and when she awoke her memories were gone."

"How is it that she came to be in this accident, and your care?" Lord Hanton demanded.

"That is part of the mystery that we have been trying to solve. Beth—I beg your pardon." Dr. Brant glanced at Rebecca. "Misses Hanton was in a coach that met with an accident not far from the gates of Hardwick Manor, Lord Ellerby's estate." Dr. Brant nodded toward James and then waved for his friend to continue.

"At the time we thought—" James began.

"We?" interrupted the viscount.

"My brother, Walter, and I. *We* found Misses Hanton unconscious. She had been flung from the coach. She needed help immediately, but the coachman argued. Naturally I prevailed, and had Misses Hanton brought to the manor and placed her under Dr. Brant's care."

Reeves interrupted briefly, laying out the tea and brandy.

"When was this?" Lord Hanton asked after the butler had gone.

"About six weeks ago." Caroline reached over for Rebecca's hand and gave it a brief squeeze.

"Six weeks! In all that time why, in God's name, man, did you not go to the authorities?"

James straightened his shoulders and narrowed his eyes at Lord Hanton. "Sir, we did inform the authorities, those in Welford Mills—a two-day journey from London. We had no idea where she had come from or where she was going. There was nothing in the *Times* to direct us, no gossip hinted of her loss, no mention of a disappearance. We had nothing to go on."

"I arrived at Hardwick with my clothes in tatters, covered in blood and filth. I was not the picture of a well-brought-up young lady." Rebecca felt James' hand on her shoulder. She lay hers on top of it. "Still, I was taken in as part of the family," she continued, skirting the week in the servants' wing. "I was fed and clothed and, most of all, protected from unknown foes and would-be assassins."

Lord Hanton had been listening with a grave face, his eyes

vacillating between Rebecca and James; this last sentence brought them to a standstill.

Rebecca smiled weakly. "We have had our share of misadventures. We . . ." She sighed and cleared her throat. "We came to London to escape those that mean to harm me." She looked around the room. "Now, *I* would like to know about my sister and why I have been threatened and attacked. The last time I barely escaped."

"Good Lord, Becca, my dove, what have you been through?" Lord Hanton dropped his hat to his side, raked his hand through his hair, and rose to cross the room.

James turned at his approach, positioning Rebecca safely behind him again. He was surprised to see Lord Hanton stretch out his hand.

"I apologize, most profusely, for what I did." Hanton's eyes traveled to James' red and tender nose. "And what I thought."

James took the viscount's hand and returned its firm shake. "I understand," he said quietly. He stepped out of the way to allow the man access to his daughter.

Lord Hanton looked over at the inspector. The man's head was down, scribbling a note. Waters was doing the same.

Rebecca saw the viscount eye the empty chair next to her. He pulled it out and sat down. Then he reached for her hand. Rebecca stiffened and leaned back. She shifted her hands from her lap and clasped them behind the chair. She swallowed, breathed deeply, and stared. She waited for recognition, any spark of familiarity. There was none.

Shaking her head, Rebecca was grateful that Lord Hanton understood; she saw him draw back. Still, his smile remained.

"Lord Ellerby did you a great service," he said. "You could only have been in the kidnappers' clutches a few days."

"When was I taken?"

"While out shopping on the fifteenth of April . . . with Elizabeth."

Rebecca started and frowned. She had no recollection of a sister; no face came to her mind's eye, no emotional reaction. It both scared her and upset her. "Is she younger or older than I am?"

Lord Hanton blinked in surprise. "Younger. She is sixteen."

Closing her eyes, Rebecca pinched the bridge of her nose. So, she was the daughter of a viscount and she had been kidnapped with her sister. Where were those memories? Why could she not remember anything before awaking at Hardwick? Focusing on what she had learned and what it meant, Rebecca opened her eyes and stared at the man who claimed to be her beloved papa.

"I could identify the kidnappers. Yes, that's why they risked so much to regain me. But . . . two weeks ago, they tried to kill me, not capture me. What happened? Why did they not turn tail and run the moment I was free? Cut their losses, change their plans?"

"Perhaps because they still hoped to succeed." Lord Hanton tipped his head slightly to the side.

"They still wanted their money?" James' question was a dis-embodied voice from above. "The ransom was worth the risk?"

Lord Hanton shifted his gaze to James. "The demand was not for money. The villains ordered me to use my influence on a bill going through the Lords, one that I support. They wanted it defeated. I could not do it. The bill is needed to stop privateering. I withdrew from the House instead. I prayed that it would be enough to satisfy their demand." He looked back to Rebecca. "But there was no further correspondence, no other demand. Nothing. Nothing at all, day after day. I thought we had lost you."

Rebecca's pulse quickened and she swallowed before asking. "*We?* Who is *we?*"

A brief frown flashed across Lord Hanton's face. "Your brothers and I."

"I have brothers?" She looked up at James. "I have brothers."

"Two brothers," her father explained. "Matthew is the eldest, at one and twenty, and Jeffrey is twelve."

"And how old am I?"

"Nineteen by Michaelmas."

Rebecca tilted her head. "We were right." She waved her hand in the direction of Caroline and Dr. Brant. "I'm eighteen." And then realizing how frivolous such a comment was in the face of all their uncertainty about Elizabeth, Rebecca snapped her mouth shut. She might not remember her sister, not how she looked, or what they mean to each other, but deep in the pit of her being something cried out in sorrow and loss. Where was Elizabeth? Was she safe?

Was she alive?

———— ◆ ————

LORD HANTON AND James sat in the study before a low fire. It was now the middle of the night and the late spring air, as well as the day's proceedings, had brought enough of a chill to warrant the fire. The peelers had departed some hours ago.

"The inspector will be here in the morning to continue our discussion," Brant explained as he returned to the drawing room after seeing the ladies to the top of the stairs. "We need to recover from our surprises first. I have offered Lord Hanton a room for the night, James. I extend to you the same invitation."

James let out a deep breath. "Thank you, Brant. I accept. I do not think I will get a lick of sleep otherwise."

Brant chuckled and nodded. "Good! I shall retire, then, and leave you two to talk. But try not to solve all our problems this evening. We have to have something to do in the morning."

James continued to stare at the glowing embers of the fire. Silence echoed around the room for some minutes.

"What is the relationship between you and my daughter?" Lord Hanton asked finally.

James sniffed in self-mockery and then altered it to a stifled yawn. His eyes never left the fire grate. "I thought you might have noticed."

"I'm not blind." Making a sound that was half sigh, half harrumph, Lord Hanton shifted in his chair. "Your relationship?" he asked again at length.

James turned his gaze to Lord Hanton. "There is none, sir. Beth . . . Misses Hanton is my sister's companion. Or at least she was until this evening. I will admit a partiality toward her, but as I did not know her marital state, I could not pursue any relationship other than friendship."

Lord Hanton drummed his fingers on the arm of his chair for a long minute or two. "Becca is not married, neither is she engaged," he said eventually.

James dropped his head back and stared at the ceiling. He drew in great gulps of relief as quietly as possible, but he was sure the man next to him could hear his ragged breathing.

"Not for want of suitors, I must tell you. But none had excited more than her mild interest. She has such firm opinions and lively conversation that she found no interest in the mild milk-sop puppies at her knee. 'No character,' she used to lament."

"Excellent," James said quickly, without thought. He blinked, surprised, not by his reaction but by the verbalization of his feelings.

Heat rose up his cheeks and he smiled feebly. Perhaps it was best to end the night before he embarrassed himself further. "I believe, sir, if I stay up any longer, I will not leave this chair till morning. I am off to bed."

Lord Hanton rose to do the same, and as they quit the room together a thought occurred to James. It was a subject that could not wait until morning. "I must warn you, sir, Beth—Rebecca— Misses Hanton has terrible nightmares."

Lord Hanton frowned. "She has never suffered from them before."

"We gathered as much. But she does suffer them now, rather cruelly. While it is not every night, it is almost so. She not only must endure the dreams themselves but the embarrassment of them. She prefers them not to be acknowledged—so if you were to be awoken . . ."

"Awoken?"

"By her screams."

Lord Hanton's eyes widened in distress.

"It would be best not to go to her." James stared sightless at the wall. "It is very difficult not to, believe me."

James and Lord Hanton continued up the stairs in silence. James prayed that exhaustion would allow Rebecca a tranquil and restorative rest.

It was inevitable that he was to be disappointed.

———•—•———

SHE RAN. She called a name. It echoed, bounced from wall to wall. She called again and again, until one echo fell on top of the other, a cacophony of words. She tried to run faster but the floor tipped. Slippery flakes of sawdust snowed from the ceiling and the floor now tipped so sharply that she fell fast and forever . . . until she hit the bottom.

Winded, she lay gasping for breath. A scream filled the room, but not from her lips. Hands grabbed at her, yanking at her fingers. Rings slipped to the floor, covered in blood. Hair fell onto her face, screening her view. She called again and felt a sharp pain burst in her cheek.

A great weight pulled at her head, bending it down. A red drip grew into a river. A creature rose from its depths and advanced toward her. She felt the gentle touch of a feather across her cheek and the hum of rapid wings, and bile rose to her throat. Darkness hovered and deepened, but just before it consumed, it dissolved.

Silence. As if she were suddenly deaf. But not blind. A hand reached forward, toward her. It held a shiny and honed form.

Her eyes locked on the dark wood hilt gently curved into the shape of a hummingbird. It smiled a gentle, sad smile, blood oozing from the corners of its upturned beak.

She whispered a name and the bird began to laugh.

JAMES COULD TAKE it no longer. Hastily donning his trousers and slipping on his boots, he opened his door to the hall. The creak and squeak of it sounded much louder in the stillness of the night and he glanced in both directions to ensure that it had not disturbed the other sleepers. He need not have worried, as the sound of Rebecca's nightmare filled the corridor, eclipsing any sound that he might make.

A door closed up ahead and moments later the screaming stopped. He breathed a sigh of relief and tiptoed down the hall until, at last, he heard muffled sounds from behind one of the doors. James paused and listened. With no intention of making his presence known, he lightly touched the wooden divider between them. When he heard Rebecca start to sob, it took all his control not to throw the door open.

Breathing deeply, he leaned his head onto the oak frame and closed his eyes.

"I am very glad you warned me." Lord Hanton stepped out from the shadows as James wheeled around. "I would, indeed, have rushed in like a bull in a china shop." Hanton sighed deeply. He slowly shook his head. "Doing nothing is agony."

"This is a particularly bad one." James clenched his jaw.

They lapsed into silence, each leaning against the wall on either side of the door. They stayed there until, some time later, Caroline crept out.

She was not in the least surprised to find them there. "She is asleep now," she whispered, gently closing the door behind her. She led the way back down the hall and quietly wished them good night.

Sleep eluded James for some time, and even then it was not restful.

CHAPTER NINETEEN

Much to Know

Walter flexed his shoulders, first one way and then the other. His only diversion was a piece of fluff that he had pulled from Henry's coat. He set it afloat in the sunbeam and yawned again.

"Well, I must say, this is not quite the high adventure I thought it would be," Walter muttered to his equally sleepy companion.

"Not high adventure? This is not even remotely entertaining!" Henry pursed his lips, sputtering in what could have been termed a raspberry. "A mysterious man, indeed! Dangerous sleuthing, you promised. Capital excitement, you said. Well, it's not! This is bloody boring."

It was all Mr. Strickland's fault. He had cast aside Walter's noble intentions to help with the investigation with a casual flick of his wrist. He recommended that the boys refrain from interfering.

The nerve.

Considering all that had transpired, the casual rejection was an insult. Walter easily persuaded Henry that they should set out on their own, where greater adventures and better appreciation was to be had.

Besides, Walter had only spoken to Mr. Strickland as a courtesy, a professional courtesy from one exceptional investigator to another. Still, while the deputy hadn't accepted their talented assistance, he had updated Walter on his progress.

They now knew that Joe Smythe had stated that he was in Welford Mills for a rest. The man complained that his journey to Plymouth was of such a taxing nature to his fragile form, that he was required to rest in towns along the way. Welford Mills was a stay of short duration, a town he had only just stumbled upon.

Poppycock!

The man was in his early twenties and didn't look in the least fragile! In fact, he was rather robust. He had also said he was not interested in Miss Dobbins. His questions regarding new arrivals in Welford had been misconstrued.

Poppycock again!

The man looked very little like a tourist. These were lies. The slippery devil had pulled the wool over the deputy's eyes. But not Walter's, no. And not Henry's. No indeed; they were made of wiser stuff.

The first order of business was to watch the bounder, but herein lay the problem.

Mr. Joe Smythe was ensconced in his room at the Horn and Thistle. He had been there all morning. Through Walter's earlier inquiries, they had learned that the man had risen at eight, eaten a hearty meal, and then returned to his room.

This was splendid, Walter had thought. The man was fortifying himself for some nefarious deed.

They found themselves a vantage point at the milliner's window to watch the Horn and Thistle and had settled down to wait.

So it was that Walter and Henry sat comfortable and lazy upon the cushioned seats of Dodd and Tobin's best chairs for the better part of two hours. Initially, they had only perched—ready to spring into action, ready for an immediate response to Joe Smythe's departure, ready to sleuth.

They anticipated running out to the street and following either on foot or using Walter's curricle, sitting just outside. However, as they approached the third hour, Walter was much less comfortable. For while the door to the Horn was seldom still for long, Mr. Smythe had yet to put in an appearance. Tradesmen, travelers, shopkeepers, and even the squire had come and gone, but of Mr. Smythe, there was no sign.

Walter was getting increasingly tired of Henry's complaints. After all, it wasn't his fault that the blackguard had taken all morning to put his wicked plan into action.

Walter sighed from the bottom of his boots.

Again the bell tinkled as yet another customer entered the milliner's shop, but Walter was not interested. His gaze did not waiver, his intent unchanged. Distraction was not an option.

"What do you think you boys is doing?" asked Mr. Strickland, standing next to Walter's chair. The man's face was stony and his address rather clipped.

Walter looked up quickly and then returned his eye to the inn. "Watching for Mr. Smythe," he whispered. "In secret." He saw another tradesman enter the Horn; the man's new boots gleamed in the sunlight. "When he comes out, Henry and I are going to follow him. We will let you know what we find out."

"Mr. Smythe is not in his room; he has been gone for some time." The deputy's voice remained frosty.

Walter dragged his eyes away from the bland scene before him. He stared at the deputy's face for some moments, trying to verify the truth of his rather bald statement.

"But we have been watching—"

"That I know, but the man has been gone for two hours."

"What!" Henry shouted with indignation, directed— unreasonably—toward Walter. "You mean—" A gesture from Walter forced Henry to lower his voice. "You mean that we have been staring incessantly at that blasted plank door for nothing?"

"And," Mr. Strickland pronounced through clenched teeth, "attracting plenty of attention while doing so. Not only can your faces be seen from out of doors, but you left a calling card just there."

Mr. Strickland pointed through the window to Walter's curricle. Traffic was slowly wending its way around the ill-positioned, well-known vehicle. The boy securing the reins ignored the angry calls, almost asleep on his feet.

"Please, Mr. Ellerby, Mr. Thompson, go home. Allow me to do me job." Mr. Strickland tipped up the back of Henry's chair, propelling him to his feet.

The deputy reached over to do the same with Walter but Walter splayed his legs and prevented the undignified act. He rose with exaggerated ceremony as he pulled down his waistcoat. He brought his chin up and tried to look down on the taller man. Then turning without a word, he bowed deeply to the patrons of the shop. With Henry at his heels, Walter pranced down the steps and acknowledged each and every soul watching on the street. With a flourish, they pulled themselves onto the seat of the curricle.

Walter paid the boy an excessive amount and turned his carriage not once but twice, waving and causing even more congestion in the backlog of traffic.

Faces were angry, disgusted, and indignant, but the look of curiosity was gone.

<hr />

"Good morning." Rebecca entered the morning room as the last to rise. She went straight to the sideboard and filled a plate from the still piping-hot platter, then carried her overflowing breakfast to the table.

The room was cozy, and the guests formed a tight, comfortable group. Rebecca avoided the empty seat by her father, choosing a chair opposite, between Caroline and James. She smiled sadly to the company and finally glanced down at her meal. Her fork hovered in the air and then slowly returned to the table.

Her plate was loaded with kippers and kippers alone.

"You have a great appreciation for fish this morning, my dear," Lord Hanton commented, casually waving his fork at her dish.

"Not really." Rebecca passed the plate full of kippers up to the ever-vigilant Reeves, who replaced it with her usual eggs and ham. "I can't stop thinking . . . trying to remember. Elizabeth needs me to remember."

James offered her a lopsided smile and placed his hand gently on top of hers. Then he jerked his hand away, blushing, as if just realizing what he had done. Rebecca reddened as well and looked to see her papa's reaction.

"Eat for now," the old gentleman said as if unaware. "Davis will be here soon. We will go over it then. I'm sure . . ." His voice petered out and he stared at his plate.

Rebecca stilled, swallowed, and quietly lay her fork down. She had no appetite—doubts about Elizabeth's well-being had killed it.

After the strained meal, Dr. Brant suggested that they abandon the morning room to find more comfort in the freshly cleaned drawing room. It no longer resembled the broken mess of the previous evening. Waiting upon the peelers seemed long, but it was likely only a quarter hour before Reeves announced Inspector Davis and Sergeant Waters. They entered a serious and silent room.

Rebecca sat with James on one of the settees facing Caroline and Dr. Brant, who perched on the other. Lord Hanton had moved the cushioned occasional chair from the corner by the windows next to Rebecca.

"We shall start on Brook Street, on the fifteenth of April," Inspector Davis said after the appropriate bows and curtsies. He stood beside the fireplace and raised his eyebrows in the general direction of the Hantons.

Lord Hanton shifted, meeting Rebecca's gaze. "I was out on business for the day with Matthew, and Jeffrey was up to some mischief or another." He shifted his eyes to James' briefly and then back to Rebecca. "After luncheon, Mrs. Trimmer, your governess, and Elizabeth and you had planned an excursion to Regent Street. Elizabeth can shop every day of the week." He paused, swallowed visibly, and then continued. "But you find it tedious. You always have it planned in such a way that you will not waste time. No browsing or dilly-dallying for you, Becca my dear."

Rebecca shifted in her chair, made uncomfortable by these unfamiliar references. They seemed to be stories of another person. "Mrs. Trimmer was with us when we were kidnapped?"

"No, actually, she fell just outside the front door of our

townhouse. A child's toy had been abandoned on the narrow bottom step. We realized later that it had been left for just such a purpose. Mrs. Trimmer is always the first out the door and she has a weak ankle. Naturally, this gave it a nasty turn. Elizabeth was so disappointed, Mrs. Trimmer encouraged you to go on without her."

Inspector Davis interrupted. "Misses Hanton kept an agenda. A type of journal. That was how we knew what shops they visited that day."

"Really?" Caroline said. "We found a list of appointments in the brown cloak. James"—she turned to her brother—"where did it go?"

On the other side of the settee, Dr. Brant cleared his throat. "Were we not tossing it about just before dinner?" He cast his eyes around the immaculate room.

Caroline gulped and then jumped to her feet, rushing out of the room. Her rapid footfalls faded as she headed into the back regions of the townhouse.

Lord Hanton frowned. "What is its significance?" The question was directed to James.

Inspector Davis leaned forward and fixed James with a similar quizzical stare.

"It is a list of shops, down Regent Street. There was a time noted for Fitzroy's but for none of the others." James rubbed at his brow; he told the inspector about the trunk, the cloak, and his visit to Ellingham. A hush fell over the room as these details were absorbed and Rebecca listened with anticipation for Caroline's return.

But Rebecca's father was not attending; his gaze was locked on the door. Rebecca reached over and touched his hand. He looked up with a start and then quickly glanced around the room.

"That evening?" Rebecca prompted. "The day we disappeared?"

"Yes, right. That evening, I returned home to find Mrs. Trimmer moaning of neglect. It was not like you to leave her unattended and uninformed. So I sent Matthew and Jeremy—Jeremy Osborne, who is *always* in our midst—in a cabriolet to assist you with your packages. However, they returned empty-handed. The evening came and went without either of you returning or a message being delivered." Lord Hanton cleared his throat.

"Finally, I sent Lord Whitten of the Home Office a frantic note. Within the hour he arrived with Inspector Davis. There was very little we could do at that time of night; we had to wait for the morning. Then, even before the shops had opened for the day, Inspector Davis was back with alarming news. He was able to ascertain that you . . ." Lord Hanton took a deep breath.

Rebecca placed her hand back on his arm. It wasn't much solace, but it seemed to help, for his next words were not as forced.

"You had, indeed, been on Regent Street shopping. You had made several purchases. Merchants remembered Elizabeth's enthusiasm and enjoyment. Just before two, a coach pulled up in front of Fitzroy's. The manager waited expectantly, hoping for a new customer. When no one alit, he ignored it. He was also disappointed that you did not arrive for your appointment.

"However, while he did not see you approach the shop, others did. They said that as you advanced up the street, a man got down from the coach. You seemed to know one another. After reading a slip of paper that he had passed you, he relieved you of your parcels and handed you and your sister into the coach. Then he entered as well, and the coach pulled away. No one heard the conversation nor recognized the man in question. Inspector Davis got many descriptions, but no two alike."

"The whole incident was so unremarkable in every particular that it was difficult at first for most witnesses to recall anything." Inspector Davis shook his head. "They did agree, however, that the man had the presence of one who has no occupation at all."

"A gentleman?" James sounded surprised.

"I am afraid so," Lord Hanton sighed. "It became all the more obvious when the note arrived."

"Note?" Rebecca took a deep breath, trying to control the tremors that were coursing through her limbs.

"Yes, it was slipped through the mail slot and discovered when Jeremy came to inquire about you and your sister. It did not demand money as we had expected. It ordered me to change my position on the letters of marque—privateers—and influence other members of the House to do likewise."

"Did it mention Elizabeth and me?" Rebecca saw her father look away just before he nodded. "What exactly did it say?"

"It wasn't what it said—although, that was bad enough . . ." Lord Hanton glanced up at Davis.

"It wasn't what it said or even the note itself, Misses Hanton, that caused the most grief," repeated the inspector. "In the envelope were your rings and those of your sister. Also, clumps of hair. All encrusted with blood. Even the note was stained with it."

Rebecca reached blindly for James' hand. "Hair, blood, and rings," she repeated. She felt the warmth of caring fingertips on hers, and the spiraling tension abated.

Hair, blood, and rings. It was more than a coincidence. The substance of her dreams . . .

Rebecca turned to Dr. Brant. "Do you think we might return to Dr. Fotherby today?" Her shoulders shook with an unexpected shudder. "I believe we should explore my dreams from a different aspect." Perhaps Dr. Fotherby would help her discover the meaning of her dreams that were looking more and more like memories. Memories that could help them find Elizabeth.

———•———

"Ah me," sighed Mrs. Fogel, with a contented and wistful smile. She peeked out from the framework of the dining room window. Before her in glorious beauty was the rolling drive, the cheerful front gardens, and the tranquility that she no longer took for granted. But it was not this wholesome view that elicited such a response from the busy housekeeper. It was the sight of a young gentleman bumping along atop the ungainly stride of the old pony, headed back to Welford Mills. His face was full of excitement, his step lively, and his manner dramatic and comical.

Mrs. Fogel could see the wild spirit of the boy returning, albeit, his costume was quite the reverse of his normal immaculate apparel: a borrowed plain brown jacket from Robert and a rather disheveled, somewhat soiled hat from Paul. And that mount of his . . . Why on earth would he choose to saddle up the old pony? Well, Mrs. Fogel could only guess that he and Henry were up to a mischief.

She turned from the window and back to the problem at hand. What to do about the piano? It was now quite out of tune. The man that had shown up at the kitchen door this morning had been the most inept tuner that she had ever encountered. He had talked and asked more questions than all the tuners she had dealt with over the years, combined. Normally they were quiet, solitary men, listeners, uncomfortable in conversation. This rascal had talked incessantly, and although he plunked at the piano, it did not seem to be the strings that interested him.

No. Mrs. Fogel had sent him packing with nothing to show for his work. The piano sounded no different than it had when the tuner had insisted its scales were off. She believed him a charlatan, trying to make a living with no aptitude for his field.

She should have known better. If nothing, his clothing should have given her a clue. The scoundrel was a mishmash. His jacket was ill-fitted while his shoulders were proud—and his walk almost insolent. And he was wearing the most inappropriate footwear. Shiny boots! Such vanity! They would not traverse the dusty roads for long. No, she didn't know what manner of game this wastrel was playing, but she wouldn't be the least surprised to learn that he had never tuned a piano in his life.

And she had said as much to Walter.

———— ◆ ————

CAROLINE PASSED THE scrap of stained wrinkled paper to Inspector Davis with both hands. "I don't know what help it could possibly offer, but there it is." Caroline was slightly out of breath, but it was as much from the fear of failure as the rush up the stairs. She returned to her seat and placed her trembling hands in her lap.

Inspector Davis pursed his lips and stared at the list for some moments. "Quality paper," he finally said. His voice rang out loudly in the silent anticipation. "Weathered but not torn. Not scribbled in a hurry, for the lettering is well-formed, slightly flowery, but not overly so. Not easily discernible as to whether it is a man or woman's hand." He passed it to Lord Hanton for another opinion.

With a shrug and a shake of his head, Lord Hanton passed it back.

Caroline turned to Davis. "Have you no suspects—not at all?" She hadn't meant it to sound like an accusation.

"Who would benefit the most were you to support the letters of marque?" James asked.

Lord Hanton lifted his shoulders in a quick shrug. "It's all about money, of course. Privateers are licensed pirates, for all intents and purposes. Most of the ship owners who fund the privateers are based in the West Indies, but certainly not all. Whoever decided to kidnap Rebecca and Elizabeth thought the vote in the House of Lords too tight, and that my influence would tip the balance in their favor."

"Someone who was prepared to risk all," Rebecca said quietly.

"Yes, indeed," Davis said. "But there are many who keep their cards close to the chest. Never revealing their true purpose. It is difficult investigating a crime that no one knows of except, of course, the criminals." Davis' voice barely contained his frustration as he glanced in Lord Hanton's direction. "It was put about that the Misses Hanton were visiting an aunt in Scotland. We have had to fabricate a stolen brooch as our pretext for inquiry."

Lord Hanton sat back in his chair and rubbed his forehead with vigor. "We have narrowed the field somewhat." He nodded to the inspector.

Davis took his pad from his pocket and flipped from one page to another, shaking his head all the while. "But nothing stands out. Perhaps if you were to enlighten us with your own *misadventures*, we might be able to piece some of it together."

Rebecca tried to describe the events leading up to their dash to London, in a detached neutral tone. Were it not for Daisy's demise, she might have succeeded. Still, Rebecca made it through the tale with only a few pauses and tears.

"Very wise," Davis said, upon hearing of the decision to put forth the story of Elizabeth Dobbins lying on her deathbed. He had been nodding throughout most of the narrative. "I wouldn't be surprised if the culprits did go into hiding initially. When no hue and cry went out with your recovery, they must have been puzzled. That would explain the time lapse before the first incident, which I know you believe was the attempted burglary, but it was likely your maid's disappearance."

Davis closed one eye and squinted the other, as if trying to read something from a great distance. Then he straightened up, easing his frown as he did so.

"The burglary took place the night of Daisy Bartley's half day. That would mean that they had questioned her and learned that Misses Hanton did not remember who she was, and certainly not who *they* were. That likely made them bold. But what Daisy couldn't tell them was that you were no longer in the servants' wing. You had switched to the other side of the manor."

Rebecca found it difficult to listen to Inspector Davis speculating about Daisy's last hours with such little pathos. She glanced away, staring sightlessly at the floor until a subtle touch distracted her. James hooked their little fingers together. It was a simple and deeply understanding gesture that brought a sliver of comfort.

"Still determined," Davis continued, "they tried to capture you after the funeral. But I must say that ploy of Paterson's was getting desperate. Although I can tell you why—the agent that Paterson made reference to was *our* agent." Davis nodded toward

Lord Hanton. "Paterson must have heard of the inquiries and realized that your recognition was imminent, hence the unsuccessful deception. Then in desperation, the murder attempt."

Rebecca faced her papa. "They thought me dead. But that assured them of their safety, and now they could use Elizabeth as their pawn. So they sent you another demand?" She saw the look passed between the inspector and her father; one nodded and the other said, "Indeed."

"What did this note say?" Rebecca asked.

"It was short and to the point. Made no reference to either you or Elizabeth," Lord Hanton replied. "It said I had to ensure a 'no' vote or else."

"That was all?"

Again the look.

"What do we do now?" James asked.

"The story of the Misses Hanton being in Scotland still stands, as long as word about last night has not gotten around." Inspector Davis' glance toward Lord Hanton was almost a reprimand. "I will increase the guard around the townhouse, but I think it best if you, Misses Hanton, remain behind closed doors as much as possible. With the exception of your visit to the doctor, of course."

Rebecca frowned at her father. "Lord Hanton . . . Papa," she said, the name feeling far from natural. "I am sick with worry about Elizabeth. I might not remember her directly but . . . she is my sister. I . . . I . . . All alone. No one to look to. Does she feel abandoned? Is she alive?" Becca lifted her hand, covering her mouth. Overwhelming nausea clawed up her throat.

"No, Becca, stop," her father said in a raw voice. "It will tie you in knots if you think about it too much. You will be unable to function, unable to do anything but fret." His words echoed with experience. "Better to imagine that Elizabeth is just fine, and it will not be long before we are all together." But tears swam in Lord Hanton's eyes, showing that his true thoughts brought him pain and sorrow.

———•———

"Keep talking, dear," Dr. Fotherby encouraged. "Don't lose yourself in what you are seeing."

Rebecca frowned. Easier said than done, much easier. The images and visions swirling before her closed eyes were clearer now than they had ever been. And clarity was proving to be more frightening than the shadows; the violence was no longer omnipotent but directed at her, and the pain was more acute. But, despite the fact that she could now read the labels on the boxes and describe the slats on the door, the men were still faceless and their words were without meaning.

Worse still, there was no sense of her sister.

"What does that mean?" Rebecca opened her eyes. She glanced at Caroline, who was standing by the door ready to intercept another dash of escape. Her friend raised her shoulders and pinched her lips.

"Nothing, my dear. Nothing at all." Dr. Fotherby sat back. "This is not a memory, but an interpretation of a memory. I think the harm you received at the hands of your kidnappers was so foreign to you that your mind is trying to make sense of it. You can't deal with parts of it, as yet. The fact that your recollection of this dream is becoming clearer is very hopeful. It tells us that you are able to handle more and more of what happened to you."

Dr. Fotherby had been pleased to learn that his nameless forlorn patient had been identified. He professed a belief that a full recovery was likely. Although "when" was the question that he could not answer.

"Let us not belabor that brain of yours anymore today. Rest yourself."

"Oh no, we cannot stop now. I must learn what I can of her." Rebecca shook her head and squeezed her eyes tightly together.

"Too much too soon might hinder more than help." Caroline touched her arm, rousing Rebecca from the chair.

With a nod of agreement, Dr. Fotherby smiled gently. "Yes, exactly. It would be best if you did not think on this until our next meeting. Then we can approach it with fresh eyes and ears and, perhaps, glean a little more."

Rebecca scrubbed at her temple. "But we cannot delay. My sister—"

"Yes, I know, dear. Truly, I understand the necessity of immediate action, but the brain is a tricky organ and, through my studies, I have learned that it is an ornery one as well. Push too hard and we might find ourselves propelled backward instead of forward. Or even worse, obliterating the recollection altogether." He raised his brows. "Come tomorrow. That shouldn't be too soon. We will try again."

Rebecca squared her shoulders, smiled wanly, and pulled down her veil. Caroline did the same and they left the doctor with deflated words of thanks. They joined Dr. Brant waiting in the outer office. With an acknowledging nod to the white-haired gentleman, Dr. Brant opened the office door and escorted the ladies to the waiting carriage.

Just moments after the departure of his last patient and her escorts, Dr. Fotherby heard his waiting room door open again. The office was now closed, and he was expecting no one. Looking around the room, he could discern no article left behind, nothing that needed retrieval.

"Dr. Fotherby?" a stranger's voice greeted him. It was an educated voice—that of a gentleman—and the doctor rose to meet him.

CHAPTER TWENTY

Kickin' up a Lark

The shifty, vile deceiver leaned nonchalantly over the children. He patted the fair-haired mop of one urchin, smiled, and handed the older one a coin. Walter could not hear the words but he knew that something, at last, was afoot.

Walter and Henry had watched Joe Smythe for the better part of a day and then for some hours this morning. Disguised and—of course—discreet, the boys had followed the villain through his trite conventional day. But once again, the results of their surveillance had proved to be less than noteworthy. Joe Smythe was extremely tedious in his habits, amiable in his greetings, and verbose in his conversations. He hid his treachery well.

Walter squinted at the urchins, now carrying the treasured coin into the bakery, and wondered at their involvement. He watched Smythe casually stroll down to a small clutch of villagers gathered before the inn and felt his expectations fade.

There was no need to poke Henry awake. Instead, he entertained the possibility of joining his friend for a few moments of shut-eye. Although Walter wondered at Henry's ability to do so leaned up against the stucco of the apothecary wall.

"Beggin' yer pardon, mister."

Walter and a suddenly wide-awake Henry turned to face the two young urchins that were addressing them. One boy was fair-haired and the older boy held up a package wrapped in newspaper. "This 'ere's fer you."

Instinctively, Henry reached out. Walter grabbed his arm. "What is it?"

"Crumpets," the boy said as if it were obvious. "The fella across the street asked us to gives 'em to ya."

"Don't forget what he says to say, Georgy." The younger boy's voice was quiet but firm.

"Ah yeah! 'E says he'll be havin' a bite in a tick and he thoughts you might be needin' somethin', too."

Walter lifted the edges of his mouth in an imitation smile. He grabbed the bag from the boy's hand and saw them scamper away with large grins on their faces. Turning to face Henry, Walter shook his head; his friend stared into the sky looking thoroughly disgruntled.

"He knows we are following." Henry ran his manicured hand down the sleeve of his jacket. A cloud of dust puffed out from his squared shoulders and then slowly dissipated. "What gave us away? How?" he muttered as he scuffed his stylish kid leather boots in the dirt.

Walter tossed Henry the package of crumpets and turned back to their quarry. He heard the ripping of paper behind him and the sounds of chewing. Out on the street, Mr. Smythe was no longer gabbing to Mrs. Cranley. In fact, he was no longer in sight.

"Henry, Henry!" Walter tried to distract his comrade from the interests of his stomach. "He's gone!"

Henry joined him at the corner; only their heads could be seen from Main Street.

They glanced in both directions and spotted a man standing by Dodd's and Tobin's. His body faced the store, as if he was interested in the bonnets in the window, but his head swiveled from side to side as if he too were seeking a face.

"Is that him?" Henry whispered so close to Walter's ear that it made him start.

"No," Walter hissed with disgust. "I believe that is Mr. Strickland. So much for—"

"What about *him*?" Henry interrupted, pointing.

Walter glanced in the direction of Henry's finger. A man with a cap pulled over his eyes stood partially hidden in the alley just past the Horn and Thistle. He leaned on the building next to him, emoting disinterest.

"Well, it's certainly not Smythe—" he started to say but, as the capped man glanced around, his gaze hesitated on the form of Mr. Strickland. Then the man turned his gaze directly to Walter and Henry.

As the man sensed their scrutiny, he raised his chin just enough for the sunlight to flood beneath his cap brim, illuminating his face. Black-and-gray peppered hair fringed a deeply tanned pock-marked face. It was a face that Walter could not forget—the coachman at Beth's accident. His eyes were hard and cold and he immediately lowered his chin, turned and hurried down the alley.

Walter ran across the street and down the alley after the coachman. Mr. Smythe was all but forgotten. Henry dropped the crumpets in his haste to follow Walter and dodged the wagon that had just avoided his distracted friend.

Walter arrived at the other end of the alley with an extra layer of grime, as his attention was not on the filth at his feet but the figure before him. He was just in time to see the capped man entering a neighboring lane, one that led out of Welford and back to the London road.

Henry, just steps behind, saw a dark form emerge from the shadows next to Walter. Henry called out a warning but not in enough time to prevent Walter from slamming into the shadowy figure. He tripped over a protruding cane and tumbled into a great heap. The sounds of the running coachman faded away.

———✦———

JAMES ROCKED WITH the motion of the carriage, but it did nothing to lull his thoughts. The case, as the inspector called it, was out of his hands now. His role was that of a spectator. It was a position that James loathed and as such rebelled, albeit in a very minor capacity.

James had told Davis of his suspicions about Hugh Derrydale's cousin, but from the outset Davis was not interested. James felt that he was onto something, but as his experience in these matters was limited, he had nothing other than his gut feeling to go by. James had not heard from Hugh since their encounter some days ago. It occurred to James that while Hugh could ask his mates about the ships and then report back to him, it would be much more efficient to pay a visit to the custom and excise house. They certainly would have the ship listings and their cargoes. If the passenger manifesto was not with them, they could tell him where it could be obtained. James was soon undertaking an excursion to St. Katherine's Docks.

This time the delay through the gates was slight. It became evident why that was so when, after passing under the warehouses, James noted that two of the larger ships docked there were fully loaded, awaiting the turn of the tide.

Sam made inquiries and stopped the carriage in line behind another. As James alit, he spied the figure of a young lady standing beside the carriage ahead. She shifted and craned her neck in every direction, watching the activities around her with fascination. She obviously enjoyed the bustle of the warehouses and docks, enthralled by its diversity and foreign nature.

When she looked in James' direction, he was shocked to recognize Miss Sophia Thompson standing on St. Katherine's Docks without a chaperone in sight. He stepped forward to offer his assistance when he heard a rustling within the carriage and a face emerged at the window.

"Lord Ellerby!" Mrs. Thompson squealed. Even Sophia flinched at her shrill tone. The large, frilled matron heaved herself off the seat and placed a pink-slippered foot on the step. She held her arm out as she allowed James to hand her down, and then simpered through the niceties of weather and health.

But Mrs. Thompson was all atwitter with anticipation and could contain herself only so long. "I hear your sister and her friend have come to Town." She glossed over James' inquiry of their locale with a quick reference to her brother's business, and launched herself straight into prying. "I had hoped to call on Miss Ellerby within a day or two."

Mrs. Thompson waited, looking hopeful. It was as if she expected an invitation.

"Do not trouble yourself, Mrs. Thompson. Miss Ellerby is staying with friends. She is not with me in Berkeley Square."

Mrs. Thompson's eyes grew wider. "Oh my, I hope there has not been a parting of the ways. Your family has always seemed to be so attached."

"Not at all, Mrs. Thompson, merely a gathering of school chums. They are all reminiscences and recollections, and as far as I understand having a grand time of it." James glanced toward Miss Thompson, hoping for a change of subject.

Sophia complied, but the topic was not far enough from its source. "Might they be going to the Blakeney Assembly tomorrow? Mama has talked of nothing else for days."

The girl's sigh was rather transparent. James knew that she had yet to be presented and had to live vicariously on the skirts of others until she could acquire her own standing.

"It must be the social event of the year," Mrs. Thompson added with sincerity.

"I believe there has been discussion about attending a concert at Vauxhall Gardens. Another event not to be missed. Quite a shame there is a conflict."

"Yes indeed, quite a cruelty to those who would have to be seen." A man, who looked to be Mrs. Thompson's brother, Mr. Gilbert Renfrew, had joined their group and their conversation.

Mrs. Thompson provided the introductions and James found himself pleasantly surprised. Mr. Renfrew, who was visiting from the West Indies, was as sturdily built as his sister, but his manner of dress hid rather than accentuated his bulk. His expression and easy conversation gave him the air of a man sure of his place in the world, and his ready smile held no guile.

It was no wonder that Walter had found the man affable, and

James felt comfortable with him immediately. It was hard to imagine that his closest kin was none other than the extravagant Mrs. Thompson.

"It is a great pleasure to have finally met you. My sister has often mentioned your name with delight, and I did so hope to make your acquaintance." Mr. Renfrew glanced over to his niece, who was not attending the conversation but instead watching the rough-and-ready men heaving their burdens from a nearby barge. "But perhaps now is not an ideal time."

James recognized the inappropriateness of the situation. He was not surprised when the gentleman bowed, and hustled the gawking Sophia and now-petulant Mrs. Thompson into their carriage. The whining plea to an inaudible remark could be heard as the carriage pulled away.

"But I thought it harmless, Gilbert. Oh my, don't be piqued with me."

The custom and excise house was a busy place, full of hustle and bustle, and clerks with so much more to do, now that a young gentleman had crossed their threshold. James was directed to an intense man whose desk was overcrowded with ledgers and papers. He looked as if he were in desperate need of his day off, and James was unsure if his request would add to the man's burden or if the change would bring relief. It was soon apparent that his presence represented the former rather than the latter.

"This is not my day for frivolous requests!"

James smiled, believing the man to be in jest, but he was not.

"Come back tomorrow. I have much to occupy me today."

"That would not be convenient." James kept his voice smooth and without rancor. "Perhaps if you were to allow me to look over your ledger, you could go about your routine with little disturbance?"

"Right, then!" The customs officer pushed not one, but a pile of ledgers toward him. "They are based on cargo. Do you know what it was that the ship carried? No, I thought not. Just an approximate date."

James flipped open the topmost book and within a few pages saw that it was going to be a formidable task, especially to someone unfamiliar with the abbreviations and codes. He snapped it closed and passed the smirking man his card.

"Send the names of the ships and their passengers to this address by day's end." James gave the official no time for further comment but immediately turned, replaced his top hat, and marched back out to his carriage.

———◆———

WALTER LAY SPRAWLED and perplexed in the dirt. One leg was bent uncomfortably beneath him, and his face was just inches from the ground. How on earth had he ended up in such a position? He pushed himself up onto his knees and took an assessment.

Both hands were encased in a combination of mud and manure. It was disgusting! He shook his hands to free them of the heaviest globs and then wiped them down the sides of his legs, leaving brown streaks across the dark material.

Robert's old coat was now completely soiled and split at the seams. Paul's hat had landed beneath Walter, crushing it beyond the possibility of reshaping. Although Walter was unhurt, he was slightly dazed. It took him a few moments to recall that he had been in hot pursuit of the mysterious coachman when he had tripped. Tripped over . . . over . . . was it a cane?

Walter's awareness returned to his surroundings and he was suddenly conscious of a set of flailing arms. It was Henry trying to protect his fallen comrade. With the best of intentions, Henry threw his arms about, as if to ward off invisible blows, all the while backing closer to his stricken friend and doing more harm than good.

It was no surprise that the menacing figure stepping out of the shadows was none other than Joe Smythe. "Are you all right? I am most dreadfully sorry. I did not see you there. I had expected you behind me, not before me." His words dripped with sarcasm and hypocrisy.

Walter felt a swell of outrage. He stood and grabbed Henry's arms, pinning them to his sides. He opened his mouth to deliver a proper set-down, then caught a glimpse of his dirt-embedded hands. His planned tirade was cut short by the realization that his manner of dress did not secure him the position he needed to vent his anger.

It would undoubtedly bring about questions for which he had no time. No, perhaps it was better if the man thought their interest a mere prank. That would allow them to continue their pursuit posthaste.

"Ne'er bet'er, sir." Walter used a broad accent that would have sent shudders down Caroline's spine had she heard him. "G'day." He turned in unison with Henry, but while facing the right direction, their feet could not get the grip they needed. Both were being held fast by the scruff of their collars.

"Not so hasty, my friends." Mr. Smythe's smile was less than genuine. "The boot is on the other leg. We need to talk."

Walter twisted and pulled, freeing himself from Mr. Smythe's grasp. "Sir. We 'as ta be goin'."

Henry tried to do as Walter had, but he found himself raised up just enough to feel great discomfort with the tight collar of his shirt, and breathing rather than freedom became his major consideration.

"Then you are in a bit of a predicament, are you not? Unless you can be in two places at the same time, for I mean not to let your friend go until you have answered some questions."

Walter met Henry's wild eye. "Nuffin' to talk h'about there, sir. We was just kickin' up a lark." He made a sudden lunge for the front of Henry's coat and jerked with all his might. For a moment it seemed the effort had been futile, but then Henry almost tumbled on top of him. They caught themselves just in time and became fleet of foot. They rounded the next corner and ran into the lane. There were no sounds of a chase.

Walter tried to talk as he ran. "Did you see . . . which way he went? The coachman?"

Henry shook his head and pointed at the same time.

Walter didn't understand the conflicting message but he continued to race up the street. The lane ended at the London road; a neighboring street led back into town. With hands on knees, they gasped for breath and agonized over which way to turn. This was the only breakthrough they had had thus far, and now it looked to be another dead end, thanks to Mr. Smythe.

Henry listened for running feet down the next lane while Walter scanned the road, looking for any kind of movement. After Walter's hopes had been raised and then dashed by a squirrel and a bluebird, he caught sight of a bobbing head. It was high up on the road, almost hidden by the thicket, but even from below, the hat atop the two-toned hair was visible.

"There!" he shouted. Before the word was out, he was back on the chase. The man continued apace and, if they were to have any chance of catching him, they had to narrow the gap. The figure up ahead disappeared behind the trees and Walter was afraid that, eventually, it would fail to reappear.

Walter knew the London road to have three turnoffs before it made its long and winding passage to Kirkstead-on-Hill. Just before the Torrin Bridge was Old Risely Road, just after it Mill Road, and then their own drive at Hardwick Manor. While two roads led to the great houses, Mill Road led to fields, cottages, and other paths.

When Walter and Henry arrived at the spot they had last seen the coachman with no one in sight, Walter did not despair. He ran past Henry and quickly crossed the bridge. "Come on," he called back as Henry hesitated, glancing around.

"Thought I saw someone behind us!" Henry called after his friend.

"Nonsense!" Walter shook his head. Really, there were times he quite despaired of Henry. "That makes no sense. We're the ones doing the following." He put on a burst of speed despite his aching sides, and turned down Mill Road.

———— ⋅—— ————

STANDING BEFORE THE large townhouse at No. 17 Brook Street, James was only vaguely aware of its grandeur and classic Greek lines. His mind was focused on the persons behind the facade— one in particular. This was the home of one Miss Rebecca Hanton. He could almost hear her laughter and see her younger self, peeking out from behind the draperies. It was the thought of the other face that should be standing beside her that urged him up the steps to request an interview with Lord Hanton.

James was led to the first floor study. The room was lined with countless tomes and was occupied not by one person but by three. Sergeant Waters stood sentry by the door, nodding to James as he entered. The other two stared at him from the other side of a massive desk.

Lord Hanton had been pacing, evidenced by his stance, which had come to a standstill with James' announcement. Inspector Davis, notebook in hand, had been making some sort of report. Their faces displayed expectation mingled with surprise.

Lord Hanton finally spoke. "Glad you are here, Ellerby. We are expecting Jeremy at any moment. There have been a few developments since we last met." He waved toward one of the mahogany leather chairs. "Sit, sit."

The tense atmosphere in the room overshadowed James' sense of urgency in regard to Hugh's cousin, Greg Brill. Instead of soliciting support for further inquiry into the man's whereabouts, James found himself caught up in the vortex of their anxiety. His first thought was of Rebecca. "Is all well in Marylebone?" he asked, sitting as directed.

"Yes, yes, indeed. Sergeant Waters has just returned from Dr. Brant's," Lord Hanton replied. "All is well but, under my orders, he did not inform them of the latest tragedy."

James blinked and then swallowed slowly, trying to control his surprise and concern. "Elizabeth?" he asked. But even as he uttered the name, James observed Lord Hanton, noting that the man's appearance was not that of deep mourning.

"No, no," Lord Hanton confirmed. He took a deep breath again before speaking. "Dr. Fotherby has been murdered. I have never met the man, but by all accounts he was an admirable and caring human being. It is a great shame."

"Oh no. How, when, why—" James was staggered, overwhelmed by questions.

Inspector Davis flipped back a few pages of his notepad and addressed the room in general in a gravelly, emotionless tone. "Dr. Stewart Fotherby's body was found yesterday evening by his maid-of-all-work just prior to eight. He had been left behind his desk in his inner office."

The inspector paused slightly. "As the doctor worked with many unstable and at times unsavory patients, this incident could have been unrelated to our investigation. However I had, of course, to verify that. What I found was just the opposite.

"Dr. Fotherby had a very regimented style of filing. Waters searched the office thoroughly and could not find Misses Hanton's file, not listed under her own name or that of Miss Ellerby, Miss Dobbins, or simply Miss Beth. According to the appointment book, Miss Ellerby and Misses Hanton were the last to see Dr. Fotherby the night he was killed."

James remembered the faith Rebecca had placed in Dr. Fotherby's abilities and knew that she would be devastated to learn of his death. As much as he regretted the need to speak to her about the tragedy, James had no intention of withholding the information from Rebecca. Though he understood why her father had done so.

Davis flipped his book shut with a *snap*. "I believe he was killed because of his help to Misses Hanton. We did not foresee this development. Few knew of Misses Hanton's memory loss, and even fewer knew of Dr. Fotherby's involvement."

The room was silent as James considered the implication. Could their actions somehow have brought about the doctor's death? It was a horrifying possibility.

"Besides the police, only your family and hers knew of the appointments." The inspector's stiff stance and sharp tone offered a sharp rebuke—almost an accusation.

James shook his head, frowned, and then shook his head again. "No, no one would say anything. No one."

Another pause allowed the inspector time to reconsider and adjust his tone. "You would be surprised how easily people pick information up: the housekeeper, boot boy, or cabriolet driver. While in most cases it would fall on disinterested ears and be forgotten, if it were whispered in the right direction . . . a great deal of information could be gleaned from a small observation."

James didn't believe this kind of thinking to be of any help at all. By following this hypothesis, all of London was suspect.

"Let us turn to the shopping list that was discovered in the cloak," Lord Hanton suggested. He pulled the piece of paper from atop the desk and waved it in the air.

Puzzled by the abrupt change of subject, James curled the corner of his mouth up in concentration and took a quick breath. He masked his huff by clearing his throat and shifting in his chair.

"Bear with me for a moment . . ." Lord Hanton hesitated, leaning toward the door. "We have learned that the writing on this paper is none other than that of our Jeremy Osborne. Mrs. Trimmer recognized the hand, and my housekeeper confirmed it. Jeremy, who visits this home daily at exactly the same hour. Jeremy, who knows where Rebecca keeps her journal. Jeremy, who rushed to inform us that he had spotted Rebecca just two days ago. And where had Jeremy seen her?"

"Outside Dr. Fotherby's office."

Lord Hanton and Inspector Davis nodded.

"You believe your own nephew would be associated with a plot to defeat a parliamentary vote and threaten the lives of your daughters?" James asked, his tone incredulous.

Lord Hanton nodded, his shoulders rigid and square. "Right from the beginning, it has been obvious that whoever is responsible knows the family. Jeremy arrives every day at this hour, whether it is to ingratiate himself with my daughters or simply provide himself with a meal, I have never determined. But today . . . he will answer a few questions."

Fury suffused Lord Hanton's face, and James wondered how Davis would control the viscount long enough to prize out those answers. However, James soon realized that Lord Hanton could keep himself in check, if circumstances demanded it. When the door finally opened to admit Osborne, Hanton greeted his nephew without any visible animosity.

"Good afternoon, Jeremy. I was beginning to wonder if you were going to put in an appearance today."

The skittish young man twitched his thin mustache as he glanced up at the clock on the mantel. It showed only a few minutes past four. He apologized needlessly and at length before noticing James and the inspector. He nodded a greeting, completely unaware of the tension in the room.

"Ah, so glad to see you again, Davis. I have been giving this situation a great deal of thought since . . ." Osborne's face contracted.

"What situation is that, Mr. Osborne?" Davis reopened his notepad.

"Politics and kidnapping. You know, privateers and all that. I wondered if there were any discussions about the letters of marque among our acquaintances."

Lord Hanton cringed when Osborne included himself as a member of the household.

"Then I recalled a discussion about that very subject just yesterday." He looked so triumphant that it was impossible to think of him as a great conspirator, unless he was a great actor as well.

"Really?" asked the inspector, displaying no true interest.

Oblivious, Osborne continued. "I happened upon Mr. Grey yesterday." He turned to his uncle. "Do you remember the two students from Lincoln's Inn, suitors of Becca's, studying law and full of opinions?"

Lord Hanton rubbed his forehead as if trying to think. James thought it likely that the man was trying to control his urge to strangle the boy. He pointed to the chair beside James. It put more distance between them. "Mr. Grey and Mr. Saunders."

"Yes, well, I had forgotten about them until yesterday. You know how bad I am with names." Osborne looked around the room. "Yes, indeedy, we talked politics. Are there any biscuits or sandwiches about?" He sighed dramatically when no one answered. "Do we know anything about Elizabeth yet?" he asked as an afterthought.

Davis shook his head. "Mr. Osborne, do you remember showing us the location of Misses Hanton's journal?"

"Yes, indeedy."

"At the time, I did not ask how you knew where it was."

Osborne waited and then realized it was a question. "Oh, Becca was going to pick me up a new set of gloves." He held his hands aloft, palms up; loose threads ran riot across his wrists. "She saw that my best pair were frayed and wanted to replace them. She was always so considerate. It was when she noted it in her journal that I saw where she put it."

"Did you yourself ever use the journal?"

"No indeedy, not. Why would I do that?"

Davis indicated to James that he should pass the list over to Osborne and they all watched as he looked it over. As he did so, a flush set his pale complexion ablaze.

"Oh, you don't mean write in it but"—Osborne kept his head down, not meeting anyone's eye—"read it." His voice was almost a whisper. "I didn't think it would be a problem." He handed the paper back to James quickly.

"Did you write that list?"

Osborne found the window of great interest. "Yes." His answer was rather clipped. "Copied it . . . from the journal."

Davis showed surprise at the young man's candor. "Why?"

Osborne offered them a deep sigh. "It all sounded so romantic."

"I beg your pardon?" Lord Hanton's voice was low and dangerous.

"He said he wanted to spend the afternoon with Becca, but he wanted it to seem like an accident. Have time with her away from all the others." He looked up, his eyes wide and dreamy. "There were always so many people around. I understood his need to impress her."

"Why did you not mention it earlier?" Davis asked.

"To what end?"

"How do you think the villains knew where the two Misses Hanton were going on the day she was kidnapped?" Davis demanded.

"You think this list was party to the abduction?" The look of horror that slid across Osborne's face showed that he, indeed, had not made the connection. "No, it could not be. Why—I saw him just yesterday."

Lord Hanton started. "Who, man, who?"

James stopped breathing as he awaited the answer, nerves taut and shaking from the effort to remain seated.

"Why, Mr. Grey, of course. I just told you. We happened upon each other just outside my rooms. Why, we even went to the pub together."

Davis stepped closer, almost menacing. "Did you happen to mention the Hantons?"

"Yes, indeedy. Why would we not?" Osborne said sounding indignant. "That was how we are acquainted. But I am not a complete fool; I did not mention the kidnapping. He thought Rebecca to be in Scotland and merely remarked that he was surprised to see her on Newman Street the other day. I said she was back visiting friends. I did not tell him where she was."

"Did Dr. Fotherby's name come up?"

"Yes, although I cannot remember in what capacity." Osborne looked up at his uncle hovering near his chair. "I was very general in all manner of topics." His voice had taken on a righteous quality.

"Jeremy, think very carefully. Did you mention the doctor's name first or did he?"

Osborne was silent for some time and then, again, his complexion began to darken. Without a word spoken, it was entirely clear that Jeremy Osborne had been manipulated and duped not once but twice. The young man had contributed, albeit unwittingly, to the kidnapping of his cousins and the murder of a worthy man.

CHAPTER TWENTY-ONE

Nightmare Revelations

With a shove, she stumbled into a room. Rough pale wood, signs and labels, boxes and crates surrounded her. She called a name: Elizabeth. She called and cringed with the blows that followed. Slippery flakes of sawdust danced under her feet. She hit the floor with a force that winded her; she lay gasping for breath.

A scream filled the room, but not from her lips.

She fought for air, still crumpled in a heap, sawdust in her mouth, her arms tied behind her back. Hands pulled her to her feet, yanking at her rings, cutting into her swollen fingers.

She called again and felt a sharp pain burst in her cheek. Another scream. Through a veil of hair, she saw a girl. Her expression was fury. And the fury spewed threats and curses.

A motion caught her eye. She watched the hummingbird dagger swing from hand to hand, side to side. She stared as it neared the source of fury.

She saw the danger. She shouted a warning, but it was unstoppable.

It lashed out. The girl crumpled; her hair floated out around her like feathers caught in a breeze.

All sound ceased as a red dribble grew into a puddle. It streamed across the floor, wending toward her, reaching for her.

A great weight pulled at her head, bending it down, and down again. A rough cloth came over her eyes.

She whispered the name and the bird began to laugh.

JAMES IGNORED EVERYONE in the room but Rebecca; he reached across the settee and held her, tucking her head under his chin. He rocked back and forth. He felt her shudder as her last words echoed in the silence of the drawing room. He glanced over her head to Caroline sitting beside Brant on the other settee. His sister's expression was not one of reproach or disapproval for his closeness to Rebecca, but rather horror at her description. The dream offered little hope of Elizabeth's survival.

Caroline eventually broke through the heavy silence. "The nightmare . . ." She cleared her throat. "The nightmare may not be what it seems."

It was just after luncheon, a meal in which James had been invited to join when he had come to deliver the sad news of Dr. Fotherby's demise, and the good news of the impending doom of their adversaries. He anticipated the announcement of the arrest and questioning of Mr. Grey very soon.

By the time James had left Grosvenor Square the previous day, it had become a hive of activity. Officers had been dispatched to the court of Lincoln's Inn and the rooms that many of the university students occupied. Still others were sent to question them and barristers at various haunts, such as pubs and gathering clubs. Their purpose was not only to apprehend Mr. Grey but also to inquire about his habits, company, and character.

The inspector, and thus Lords Hanton and Ellerby, were informed that Mr. Grey was a flamboyant gentleman with a leaning toward materialism. He was from a less than affluent but well-born family in Kent. However, the most intriguing information was that while Mr. Grey tried to hide his immoral behavior, he did nothing to mask the fact that he was a zealot, a man consumed with fervor, and deeply into the craft of debate. His choices of topics for argument were wide and varied, but among them, the letters of marque ranked high.

James had spent a fitful night awaiting word of Mr. Grey's arrest. Midmorning the next day, Davis' note finally reached Berkeley Square. James had immediately set out for Harley Street, dispatch in hand, to share the news.

Caroline and Brant were overjoyed to hear that Mr. Grey had been located and his arrest was imminent. But Rebecca was restrained, and when she recounted her nightmare, the room grew quiet—very quiet.

"Not a dream . . . not even a nightmare," Rebecca said, sitting up straight and meeting James' worried gaze. "It was a memory . . ." Words stuck in her throat and choked her, but her thoughts carried her further, beyond the memory, to the truth behind it.

Elizabeth was dead: The fury and the blood had been hers. Rebecca's sister had been murdered in front of her. Her only consolation was the speed with which Elizabeth had met her end.

It was not much of a consolation.

—— · ——

"IF YOU WOULD just listen to me," Walter tried again.

The parish deputy had found the boys, thus far, of little help and a great hindrance as he tried to carry out his new duties. They were constantly in the way in thought and in person. Had their families been from a lower class, he would have boxed their ears and given them a good dressing down. As it was, Mr. Strickland had only one recourse: He had to listen.

The deputy ushered the boys to the back office of the apothecary. It was not large and was serving a dual purpose for both shop and parish business. There were numerous piles of scribbled letters, notes, lists, and ledgers amassed and overflowing across a small rudimentary desk in the center.

Mr. Strickland pushed his spectacles up at the bridge of his nose and twitched his mustachio as if it itched. "Well?" he prodded.

Both boys spoke at the same time, but eventually Henry fell behind and Walter became the sole proprietor of the saga. "He was gone and any clue of him or his purpose has gone with him," Walter concluded.

Mr. Strickland looked at the solemn young men. He was glad to see that they had returned to their normal attire. They, in fact, stood out far less in their bright waistcoats than they did in their brown jackets. "You sure it be the coachman?"

"Without a doubt. Not only did we see him clearly, but he recognized us."

"What of Smythe? Was he not the man you thought part of the troubles?"

"They must be working together," Henry said, after a quick glance to his friend. "Had he not tripped Walter, we would not be here arguing the point."

"Strange, what with Miss Beth's removal, that they didn't vacate themselves. Yes, strange indeed." He was silent for some moments.

The clock ticked on his chimneypiece and muted voices drifted beneath the door. "Could Mr. Smythe and Mr. Paterson be one and the same?" Mr. Strickland asked.

"No," Walter said, shaking his head. Henry mimicked the motion.

Mr. Strickland curled his upper lip beneath his large mustache and nodded several times in succession. "All right. Then why do you think he headed for Mill Road?"

"Where else would he have gone? To return to town meant passing us."

Mr. Strickland smiled at the anxious faces. "Well, he could have jumped into the woods and hidden in the shadows. He could have run underneath the bridge and waited until you passed. He could have hidden behind the manor gate and reentered town after you had gone down to the mill, or he could have gone up Old Risely Road."

Henry shook his head. "That only leads to our hall."

"No. Lord Ellerby and I—" Mr. Strickland stopped, his eyebrows joined above his spectacles. "Lord Ellerby and I—" he repeated and then stopped again. He straightened. "You know there may be something. Lord Ellerby and I found a path. It led to the new ruins." His frown deepened and he turned to Walter. "Could we use Lord Ellerby's retriever? He was quite helpful last time. If we hurry, the track might not be gone."

"Of course, I will get Jack and meet you at Old Risely Road," Walter said.

Henry and Walter almost ran from the office, knocking into

Mrs. Cranley as they flung the door wide. Walter apologized as he helped the woman remain steady on her feet and then hastily made an exit.

Henry was already on the seat of the curricle, reins in hand. Walter had just enough time to leap up beside his friend before the horses were urged forward, cantering at first and then prodded into a run.

Walter whooped in delight. Delight with the speed, delight with the prospect of furthering the investigation, and delight with the day in general. The quest for clues and the apprehension of the criminals was once again at hand. Walter felt his blood quicken.

He ignored the critical stares of the townsfolk. High spirits were seldom appreciated.

Walter thought he saw the figure of Joe Smythe watching from a clutch of tradesmen chatting by the side of the road, but Walter cared not. He was off to catch a villain. Joe Smythe was of little consequence when placed next to the dastardly coachman with salt-and-pepper hair.

BRANT WAS APPALLED. "The cold and calculating cheek. It's monstrous!" He shook his head in disbelief. "To sit under the Hanton roof, to drink from their cups and eat their cakes, all the while watching and hatching a nefarious plan!"

James nodded in agreement. "Not only that, but Grey was considered one of Rebecca's suitors. He fooled her into thinking he had formed an attachment."

James and Brant had sequestered themselves in the Harley Street study.

"It does explain why she got into the carriage without hesitation," Brant remarked. "She would trust him. He had but to say there was a problem with the family and she, along with Elizabeth, would have been grateful for his help. Can you imagine, grateful—that murdering wretch! Hellfire and damnation, they had better catch him soon!"

There was a slight tap at the door, and before either had a chance to answer, it opened.

Caroline's head peeked round the edge. "Is everything all right?"

"Yes, of course," Brant answered, too quickly.

"That is good to hear," she said. "This was just delivered for you, by way of Berkeley Square."

James took the offered papers with a quizzical look. He tore the seal and found not one but two sheets inside from the Customs and Excise Office. Both were covered in lists—vessels of every shape and size in or around the port of London in April. The clerk had had his revenge, supplying too *much* information. The lists would require a thorough study to glean anything. James snorted, folded the papers, and stuffed them into his pocket.

"I thought to learn," James explained, "of Greg Brill's accomplice through dock records, but now that we have Grey's name, we have no need."

"What leads us to believe that Mr. Grey is indeed the man behind the kidnapping?" Caroline asked him with an eyebrow arched.

Before James could reply, Lord Hanton pushed the study door open fully and entered with Rebecca on his arm. "I have news," he told the group. "Grey has been apprehended. And, even as we speak, is on his way to Scotland Yard where Inspector Davis will be questioning him. Elizabeth will be returned to us soon." Lord Hanton patted Rebecca's arm.

James watched Rebecca turn her lips up in a halfhearted attempt to look hopeful. She did not expect a happy reunion. Had he been closer, James would have taken her into his arms to offer creature comfort . . . not in front of her father—a pat on the arm would have had to do—but he was too far away and a pat would be unimpressive. Rebecca's father would have objected and it was all moot as they seemed to be going back out the door. James sighed and tapped Lord Hanton on the shoulder to get his attention. He quietly asked if Grey's accomplices had been caught.

Lord Hanton glanced at Rebecca and then at Caroline. "It might be best discussed when the ladies are out of earshot."

"Really?" Rebecca looked nonplussed. "After all that has transpired? Surely I have proven my ability to withstand shocks. After all, if I can survive being kidnapped, I can certainly deal with a discussion about it."

"Yes, yes, quite right." Lord Hanton still looked uncomfortable. "Though this is not truly about the kidnapping. It's more about . . . ahem . . . well . . . Grey was found in a house of . . . a house of ill repute. There were others with him, mostly students, but there was"—his eyes grew larger—"an older man with them. Sergeant Waters couldn't say much but that he was described as going gray. A salt-and-pepper shock of hair."

Hanton started across the hall but turned back for another quick comment. "I wouldn't be surprised to learn that we not only have your Mr. Paterson in custody, but the coachman as well."

With that, Lord Hanton disappeared into the drawing room.

Just as James was about to do the same, he felt himself held back. He looked down to see Brant's hand on his arm, pulling him aside.

"I have been wondering," his friend said in a hushed tone, "and questioning why it was that Grey did not kill Mr. Osborne."

James nodded. "I had wondered about that, as well. Perhaps he had no opportunity, too many people around or some such."

"It is a strange and twisted mind that would conceive to kill a man," Brant said, "who might identify you as a murderer, all the while letting go of another man who would."

"TRY TO THINK of something else, Rebecca," James whispered softly. They were standing before the tall row of windows of the Harley Street drawing room, close but not touching. She had drawn back the draperies under the guise of getting a better view of the busy street below. But, in fact, she was more aware of the small group gathered in the center of the room than the scene before her eyes.

Lord Hanton had taken a position beside the settee on which Caroline and Dr. Brant were seated. They discussed the weather; it was a banal, distracted conversation. The wait was difficult for everyone.

The imagery of her dream replayed in her head. She needed to understand. She wanted someone to tell her that she was mistaken, that it wasn't a memory, that she didn't watch her sister die.

Turning her head, Rebecca looked back into the room. The topic was now a concert that evening at Vauxhall Gardens, a performance of Handel's *Water Music*. She shook her head, frowning; a concert was incongruous, frivolous, unworthy.

"You need . . . *we* need a distraction," Lord Hanton explained, and then scrubbed at his face. "There is nothing we can do until . . . I would not see you sick from waiting. Your poor brain is only recovering."

"I will not collapse with worry, Papa. I am made of stronger stuff."

"Yes, indeed. But a distraction can do nothing but help." He walked over to Rebecca still standing by the window, and took both her hands into his own. "You must go."

At first, Rebecca couldn't believe him to be serious. "I couldn't possibly." But she saw that any reference to her highly charged emotional state would only make him push the point further. "It would not be safe," she finished lamely.

"Grey is deep within the hollows of Scotland Yard and his henchman with him. Still, I could engage the peelers to follow you to the concert. I will return to Grosvenor Square to await word." He squeezed her hands in what was likely meant to be reassurance, but he ruined the attempt by swallowing visibly and lifting his cheeks in an entirely false smile.

———⋅———

James was in a quandary. While on one hand he understood Rebecca's distress, on the other, he, like Hanton, saw that it could be detrimental to her heath. She needed to put her mind on something else. It was no longer dangerous to venture out—certainly not with the peelers in tow and Grey in jail.

As Hanton pressed for an agreement from his daughter, James saw the plaintive look that Rebecca cast him. He took Rebecca's hand, entwined their fingers, and led her to the next window. Lord Hanton snorted and returned to the center of the room.

"It might help *his* distress, Rebecca. To believe—even if

falsely—that you are occupied. That you are not suffering, as he is. I believe he wants to protect you." James lifted her chin so that he could stare into her eyes. The ache there almost undid him. He caressed her jaw with his thumb, wishing her father were not just feet away. He wanted to kiss her, gently, tenderly. Help her forget, even if only for a moment.

He resigned himself to a smile. "Your father believes the end is in sight. To him, we are just hours away from knowing about your sister—for good or ill, at least we will know." He had to hold her hand tightly as she tried to pull away. "He sees your keyed-up state and wants to alleviate it. There is nothing any of us can do but wait—distraction might make the time go faster."

"It won't," Rebecca said firmly, and then she closed her eyes briefly. She took a deep breath before continuing. "But if—" She glanced over at the forlorn figure in the middle of the room. "But if my going to Vauxhall tonight will relieve him, even for a moment, then I will do so. For I believe we are heading into dark days when something such as a frivolous concert will provide no reprieve at all."

NATURALLY, Henry was the first to declare their search worthless. He had no emotion, other than ego, vested in the project. "We have been looking for hours, and more important, I have missed tea."

Walter thought that his friend had also missed the intent of sleuthing entirely, and was not impressed. He, on the other hand, had not expected an easy game of it. More than two weeks had passed since the original discovery of the trail, and in that time nature had filled in as many nooks and crannies as it could in the spirit of rebirth. There appeared to be no broken branches or mis-shapen shrubs anywhere.

Eventually, Jack had found the scent and tracked it to the ruins, but from there, he was stymied. Starting off in one direction, the dog would then turn and head in the opposite. Clearly, the retriever was baffled, forcing the deputy and the boys to walk the open ground, heads down, looking for a trail, but the hard earth gave up no clues.

Walking across to the cliff edge, Walter postulated that a cave or opening of some sort might provide a refuge or at least a wait-ing spot for the coachman. But try as he might, he could not find a way down the cliffs. It seemed virtually impossible.

"I believe we must call it a day," Mr. Strickland said as they turned from the cliffs and stood facing the hall. It loomed large behind the ruins; light was beginning to show through the lower windows as the evening came on.

They stood and stared for some minutes.

"Has there been any new hires at Risely?" Mr. Strickland asked eventually.

"No idea." Henry shrugged. "Workers for the ruins, of course, but other than that you'd have to ask Dipple." He referred to the family butler.

"Indeed." Mr. Strickland left the boys where they were stand-ing. Walking back over the field, his expression was thoughtful, distracted.

Walter shook his head and looked around. "Henry, have you seen Jack?" The retriever had disappeared.

Henry pointed to the other side of the drive. "He was there, last I saw him." He turned away from the sight of Mr. Strickland's receding back. "I'll help you look," he sighed. "But lawks, I'm done to a cow's thumb."

With slow, tired steps, they made their way back across the heath. As they reached the drive, they could hear echoed barking.

Walter laughed. "He's gone into your ruins." He whistled for Jack to come.

Henry perked up. "Do you want to see them?"

"Henry, I hate to point out the obvious, but I can see the keep from here."

"Not the inside."

"Inside?"

"Yes . . . I am not supposed to go in." Henry glanced up at the hall. "But I have been dying to take a look. I'm *sure* it's safe."

"Lawks, really? You never told me."

"I did, too, but your mind was on other things. Kept interrupting me. Cared more about the color of your waistcoat—not that I blamed you."

Walter ignored his friend's sullen tone and waved for Henry to show the way.

One of the walls had been built as if the foundations had fallen and now lay scattered at its sides. They provided stepping-stones up the five-foot climb and then down into the enclosure. It was a clever way to hide the entrance.

The center of the keep was open and featureless, the edges lined with fractured half towers and crumbled windows, but in the northeast corner, the tower seemed partially intact. An arched opening led underneath, and once inside, the facade of antiquity faded away. Walter paused to allow his eyes to adjust to the half-light and he listened.

Jack's barking was no longer continuous but irregular and sounded just as distant.

"Could he have fallen down something?" he asked Henry.

"There is a dungeon."

"A dungeon?"

"Yeah. *She* wanted to add something no one else would have in their ruins." Henry seldom referred to his mother by name; he snorted. "Uncle wrote to suggest a dungeon. I know he was kidding, but *she* took him seriously and the dungeon was added."

The barking was getting weaker and staccato. "Where is this bloody dungeon?" Walter could feel his pulse quickening; Jack's bark was suffused with alarm.

"*I* don't know. I've not been in here before."

Stumbling to the back wall, Walter ran his hand across the rough surface, feeling his way forward. He almost fell when the wall opened up into a stairwell. Jack's barking echoed up from below. Rushing ahead of Henry, Walter saw a light below, making his journey easier as he descended. They ran down the passage, following the sounds of the dog.

If they had been less concerned, they would have been thinking a little more clearly and paused to consider the existence of lit torches in an unoccupied tunnel. However, Walter entertained no thought of his own danger or conceived of what else he might find, until he ran past a thick wooden door and into the heavily shadowed room beyond. Here they were forced to stop and recognize the folly of their actions, for the retriever was not alone.

Three sets of human eyes were locked on them. The pockmarked face immediately caught Walter's attention; the coachman's expression was not of surprise, but of satisfaction.

CHAPTER TWENTY-TWO

Trapped

As the last strains of the violins faded into the cavernous dome of the rotunda, Rebecca breathed in deeply. It had been a mistake; she should never have relented. The concert was not a distraction; it was an intrusion. She had not stopped thinking of Elizabeth through the entire performance. She felt twitchy and wanted to return to the carriage immediately. The excursion's only value had been a *slight* lifting of despair in her father's expression as he had waved them off.

Rebecca shifted forward on her seat so that she might catch Caroline's eye, hidden behind James. "Lovely. Shall we go?" she asked her companions, realizing the rigidity of her back over the past hour.

"I believe this is the intermission," Caroline said. "Do you not wish—?" Something in Rebecca's expression answered her query before it was fully expressed. Caroline laid her arm on Dr. Brant's and they all rose. "We can admire the gardens on the way to the gates," she said airily.

Outside, the small gaslights twinkled brightly, eclipsing the stars far above. The smell of the famous Vauxhall ham wafted through the air, increasing Rebecca's unceasing nausea. The crowds were full of the indulged and the indulgent, replete in the latest fashions, talking to one another with great animation and little decorum.

With few known acquaintances, Rebecca's small party of four could expect no interruption as they followed the Grand Walk to the front gates and the waiting carriage. It was a joy to be so judiciously ignored.

Then Rebecca caught a stare from the shadows, and she stiffened and tripped. She clutched at James' arm for support.

"Is all well?" Caroline asked.

"Yes, of course," Rebecca answered mindlessly, her eyes lingering on the shadowed figures of the policemen, watching them from the crowd. "I am just unaccustomed to living in a glass bowl," she added.

James placed his other hand atop her arm while glancing into the crowds as well. "Not much longer," he said quietly. "I'll let them know that we are leaving early." But before James could do so, they were accosted by an overly loud and high-pitched voice meant to demand attention.

"Miss Ellerby, Miss Dobbins. How grand to see you!" Mrs. Thompson shouted as she stepped into their circle. A man of similar build and slight resemblance stood quietly at her side. "Oh my, I knew, I just knew there would be a happy meeting. And look, here we are, all together."

"Mrs. Thompson, this is a surprise. I though you were attending the Blakeney Assembly this evening."

The gentlemen bowed, the ladies curtsied, and James introduced

Rebecca and Caroline to Mr. Gilbert Renfrew. Rebecca noticed that James still referred to her as Miss Dobbins. Discretion and Mrs. Thompson were not likely to sit well together. Any resulting confusion would be resolved at a later date.

"No, well, yes but . . . I heard that the Assembly was to be a terrible crush. And being that I am so much more of a musical person, I persuaded Mr. Renfrew here"—she patted his arm as if they would not know to whom she referred—"to forgo the ball and have a quieter alfresco in the Gardens. There is no brother kinder."

"Besides," Mr. Renfrew added with a perfectly straight face, "it is one of the social events of the year."

"Oh my, yes."

Mrs. Thompson seemed completely unaware of her brother's sarcasm, as well as the wink he sent in Rebecca's direction.

"Why, I just bumped into Lady Charlotte, and who should be with her but Lord Ingham's daughter? Well, I must say . . ." And she did just that. Suddenly the bastions of society were laid bare by the probing and tattling of Mrs. Thompson.

"I beg your pardon," James interrupted, turning toward Rebecca. "I must leave you for a moment . . . before we set off." Without mentioning the necessary, it was implied that James needed to answer the call of nature; Rebecca knew his desertion was, in fact, to inform the peelers that they were heading to the gates.

Mrs. Thompson sniffed. She snapped her jaw shut and pursed her lips.

"I will go with you," Brant said. "See a man about a horse."

Rebecca almost laughed at his desperation to get away from Mrs. Thompson's prattle.

James turned to Mr. Renfrew. "Would you mind if we left our lovely ladies in your capable hands for a few moments?"

Mr. Renfrew looked pleased. "Most willing to oblige." He bowed.

The moment the gentlemen left their company, Mrs. Thompson resumed her blathering as if there had been no interruption. Mr. Renfrew caught the movement of Rebecca's shoulders lifting in a sigh. She straightened immediately, but the man just smiled. He scratched at his cheek and then turned his head, squinting at one group of revelers and then another, dismissing each with a headshake. Eventually, Mr. Renfrew's attention wandered to something behind them.

He frowned and quickly bowed to the others. "If you will excuse me."

Rebecca was quite surprised by the hurried leave-taking, and looked over her shoulder. She watched as Mr. Renfrew rushed to meet James and Dr. Brant. Their conversation appeared animated, but the words did not carry across the path. She wondered at its meaning.

Caroline tipped her eyebrow in Rebecca's direction but said nothing. Instead, Caroline turned back to Mrs. Thompson. "You were saying?" Neither Caroline nor Rebecca were particularly interested in the woman's dissertation about the similarities of various flower beds but it was politic to appear so.

When Mr. Renfrew returned to the group moments later, neither James nor Dr. Brant accompanied him. Rebecca turned to see where they might be, witnessing their hurried departure around the side of the rotunda. She turned to frown at Mr. Renfrew, asking for an explanation.

Mr. Renfrew opened his mouth and then closed it again. There was a hesitance to his manner. "I am afraid—" Mr. Renfrew glanced first at his sister and then directly to Rebecca. "I am afraid that Dr. Brant and Lord Ellerby are going to be unable to join us for the remainder of the evening."

Rebecca's pulse began to quicken, her stomach churned and her mouth went dry. There was no reason to think that this odd situation had anything to do with Elizabeth, but Rebecca had thought of little else all evening.

"Well, really. How singular!" Mrs. Thompson huffed.

"In fact, my dear." Again he turned to Mrs. Thompson. "We have been requested to escort Miss Ellerby and Miss Dobbins home."

"Oh my, before the end of the concert? You cannot be serious."

Mr. Renfrew straightened his shoulders and his waistcoat. "Yes, Margaret, I am serious. It seems to be an urgent matter and I was asked to undertake it." He offered his arm to Rebecca.

"Perhaps it would be best to look for a hackney carriage. Your carriage, Miss Ellerby, will be near impossible to extract."

Mrs. Thompson was not impressed or compliant. "Oh, Mr. Renfrew," she whined to her brother, "there will not be room for everyone. We will be terribly overcrowded."

Rebecca felt the stiffening muscles of Mr. Renfrew's arm beneath her own but he did not, as she feared, create a scene. "You are right, my dear. I cannot ask you to miss the concert while at the same time threatening your health in an overstuffed hackney. Three is possible; four would be horrendous. I could not do that to you."

Mrs. Thompson simpered.

"It would not suit," he continued in his calm tone. "The answer is obvious: I will find another party whom you can join. No need for you to forgo the pleasures of such a night."

"But—but—" Mrs. Thompson sputtered.

Mr. Renfrew ignored her protest. "That way, you will have the enjoyment of the music and plenty of room in the carriage home." He took his sister's arm and placed it on his own. Then he pulled her across the walk to a group of revelers that she had, only some moments ago, been criticizing. Mrs. Thompson greeted the party with great enthusiasm.

Rebecca and Caroline waited patiently . . . with the *appearance* of patience. They had not waited long when Mr. Renfrew returned and offered them each an arm. The three strolled companionably toward the garden gates.

Rebecca had restrained herself thus far, knowing the proximity of the other attendees was too close for intimate conversation. However, as they approached the gates, the crowds were sparse, and she felt it now possible to inquire. "Please, Mr. Renfrew, what exactly did Lord Ellerby say?"

The stocky man looked down at her as if just realizing the tension that he had caused. "My dear, nothing untoward." He squeezed her arm. "Though he did request that I not leave you alone and take you back to Harley Street right away."

"Nothing else?"

"Well, he did say a few other things." He patted her hand. "Perhaps they will mean more to you than they did to me." He paused for a moment as they entered the gates one at a time. "Lord Ellerby said something about encountering an inspector."

"Inspector Davis?"

"Yes, I believe you to be right. He apparently gave Lord Ellerby some sort of information. It required him to leave right away. I assume it must be serious, but nothing to worry your pretty little head about."

Rebecca could only wish that were true.

Beyond the gate, they wound their way through the numerous barouches, cabriolets, and broughams. Mr. Renfrew guided them to the outer circle, toward a serviceable, if not stellar, hackney carriage.

Rather than wait for the coachman to jump from his seat, Mr. Renfrew opened the door himself and handed them in. He then jumped aboard, shouting, "Harley Street, and be quick about it!"

Rebecca and Caroline, squeezed almost on top of each other, turned to stare at Mr. Renfrew. "Did my brother say where he was going?" Caroline asked.

Mr. Renfrew was looking out the window, watching the maneuvering of the coachman. He turned back to Caroline. "Yes, my dear."

"Could you take us there instead, please?"

Mr. Renfrew frowned and started to shake his head.

"Yes," Rebecca pleaded. "Yes, could you take us to where the gentlemen are going? As you intimated, we are aware of the cause of Lord Ellerby and Dr. Brant's abandonment. It is serious and involves us directly."

Mr. Renfrew sighed. "It is against my better judgment but—" He nodded a sharp jerk. "Fine. If, however, we encounter any problem or any unsavory conditions when we get there, we will immediately turn about." His jaw was set and his voice firm.

Rebecca glanced out the window. The carriage had pulled free and was passing the stationary tangle of waiting vehicles. Sam, halfway down the line, was sitting on the box of the Ellerby carriage, feet up, relaxed, and chatting with his neighbor.

She wished that there were some way to inform him that James had gone with the inspector, but she knew that her voice would not carry. However, Sam looked up just at the right moment and Rebecca lifted her hand in recognition. She was considering the indelicacy of shouting when Mr. Renfrew leaned out of the window, blocking her view.

"Driver, Driver!" he shouted. "Change that to St. Katherine's Dock. Hurry!"

The carriage jerked slightly as the driver urged the horses to a faster pace.

Rebecca let out her breath. Finally, she had time to consider what it was that might have happened. There was the unspeakable, which might explain why she and Caroline had been directed home. But there was also the possibility that while Elizabeth's location had been pried from Mr. Grey, it had not yet been verified. She felt a touch and looked down to see Caroline's hand on hers. Rebecca squeezed it in reassurance and then leaned back. It might be a long night.

———◆———

"THIS IS THE night for visitors, huh, Roy! I mighta guessed how it would be." While the pockmarked coachman was smiling at his guests, he was also slowly drawing a knife from its sheath at his waist. The blade was wide, honed, and lethal in appearance.

It also bore no resemblance whatsoever to a hummingbird, causing the mixed sensation of relief and disappointment in Walter.

The room was not overly large, and despite its lack of age, already had a dank smell as well as the pungent odor of filth. The torches, while providing some light, cast enough shadows and smoke to confuse Walter at first.

When accustomed to the gloom, Walter saw that the dungeon was strewn with straw, bedding, and foodstuffs. Crates and boxes served as tables and chairs, and extra torches were piled against the stone wall.

The ceiling was high above them and there was a small, ineffective window well beyond their reach. The only other exit from the room, besides that from which they had entered, was opposite the boys, but it was both grated and bolted. The bolt was accessible from this side of the room, suggesting that it was an enclosure beyond, not a hall.

Walter and Henry were poorly placed in the center of the room. To the right of them, Mr. Smythe knelt beside Jack. He patted the dog calmly while staring at the boys. His left hand, around Jack's collar, was holding the dog fast.

The coachman was only a few yards ahead of Walter. His sneer grew larger and more malevolent with each passing moment. That put the man the coachman had referred to as Roy by the door. It was not surprising when Roy used his advantage to kick it shut, closing off their only retreat.

The *bang* echoed ominously.

Walter swallowed hard and tried to think of their options.

Henry was closest to the door but also uncomfortably near to the fairly tall, ill-shaven Roy. There was something familiar about his toothless grin and fringed hair.

Henry must have been of the same mind. "Mr. Norton, is that you?" Henry almost looked relieved. "I didn't recognize you at first, in this half-light. I thought you had left town when the ruins were finished."

Henry's tone became less fearful and more conversational with each passing consonant. "It's me, Henry, Henry Thompson." He smiled at the man and his posture began to relax. "You've done quite the job down here. Amazing! Indeed, quite the thing."

"Oh, I know who you is, Mr. Thompson." Roy Norton's tone fell far short of a welcome. "You an yer mate over there has been plaguing us since the day this here venture started. It were planned for months an' months. Then along comes you two dolts, getting in the way. Causing h'accidents, an' stopping us from getting that which belongs to us. If it weren't for you twos, I wouldna been living down here, like a rat, for the better part of a month." Roy's gravelly voice was eerily calm.

Henry swallowed and, even in the dim light, Walter could see him turn pale.

Roy leaned forward and the torchlight shone off his partially bald head. Walter realized where he had seen Mr. Norton before and it wasn't as a newly hired builder at Risely. No, this was the man that he had horsewhipped away from Beth. This was one of the men that had attacked them on Mill Road.

Now Walter *knew* they were in trouble. Three against two. Three with more weight, years, and experience, not to mention the knife.

"Well, we certainly didn't mean to disturb you. Just our boyish curiosity, is all. Most rude of us, really. We had better be going and get out of your way. We can see that you are busy." Walter glanced over with supposed interest to the cribbage game laid out on the nearby crate. "Red is in the lead." He took a half step back.

"Ah, ah, Mr. Ellerby. We has only just gots ya here." The coachman waved his knife in Walter's direction. "You can't be leaving just yet. Not when it's taken us so long to gets you here. Thought you'd never figure it out."

Walter swallowed and leaned back.

"Get us *here*?" Henry's voice was more of a squeak.

"Lawks, yes! You bacon-brained puppies! It were hard getting your attention. Thicker than the bible, you two!"

"Why—?" Henry croaked and then cleared his throat. "Why would you want to get our attention?"

Roy Norton laughed none too kindly. "We just wanted to thank ya proper is all, for yer meddling. But we had our orders an—"

"Nothing were said," the pockmarked man interrupted with enthusiasm, "about if you were to find yer way down 'ere."

The maniacal glint of excitement in the coachman's eye was not lost on Walter.

"Buts I gots a question afore we gets down to thankin' yer."

Mr. Norton opened and closed his fists several times as if in preparation.

Henry looked around, likely for a weapon. The only thing within easy reach of him was the broken lid of a crate.

Walter's options were about as useful: the torches against the wall or the straw at his feet. He shifted in his boots, wondering if agility would help. "Certainly. What question would that be?"

"Who's yer buddy here?" The salt-and-pepper head jerked toward Mr. Smythe.

Walter frowned. "He's with you."

Mr. Smythe was still kneeling at Jack's side. He continued to pat the dog slowly and methodically. He stared back at the inquiring eyes with a nonchalant manner.

"All right's then, who are ya?" the coachman barked. "And make it snappy, or yer gonna feel this steel."

"Really, my good man," Mr. Smythe said casually. "Were you to stab me, you would lose what little advantage you have."

Walter was impressed with Mr. Smythe's bravado, but the coachman was obviously not.

"Stupid gaffer, I gots all the advantage."

Joe Smythe dropped his hold on Jack and slowly rose. "I do not think you do."

The retriever bound over to wiggle and waggle around Walter's legs. But he was not paying attention to the dog.

All Walter's focus was centered across the room. He stared at the gentleman with the flintlock pistol in his hand.

As THE CARRIAGE left Vauxhall Gardens farther and farther behind, the traffic dispersed and the delays became fewer. When at last the rocking motion became rhythmic and constant, Caroline sat back against the cushioned wall. They were moving along now at a good clip, cutting across the south shore of the river toward the London Bridge.

Caroline was pleased to note that, though subdued, Rebecca showed little sign of being distressed. She simply remained silent while Mr. Renfrew chatted about the West Indies.

"So, do you plan to stay in England for the summer, Mr. Renfrew?" Caroline asked. She glanced out the window, willing the bridge to come into sight.

"Yes, I believe so. My business might require me to remain until Michaelmas, but I cannot stay much longer. Cannot leave Saunders alone on the island for too long."

Caroline frowned, not understanding. "Saunders?" she asked.

Mr. Renfrew laughed. "Nathan Saunders. He is my partner in Jamaica. We go back to the days when we were not much older than you are now. We were wild and impetuous."

It was hard to see this smiling, middle-aged gentleman as a wild, impetuous youth but then perhaps, Caroline thought, her future children might not believe her own story of murder and intrigue. Time would tell.

"Yes, we left England to make our fortune in foreign parts." Mr. Renfrew patted his generous belly with satisfaction. "And while it didn't happen right away, it did happen eventually."

Caroline found it hard to focus, even though his continuing stories of island life were humorous and urbane. Finally the sound of the horses' hooves upon the road changed, and she looked out to see that they were approaching London Bridge. She glanced over to see Rebecca pulling her gaze from the window as well, and they lifted their cheeks at each other for reassurance.

It was just a short distance from the north side of the bridge to St. Katherine's Docks, but it felt interminable. As they approached the gates, the conversation lagged. The streets were quiet. The night was well advanced and a change in temperature had brought with it the inevitable wisps of fog.

Mr. Renfrew alit to speak to the gatekeeper and then rejoined them with a serious face. The carriage passed under the warehouse arch and turned left. It passed row after row of warehouses and sheds built tightly together with few alleys and walks.

"Well, now that we are here . . . ," Mr. Renfrew interrupted the silence. He glanced from Rebecca to Caroline, his face clouded. "I apologize if this is an indelicate question, but might you explain why we are here?"

Caroline felt the pace of the horses ease off, and the carriage came to a standstill.

—•—

REBECCA SHIFTED TOWARD the door. "I am afraid I cannot explain fully as yet, Mr. Renfrew. But I can say that Inspector Davis and Lord Ellerby are trying to help me retrieve a lost item. They are most diligent men and to have relied so heavily upon your good favor, to see us safely home, could only mean that it has been found."

"Really! But, my dear, why do you need to be present when it is found? I believe I should not have been persuaded. I should have taken you straight to Harley Street as Ellerby requested."

"Oh no, sir." Rebecca grabbed the door handle and stepped out of the carriage before she had finished her sentence. She was deathly afraid that the kindly gentleman would order the carriage away. "I need to be there when—"

Rebecca looked down the street, ahead of the carriage. She couldn't see any movement. She turned her head so that she was facing the direction from which they had come. Still nothing moved.

There was no activity at all. No other vehicles waited nearby and no steps echoed through the night. She faced the warehouse, looking for a light or telltale movement that might inform them where James and Dr. Brant waited. But all was still.

"It is very quiet here," Mr. Renfrew said, echoing her thoughts.

Rebecca scanned the building in front of them. A door, not ten yards away, was ajar. It led into a dark warehouse, yet somehow it seemed like an invitation . . . somehow it felt familiar.

"Misses Hanton?" Mr. Renfrew said, trying to get her attention.

"Rebecca?" Caroline's voice was apprehensive. "Rebecca, are you—"

Rebecca picked up the full skirts of her evening gown and rushed to the warehouse door. She pushed it open fully and heard the *bang* reverberate through the large, hollow building. She sensed rather than saw her companions behind her, but she didn't glance back.

Inside, the spacious hall was wide, and when her eyes adjusted to what little light was shining through the windows, she saw that the walls were many shades of graying cedar. Her mind was filled—her mental void was heaped to capacity with thoughts and emotions—memories of family, friends, laughter, and sorrow. Memories of this very place where the horror had begun.

"Caroline, this is it!" Rebecca shouted. She didn't wait for an answer but plunged ahead.

The warehouse was full of signs and labels, boxes and crates all in rough pale pine. There was a sweet smell to the air, a mixture of cane, fresh wood, and sawdust. She ran to the back of the warehouse and easily found the other door. It led into the smaller room with a high ceiling overcrowded with more boxes and crates, more than she remembered being here three fortnights ago.

The floor was still covered in sawdust, and in the center of the room was the very crate that she had been forced to sit on. Forced to watch . . .

Mr. Renfrew lit a lamp by the door and Caroline rushed to her side. Slowly the room began to illuminate.

"Rebecca, are you all right?" Her voice echoed, bouncing down from the ceiling.

"This is it, Caroline." Rebecca's voice was shaky but not weak. "This is the room in my dreams. This is where—" She twisted her head, trying to peer around the stacked crates. "Where do you think . . . ?" Finally, she looked toward the door.

Another man stepped out of the shadows and stood beside Mr. Renfrew, blocking the only exit. His hair, straight and dark, was brushed backward on the sides, falling just below the nape of his neck. He had hazel eyes and a characterless face, except for a small scar on his chin. He looked all too familiar.

Neither of the men had said anything. They were simply waiting, and Rebecca knew why.

Renfrew had called her Misses *Hanton* in the carriage. He had not been surprised by the empty street or shocked by her blind race through the warehouse. He was simply waiting, waiting to see if she remembered.

And she did.

Caroline stared slack-jawed at the man standing beside Mr. Renfrew. "Mr. Paterson?" She sounded incredulous.

"No, indeed. I'd like to introduce . . ." Renfrew laughed in a sharp, unpleasant staccato. "*Re*introduce, Kyle Saunders, my partner's son. Though I do say he did a credible job playing Mr. Paterson."

Rebecca straightened and swallowed against the sour bile that had crawled up her throat. She grabbed Caroline's hand tightly and pulled her close. She tried to place herself in front of her friend but Caroline resisted, not understanding. Rebecca slowly backed up, taking Caroline with her until they could go no farther.

"Is something wrong, Misses Hanton?" Mr. Renfrew smiled none too kindly.

"What have you done with Elizabeth?" Rebecca asked. She heard Caroline stifle a gasp.

Mr. Renfrew exuded as jovial and harmless a nature as ever. "Oh dear, you were right, Kyle." His eyes turned for a fraction toward the man in question as he chuckled. "She remembers. I had so hoped to avoid this unpleasantness."

"Perhaps you should have continued referring to me as Miss Dobbins."

He laughed. "Is that what gave me away?"

Caroline clenched Rebecca's hand so tightly she thought she might lose sensation in it.

"That, this room, and my memory."

"An abundance of reasons, my dear." Mr. Renfrew shook his head. "I guess we were doomed from the start."

"Doomed," mocked Mr. Saunders as he reached into his boot and drew out a slim, finely honed dagger. When the light caught it, neither Caroline nor Rebecca was surprised to see that the dark wood hilt gently curved into the shape of a hummingbird.

CHAPTER TWENTY-THREE

Dungeons and Daggers

"I believe it is my turn to ask questions." Mr. Smythe didn't look as smug as he sounded. Perspiration dripped down his temples despite the less than balmy temperature of the underground chamber. "Where are Rebecca and Elizabeth?" He aimed his pistol at the coachman.

Roy interrupted with a wail. "Golly, we is in fer it now!"

"Shut yer yap, Roy. We don't know nothing," the coachman, Greg Brill, snapped. "Don't know no Rebecca or Elizabeth."

"I believe you do." Mr. Smythe lifted his arm to chest height. "Where are Rebecca and Elizabeth?"

"Beth?" Walter turned to stare at the man. "You are looking for Beth? Are you a relation, or . . . her . . . husband?"

"Husband?!" Smythe's jaw clenched. "She is just sixteen."

"Rot!" Walter snorted in disagreement. "She's older than that!"

Keeping his eyes on Greg Brill, Smythe frowned. "Elizabeth is sixteen, Rebecca is eighteen." He raised the pistol to the coachman's eye level. "*Where* are they?"

Walter, oblivious to the hostilities, rubbed his temples and stared into the air. "Does Rebecca have thick straight brown hair, hazel eyes, and a tendency toward obstinacy?"

The corners of Smythe's mouth twitched. "Indeed."

Walter snapped his tongue and shouted, "Aha!" thereby distracting Smythe, who turned slightly toward Walter.

Brill lunged. He twisted the pistol in Smythe's grasp, but it fired before either had control. The horrendous report almost covered a yelp of surprise and pain. Walter grabbed Henry's arm just in time to slow his fall; Henry's legs buckled and he sat heavily on the floor. Blood streamed through Henry's fingers. Jack ran to his side, pushing his muzzle into Henry's face.

At the same time, Roy reached for the door. He tried to shove aside Henry and Jack, who blocked his way. He had almost succeeded when Walter slammed the man's head into the wall. Staggering, Roy wiped at the blood now dripping from his forehead, and then swung his fist at Walter.

The blow to Walter's jaw sent him reeling backward. Grabbing an unlit torch from the floor, Walter swung it double-handed at Roy. The man dropped to the floor and lay unconscious across the threshold.

Turning quickly, Walter saw that Mr. Smythe was in trouble. The firing of the pistol had taken the advantage from him. It lay powerless on the stone floor, spent and forgotten. The contest was now for the knife. Both Smythe and Brill had their hands locked around the hilt, but it was inching its way closer and closer to Smythe's chest.

Walter lifted his torch to shoulder height, but just as he had the coachman in position, the men contorted and twisted. For several moments the two struggled, shifting constantly, never allowing

Walter the chance to change the odds. Finally Walter dropped his useless weapon and seized the back of Smythe's coat. With all his strength, he yanked the man back.

All three men fell to the floor. Regrettably, the coachman retained the knife and Smythe sported a nasty cut on his hand. However, the advantage was theirs again, for Walter and Smythe— and in his own way, Henry—stood between the coachman and the door.

Walter and Smythe were quick to their feet. Brill's movements were slow and furtive; his eyes darting between them and the opening.

"Where are they?" Smythe asked again.

Brill's smile was repulsive.

Walter picked up the torch and swung it just inches from the coachman's nose.

The man didn't flinch. "I don't know what you're talkin' h'about. I'm just a poor harmless worker, trying to earn a decent living." The man inched slowly around the wall as the lies spilled from his mouth.

Walter wanted to hit him just so he would shut up. But the pounding in his ears was getting more and more distracting. He shook his head to clear it, then realized that the sound was not coming from inside his brain, or even inside this room. The non-rhythmic thumping echoed in spits and spurts. It was odd, very odd.

Smythe squatted and pawed at the floor around him, trying to locate his pistol without looking away from Brill. Before Smythe could find it, the coachman ducked under Walter's torch and threw his shoulder into Smythe's chest. It sent them both sprawling across the floor.

Walter threw his weight into a tremendous swing of his torch but the coachman rolled to safety at the last second. The momentum twisted Walter around and he landed on his knees, his head banging against the iron grate door. Shaking his head gingerly, Walter turned to watch the struggle for the knife begin anew.

Brill fell on Smythe, but the younger man met the coachman at every turn. With each lunge, Smythe forced Brill into a stalemate. Then Brill jerked the knife up, out of Smythe's hold, and sliced down into his thigh. By the time Smythe shouted out in pain, Brill was halfway to the door.

Henry still sat where he had fallen, blocking the threshold, his sleeve soaked in blood. As Brill jumped over him, Henry let go of his wound and grabbed. The limb slipped through his grasp but the pant leg did not. The man tumbled over Henry's back. The coachman must have landed on Roy, for the sound was more of a *thud* than a *crash*.

About to shout *hurrah*, Walter saw a foot come up behind Henry. He had no time to warn his friend; Henry received a vicious kick to the head. He dropped the pant leg and rocked with the force of the blow, his eyes wide with pain.

Walter grabbed the grate, ignoring the pressure of a goose egg forming on his temple. He used the iron bars as leverage and pulled himself to his feet. When at last he was upright, he pushed himself away and turned.

The door was open and Brill was gone.

———◆———

"I AM SORRY for all the bungling this past month or so, my dear. This is certainly not the way I had planned it." Mr. Renfrew looked as cordial as if he were discussing the weather. "It has just been one mistake after another. I have come to the conclusion that people never do what you expect them to do. Well . . ." He laughed and stepped farther into the room, then dusted off a crate and sat down. "Most don't."

Mr. Saunders remained standing. The hummingbird dagger swung from hand to hand, side to side.

Rebecca tried not to look at it. She knew that if she did, she would be lost in the motion.

"My sister seems to be the exception," Renfrew continued. "I knew she would be incensed at the idea of leaving the concert early. Her dissatisfaction about the seating arrangements was just the added touch that I needed. Quite handy."

He looked into the air above their heads as if reliving the scene in his mind. "Yes, this evening my plans finally worked out." He turned his eyes back to them. "The driver was, of course, paid to bring us here no matter how we directed him. How delightful that you allowed us to do so under the auspices of fulfilling your wishes. It made the ride so much more affable."

"Glad we could oblige." Caroline's voice was cold—downright frosty.

Mr. Renfrew saw Caroline step out from behind Rebecca and misunderstood. "Sit, sit, Miss Ellerby, Misses Hanton, if you are tired. We may have to wait awhile." He turned to Saunders. "When did I say they were coming?"

Saunders' eyes never left Rebecca's. "Just before midnight."

Renfrew drew out his pocket watch and consulted it. "Plenty of time." He tucked it away carefully. "I thought it would take us longer to maneuver the men away. But they were so eager to escape Margaret. Poor Margaret, her own worst enemy." He noticed that Rebecca had not moved. "Sit, ladies, be comfortable. We have at least half an hour to kill, if you'll excuse the expression." He snick-ered as if at a private joke.

They didn't move. Rebecca found it easier now to concentrate. Caroline's move had partially blocked the swinging motion from her peripheral vision.

"You do realize that you have played your hand too close to home this time," Rebecca said. "Whatever your plans with us, Lord Ellerby and Dr. Brant know who you are. You will be apprehended."

"Come, come, my dear. You should think better of me than that." Renfrew sounded disappointed. "The wild goose chase that I sent your men on was on the pretext of a stranger's infor-mation. It took very little to elicit a request to return you to Harley Street. They likely believe it was their idea. So you see, I am a good Samaritan. In the morning, I will be found dazed and disheveled, having been thrown from the carriage. They know nothing of Kyle."

"Such a masterful plan." Rebecca took a deep breath. "But the police already suspect Mr. Saunders. They know that it was he who kidnapped Elizabeth and me."

"No, Misses Hanton," Saunders interrupted. He smiled a slow, superior grimace. "They suspect Grey. The name that I gave to them. Osborne is such a fool; he could barely recall who I was, let alone my name. I simply reintroduced myself as Grey." Saunders' laugh had nothing to do with humor.

Rebecca swallowed hard and bit her bottom lip. "Why are you doing this?"

"I am trying to prevent a great travesty; and as always, there are sacrifices to be made for the greater good." Mr. Renfrew sounded genuinely regretful. And then he grinned. It sent a chill up Rebecca's spine. "If the letters of marque are repealed, the fortunes of the ship owners in the West Indies will be in jeopardy. It will bankrupt the entire country. I am the owner of three such privateer ships. This legislation will wreck us all. I simply will not have it."

"If you feel it is ruinous for the islands, why not argue through the proper channels? Lawyers, lobbyists, clergy?" Rebecca asked with a shiver of revulsion. "Why bring to bear such pressure on my father? Kidnap us? Surely, the vote of one man will not make a difference."

Renfrew squinted and smiled in an odd parody of an amiable man. "Oh . . . but you are so very wrong. These great gentlemen are like sheep; they huddle together in groups and follow. Lord Hanton will have no problem convincing others to vote against the repeal. With his support, the letters of marque will still stand. We will be able to continue attacking foreign ships with impunity.

"If there had been another way, we might have taken it. But the vote is too close—and this is too much fun. Threats and fearful faces . . . You look quite terrified, my dear. It's most stimulating." He snorted and then chuckled under his breath. "We *need* the letters of marque to stand—they are our life blood." He laughed heartily at his own words. "So you see your father, being a man of great respect, will lead the sheep. Though it *is* unfortunate for you and your sister."

"Unfortunate for us as well," Saunders remarked with a fair amount of acid.

Mr. Renfrew glanced over to the younger man. "Yes, well, we thought Lord Hanton's affection couldn't be overridden by principles. We never thought that he would simply withdraw." He looked over to Rebecca, still standing stiffly beside the crate. "So you see, we are back to where we started. People never do what you expect them to do. But I still believe he can be persuaded."

"Why did you kill Daisy?"

"Well, my dear, she guessed who I was. The girl was far too intelligent for her own good. Saunders had but asked a few benign questions. They were simple queries of you and the manor. Not only did she refuse to enlighten us, she also replied with too much sass for Saunders' liking. Feisty, that girl, but it was rather irritating. Besides, Kyle has a temper." He sighed as if he meant it. "Such a shame. He really needs to get that under control."

Saunders smiled in such a way that Rebecca knew he had no intention of getting anything under control. He clearly relished the feel of unbridled anger.

The dagger continued to swing.

"And as I have said, Mr. Saunders played the role of Mr. Paterson, too," Renfrew continued. "Although he was ultimately unsuccessful in that role as well." He hesitated as if something had just come to mind. "Tell me, my dear, when did you get your memories back?"

"Bits and pieces have been coming back to me for some time now," she fibbed, dropping her gaze to the sawdust on the floor. "Elizabeth . . . How could you do that to Elizabeth?"

"Ah yes. Well my dear, we'll have to put that down to Kyle's temper again. I never—" Mr. Renfrew left his sentence hanging and quickly turned his head toward his accomplice. "Did you hear that?" The slow but stealthy sound of footfalls echoed in the larger warehouse.

"They are here."

"Then they are early." The gentleman pulled out a small pistol from his pocket and cocked it. He pointed it at Rebecca and Caroline. "Go check," he ordered his partner.

"For whom are we waiting?" Caroline asked when Saunders closed the door behind him.

Mr. Renfrew smiled. "We are waiting for some business associates. I came by the other day to make the final arrangements. You see, as much as you may think otherwise, I really do not stomach murder well. I had never intended to do either of the Misses Hanton harm but had devised a rather ironic, truly fitting end to this scenario."

He raised an eyebrow at Rebecca's confused expression. "You didn't think that had your father complied, I would have returned you to him? No, no, that would not do! I would have been arrested before I had stepped into my carriage, let alone onto a clipper."

Just then the door opened, admitting two roughly dressed men. One had a short craggy beard and the other had a potbelly and a fleshy jaw. They were unkempt and smelled of fish and alcohol.

Saunders followed them in and closed the door.

"You are early," Renfrew complained.

"Right you are there, gov'ner." The jowly man reached into his pocket, his loud voice echoing from the rafters. "Let's get this business over, then. Something is going on out there. People milling about when it's usually as quiet as a rat's fart." He pulled a small jingling bag from his pocket. "Where is they then?"

Mr. Renfrew sidestepped even though Rebecca and Caroline were already in full view. "Right here."

"What, them?" The man seemed astounded. "They's too old."

"What are you talking about, man?" Renfrew's voice was sharp, his body tense. It was the first hint of temper that Renfrew had displayed thus far.

"They's too old. Can't sell them. These would be nothing but trouble." He glared at Rebecca, who glared back. "See what I mean?" His jowls bounced as he nodded his head.

Mr. Renfrew's face hardened. "Do you want them or not?"

The man eyed Rebecca for a few moments. "Nah. Not even if they was free."

The moneybag jingled again as it was returned to his pocket.

Mr. Renfrew shook his head in disbelief and Saunders' smile grew.

"How does it feel to be rejected, Misses Hanton? And by the scum of the earth. You could hardly get any lower." Saunders' voice was smug and superior.

The slave traders pivoted. "Who's callin' who scum, you Bond Street fripple!" The jowly man spit at Saunders' feet and reached beneath his soiled coat. He drew out a large knife and used it to point at Saunders' dagger, still swaying from side to side. "What you got there?" he taunted. "A toothpick?"

With a quick, deft movement, Saunders slashed at the man, catching him across the mouth. The trader grabbed at his wound, making a ghastly gurgling sound as blood poured through his fingers and rained onto the floor. He tossed his knife at his companion just as a loud *bang* rent the air; the blade fell uselessly to the floor. Renfrew had fired his pistol into the wall above their heads.

"Enough," he growled.

The traders turned, anger in their eyes, ready to take him on . . . but they hesitated.

"Enough," Renfrew said again in a whisper. A dangerous, deadly threat.

The uninjured trader lifted his chin, gripped his companion

by the front of his coat and dragged him from the room without a word.

FROM A CRACK between the crates in the darkened corner farthest from the light, Rebecca and Caroline watched Renfrew turn back to the center of the room and realize that they had disappeared behind the dubious protection of the maze of boxes. The man laughed, and Rebecca closed her eyes for a moment and swallowed.

"Come, ladies, the room has but one door," Renfrew scoffed. "Let us not play games."

Rebecca looked above her to the crates piled high. She pushed gently on the closest, but it didn't budge. She motioned to Caroline. Sign language and intuition aided their wordless conversation, leaving Rebecca to question Renfrew while Caroline climbed.

"What are you going to do with us now, Mr. Renfrew? Do you have an alternate plan?" She spoke loud enough to create an echo; it marginally disguised her location—marginally.

"Always my dear, but it is not one that I wanted to implement."

"You can't kill us; you would have no leverage with my father. You will never persuade him to take up your cause that way."

"My dear, how totally selfish of you. Do you think your sister has no value in your father's eyes? Now please, come out so we can talk face-to-face like civilized people."

Caroline had climbed halfway to the top of the crates. Rebecca looked up and met Caroline's wide eyes. She put her hand over her mouth to prevent any sound from escaping and nodded to Rebecca.

Rebecca's stomach roiled. "Elizabeth isn't dead?"

"No, no, my dear. I will admit she is not doing very well, but she is alive."

Rebecca slipped between two boxes and then stilled. Had she heard correctly? Had he just said that Elizabeth was alive? Could she believe him? She looked up. Caroline's smile was so wide it spread beyond the confines of her hand. In fact, she was having a hard time holding on, she was shaking so badly.

Dragging in a gulp of air, Rebecca started to tremble as well and fought to remain standing. One thought, one statement played over and over in her mind: *Elizabeth is alive!* But where *was* she?

<hr>

"IT'S ALIVE!" Walter shouted, jumping back as if he'd been burned. Slowly, ignoring the groans behind him, he crept back to the iron-grated door. He peered into the darkness. Jack joined him, wagging his tail. There was no mistake: Something was moving in the small cell beyond, and it seemed to be responsible for the thumping.

"Henry, Smythe, there is something in here."

Walter turned his head enough to use his peripheral vision.

Smythe still sat where he had fallen. The man was panting. In pain or from the exertion of his struggle with Brill, Walter couldn't tell. He watched as Smythe yanked off his neckcloth and tied it around his leg.

"Then find out what it is!" the man barked as he planted both hands hard against the weeping wound.

Walter nodded slightly, took a deep breath, and pulled back the bolt. The door slid quietly and easily toward him. Jack leapt ahead to the far wall where a bundle of rags lay.

As Walter crept closer, he was confronted with many odors,

all of them foul. The most prominent among them was that of putrescence. As he neared the pile, he realized that it was a person, curled up and covered and very sick.

He slowly drew back the thin covering. The pale face of a girl emerged; her eyes were only half open, but her lips were weakly smiling. As he pulled the covers back farther they revealed a swath of filthy bandages wrapped around her throat; the stench was overwhelming. In her hand was a small tin cup. Even now she was banging it against the floor as if afraid that Walter would disappear were she to stop.

He gently opened her fingers and eased the cup from her. "It's all right. You can stop now," he whispered.

Her nod was barely perceptible.

Walter pushed Jack away, drew back the miserable rag of a covering and as gently and heedfully as he could, reached beneath her knees and around her back. She was light—hardly any weight at all. He squinted as they emerged, the dull torchlight bright in comparison to the hole that had housed her.

Smythe was in the process of tying a wad of cloth torn from his shirt onto his leg when he looked up. On seeing the bundle in Walter's arms he tried to jump to his feet, but his leg wouldn't hold him and he sat back down. "Elizabeth?" he cried. "Lud, is it Elizabeth?"

Walter frowned, confused by the question and the emotion on Smythe's face. He stepped toward Smythe and turned just enough for the girl to see the man who had addressed them.

"Matt!" she shouted. It was hoarse and painful, but she flailed her arm as if trying to reach Smythe.

Walter lowered her to the floor beside the wounded man.

"Oh Lord, Funny Face, what have they done?" Smythe lifted

his hand as if to touch the bandages at her throat but stopped and put his arm around her instead.

The two huddled together. In the hushed atmosphere of the room, their emotions were all too evident.

Finally Smythe wiped his face on his sleeve and looked up at Walter. "Thank you, Mr. Ellerby, for your help. I apologize for the subterfuge. I was unsure of your place in these matters." He held up his one free hand and although it was his left, Walter was not insulted. "This is Elizabeth Hanton, my sister. My name is Matthew Hanton."

Walter stared, mouth agape, trying to make sense of her name. The villains seemed to have an affinity to girls called Elizabeth. The room was silent for some moments as the boys absorbed the news, and it was just as well, for a voice called from above. "Mr. Ellerby, Mr. Thompson, answer me!" Mr. Strickland must have been calling for some time. "Are you down there? Be this a prank?"

"No!" the three young men shouted, and there could be no doubt that it was heard. Footsteps echoed through the halls, bouncing down to them.

Walter looked over to the Hantons, disturbed to see Elizabeth flailing her arm again. Her brother leaned closer and she whispered something to him.

Matthew Hanton looked to Walter, his expression troubled. "Rebecca, where is Rebecca? Is she all right?"

"Rebecca?"

"Yes, Rebecca. Straight brown hair, oval face, looks somewhat like me. Our sister Rebecca. Is she all right?"

Walter paused, thought, and then nodded with great vigor. "So, Beth's name is Rebecca. And you are her family. Well, that is most excellent." He waved his hand at them and smiled. "She is fine.

Rebecca is fine," he said loftily, rolling the name around in his mouth as if getting used to the sound. "Safe and sound with my brother and sister in London. They are likely sipping tea in the drawing room as we speak."

———•———

REBECCA, lost among the crates in the cavernous warehouse backroom, sobbed silent, joyful tears. The scene in her mind was of her first visit to this monstrous room. Elizabeth's injury kept playing over in her mind. How had her sister survived such a wound? Where was she now?

"Oh, my dear, I am most sorry. I did not realize that you believed her to be dead. I would have told you straightaway. She is at Risely. No wonder you were so out of sorts." Renfrew continued to maintain the ridiculous attitude of benevolence in the face of his atrocities.

Rebecca almost found the affectation more revolting than the cold menace of Saunders. "And when would you have done that? At Daisy's funeral?"

In the brief lull of their voices, Rebecca heard a creak to her right. She looked up to see Caroline still moving higher. She took a deep calming breath and wiped the tears from her eyes. Through the crack she could still see Renfrew, holding the reloaded pistol, but of Saunders she could see nothing. She moved her head this way and that, straining.

"Yes, indeed. I see your point." Renfrew laughed and sounded genuinely amused. "Well, let me clear it up for you now. Saunders would likely have killed your sister had I not seen it coming. So, in fact, you have something to thank me for."

Now that Rebecca was listening for it, she heard another creak.

This time it was slightly closer and she understood Renfrew's chattiness; he was trying to hide Saunders' stealth. She would have to move again. Hiking up her skirts, Rebecca tucked the hem into her bodice. She grabbed the crate ahead of her, ignoring the sharp slivers of wood and asked one last question, in the hopes that the echoes and Renfrew's babble would cover the sounds she would inevitably make climbing to the other side. "And why would I thank you?"

"If I hadn't grabbed his arm and pulled it back, instead of cutting her neck he would have slit her throat. But the blood, oh my dear, it was no wonder you were misled. What a mess that was! We had to put the cloth meant for her mouth, around her throat. I have to admit, though, that the trip to Welford Mills would not have been so calm were your sister not unconscious. A little spitfire that one. Yes, with you trussed and her senseless, the trip was not all that unpleasant.

"We were mere moments away from Risely when the accident occurred. We were so close. Really, a most inconvenient happenstance. We can only lay the blame at the feet of your younger brother, Miss Ellerby. He is too wild and needs reining in. Your mother has left him to his own devices for far too long."

Renfrew was taunting Caroline to speak, but Rebecca knew she was not easily provoked.

"There were so many times that Kyle wanted to introduce his flashy dagger to Walter. But I am a man of integrity; I would not let him throw away the true purpose of our scheme. I hope you appreciate that."

Climbing over the top crate and down the other side, Rebecca dropped her skirts back to the ground and silently inched through the narrow opening between the boxes and the wall.

"You must have known this to be futile."

Startled, Rebecca half turned toward the voice, but Saunders grabbed her from behind. He wrapped his left arm around her and raised his right hand to her throat. In it he held the hummingbird dagger.

"Go ahead," she taunted, surprising herself.

Saunders laughed, his mouth beside her ear, his breath warm and repulsive. "Not yet," he whispered. "Not yet." Instead, he walked her forward into the light. Something bumped against her boot as he pulled her to a stop; it made a soft metallic scrape as it shifted.

"Ah, there you are at last," Renfrew sighed. "The conversation was becoming tedious." He turned to the middle of the room and looked up into the dark. "You can come out now, Miss Ellerby. We have Misses Hanton."

Rebecca prayed that Caroline stayed hidden; it was their only strength, their only weapon . . . Or was it? With a quiet gasp, Rebecca rolled her foot sideways. She found the object she had nudged and once again heard the soft scrape of metal. Straining to see, Rebecca lowered her chin, ignoring the sharp prick on her neck and slow dribble of blood.

She couldn't see the entire object—just the hilt. The hilt of the trader's knife.

"Miss Ellerby, I tire of this game!" Renfrew's tone and stance showed that it was true. The real Gilbert Renfrew was emerging. He turned his head toward Rebecca, eyeing her predicament with relish. "Well, my dear, it seems we must do this the hard way."

"WHERE HAVE THEY GONE?" James' voice had risen in volume with each repetition of the question; he was fairly shouting by the time they reached the Vauxhall Garden gates. Brant was unhelpfully silent. "Renfrew said he would wait for us here and yet here he is not!" James huffed and glared at any and everyone around them. His glower cleared the promenade, making it even more apparent that the ladies were nowhere to be seen.

Renfrew had lied. "He lied!" James shouted to no one in particular.

"About many things," Brant said quietly, cutting through James' panicked rage. "The peelers were not looking for us; he is not waiting where he said he would be, and I don't believe he persuaded Mrs. Thompson to forgo the Blakeney Assembly because it would be a crush."

"Absolutely not!" James said. He shook his head and swallowed several times in succession. His heart pounded; he was desperate to find Caroline and Rebecca. He could not lose her—would *not* lose *them*! Where were they?

"Sir!" a voice accosted them from the other side of the gate.

"Sam." James jumped over the turnstile, brushed past the protesting ticket man, and stepped out onto the street. Brant was right behind him. "Sam, have you seen Miss Ellerby?"

The coachman looked over his shoulder toward Colyhurst Road. "Yes, m'lord. She an' Misses Hanton was squeezed in a hackney with an older gent. They was rushin' off somethin' terrible. The driver was flicking 'is whip before they even gots to the road."

"Did you recognize the gentleman with them?" James felt sick. Disaster had befallen. Rebecca and Caroline were gone— kidnapped!

Sam shook his head vehemently. "No, sir, but I heard him yell to the driver. 'To St. Katherine's docks.'"

"Oh, Lord," Brant said, "if they are taken onboard a ship we'll never find them. They could sail anywhere."

"Get the carriage free, Sam." James turned to the eavesdropping ticket seller. "When the peelers get here, tell them where we have gone." He didn't wait for a reply but turned back. "Go, Sam. We are right behind you!"

———————◆———————

REBECCA HEARD A low rumble in her ear and realized that Saunders was chuckling. She shivered with revulsion and his laugh became colder. He tightened his hold on her waist and pulled the knife away from her throat to show her the red tip—her blood dribbling down the blade of the hummingbird dagger. It was terrifying—the stuff of nightmares.

Rebecca dropped. Straight down, she let her legs do what they had wanted to do for sometime, collapse. She felt the dagger swing just over her head and threw her shoulder into Saunders' legs, knocking him off balance.

Suddenly, boxes and crates tumbled from their perches—helter-skelter, raining down on them. Rebecca rolled aside, grabbing the trader's knife as she did. From the corner of her eye, she watched Caroline jump down on Renfrew, knocking him and his pistol to the ground. Caroline landed hard on her knees beside the villain and pummeled the man about his head.

Like a top, Saunders wobbled unsteadily and then righted himself. He ignored Renfrew and Caroline, staring at Rebecca with an inhuman glint. He tightened his grip on the hummingbird dagger and advanced toward her with increasing speed.

Behind him, Caroline grabbed up the pistol and fired at Saunders.

The ball shot wide, but it and the simultaneous shout from the door threw him off-kilter. One leg remained true but the other skidded through the slippery blood from the trader's wound. He hit the floor in a sprawl, half kneeling. But the momentum pitched him forward and he put his arm out to protect his face. He hit the floor hard, twitched, and then lay still.

Rebecca looked up at the doorway. James and Brant. A finer sight she had never seen.

One moment she was on the ground, the next she was in James' arms. "Risely," she said in a shaky whisper as he held her tight. "Risely. Elizabeth is at Risely Hall. She's wounded."

"Davis!" James shouted over his shoulder, still holding Rebecca close. "Send someone to Risely for Elizabeth immediately! She's been hurt. Tell Lord Hanton!" Turning back, James touched their foreheads together, breathing deeply. "Soon, my love. All will be well very soon." Her body molded to his and she lost sense of time. She didn't want to think anymore. Couldn't think anymore.

All too soon, noise broke through her fog. All too soon they had to return to a warehouse full of boxes and men in blue uniforms.

Four constables hauled Renfrew from the floor while he struggled and shouted his innocence. He accused Saunders' of coercion, but his words fell on deaf ears and he was dragged to the outer warehouse without any deference to his title.

James led Rebecca in a slow, solemn procession to the door, ahead of Caroline and Dr. Brant. Just before Rebecca stepped across the threshold, she looked back. Saunders had been flipped over and now lay on the floor faceup. Inspector Davis saw her glance their way and, with a sharp command, ordered the peelers to obstruct her view.

But they had not moved fast enough.

Rebecca had seen what he had tried to shield her from.

For a brief moment everything else had ceased to exist. Her eyes had locked on the menacing beauty of the hummingbird dagger. The dark wood hilt curved into the body that had once been Saunders. The long bill that had been fashioned to drink the nectar of life had done its job again. Blood wept to form a puddle beneath him, blending and mixing with the trader's blood that had been his doom.

Rebecca laid her head on James' shoulder and together they left the warehouse and hummingbird dagger behind forever.

CHAPTER TWENTY-FOUR

The Aftermath

Despite the number of persons ensconced in the drawing room of the Brant London townhouse, the silence was overwhelming. Rebecca glanced at Caroline sitting next to Dr. Brant, and James, who was glassy-eyed, leaning on the mantel. She wanted to say something witty to distract all from their worries, but her thoughts were muddled and dominated by questions about Elizabeth—her safety and whereabouts. Only a knock at the front door roused them from their lethargy.

They had returned the day before with smiles and light hearts, ready to celebrate having survived the horrors at the warehouse. But no sooner had they started to relive their experiences, than the lack of knowledge about Elizabeth had torn them asunder. A long evening and a sleepless night had followed.

"All is well!" a voice shouted from the doorway as it slammed open.

Lord Hanton stood beneath the frame, his chin up, his chest

puffed out, and a wide smile on his face. He strode into the room, took Rebecca's hands in his own, and pulled her to her feet. "Elizabeth is safe at Hardwick. I just received word . . . from a Derrick Strickland."

Rebecca squealed her happiness in a most indelicate way and was about to beg everyone's pardon, when she heard Caroline do the same—and then James hurrahed. Suddenly, the room was full of noise, voices, and laughter.

"Pack, everyone, pack!" Lord Hanton ordered. "We are Welford bound." Then he gulped and turned to look at James. "If you are amenable, of course."

James smiled broadly and glanced at Rebecca. "Absolutely."

"Excellent, excellent! I shall follow directly." Lord Hanton nodded.

———

REBECCA SPENT THE entire journey back to Hardwick Manor trying to recall her sister. Disjointed memories came in spits and spurts without any continuity, leaving Rebecca as befuddled as ever. When the carriage finally drew up in front of Hardwick, Rebecca stepped into the manor anticipating an uncomfortable reunion. She found Elizabeth in the morning room, lying on the settee, a collection of pillows behind her back. A scarf was wrapped around her neck, a cup of tea sat on the table at her elbow, and a light throw covered her legs.

"Rebecca!" Elizabeth's voice was scratchy and strained but her smile offered a full welcome.

Rebecca stood in the doorway of the morning room and stared. One moment the girl on the settee was a stranger, the next she was Elizabeth: sister, friend, and companion. A rush of memories crowded into her mind, and suddenly Rebecca's life before Hardwick was returned to her. It was so abrupt and so unexpected that Rebecca stumbled, nearly tripping. Righting herself, she reached for the wall beside her for support and dragged in a ragged breath. She stood for some moments trying to still her racing heart. She swallowed against the lump in her throat.

Scenes of running down a country lane together as young girls, discovering a frog in the garden, their first horseback riding lessons, and countless other memories streamed past her mind's eye. Some recollections were of happy days, others were of them squabbling, and still others of the pranks they played on their brothers. They were the best of friends or the fiercest of enemies depending on the day. However, there was no doubt about their deep affection for each other.

"Elizabeth," she croaked, and then rushed across the room. Rebecca dropped to her knees in front of her sister and wrapped her arms around her. She was thin and frail, and Rebecca worried that she might be squeezing too tightly, but Elizabeth clung to her until they both broke into sobs.

Eventually Rebecca stood, grabbed a nearby chair, and pulled it beside the settee.

"There is so much to say I almost don't know where to start," she said.

Elizabeth smiled, a hint of mischief in her eyes. "Then I'll start first."

Behind them, James sighed with great relief and quietly closed the door to offer them some privacy.

A TALL YOUNG man, who looked remarkably like Rebecca, stared at James from the bottom of the stairs. He held on to the banister as if in need of support.

"Matthew Hanton, I presume," James said, putting out his hand to greet him. "I am James Ellerby. Your father told me you were in Welford Mills."

"Did he come with you? Is he here?"

"Not as yet," James said with a smile. "He will be here tomorrow. Just a few things to clear up in town." Not as frivolous as it sounded, Lord Hanton was verifying Mr. Renfrew's arrest. "I'm sure he will set off directly. He is anxious to see Elizabeth."

The young man shifted. "Yes, I imagine so." He placed a walking stick in front of him and wobbled forward.

"Oh," James said, "I didn't . . . here, let me help." He took Matthew's arm, offering support and led him to . . . "Where are we going?"

Matthew chuckled. "I was in the drawing room when I heard the commotion of your arrival." He glanced at the closed morning room door. "I should probably return there."

But before he could start up the stairs, Caroline and Brant stepped through the front door.

"There is no need." Caroline said as she turned toward her brother. "Is there, James? Dr. Brant need not hurry back to Kirkstead-on-Hill. He should join us . . . Oh, hello," Caroline addressed the stranger in their midst. "James told me we had guests. Would you be Matthew Hanton?"

When all the introductions were made, James and Brant helped Matthew up the stairs and they were soon relaxing in the drawing room. Mrs. Fogel promised tea and cakes.

"And where might Walter be?" James asked, looking around.

He was surprised that Walter had not met them at the door. Matthew shrugged.

"I am here!" a pompous voice called out. "I was out with Henry, touring the neighborhood. Checking on our incarcerated villains. Making sure that all was well." And then he added as an afterthought, "Got to keep Henry busy; don't want him stewing about his uncle." He flopped onto one of the chairs by the fireplace.

Caroline nodded. "And might you enlighten us about how you came to find Elizabeth? Your note only said that you had."

Walter explained, describing the circumstances of Miss Elizabeth's rescue in such florid detail that he was rather pleased with the expressions of horror on the faces of his nearest and dearest. He also told them that Elizabeth needed the special talents of Dr. Brant. Mr. Strickland had prescribed various potions, but her recovery would be better assured with the care of the good physician.

Walter was also pleased to report that Mr. Strickland had taken the protesting coachman and dazed builder into custody. He praised the deputy's keen sense of logic and curiosity that had sent him rushing to the new ruins upon hearing the reverberation of the pistol shot. If he had not been so timely, Greg Brill would have escaped and their feelings of accomplishment would have been tempered.

In the midst of the celebrations, Matthew Hanton explained his presence in Welford with some amusement. It seems his suspicions of the Ellerby involvement began with the report of a Miss Dobbins staying at Hardwick under mysterious circumstances. Matthew had been dispatched to verify if Miss Dobbins was indeed one his sisters, only to arrive after she had left for London.

"I would not have left you to handle all this on your own," James said to Walter. "Had I known . . ."

"But I did just fine, James." Walter winked saucily at his sister. "I rescued Elizabeth and prevented the villains from getting away. Not bad for a day's work."

James chuckled and nodded. "Too true, Walter. Not bad at all."

———◆———

NOT ALL THE Welford Mills' homecomings were pleasant. Mrs. Thompson's discomfort was extreme, for not only would she now have to live with the shame of her brother's actions, but the realization that all those around her would know of it. Gilbert Renfrew had been found guilty of kidnapping and was being transported to Australia.

James, after turning one and twenty, journeyed with Lord Hanton into town to ensure the successful repeal of the letters of marque—legalized privateers would soon be at an end.

Upon their return from London, a small gathering was held to celebrate the event.

It was a congenial affair, held in the saloon of Hardwick Manor. For Henry's sake, the Thompsons had been invited; while Henry was happy to join the celebration, Mrs. Thompson declined. The company bore the loss well.

———◆———

WALTER GREETED HENRY at the front door, and then led him into the saloon. The boys strutted in a style that had become less common for them now. However, it was one of those days and they were doing it up proud. And with a touch of panache, the boys were clothed in the same wild waistcoats and jackets as the day of the accident.

James rose and greeted Henry as they entered the room. But just as Henry was about to perch himself on the settee, he found Lord Ellerby staring at his waistcoat.

"Lord Ellerby?" Henry's eyebrows met above his nose.

James smiled and fingered one of the silver buttons on Henry's waistcoat. "You are missing one." He pointed to the last button-hole, conspicuously empty. And then seeing Henry's discomfort, patted him on the shoulder. "I have it." He laughed and with great enjoyment turned to Rebecca. "I thought that it was a clue at one time."

Rebecca tilted her head and smiled. Sitting on the settee beside her in an apricot high-necked gown, Elizabeth whispered a comment that brought Rebecca to blush and then she too laughed with the company.

James felt great comfort in the sound. He loved Rebecca's laugh, and now it was unrestrained. Gone were the shadows; they had been banished—banished and replaced with childhood memories. Even her nightmares were milder and fewer. It was likely that they would soon disappear entirely. It was a comforting thought.

Someone cleared their throat. And then again, louder.

James turned.

A woman stood at the saloon door, dressed in the latest fashions, with a tall ostrich plume tucked into her turban. Her shoulders were back and her chin was in the air; she exuded poise and hauteur.

"We have guests? Are we having a party?" she asked, looking with a quizzical gaze. She stared at one face after another as the room became quiet and still. "Did I miss something? Something important?"

Caroline stepped forward. "No, Mother, nothing out of the ordinary."

At Caroline's denial, the room burst into laughter and the chatter resumed. A good time was had by all well into the night.

After

The next morning, Rebecca raced to the drawing room, bursting through the door with no ceremony or announcement. She stopped and looked around, knowing that James was waiting for her; the butler had said as much. The room seemed empty until Rebecca saw a figure standing very still by the glass doors that led out to the terrace.

"James," she said, her voice a sigh of contentment as much as recognition. She stepped closer, swaying her hips in what she hoped was an enticing manner. And yet James had not spoken, not moved . . . still as a statue. A very handsome statue. A very handsome, well-dressed statue.

Clothed formally in a morning coat with a red-striped waistcoat and charcoal-gray trousers, James looked stunning and . . . well, uncomfortable. It was odd to see him less than confident. He had a fistful of flowers in one hand and a small piece of paper in the other.

Finally, he moved. He shifted from one foot to the other and cleared his throat. "Good morning, Rebecca," he said in a formal tone, then lifted the bouquet toward her. "These are for you."

"They are beautiful," Rebecca gushed, taking the flowers and holding them to her nose. "And they smell divine."

James returned to his statue stance.

Frowning, Rebecca laid the flowers gently on a nearby table and approached James. "Is all well?" she asked, standing only a few feet away.

"Yes," he said woodenly and then glanced down at the paper in his hand. "I wanted to speak with you."

"Yes." Rebecca giggled. "It would seem so."

"We have something of great importance to discuss." He took a deep breath and lifted the paper again, this time reading. "I know it is perhaps too early and that the stresses of these past days have just been resolved . . . no, no, that doesn't sound right." He shook his head and ran his finger down the paper. "I practiced this for hours and yet, I'm still not doing it right."

"What, exactly, are you doing?" Rebecca asked, smiling encouragement.

"Proposing." He ignored her gasp and continued. "But I cannot help—no, cannot resist . . . yes, that sounds better. I cannot help . . . resist making our attachment official—"

"James."

"So I would suggest . . . no, I would ask. There, that's better, don't you think?" He gulped and drew another ragged breath and finally looked up at her.

"James, you know how I feel about you. I have not hidden my feelings."

He blinked and then nodded. "Yes, but it is still not a given that you would want to spend the rest of your days with me. That you would marry me."

"Yes, it is." Rebecca leaned closer, plucked the note from his hand, and tossed it behind her. "Now, try again."

"But, but . . . I need my note. I had it all written out. Quite eloquent, if I could just read properly."

"You don't need to be eloquent. Just tell me how you feel."

"But . . . but . . . are you certain? A lady should have a perfect proposal. Something to remember all her life."

"I don't need perfection, James, just you. But I can't say yes if you do not ask the question."

With a snicker of self-deprecation, James shook and then nodded his head. He licked his lips, shifted his balance from one leg to the other once again, opened his mouth and then blurted it out—the most beautiful words she had ever heard.

"I love you, Rebecca. You are in my thoughts from the moment I awake until the moment I sleep. I want to be at your side throughout life, the good times and the bad. You are my strength and I would like to be yours. Will you marry me?"

Rebecca closed her eyes and sighed very deeply. "That *was* perfection." There was a dreamy expression on her face when she opened her eyes again. Wrapping her arms around James' neck, Rebecca lifted her face, expecting a kiss.

But James hesitated.

"James? Why are we not kissing?"

"I thought an answer first was in order."

His breath brushed across her lips, sending tingles down her spine.

"Of course." Rebecca laughed and stood on her toes, again waiting for her kiss.

"Do you mean *of course* you think an answer is in order? Or do you mean *of course* you will marry me?"

"James, kiss me! We'll work out the semantics later . . . perhaps after we are married."

James laughed and pulled her tighter. Lifting Rebecca off her feet, he twirled her around the room. And then, he kissed her.

Finally.

HISTORICAL NOTE:

Separating Fact from Fiction

LETTERS OF MARQUE authorized the attack and capture of enemy ships by civilian vessels. The sailors and licensed ships were called privateers, and it was considered an honorable and patriotic occupation at the onset. The privateers' heyday took place during the Renaissance; they did not lose their respectability until the 1830s. Still, the practice of using the letters of marque to legitimize piracy was not renounced until 1856 by the Paris Declaration.

A bill abolishing the letters of marque was neither introduced nor defeated in 1833 in the British House of Commons. (But the possibility was excellent fodder for a fictional kidnapping.)

Acknowledgments

THE HUMMINGBIRD DAGGER is a favorite among my beta readers and as such, I faced a mutiny if I did not polish it and present it to Swoon Reads for publication. It was fortunate that my editor, Emily Settle, was equally enthused about the book. And so I wish to acknowledge and thank all those involved in this publication, beginning with the helping hands at Swoon Reads.

Thank you, Emily, for your advice, patience, editing skills, and author management. You are amazing! Thank you, Jean Feiwel, for your leadership and guidance on this project, and Lauren Scobell, for championing the book and working toward a cohesive vision. Rich Deas, as always, the cover design is outstanding! It conveys the atmosphere and drama perfectly. I would also like to thank Mandy Veloso, my production editor, and the marketing team of Melissa Croce and Teresa Ferraiolo. As well, many thanks to my publicist, Kelsey Marrujo. I am privileged to have such an eager and talented team to direct me along the way.

Thank you, fellow Swoon Reads authors; a better support

group could not be found. And to my readers: Thank you for your encouraging Twitter and Facebook comments.

To my family and friends: Thank you for seeing me through the turmoil. Mike: You are my rock—I'm almost speechless when I think of all that you do to keep us trucking. Christine: Here it is! The one you've been waiting for. *The Hummingbird Dagger* would not be in print were it not for your faith and willingness to reread the manuscript—over and over . . . and over. Deb: Thank you for your help catching the *many* inconsistencies and your advice along the way. Dan, Mom, Steve, Stew, Trudy, Dillan, Matthew, Sue, Paul, Ginny, and Mel: Thank you for your encouragement and enthusiasm.

Check out more books chosen for publication by readers like you.

DID YOU KNOW...

readers like you helped to get this book published?

Join our book-obsessed community and help us discover awesome new writing talent.

1

Write it.
Share your original YA manuscript.

2

Read it.
Discover bright new bookish talent.

3

Share it.
Discuss, rate, and share your faves.

4

Love it.
Help us publish the books you love.

Share your own manuscript or dive between the pages at **swoonreads.com** or by downloading the **Swoon Reads app.**